I0722059

Florida Keys' Watercolor Kapers

A Compilation Of Adventures
Inspired By Key West Watercolors

Layout, Stories, and Watercolors
By Bob Kranich
Edited by Joanne Mary Kranich

Published by: Bob Kranich
White Post, Virginia

Book design by: Bob Kranich
Edited by: Joanne Mary Kranich

Published by: Bob Kranich
White Post, Va.

Printed in the United States of America

Publisher's Cataloging-in-Publication Data

Names: Kranich, Bob, author. I Kranich, Joanne Mary, editor.
Title: Florida Keys' watercolor kapers : a compilation of adventures inspired by Key West water colors /
layout, stories and watercolors by Bob Kranich ; edited by Joanne Mary Kranich
Description: Includes bibliographical references and index. I First Paperback Edition I White Post, VA:
Bob Kranich, 2019.
Identifiers: ISBN 978-0-9716515-7-9
Subjects: LCHS Kranich, Bob. I Key West (Fla.) —History. I Key West (Fla.)—Social Life and customs. I
Florida Keys (Fla.)—History. I Florida Keys (Fla.)—Social life and customs. I Florida—Pictorial works. I
Florida—History, Local—Pictorial works. I Key West (Fla.)—Fiction. I Florida Keys (Fla.)—Fiction. I
Florida—Fictiion. I Short stories, American. I BISAC HISTORY / United States / State & Local / South (AL,
AR, FL, GA, KY, LA, MS, NC, SC, TN, VA, WV) I BIOGRAPHY & AUTOBIOGRAPHY / Personal Memoirs I
FICTION / Short Stories (single author)
Classification: LCC F319.K4 .K73 2109 I DDC 975.9/41064/0222

Library of Congress Control Number: 2019900494

First Paperback Edition

Florida Keys' Watercolor Kapers
A Compilation Of Adventures,
Inspired By Key West Watercolors

This book is dedicated to
Norman and Dolores Kranich.
A Great Uncle and Aunt.
They loved Key West,
God Rest Their Souls.

I am greatly indebted to my Uncle Norman and Aunt Dolores. Their home was my final destination in my hike across Florida. I was welcomed into their home for an entire month. They were so pleasant and helpful as I explored Key West with the bicycle they rented for me and painted water colors.

I remember my Uncle Norman always having excellent advice for all of us kids. My uncle was always concerned about all his nieces and nephews. My aunt was such an enthusiastic person to be around. She had that slight German accent, and I can't forget….she was a fantastic cook!

Of special note, I would like to thank Norman McGlothlin who was very helpful in his military review of two stories: *No Name Key* and *Island Flavor*. My granddaughter, Madyson Elsea, helped in editing some of the stories in this book. Thanks, Mady!

Great thanks goes out to Charlotte Osterman for her review of the manuscript of this book. Again, as in my first book *A Walk Across Florida,* her PhD in English made all the difference.

In addition, my sister Denise, also lent her literary experience to this work. As I have learned through the years of writing, you just can't review too many times.

Lastly, I would like to thank my wife and my editor. She never tires of encouraging me and keeping me on track.

Thank you Joanne! I love you!

Bob

Table of Contents

Introduction

After I finished my 750 mile hike across Florida from Georgia to Key West, I ended up at my Uncle Norman's and Aunt Dolores's house. They knew that I was on my way, so my Uncle Norman was very gracious. Of his own accord he rented me a single-speed bike to tour the island the month I was there.

I roamed around and made a lot of sketches and watercolors. Later I would print out these pictures of Key West scenes, frame them, and give them to my family members for Christmas presents.

My sister, Denise Kranich, suggested that I needed to put all of my watercolors in a book, and print it. That is how this book came to be.

Each watercolor is an inspiration for a story. Some of the stories are true, such as *Western Union Cable Repair Schooner*. In fact, it is probably an historic item because I interviewed both Captain Dick Steadman and his First Mate Jack. They told me about their true adventures. The story *The Girl On The Bridge* was told the best I could remember. It is funny today, but was frustrating to me at the time. (No matter what happened, I have always loved my Uncle Norman.) Lastly, *The Met* is partially true. Uncle Norman did have a little Nash Metropolitan, although I did take some 'writer's permission' with the tale.

The rest of the stories are fiction, with both historic and locational facts.

Some stories were supposed to be short stories, but I couldn't stop! As many authors will tell you, stories have a way of taking on a life all their own. I did do a lot of research. For example, it took reading six books about the Bay of Pigs to get all of the historic and political background for *No Name Key*.

When I was finished, I wondered just where did all of this come from? I wish to thank and praise the Good Lord for it all!

Here's to good reading,

Bob

Prologue

What was that? I was coming up out of a deep sleep. It was music... melodic strains of piano music were drifting in the window. I could hear each stroke of the keys. Where was I? Looking around, I could see that I was in a very confined space. As I sat up, I remembered. I was in my uncle's and aunt's small camper trailer right next to their house. My Uncle Norman was playing the piano.

As I sat there it all came back to me… it was yesterday I had completed my *A Walk Across Florida*. It was 750-plus miles. This was the first bed I had slept in since I left home in Tampa, Florida, and started on my hike 5 and 1/2 weeks ago.

Hurriedly I dressed, combed my hair, and brushed my teeth. I didn't want to miss one of my Aunt Dolores's meals. She was a great cook.

My uncle's piano stopped as I walked by the coconut palm and went into the screened porch. This porch was on the back of the house, and as I remembered from many years ago, this was where they ate all of their meals. With the heavy wooden Key West hurricane shutters and the screens, it was just like being outside. This room was at ground level, and you had to go up about five steps to enter the kitchen.

"Hi Bobby," my aunt said, with her slight German accent, beaming down into the porch area. "Have a seat. We are about to have breakfast."

My uncle appeared smiling, " I played to wake you up. How was it?"

"Uncle Norman, it was even more beautiful than the birds' sounds I had wake me up on many of my hike mornings!"

"Now Bobby, I don't know if I can compete with nature!"

One of Aunt Dolores's daughter's two girls they were raising came in and greeted me. They were my nieces. Sandy was the older of the two, about 12, and Robin who next appeared, was about 8 years old. We all sat down, and Aunt Delores brought in our plates of sunshine eggs, as she called them. "These eggs are cooked Cuban style, Bobby," she said.

The Cuban culture has played an important part in the history of Key West. In fact, Key West was a stepping-off place as Cuban people moved on to the US mainland. Besides bringing the manufacture of cigars, they brought their many other skills and customs along with them.

After we said grace, Uncle Norman began to speak, "Bobby, I have rented a single-speed balloon tire bicycle for you. It's not very impressive, but it will get you around this island. After all, Key West is only about four miles long by one and a half miles wide."

"Thanks, Uncle Norman, that will be great! I want to get started today. I have been sketching as I hiked down here, and if I can find some watercolors and art paper I'll do some painting."

"There is a store, I'll draw you a map," he said. "Actually I have a tourist map from one of the restaurants. I'll just point it out to you and you will be able to easily locate it."

After breakfast he showed me the location of the store with art supplies on the tourist map and then the bicycle. It wasn't fancy, but it had a basket on the handle bars that would be useful to transport my necessary supplies. As I was filling one of my canteens I had used on my hiking trip, both Uncle Norman and the girls left for work and school respectively. My aunt gave me a sack lunch, and down the street I went.

As I headed towards town, I noticed that the houses were small and close together. This is the way I found everything in Key West, both the old and the new. There just wasn't any more land. I came to the end of Fogarty Avenue, glanced at my map, and wandered towards town until I came to Duval Street. It was easy enough then to find the artist supply store. Uncle Norman was right. They had everything I needed.

I bought a couple of watercolor pads, watercolor tube colors, a couple of brushes, a sketch pad, pencils and eraser. I was now in business!

According to my map I was very close to the Key West Bight. I found

out later that a "Bight" was a Key West name for harbor. This was where the Coast Guard and the Turtle Crawls were. I wanted to see the Turtle Crawls. This is the place where the sailing ship from the Cayman Islands docks and unloads their catch of green turtles. In fact I could see the masts of the Cayman Island ship, the A. M. Adams, in the distance.

I came to the docks, got off and had started to walk my bike toward the masts when I came adjacent to a beautiful old two-masted sailing ship. It was tied up to the pier that was jutting out from the concrete dock. There were a couple of guys working on a small piece of mechanical equipment right there on the pier. This was the only ship tied up there, so the natural assumption was that they were the crew of this ship.

I parked my bike and walked out onto the pier. I eased up to the pair, and just got down on my haunches like they were doing. They were concentrating on the piece of mechanical equipment. It appeared to be a small cable winch. All sorts of tools were strewn about the pier.

"What do you think mate, will we be able to salvage it?"

"Well Cap'n, if I can't find something to jerry-rig it in the local hardware store, we'll have to order some parts."

"It's old, but if we can fix it, we can save the firm money," Jack said.

The captain looked up, "What do we have here?" He looked right at me.

"It's a landlubber," the mate said.

"Who are you, young fella?" the captain asked.

"I just finished a long walk down to Key West, hiking and camping. I'm visiting my uncle and aunt on Fogarty Avenue. That's my bike over there on the dock. My name's Bob, and I am interested in your boat."

"Nice to meet you," the captain said, standing up as he wiped his greasy hand on his pants and extended it to shake.

"I'm Captain Dick Steadman, and this is my First Mate, Jack Fryer."

I didn't hesitate and took his hand in a good shake and then did the same with the First Mate, Jack.

"I'm Bob, Bob Kranich down from Tampa."

I detected a slight English accent in both their speeches.

"So you want to know about our ship, matey. Come a'board, and we'll set a spell. Jack is going to go downtown to the hardware store after lunch for some parts."

He led the way, and Jack motioned me to go ahead and follow the captain. We crossed over the water on a gangplank and sat down on some stools set together on the deck.

"Jack, run down to the galley, and get us some Cokes. That will be good enough. I don't think this young fella needs anything stronger!"

"It is not every day that the wind blows in a visitor to see us. Jack and I are the only permanent hands on this ship. If we get a call to go out by the firm, we have to search high and low around the town to get a crew."

Jack came back with the Cokes and gave one to each of us.

"Thanks Jack," we said in unison. He nodded his appreciation.

"Jack, Bob is interested in our boat, and I'm about to tell him a couple stories of our adventures."

"Bob, get set for some tall sea-faring tales," Jack said with a smile.

"Pay no mind to him," the captain said, smiling, "Here we go, Bob!"

Schooner Western Union, 1969

(Prior to having two diesel engines
installed and removing some of her sails)
Out of Key West, Florida,
Bob Kranich

1

Western Union
Cable Repair Schooner

"A little more to starboard," the captain said.

"All right, Capt'n," the First Mate said respectfully.

Relaying this to the helmsman and double-checking the magnetic compass, Captain Dick Steadman looked forward from where he stood in the stern of the cable repair schooner named the Western Union.

The tropical, turquoise Florida Bahamian sea was a spectacular sight before him.

Beautiful day for the work ahead, he thought. Light seas, sun beaming down, and not a Nor'wester in sight. If we can just find that break in this cable and get it repaired.

The schooner is the last of a vanishing breed, including the men who run her. It is a telephone-telegraph cable-laying and repair schooner. The Western Union is out of Key West, Florida. It had been only four days since they received the emergency call from headquarters in New York. There was a break in the undersea cable heading out of Key West towards the Bahama Islands.

The two full-time, and maintenance men, Captain Dick Steadman and First Mate Jack Fryer had to hunt high and low to round up a crew. They had been fortunate that eight of the ten-man crew were old hands from the last job, six months ago. It had been a hectic preparation. Not only did a crew have to be rounded up, but provisions for ten to twelve days had to be purchased. The equipment had to be stowed, and the schooner made ready. Like most boats, she was constantly being repaired and maintained, with maintenance as diverse as painting and engine tune-ups. This kept things out-of-place and disorganized.

But now, here they were, almost on station. They had been following the cable using a Leaer-Amplifier. This piece of equipment receives signals coming from the underwater cable which are being sent by the sending station. When they are over the cable the signals are strongest.

"That's it Cap'n," Jack said.

The signal had faded out, meaning that the break was below.

"Out with the buoy!" Captain Dick yelled.

"Aye, Sir!" This is just what two of the crew were waiting to hear, and overboard it went. First, they would make sure it anchored and stayed in one place. Next, they would head back the way they had come about a half-a-mile and drop out a grappling hook. Then, they would proceed to go across the cable perpendicular to it. If they hooked it they would then bring it up to the boat.

"We'll use the sand grappling hook," Captain Dick ordered.

He knew by the Fathometer* readings the bottom was sandy. The longer hooks of the sand grappling apparatus would work in this bottom.

"Ok, let her go!" the first mate commanded.

Over the side the bulk weight of the hook and chain were wrestled by Jack and the crew. This hook and chain was fastened to a cable and threaded from the pulleys on the bow of the boat around the cable drum and into the cable hold.

If they were lucky, they could snag their objective on the first try. However, sometimes they had to try as many as eight runs to finally capture the cable lying on the bottom. They had 258 fathoms* of cable out and now were making an approach perpendicular to the cable. This could be performed in relation to the buoy lines they had set out. The greatest depth they had worked in was 380 fathoms in this Bahamain area.

By the tension of grappling cable on the dynamometer* they could tell when the cable was snagged. But, this time they didn't need it, and there was a sudden lurch of the schooner.

"Full ahead!" the captain shouts.

This was needed because if they were to drop back from the force of a wave the grappling hook could let its precious catch slip loose. The next step was to winch it up and secure it to a buoy. Then the same operation had to be repeated to obtain the other end of the broken cable.

It being impossible to stretch it back together, a piece had to be spliced in. This length varied depending on the depth of the water. A 20-foot splice was about average, and that was what they did to complete the job.

The cable schooner was two-masted and was built in a shop near the Mallory Docks in Key West, in 1939. It was one of three similar types, built according to the New England coast style. She was 92-feet long, 23.5-feet wide and drew six to eight feet of water. Her top speed was about eight and one half knots* and designed primarily for shallow water. But, just like this job they were on now, she had worked a lot of deep sea.

Because of the installation of two diesel engines and placement of exhaust stacks, the main boom and sails had to be abandoned. The foresail* and rigging were still intact and at times used to steady her in a wind, but the two diesels did most of the work. There were three other engines: one turning an electric generator for the cable equipment motors, a refrigerator engine, and a light plant.

She was equipped for a crew of ten, with accommodations for captain and three in the cabin. It was a snug, but efficient design. All types of communications gear were available, such as ship-to-shore, CB and Hallicrafter short-wave for weather reports.

It was interesting to stand around on the deck of the ship and listen to these two salty characters responsible for her performance, and talk of past days. I could tell they were just as much a part of her, as she was to them.

They could spin many yarns, but one of the most interesting was the time they were returning from a job, and they passed too close to Cuba. It was just prior to the Bay of Pigs affair.

"Captain, we're kind of close to Cuban waters."

"Jack, according to my charting, we're well out of it, at least five to ten miles."

" Don't look now Cap'n, but what is that shape heading towards us on our rear port (left) side?"

"Jack, it looks like a small military vessel. I hope it's not Cuban! Helmsman, hold your course straight towards Key West. We'll pretend we don't see him."

"That's not going to work, Cap'n. He is bearing down on us very fast.

In fact he has increased speed."

The radio man appeared, head sticking out of his door. "They're trying to get us on the radio, Captain. They want us to heave-to. I can understand them in Spanish. They are also trying to use some broken English."

"Carlos, don't let on that we can understand Spanish. Speak only in English, and when they finally say something in it, answer them and see just what they want."

The radio man stuck his head right back out, "They finally got someone who can speak broken English. They want us to stop for inspection."

"Well, all they will find is a hold of grappling hooks and cable. I guess we will do what they want."

As the ship was getting closer, the radio man stuck his head out of the cabin again. "Oh, oh, sir, they just called shore and said they were bringing us in."

"Oh no! We're not going for that. I don't want to spend some time in that Communist Cuba with Fidel Castro! Get on the ship-to-shore radio, and try to get ahold of some American authorities on the line, Carlos, and fast!"

"Aye, Aye, Captain Jack, I'm getting on that radio."

"Here Captain, I've got someone who's got us hooked up with the U. S. Navy I think," the radio man said.

"Hello, this is Captain Dick Steadman of the Western Union out of Key West. I've got a Cuban gunboat off my stern and closing fast. They just radioed their HQ and said that they were going to bring us in, to Cuba!"

"Hold on Captain Steadman, this is Captain Smithe of the U. S. Navy. Don't let them board you. You'll have a couple of jets from Guantanamo over you in a few minutes. We're scrambling right now!"

At that point the Cuban gunboat was off their center port-side and they could see what appeared to be the captain with a megaphone trying to get their attention.

Suddenly out of the low-hanging cumulus clouds came two U. S. Navy jets streaking right over them. In fact they were so close that the exhaust blast and turbulence blew their sails and violently rocked both boats.

In a couple of minutes they were coming back. Suddenly the radio crackled on.

"Western Union, this is U. S. Navy jet overhead. Can you make a run for it? We'll cover."

"U. S. Navy jet, this is Captain Steadman on the Western Union, negative. I repeat, negative. We have some large drums of fuel for the engines on the deck. We'll have to ease off."

"Western Union, hang on, we have a ship on the way."

Jack went over to the control area and stopped one of the diesel engines. He then proceeded to flood the engine, and when he tried to start it a large puff of smoke came out.

Captain Steadman yelled out, "Jack, shrug your shoulders, and make it seem that we are having trouble with the engines."

"Ok Cap'n."

Jack went into his act of gesturing to the Cubans they were having trouble with their engines. The captain slowly moved the schooner away from the Cuban gunboat using the one engine that was still running. He kept the electrical current turned off on the second engine. Then, he occasionally switched the starter on. This made it seem like he was trying to get the second engine running.

U S Navy Vought A-7 Corsair jets from Guantanamo

The Cubans' boat turned around and their captain motioned for them to follow.

The captain stuck his head out and yelled to Jack, "Try to make them understand that we have only one engine, and we will follow very slowly."

Jack continued his motions and tried to signal about the one engine.

This went on for a few hours with the Western Union slowly following the Cuban gunboat. They both could see that the Cubans were nervously looking skyward.

Then they saw a grey shape in the distance heading towards them as the two Navy jets screamed back overhead. It was a U. S. Navy destroyer. It was signaling with a blinker signal offering full protection. The Cubans must have been able to read that, because right after the boat came into view, the Cuban gunboat captain motioned for the Western Union to go on. Captain Jack didn't need a second invitation. He cleared the engine he had been playing with and it roared to a sudden start. They put the hammer down and headed straight for Key West with the U. S. Navy destroyer following right behind. In fact, the Navy escorted the Western Union the 90 miles back to Key West. They had gotten within a half mile of the Cuban coast. A very close call!

The Western Union was framed up with local mahogany lumber in the Cayman Islands by Mr. Heber Elroy Arch.* The planking was two inch thick long-leaf yellow pine brought over from north Florida. After it was framed and planked, it was disassembled and shipped to Key West on the Thompson Enterprises' 130-foot Cayman Island turtle schooner, A. M. Adams.

The keel was laid at the Mallory Docks in Key West. Everything that was built in the Cayman Islands was attached, the Oregon Fir masts installed, and the boat finished. It took Mr. Elroy who had the contract to build the boat, a brother, five Caymanians and four Key Westers to finish the boat.*

The Western Union was finished in 1939, and then it served unofficially during the war watching the Florida Key West waters for German U-boats.* It laid and repaired cables from Florida to South and Central America, the Caribbean islands and the U. S. Gulf Coast States from 1939 to mid-1974. The Captain Dick Steadman in this story was the second generation of Steadmans who captained the Western Union.*

In 1974 the Western Union was converted into a sailing ship for tours and charters. In 1984, the ship was sold and used in Philadelphia for troubled youth by the Vision Quest National organization. It was also added to the National Register of Historic Places.* The Western Union was back in Key West again in 1997 with the Historic Tours of America as a day and sunset tour and charter ship. She was used by film makers as the sailing ship in the 1997 movie *La Armistad.*

Historic Tours of America donated the Western Union to the Schooner Western Union Preservation Society (SWUPS) in 2007 on the condition it remain in Key West and be restored.* The ship went into dry dock for restoration in 2008 and did not emerge with U. S. Coast Guard approval until three years later.

The city of Key West realized the Western Union was the last tall sailing ship built on their island. Consequently it was named the official flagship of Florida by the Florida legislature in 2012.*

Today, the Western Union is docked in Key West at the city's bight at 202 William Street.* One can take a dock-side tour or a sailing trip. It is officially used by the non profit, locally supported SWUPS for day, sunset, moonlight, charter, and children's educational activities as well as charitable events.*

Robin skipped down the street right past Mary Jane's house.
She passed a small Key West cottage and noticed the Royal Poincianas were in full bloom.

2

The Stowaway

"Grandma, that was a great breakfast!"

Robin was being especially nice this morning…because she was up to something. Eight years old, she was a tomboy through and through! She was petite, and her reddish-brown hair barely came to her shoulders. But do not let her debonair disposition and sweet looks fool you!

Her grandmother Dolores and grandpa Norman were raising her and her sister, Sandra. Dolores thought for a brief moment, hum, Robin is being especially nice this morning…but then let it pass.

"Grandma, can I go over to Mary Jane's and play today? I'll come back by supper time. It's only a couple blocks away."

"Dear, you have to get permission from Mary Jane's mother."

"Grandma, I already did. Don't you remember? Last night when we were at the grocery store and we saw Mary Jane and her mom, I asked permission then."

"Ok honey, but make sure you are home in time for supper."

"Thank you, Grandma," Robin said as she stood on her tiptoes and kissed her grandma on the cheek.

Robin ran through the house to her and her sister's room. Her sister was nowhere to be seen, but water was running in the shower. Her sister always finished her meals much before Robin, and then left the table.

Robin thought…the coast is clear. She grabbed her little purse, popped open the piggy bank, took out a handful of change and dropped it in her purse. Out the front door she went.

"Bye Grandma, I love you!" she said as the door slammed shut.

Robin happily skipped down the sidewalk, right past Mary Jane's house. A block later she thought to herself, here is the street I need to take. It will bring me to North Roosevelt Boulevard. It is the one next to our school, and there is a push-button that stops the cars. I can then cross over that busy street. The street had some older houses on it, and Robin thought the red-pink flowers on those trees were really pretty.

Robin's plan she had conjured up was working. Her grandpa had promised to take her fishing in his motor boat today…but then the Navy base called him for some special work. After all, he was the base paymaster. She didn't know just what he had to do. It was something about a holiday coming up. But she thought, it wasn't fair! He had promised, so she was going fishing by herself anyway!

When she came to the corner, she could see that the boulevard was very busy both ways with cars. Tourists, she thought. She pushed the button, and shortly the white hand in the light across the street beckoned her as all of the cars on Roosevelt Boulevard came to a halt. Wow, she thought that was great!

Once across she could see her destination. About a block to the right were the charter boat docks. She had seen them lots of times while driving to Key West with her grandparents. She had also read the signs:

FISHING
FULL AND HALF DAY
CHARTER & TOUR BOATS

In this area there was room for cars to pull in and park, a very wide sidewalk, and then wooden docks and piers. There were small office shacks, wide areas with game fish weighing scales, and all types of fishing boats.

Robin walked along with the gaping tourists. There were fishermen, deck hands, and captains standing about the area. She came to a shack with a sign. She tried to read it and then remembered what her teacher had said. Sound it out…

There is the word cap, I know it, Cap...tain.
Jack, I know that word Jack. One of my friends at school is
named Jack.
Ok, Captain Jack
De...ep
Sea, and I know sea, it's water and
Fishing, that's what I want to do!
Let's see;

CAPTAIN JACK'S DEEP SEA FISHING

"This place will do," she said out loud. Now just how do I get on that boat? Then a man came out of the shack wearing a brimmed white hat with an important looking emblem on it, and boomed out, "We're ready to load!"

The people started to form a line heading towards the pier where a large boat was tied up. Robin saw a middle-aged couple holding hands in line and she got behind them, staying very close. When the three of them got up to, and passed by the check-in point, the captain looked down at her suspiciously.

Just then a loud siren went off behind them in the street. A police car with lights flashing went by. When the captain looked down again Robin was nowhere to be seen. She was out on the deck next to the couple. It is possible that even though they were middle-aged they could have been newlyweds on a honeymoon. They did not seem to notice a little girl hanging around them.

This boat they were on was named *Full Catch*. It was pretty impressive! From front to rear a total of 57 feet, with dual 750 HP each Caterpillar diesel inboard engines, and a flying bridge topping the boat off.

Tall, large, and muscular, Captain Jack had lived in Key West all his life. His parents together with 10-year-old Jack were moved there in 1935 by the U S Navy. His dad, a captain in his own right, commanded many different types of ships to include one of the submarine tender support ships. He was efficient and had all the right connections, so that he served in Key West until after the War, then retired in Key West.

After graduation from high school, Jack worked on many local fishing boats. He was a very thrifty fella and saved up enough money for a down payment on his dream boat and business, *Captain Jack's Deep Sea Fishing*. He had been at this the last 10 years and loved every minute of it. Another couple of years and he would own this boat and all the profit would then be his.

Captain Jack climbed up to the flying bridge. He caught one of his two mate's eyes, nodded and commanded, "Cast off, John."

Both John and the other helper, Chuck, unwound the ropes holding the boat to the pier and then coiled them back in place. Jack flipped the starters for both engines. Without hesitation they both blasted on with a tremendous roar!

You could hear that hollow echo from the pipes against the water. He carefully eased the boat away from its mooring, slowly turned it around, and gave the two engines a little throttle. Soon they were out of the Garrison Bight and into the channel. To keep in the center of the channel he had to keep the correct channel markers to his port and starboard (left and right).

The *Full Catch* had to swing out and around the western end of Key West. He had to keep a watch out for fishermen and an occasional Navy ship out from the submarine basin from the U S Naval Station.

Jack's two crew members moved among their 12 customers showing them chairs to sit in, conversing and tending to the ship's needs. From his perch high up on the flying bridge Jack could see that all his customers were getting settled.

Jack pushed both throttles forward. The bow of the ship came up and then, from the powerful surge of the two engines, it proceeded to come back down as the rear of the ship came up. The entire ship was leveled out. It was now planing,* moving at a fast clip and cutting the waves smoothly. Jack sure loved this action. He could feel the surge of power. He felt it through his entire body, from his fingers on the throttles to the vibration in the soles of his feet. He felt free...free as a bird, an albatross* to be exact.

With this action it was only about 45 minutes until they were past the Navy yard and on just the Atlantic side of Key West. Captain Jack pulled back on the throttles. The boat slowed and dropped in the water.

Jack came down the ladder, off the bridge.

He announced, "Now folks gather round. We've got more than enough fishing rigs for everyone. One per person. My mates, John and Chuck will help you get baited up. Then, we will ease out into the Gulf, and you will let your lines out, and we'll troll. Try not to get tangled up with anyone. If the person next to you gets a strike, please ease slightly away from them with your rig. Remember every day we get something. It may be good eating such as Mahi-mahi or even a trophy! If you don't get anything, I give you back half of your money. You will see that Captain Jack and his boys know where the fish are! Now, let the fun begin!"

Jack could see that all the customers were spread out on the sides and rear of the boat, lines out. There was one little problem. It looked like John was having a time outfitting a little girl with a rod and reel. Jack went over to them. Then he remembered...this was the little girl he had seen during loading!

"John, go up on the bridge, take the helm and start a slow troll, I'll take over here."

"Aye aye, Cap'n," John snapped to...and headed for the bridge.

"Now little girl, what's your name?"

"Robin, Sir," she looking up at a towering giant.

"Robin, shouldn't you be over with your parents?"

"They're not my parents, Sir," she said sheepishly, looking down.

"Well, then, just who are you with?" he demanded in a thundering voice.

"No one, Sir...Captain."

"So we have a stowaway!"

"What's a stowaway, Sir?"

"Leave the rod and reel here, and come with me."

"But Sir, I need to fish! My grandpa said that he would take me fishing, but they called him in to the Navy Base to work!"

"Just come with me, we'll talk about that later."
They proceeded to climb up to the bridge.

"Just keep it going John, we've got a stowaway."

"Ha," John said, "I was beginning to wonder about that."

"Have a seat there," Jack said to Robin as he pointed to an equipment chest with a padded top.

He picked up a hand microphone and punched a side switch on the radio. "What's your grandpa's name, Robin?"

"Norman Kranich," she said softly.

He spoke into the microphone, "Key West Central, this is Captain Jack's deep sea fishing boat. Over."

"We hear you Captain Jack, go ahead. Over."

"That you Sam? Over."

" Yes Jack, what you need? Over."

"Sam, I'm out on a fishing trip with a bunch of customers, and I've got a stowaway. There's no problem, but can you patch me in to Key West telephone, a Norman Kranich? Over."

"Sure can, Jack. Just a minute. Over."

"Hello, Norman Kranich residence, Mrs. Kranich here."

"Ma'am, this is Key West Central, Ship-to-Shore. Hold on please while I make a connection."

"This is Key West Central, I have Mrs. Kranich on the line. Go ahead Jack. Over."

"Mrs. Kranich?"

"Yes, speaking."

"Ma'm, This is Captain Jack of Captain Jack's Deep Sea Fishing. I have your little granddaughter Robin on my boat. It seems that she stowawayed to go deep sea fishing."

"Captain, what a shocker!" Robin's grandmother exclaimed.

"Is she ok?"

"Yes ma'am. I can't turn around right now. I'm about 3 miles into the Atlantic and working with customers. But we will see you this afternoon at 5:00 at the deep sea fishing docks, Garrison Bight, pier 7."

"Thank you Captain Jack. Wait until her grandpa hears about this!"

"You're welcome, Ma'm. Go easy on her, she seems to be a great kid!"

"Key West Central, Sam, Captain Jack here, Thanks. Over."

"Think nothing of it, Jack. Key West Central, Out."

"John, you got the helm, keep trolling. This little girl and I are going to do some fishing."

They went down the stairs and over to the fishing tackle hanging on the side of the cabin.

"Here Robin, take this rod and reel. Let's go to the stern, and I'll bait the hook for you."

Jack could see his customers had already brought in a fair amount of fish. Some of them were Mahi-mahi and some Kingfish.

"Here Robin, this is how you bait the hook with one of these larger cigar minnows like this." Jack put the hook in the minnow's mouth and then stuck it into the head.

"There now, throw the line, bait, hook and sinker in. Let it reel out like this." He showed her how to let the line out and then flipped on the drag.

"Like this, Captain?" Robin asked enthusiastically.

"Yep, you're doing good," the captain said.

No sooner had the line and bait got out about 40 yards when wham! A strike!

"What do I do?" Robin yelled.

"Hold steady and reel it in," Jack exclaimed.

REK

Just then a Sailfish broke the surface behind the boat dancing on it's tail. He could see that it was a real pull for an 8-year-old kid. She was reeling hard.

"It sure is hard to turn," Robin said.

Then the sailfish jumped again. It was a big one! Jack was getting excited!

Robin said, "Captain Jack, I don't think I can hold the rod any more. He is pulling hard!"

"Lay your rod down temporarily against the rail and keep reeling," he advised. "When the fish stops pulling for a moment we will put the rod in this holder I just put around my waist." As the fish paused, Captain Jack said, "Quick, Robin, put the rod in the holder. I'll hold the rod, and you turn the reel."

Robin was cranking hard.

Then a chorus of customers all said in unison, "Wow look at that!"

Many of the customers were bringing in their lines. Some were just watching, and others were reaching for their cameras.

Jack yelled up to John on the bridge, "Do what you can with the boat to tire this fish out!"

"Aye aye, Captain." John started maneuvering the *Full Catch* to help.

Robin was continuing to reel while Jack held the rod steady in his holder. All of a sudden, there he was…not a winning trophy, but a good size sailfish. Chuck was right there with the gaff as he hooked the fish and maneuvered it over a net which was hooked to a winch lift. Up and out it came. Robin's eyes were as big as saucers!

Captain Jack looked around at his admiring fishing customers. He asked, "Anyone not got any fish?"

"Chuck said, "They all got lots of fish! It's been a successful trip.""

"Well then, it's time to head in so we can get back by 5:00. Robin and I will take the bridge. John and Chuck, please help the customers with their fish."

"Let's go home!"

Grandpa Norman, Grandma Delores, and Sandy had just stepped out of their car. As they went on to the dock they saw Captain Jack's *Full Catch* easing up to the pier. They couldn't believe their eyes when they saw who was on the flying bridge sitting in the captain's chair waving to them.

As Chuck and John were tying up, Robin yelled, "Grandma, Grandpa, Sandy, come see my sailfish!"

Captain Jack jumped off the boat, shook hands with Grandpa Norman and said, as he tipped his captain's hat, "Ma'am" to grandma, "Could you stay around a little while, we have some advertising pictures to take."

A Key West Herald newspaper car came up and a reporter and cameraman jumped out. "Where is that sailfish? Where is that little girl?"

Jack pointed, "Right over there with my two mates, John and Chuck. They are just now hanging it up."

Full Catch was coming into the docks. Up on the flying bridge was Captain Jack manning the bridge, and Robin waving to her grandparents and Sandy on the pier.

They all walked over to the fish display area on the pier next to the small office shack. This included the bewildered Grandma Dolores, Grandpa Norman, and Sandy.

Robin was there right next to her sailfish.

"Hi Grandma! Hi Grandpa! Hi Sandy! "Come here. Look at my sailfish!" Captain Jack went over, put his arm around her as they posed with the sailfish. Light bulbs flashing!

The next morning they saw a banner headline in the Key West newspaper, Sports Section.

Eight-Year-Old Girl Catches 80 lb. Sailfish
With the help of Captain Jack of
"CAPTAIN JACK'S DEEP SEA FISHING"

I really enjoyed writing this little fictional story. It brought back memories of roaming the Key West fishing docks. However, there really was and is a Robin.

Love you and God Bless you, Robin

Bob

Manuel was out on the Key West main city dock in the early morning. He had hopes for a quiet uneventful day...What was that young fella doing? Sketching him!

3
No Name Key

Manuel had been coming down to the Key West city docks in the early morning just to sit and fish on the pier. He had been doing this the last few months since he retired at age 65. Manuel's last job had been as a civilian stevedore working on the dock at the Navy Yard Base. He had done some special planning for this day's fishing. He had bought some live shrimp for bait, an ice chest, a comfortable folding lawn chair, and his lunch. Now he could get down to some serious fishing.

Manuel was Cuban American. He came here with his parents in 1914 at the age of 10. He had two younger sisters. His grandfather's ancestry dated back to the 1400's. That's when the Spanish conquistadores made the Cuban natives slaves to work the sugar cane plantations.

His mother was a natural born Cuban native. Manuel was average height, about five foot eleven inches. He was still fairly muscular and in trim shape from the previous eight years working at the dock. He also had strong black features, and he was very proud of it!

Out of the corner of his eye, he saw a young man on a bicycle pulling up to the sidewalk next to the pier. Since it was early morning, not too many people were on the docks, especially the tourists!

Just what was this young man up to? He could see that this guy was paying close attention to him. Did he have a camera? No, he was sketching him. He said to himself, "I hope this fella is not a member of the D.G.I. (direccion de inteligencia, Cuban Secret Police).

It hadn't been too long ago, only eight years, since that April 1961, the Bay of Pigs Invasion. He was sure he had covered his tracks. No one except the C.I.A, and the Navy's Human Resources individual who hired him knew he had participated. His family didn't even know. There *was* one other person, his friend who had talked him into it. However he was sworn to secrecy.

His mind started to drift off. It was late February in 1961. He and Hector had been laid off from the old fish cannery which was located along the Key West docks. Even though Hector was much younger than he, they were good friends. Hector had been 28, single, individualistic and invincible. He was light-skinned and primarily of Cuban descent.

Every day after looking for work, they would come down to the docks and fish after supper. This particular evening they were sitting on a couple of folding chairs, poles held in their one hand, and a cold lemonade in the other.

Suddenly Hector said, "We should join the Cuban Freedom Fighters and go help kick Fidel Castro out of Cuba!"

"What are you talking about?" Manuel asked.

"I've heard that the C.I.A. is actively recruiting in Miami for a brigade of Cubans to overthrow Castro."

"Where do you get your information? I haven't heard anything about that!" Manuel exclaimed.

"One of my friend's brothers went up to Miami. He said don't tell anyone but he went up to join and hasn't returned."

Manuel said, "That doesn't prove anything. He could be partying in Miami! By the way, how do you know the F.B.I. is recruiting?"

"Not the F.B.I.," Hector said, "It's the C.I.A.! Everyone knows about it. Haven't you read the Miami Herald newspaper? Besides, I know a better way to enlist and train. Word on this island...is that some of them are training on No Name Key."

"What do you mean No Name Key? What is the name of the Key?" Manuel asked.

"No Name Key is the name of the Key next to and East of Big Pine Key," Hector answered.

"I always thought that was Little Pine Key," Manuel said. "Now just where did you get this information? Super Spy!"

"Well, smart guy, you know that I play Double 9 Dominoes with *Island Jim* down at Sloppy Joes. You know the guy that everyone's trying to beat at his own game. Jim doesn't have to get around, the whole island comes to him! That guy is definitely in the center of things at Sloppy Joe's and Key West. He hears all, knows all, and sees all. Says that some group is training on No Name Key."*

"What do you propose to do?" Manuel asked.

"Let's borrow my brother's car and drive up to No Name, and see if we can join," Hector stated. "Hey man, at least we can see just what's going on. We can't find any work. We've looked everywhere the last few weeks. Let's finally do something good for our country. Let's make Cuba free!"

"OK," Manuel said somewhat reluctantly, "What time will you pick me up tomorrow morning?"

"Let's start early, say 7 AM? It's only about a 30 mile drive."

The old '48 Ford pulled up to Manuel's drive. Manuel saw it and came down the steps of his parents' two-story classical revival house. The house had been in the family since his parents bought it after they arrived in Key West. The house was historic by the fact that it was probably cut out and assembled in the Cayman Islands and then shipped to Key West, and reassembled at the turn of the century.

Hector drove out of the old town section over to Roosevelt Boulevard and then turned right along the deep sea fishing docks. They crossed the bridge to Stock Island and were on their way. The Boca Chica Naval Air Station was on their right. There were a couple of huge Naval dirigibles outside near their hangers. These lighter than air ships were originally used for anti-submarine detection during the Second World War. Manuel and Hector could also see and hear a couple of Navy planes lining up on one of the runways to take off.

"Now Hector, what do you know about this No Name Key?"

"Well, I asked my brother, and he knows something about it. He used to fish up that way. I also talked to *Island Jim* at Sloppy Joe's, and he knew a lot about it. They say that today the island is uninhabited. But in the late 1800's, according to a census, it had 45 residents. In the early 1900's there was a school with over 20 students. The hurricane of 1919 wiped out the school.

In 1930 the construction of the last wooden bridge from Key West was completed. Because of this a lodge was started on No Name. The bridge linked Big Pine Key to No Name and on No Name there was a ferry east to Lower Matecumbe Key. The whopper hurricane of 1935 wiped out the ferry service. After that the lodge changed owners and names. It was then called No Name Key Fish Camp until the 1948 hurricane finished off the last of the old wooden bridge. With all of the accesses and camps gone through the 50's, No Name became uninhabited. The Key is about a mile wide and two miles long. What is strange is that this little Key is in places 3 to 4 feet higher than Big Pine Key which is over four times larger."

"Wow! Unbelievable! How did you retain all of that?" Manuel asked.

"You know that I like history, and besides I'm not old like you. I have a memory," Hector said with a big smile.

"Look at this, you talked so much, here's our turn, Highway 4A. We didn't even see Marathon when we went through it! There's a store on the corner. Let's stop and ask around. Maybe we can pick up some snacks and food just in case we find some freedom fighters," Manuel stated.

"Good idea," Hector agreed.

The '48 Ford eased up to an unpainted wooden building. It had a few signs out front and one old gas pump. They got out and walked in. The screen door slammed with a bang behind them.

"Howdy gents. What can I do for ya?" An older man greeted them from behind a wooden counter next to an antique cash register.

Hector replied, "We need to buy some snacks, a few supplies and then we need information about No Name Key."

"What do you need to know about No Name Key?" he asked, and then added, "Seems there were a couple of guys in here last week asking about No Name."

Manuel wandered around picking up items he thought they could use, being very particular with their limited funds.

"Well," Hector asked, "Is there any way to get over there? I guess that old wooden bridge is gone?"

"Yep, the old wooden bridge went out with the hurricane of '48 and then a fire finished what was left of it. All that remains are rows of old wood pilings. But I can tell you two a way to get over there if you don't have a boat. You don't have a boat, do you?"

"No, but we sure could use an idea," Hector said.

"You guys look like good honest customers. So I'm going to give you an idea. But don't tell anyone I told you so. When you get to the end of the road, park your car. Then face No Name Key, and you will see all those pilings out in the water. If you turn left you will see a faint trail through the mangroves. Go down that trail, and you will come to a very small beach. If no one is using it, you will see a small row boat. Everyone around here uses it. You will need these oars. I will need a ten dollar deposit and will keep five when you bring them back.”

“Wow, thanks a lot,” Hector said.

Manuel came to the front and dropped some items on the counter.

“What do you think, Hector, two cans of spam, beef jerky, a couple of cans of beans and sardines, hard candy, and a loaf of bread. That is about all we can afford. I heard about the ten dollars for the oars. How about we give you five dollars, Old Timer, and you can trust us to bring them back? We’ll give you our driver’s license numbers.”

“You look like trusty souls. I’ll let you have them. By the way, that will be $6.67 for the food, $5 for the oars, $11.67 total.”

“Add a couple of moon pies and two Cokes to that bill,” Hector said.

“That will be an additional 93 cents for a total of $12.60.”

Hector and Manuel each pulled out some dollar bills. The old man bagged up the food.

“Thanks a lot, Old Timer,” Hector said as he took the oars. Manuel carried the bag of food.

“Keep a look out for those fellers who were towing a boat and trailer,” the old man said.

“Sure will,” Hector answered.

“We will have to stick those oars out of one of the back windows,” Manuel said. “They are kind of long.”

Hector rolled down the window, closed the back door and slid the oars in. It didn’t take long to drive the couple of miles down the road and then a right turn onto the smaller road to the water. They could see No Name Key and the row of wood posts heading out to it. They parked the car on the left side of the road.

“The old man was right,” Hector said. “Look over there.”

On the right off the road behind some pine trees and brush was a ‘60 Oldsmobile with a boat trailer hooked on to it.

Hector said, “It isn’t too big of a boat. See the trailer, probably a 12 to 15 foot runabout, with an outboard motor.”

They grabbed the food and oars and went down to the shore next to the pilings. There they saw a faint trail heading towards the mangroves. The mangroves were thick, but someone had made a faint trail through them a little ways from the water. It was an old trail, with no new cuts on the undergrowth. It wasn’t far, and all of a sudden they broke out into a very small sand beach. There away from the water and tied to a gnarled pine tree was a rowboat, none-the-worse for wear, kind of like one of those early 50's plywood wonders with faded and peeling green paint.

"Captain," Manuel said to Hector, "here's the oars, let's get her down to the water and get across to yon far island."

They dropped the food and oars into the boat and dragged it down to the water.

"This boat is a lot lighter than it looks," Hector said, kind of surprised.

"Yes...thank goodness, it's the plywood, lots better than planks."

They got it in the water, and Hector got in and said, "Since I'm the captain, as you said, and I've got to row, you as first mate need to wade in the water and push me off!"

"Aye aye, Captain," Manuel replied as he threw his socks and shoes in the boat, waded in and pushed hard. The boat broke free of the sand, Manuel jumped in, and they were rocking with the waves. They were both experienced fishermen, and this was not new to them. Hector hooked the oars in the locks and pulled hard toward No Name Key.

"We'll put in next to the old bridge pilings. It should be clear there, and we can secure the boat and hide the oars," Manuel suggested.

"Sounds good to me," Hector agreed.

It was a sunny day, clear and still. There were no waves to speak of between Big Pine and No Name. In fact, it didn't look too deep. They pulled up to an abutment of pilings and old railroad ties.

Manuel jumped out before the captain could issue orders and pulled the boat up on the sand next to the pilings. Hector got out, feet dry.

"Good work, first mate," he said.

They dragged the boat up the cleared area and tied it to a stout, stunted, and bent over pine.

"I'm going to take the oars with us and then hide them," Manuel said. "The best way for us to go I think is along this old Highway 4A. I know at the other side of the island, and at the end of this road is the old camp."

They had to search hard at times to keep the deer trail in sight. The open area of what was originally Highway 4A soon turned into basically a trail. Overgrown at that! It appeared it was used primarily by the Key deer. Normally it wouldn't have taken very long to hike the approximately one and one quarter miles, but since it was overgrown it took a little over an hour. The vegetation in semi-tropical areas grows fast. Finally they got to the end of the trail and came to a small sand beach.

"Look how the coral fill goes out into the water from here. That's the old roadbed to the ferry landing. There used to be a fishing camp over there in the old days. There might be a house or cabin left standing.

The Freedom Fighters may be set up there," Manuel said,

"Look over there." Manuel again pointed north along the beach. "Just past that mangrove clump, there is a small house. It's right next to the coconut palms."

"It must be one of the old lodge buildings," Hector said. "Let's check it out."

Manuel headed along the beach towards it still carrying the oars, which he had decided not to leave. When they got there they could see it was just a small beach cabin. The front had a slight overhang. There was a rusty metal roof and weathered brown wood siding with faint traces of a long-ago painted white-wash. A screen door hung on one hinge, and since it was open, it invited a look inside. Everything about the place said old, almost ancient.

Manuel said, "There's a small building up the beach near the coconut palms."

"I'll leave these oars out here against the building."

They went in very cautiously. The darkness inside kept them from instantly seeing anything. As their eyes adjusted to the darkness, they could see that there were only two rooms. The inside wall covering was gone. There was only a wood frame skeleton with the outside boards showing. The room they were in was basically empty except for an old wooden chair near the opening.

"Check the back room," Hector pointed.

"OK!" motioned Manuel as he moved towards it. He opened the door a little at a time. The room was partially lit up from the light shining in from the one remaining window.

"We got something!" Manuel exclaimed.

There was an old wood table, three old chairs, and over in the corner of the back wall two U. S. Army camo-green rucksacks. There were also three dark green U. S. Army rolled-up sleeping bags.

"It looks like some of them are actually holed up here. I guess they are out on maneuvers," Hector stated.

"What do we do?" Manuel questioned.

"Let's go outside and have a look around," Hector suggested.

They stepped outside into the bright sunlight, blinking as their eyes adjusted. The house was set back only a little ways from the sandy beach. A couple of coconut palms on either side stood between them and the water. That was when Hector noticed something, "Look, there's a couple of coconut husks lying around the tree." He walked over to them, "These coconuts have been opened recently."

They were both bending down looking, when a voice rang out, "Hey boys! Who are you?"

Both Hector and Manuel swung around, startled. They stood up.

"Hold it right there you two! Move slow and put your hands up!"

Three men were standing in front of the house. They were dressed in Army green camouflage. One man, short and stocky, was moving towards them. The other two had what appeared to be M-1 carbines, not pointed

at them, but they were certainly in a ready position.

The man moving towards them stopped about ten feet away. They could see that he had a U. S. Army .45 in a holster on a web belt. It was unsnapped.

"Who are you two? What are you up to?" he demanded.

"We are looking for the Freedom Fighters. We came here to join up and train." Hector said.

Manuel added, "Yeah, we want to kick Castro out of Cuba."

"It sounds pretty noble," the guy said. "But I have to ask you, are you connected in any way with the law?"

"No!" they both said in unison.

"Why do you ask?" Hector questioned.

"Sometimes they don't take too kindly to us training out here," the guy answered. "If you two don't mind, I have to see if you're armed, and we'll have to frisk you. Just a precaution."

"Go ahead," Manuel said.

"Slim."

They knew now that this guy was definitely the leader.

One of the other two, a tall thin fellow, slung his rifle over his shoulder, came around behind, and patted them down.

"Clean," Slim stated.

"OK guys, you can put your hands down . Sorry I was so abrupt at first, but we can't be too careful," the leader said. "If you want to, we'll go inside, out of sight, and talk." The leader headed towards the house with Manuel and Hector following, and the two others bringing up the rear.

He stopped at the door and turned around facing them. "We'll do the introductions now because Joe will be keeping a watch outside. You know Slim, and I'm Roy. We only use first names. I'm sure you guys understand. Slim and I are over from the Keys, and Joe, the mainland. How about you guys?"

Manuel answered, "I'm Manuel, and my young friend here is Hector. We're Key West Conchs. We got laid off a month ago."
Hector added, "We'd like to do something for our homeland, and here we are."

"Joe, keep an outside watch. Slim, the door. Let's go to the back room." They went in. Roy sat down at the table.

"Pull up a chair, and we'll talk. First I can't sign you two up as Cuban Freedom Fighters. You will have to go up to Miami for that. We're training on our own. We do have a couple of contacts, but I can't talk about that. What I can give you is about two days of good hard survival training and some M-1 basics. We don't shoot much, don't want to alert anyone. But you'll each get a couple of shots. We're out of here after that."

"What do you think, Hector?" Manuel asked. "Sounds like we can learn a lot from these guys."

"Ya, sure, I'm in," Hector answered.

"We've trained here a few times before. We try to live off the land. What we'll do first is eat up that bag of food you left outside the door, so you won't be tempted later. Then you two will hoof the two rucksacks. We will travel around this island for our meals, camps, stealth and weapons training, and water source location. Now break out the food, and let's eat!"

Roy stood up, opened the door to the front room and said, "Slim, bring in the bag of food. These guys are going to treat!"

"Sounds good. I haven't eaten store-bought grub for at least three days!" Slim exclaimed.

Slim brought in the guys' food bag and set it down on the table. "I brought your oars inside, so they'll be out of sight. It's good you didn't leave them in the boat. We would have hid them." Slim proudly stated, "We saw you rowing over and followed you to the house...Let's eat!"

Hector and Manuel opened up and divided their rations into five portions. It wasn't much.

"Slim, as soon as you finish eating, swap places with Joe and let him dine," Roy commanded.

"Yes sir." Slim did a faint salute. He went out to the next room taking his and Joe's food.

"Manuel, Hector, let's get started." Roy went over to one of the rucksacks, opened a pocket and took out a *U. S. Army FM 21-76 Survival Manual.**

"You guys can have this. Read it when you have time. I've got more back in the car."

"Thanks," they both replied.

"We'll spend an hour or two here, and then we'll move out. First item in survival is water, good potable water. We're lucky here. This island is made up of oolitic limestone, and you can find fresh water in its formations. So we look for fresh water holes. Now food, that's another problem. If we were desperate we could shoot a Key deer. But here that is illegal. However, we have rabbits, land crabs, crawfish, fish, and birds. As far as plants, occasionally we find old cultivated fruit trees, sapodillas and limes. There's coconuts, some berries, and pine needles for tea."

"I'm going to take Joe's place, and he will come in here and show you how to break down and clean an M-1 carbine."

He went out where Joe was and said, "Joe, will you show Hector and Manuel the essentials of an M-1?"

"Yes sir."

Joe came in, laid his M-1 on the table and pointed it away from everyone. "You guys ever use a firearm?"

Hector replied, ".22 rifle."

Manuel answered, "Hunting shotgun, a few times."

"At least that's something," Joe noted and then went on.

"First, make sure it's on safety. Pop out the clip, like this. Eject the chamber round. Put the round back in the magazine. You can easily field strip this carbine. Like this: the three basic parts are the receiver and trigger group, barrel, and stock. You'll find the cleaning tools, rags and oil here in the stock. Brush it off, clean the barrel with this tool. A little oil on the rag. Wipe all metal down with the oil rag. Lightly! Put it all back together in this order: Snap! Crack! Click! If you practice this, you should be able to field strip, clean and reassemble in a couple of minutes in the dark."

"Now, I'm not going to put the clip in. But here's how to load and fire."

"Wow! You really know your stuff. You military?" Hector questioned.

"Drafted in '46. Korean War. Civilian now," Joe stated. "We'll let you shoot a couple tomorrow. For now each of you break it down, and go through the motions of cleaning."

He left the M-1 on the table, took the clip and went into the next room.

"Got them through it sir. They're practicing."

"Good. At 1430 (military time),* we'll head out south to the old 'M' homestead. Show them how to find water. We'll check the traps. How about you take the point? After you get your carbine back, have Slim bring up the rear."

Roy and Joe went back into the rear room.

"How you guys coming?" Roy asked.

"We have each been through it a couple of times. It will take more practice to go through it in the dark in a couple of minutes."

"You're right there! Joe is going to need his carbine."

Joe picked it up, checked it, snapped in the magazine, and checked the safety.

"I'll check with Slim and get ready sir."

"OK Joe," Roy said,

Then Joe went out.

"Guys, we're going to shove off. You each get a rucksack. I hope you don't mind, but you two need the practice. We'll leave the sleeping bags here. We've got plastic tarps and three lightweight mosquito nets in the packs. You'll have to share one of the nets. Each net is big enough to get two people under. Let's go!"

It was 2:30 exactly when Joe met them at the house and they headed back towards the trail which was Highway 4-A. Joe was out front with Roy following, and Manuel and Hector behind him lugging the rucksacks. Just back of them a short distance, Slim brought up the rear.

When they got to the 4-A they headed back the way Hector and Manuel had come in. After about a quarter of a mile Joe up ahead was pointing to the south. As they came up to him he went into the brush on what appeared to be a faint animal trail. Most likely Key deer, Manuel thought. Roy held them for a few minutes, and then they went in the same way as Joe. Manuel noticed that Slim waited until they were all started before he then took up the rear.

Thirty minutes later they broke out into an open area of brush with an occasional small pine. They could see Joe up ahead, crouched down rifle at the ready. That's when they realized they were training for war!

Roy held up his hand and dropped down. They both followed his example. Looking over his shoulder Manuel could see Slim stopped in the rear. He, too, had his rifle at the ready.

Roy scanned the area, waved his hand forward and then moved forward with a stooped profile. They were soon back in a thicket following another faint trail. The thicket gave way to a small clearing. They stopped at the edge.

Roy said very softly, "This is the old Matcovich homestead area. He settled here in the late 1800's. Occasionally you will find an old gnarled fruit tree. The cabin was in this clearing. Nothing is left now. But the depression left from the old well has fresh water."

They moved over to the center of the clearing to a small limestone depression in the ground with water in it. Manuel noticed again that neither Joe nor Slim had moved into the center with them. He figured they were at the edges of the clearing, both front and rear.

"We'll fill those four canteens in the packs with water. Now if this is too dark or looks bad, you put a couple of these chlorine tablets in each canteen and shake. In thirty minutes you can drink. Here, you guys can have this bottle of tablets. It's almost full. We've got more in the rucksacks and in the car."

Manuel and Hector did as they were told. The water was crystal clear.

"We'll set up camp in the trees over there."

Roy went about showing them how to select high and dry areas to sleep on. They would be using small plastic tarps to sleep on and cover with. The mosquito nets had one quarter inch diameter cord sewed to them so they could be tied to the nearby trees or bushes.

"Slim, will take you two and check the traps for rabbits. When you get back, Joe will walk you over to the beach area to look for edible marine life."

They found the traps, but they were empty. One had been sprung and they reset it. The marine life search was a little more fruitful, with a couple of land crabs, a few sea crabs, and a few small fish.

When they got back, Roy said, "Slim will do a fast boil of all this stuff."

As Manuel and Hector worked on the fire, Slim cautioned, "Use only dry wood, small stuff. We don't want any tell-tale smoke to give away our position."

After all the marine life was boiled, Slim took what appeared to be a bayonet and cut everything up. Scales, shells, bones and all! Whack! Whack! Then he divided it into five parts..

Roy said, "Eat what you can. If you were in a real life or death situation, this would be a feast to you! Now you can get a taste of the real thing."

Roy then commanded, "We'll each do watch on two-hour shifts: Slim, Hector, Joe, Manuel and myself, in that order. We'll sleep starting right now. Up at 4 AM, move out at 5 after a U. S. Army cold K-ration* breakfast. You guys ever have K-rations?"

"No," the guys answered in unison.

"You've got something to experience."

Manuel felt someone nudge him. "Your turn," Joe said.

He rubbed his eyes, and Joe pointed to the place at the edge of the camp he was to sit and look out for two hours.

As he sat there he thought it was sure strange being out in the middle of nowhere. Then as the night sounds enveloped him he heard crickets, the slight breeze stirring leaves, and the rhythmic beating of the waves on the distance beach. He heard an occasional bird sound and strange snaps and cracks in the forest around him. It didn't seem long, and the two hours were almost gone. Before he could stand up, Roy came over.

"I'll take over," he said.

Morning came and went. The meager share of K-rations wasn't any feast. They filled the canteens and cleaned up the camp to look like it hadn't been used.

The day consisted of a traverse of the entire island, military style. They were always on the lookout, always moving slow. Sometimes they were on the beach, then on mangrove trails and other times open pine woodland. They grazed on berries and edible plants, chewed bark, and located more limestone depressions with either fresh rain water or surface water. Occasionally they had to use the chlorine tablets. Traversing a one-mile wide by two-mile long island adds up to at least six to seven miles of hard walking, but never in a hurry and constantly cautious.

The late afternoon found them on the northeast side of No Name, close to the shore, tired and dirty.

"All right guys," Roy said. "Joe, Manuel and Hector will net us some fish. Slim, get some coals burning. I'm going to keep a watch for boats and fishermen. We'll do the same tonight, same watch order, and we'll break camp early."

Luck was with them, and they netted some fish. Slim covered them in mud and baked them in the coals.

Morning came. "Guys," Roy said, "We'll split up the remaining K-rations. Manuel, Hector, it's been short but fun! We're going down the beach a short distance. The cabin is right over there past those pine trees. You can get your oars, and we'll pick up our sleeping bags. Keep a watch on your way back. Don't be seen if possible, and you never saw us!

They moved out and Roy was right, just over there was the cabin! The three picked up their bags and took the rucksacks. Hector shouldered the oars.

"Good luck guys," Roy said.

They all shook hands and then headed in two different directions. Manuel took the lead on the 4-A trail back the way they had come in. They walked along not saying a thing, each mulling over the last couple of days and nursing their aches from the hiking and rucksacks. Suddenly they heard the start-up of an outboard motor, and then the sound of it racing across the water.

"They had their boat and motor hidden somewhere close!" Hector said.

"Yea," Manuel agreed, "They will be back, loaded and gone before we ever get back to our boat!"

They broke out of the brush. There was their boat, and they were glad to see it.

"You will have to row half the way back," Hector said. "I'm sure I won't be able to go all the way."

"OK," Manuel said.

They got back across to Big Pine, returned the boat to its hiding place and then the oars to the old man at the store.

"Did you ever see those three guys on No Name," he asked. "They just left. Boy they were sure hungry! Bought a couple of sandwiches each! Then left with a rush."

"Nope, didn't see them. Thanks for the oars and the boat, old timer," Manuel said.

"Let's get back to Key West," Hector exclaimed. "I need to get some sleep in my bed!"

They drove the 30 miles back to Key West. Hector pulled up in front of Manuel's parents' house.

"Still thinking about joining up in Miami?" Manuel asked.

"I'll get back to you in a couple of days. How about Friday at the docks?" Hector answered.

"See you then, Hector," Manuel said.

Early Friday morning found Manuel on the docks in his usual place.

"Hey buddy, how you doing?" Hector said.

"Come on over and sit," Manuel said.

"Catch anything?"

"A couple," Manuel pointed to his bucket.

"Think any more about Cuba?" Hector asked.

"I'm ready if you are," Manuel answered.

"How about I check on the bus to Miami, and call you tonight. I was thinking, we have got to get our stories straight. Let's say we're catching the bus up to Miami to go to work for, what you say, three months. It shouldn't take more time than that to kick Castro out of Cuba!" Hector exclaimed.

"Sounds like a plan, compadre! Give me a call, and I'll see how much money I can come up with," Manuel added.

Ring! Ring! "Hello, yes he's here," Manuel's mother said. "Manuel, it's for you!"

"OK, Mom, thank you. Hello."

"Manuel, it's Hector. I checked on the bus to Miami. It's $27.50 each. We don't need to think about round trip, because we will be coming back from Cuba. We'll need plane or boat tickets!"

"OK wise guy. But you're right! We should take some extra cash, for food and whatever," Manuel said.

"Manuel, I got about $60...what about you?"

"I can match that, compadre."

"We'll pack light and walk downtown and catch the 9:05 tomorrow. Tell your folks our story, and I'll do the same. See you at 8 am sharp! At your house tomorrow."

"OK, I'm with you. See you then."

"Mom, that was Hector. We're going up to Miami tomorrow on the Greyhound. Going to work three months or so."

"Manuel, Hector and you aren't in some kind of trouble are you?"

"No Mom! Just that we haven't found any work around here, and we thought we would give Miami a try."

"Now Manuel, don't let those Freedom Fighters talk you into joining up! Stay out of trouble!"

"Yes, Mom."

"Don't forget to call me!"

Manuel went upstairs to his room, got his money out of his top drawer and took a small gym bag out of the closet. He folded a couple of t-shirts, a sport shirt, a couple of socks and boxers, and stuffed them into the bag.

In the morning, he was up early. His mom was in the kitchen.

"Mom, I need a couple of tacos for a lunch."

"Don't worry, here they are. I have them packed for you, mi hijito."

He ate fast, kissed her, grabbed the paper sack and his gym bag.

"Bye, Dad." Out he went.

It was 8 am sharp, and Hector was walking down the sidewalk. He only lived a few blocks away. When they worked at the fish cannery they used to walk to work and back every day.

"Are you ready, Manuel?"

"Yes, I am. Got your money?"

"Yes, I didn't forget this time. I know I used to bum change from you for the Coke machine at work. Used to say I forgot my money," Hector laughed.

"Didn't you forget it?" Manuel asked.

"Not all the time!" Hector laughed again.

"There's the bus station."

"Just trying to change the subject," Manuel teased.

"No, there it is! Let's get our tickets before they leave without us!"

At 9:05 the Greyhound pulled out of the station drive and pulled up onto the city street with a roar.

"Manuel, the good thing about this trip on this bus, is the station is right downtown in Miami. Right in in the middle of little Cuba. All we have to do is ask around for the recruiting station."

"It all sounds too easy. But we'll see, we can make it up as we go."

They both settled back and closed their eyes. They were lulled to sleep by the bump ba-bump...bump ba-bump of the bus's three sets of huge tires. As they slept, they were missing the views of the beautiful turquoise water and each of the highway bridges built on top of the old Flagler railroad bridges. This was an enormous construction feat on top of one of the nation's vast amazing wonders.

The next thing they knew the bus was stopping and starting as it wandered through the inner-city streets of old Miami. It made a sharp turn, went up into a depot parking lot and came to a stop in front of the Miami main bus terminal.

People were moving down the aisle. They got up, grabbed their gym bags from the overhead, and down the steps and out of the bus they went. They could see the driver was already busy unloading the outside bins and checking people's baggage ticket stubs. It was all a bustle of activity.

Over all this noise and the sudden honks and screeches of the city traffic, Manuel hollered, "Where do we go next, Hector?"

"I'm just going to ask somebody." He walked right up to a young adult standing there, "Hey Amigo. Do you know where the Freedom Fighters recruiting station is?"

"Hey man, you must be from out of town! Just two blocks down that way. You can't miss it, on this same side of the street."

"That takes care of that," Manuel said. "Thanks."

There were all kinds of things in the way on the sidewalk, fruit vendor carts, sweet ice carts, and little stalls of merchandise jutting out into the sidewalk from each store, people coming and going.

Halfway down the block, one of the store display windows had a brown paper sign pasted to it:

Fuente De Liberation of Cuba!

They went up to the door. It was locked.

"Look there, Hector. The sign says closed," Manuel said.

Hector cupped his hands and put his face next to the glass. "There is someone inside. I'm going to knock." His knock was more like a battering ram!

"If you knock the door down, we can just walk right in," Manuel laughed.

A young fella in his teens came to the door. "We're closed. What do you want?"

Hector said, "We just got off the bus from Key West, and we're ready to sign up!"

The latch clicked, and the door opened.

"Come in, take a seat. I have to call my brother. He is in charge. He had to go home for something. I'm just watching the place. I can't sign you up." He locked the door.

"We'll wait," Hector said.

He went to the back room. They could hear him dialing the phone. The room was bare except for some old wooden chairs against the wall and a wood desk in the center with two chairs next to it. There were posters on the walls, "Liberate Cuba" and "Democracy for Cuba." There was also a large map of Cuba.

"Hello, it's Sammy. There's a couple of guys just came in from Key West on the bus. They want to join up. Yeah, Ok. See you."

The guy came back in. "He should be back in about ten minutes. Sammy said you could start filling out the information forms."

He sat down at the desk and pulled out a drawer and put a form down on the table top with a pen. Manuel went forward from his seat on a chair against the wall and sat at the table. Hector was engrossed in the Cuban map.

Manuel said, "You're next Hector, as soon as I get this filled out." He came over to the table still looking at the Cuban map over his shoulder.

Manuel looked over the form and started filling it out, "Looks alright to

Fronte de Liberation of Cuba
Name:___________________________
Date of Birth:___________________
Place of Birth:___________________
Citizen of Country:______________
I believe in democracy for Cuba.
I do not support Castro's government.
Everything on this form is true.
Signed:_________________________

me," he stated.

The ten minutes went by fast. The next thing they heard was the loud sound of a car with dual pipes backing down. Blat..Blat..Blat. A convertible pulled up in front. That was about all they could see from their vantage point and around the brown paper sign plastered to the front window. Sammy went to the front door and unlocked it.

" Hi Ed, Hi Sylvia."

Ed and a young woman walked in.

Sammy did the introductions, "Ed, these are the guys I told you about, Manuel and Hector."

They all shook hands.

"They have already filled out the forms."

He handed the two forms to Ed.

"Looks good to me. Ok guys, we'll run you out to the embarkation point. I took three guys over day before yesterday."

"Sammy, keep a watch on the shop. You can call at Opa-Locka if you need me. Otherwise, flip the closed sign and shut it down in a couple of hours. Sylvia and I are going to run these guys out to the airport."

"Ok Ed, I'll cover," Sammy said, trying to sound important.

They went outside, as the latch clicked shut behind them.

"Guys climb in the back," Ed ordered.

They were looking at a '57 Ford convertible, top down. A low rider. Probably lowered a couple of inches in the front and a full six in the rear! Sylvia opened the passenger door and pulled the seat forward so Manuel and Hector could get in. Ed threw their gym bags in the trunk.

Ed fired the Ford up and a sudden sound blasted out of the dual chrome pipes in the rear. Rupp-ah, Rupp-ah, the car roared as Ed swung out into the street from the parking space in front of the store.

"Cool car," Hector said, "Will she move?"

"You bet!" Ed exclaimed, "I'll give you a sample when we get out to the highway."

When they got to the highway, Ed poured it on.

Ed looked over his shoulder and had to say kind of loud, over the roar of the dual pipes, "We're going out to Opa-Locka. It's an old deserted Army Air base in north Miami. There are some old barracks near the flight line. The flights are going out at night, lights out."

"Who is and to where?" Hector asked.

"Sorry Hector, can't answer either of those questions. It will be best if you guys don't ask anything. Just go along with the program."

"Well Ed, we appreciate you getting us both right out there because we don't have any place to spend the night," Manuel said.

"They'll take care of you, don't worry," Ed replied.

They must have been doing 80! Ed slowed down for a turn. "Bam, Pow, tha...tha...tha, the Ford complained. A short distance from the main road in what appeared to be a deserted area, they came up to a gate across the road. A sign on the gate read:

**DEAD END
U. S. GOVERNMENT PROPERTY
KEEP OUT
TRESPASSERS WILL BE PROSECUTED**

There was a chain-link fence going to the left and right as far as they could see. Brush was growing on both sides of the fence. It sure looked deserted.

"Hector, will you take this key and jump out, unlock and open the gate. Please shut and lock it after I pull through," Ed ordered.

Hector jumped back in and gave Ed the key. They drove down the road. There was a lot of trash on the road, and it was overgrown on both sides. They soon started to see deserted Second World War wooden barracks buildings, windows boarded up and glass broken out. Some were one and others two-story. They were all decorated with faded and peeling paint. It was a desolate scene. At one time this was a bustling and first class Army Air Base.

In 1927, the city of Opa-locka* was founded by the retired aviation pioneer, Glen Curtis. He and his partner-investor James Bright also developed the cities of Miami Springs and Hialeah. Curtis then moved his aviation school to an airport he built nearby and named it Florida Aviation Camp. Curtis was instrumental in the establishment of commercial aviation such as Pan Am and Eastern Airlines. He willed the Aviation Camp to the U.S. Navy after his early death in 1930. In World War II the airport became Naval Air Station Miami and was the headquarters for the U.S. Naval Training Command.

There were at least 10,000 personnel, both military and civilians working at this base. After the war it fell into disuse. In 1959 the property was given to Dade County, and in 1962 it was renamed Opa-locka Airport.

They pulled up to a couple of single-story buildings near the flight line. These buildings appeared to be in somewhat better shape than the ones they had just passed by. Ed got out and said, "Here we are. Let's go inside and see if anyone is around."

There was a big two wheeled cart next to the door. It held a large red painted fire extinguisher. Ed knocked hard a few times. In a few minutes a face looked through the window, and the door opened up.

Ed said, "Enrique, you didn't go with the last group?"

"No, the three of us just missed the flight. They said to remain here."

Ed asked, "Did they take care of you? I mean food and clothes. I see that you have your fatigues."

"Yes, we've got plenty of food. The refrigerator is full. The cupboard is stocked. We won't go hungry."

"What did they tell you?" Ed asked.

"They said to hang tight. Frank would be here tomorrow. Didn't say when we fly out," Enrique informed him.

"What about John and Sam?" Ed asked.

"They're in their bunks, sacked out," Enrique stated.

"Then Enrique, I want you to meet Manuel and Hector. They've just joined up. Show them where the fatigues and the food are. They need both," Ed said,

"Hector, Manuel, I'm leaving you in good hands. Enrique will show you around. Is it all quiet at the administration buildings?"

"Yes, they all left a couple of hours ago...it's dead over there!"

Ed and Sylvia left. The Ford could be heard starting up and then its dual pipes fading off in the distance as they headed back to the gate.

Enrique said, "The fatigues are there in some boxes. Not too fancy. Only medium, large and x-large. I would leave your civvies and pack what you can get in your bags. Food's over there in the cupboard and refrigerator. Make yourselves at home. The back room has a bunch of bunks. John and Sam are back there sleeping. I recommend eating and sleeping because the C.I.A., I mean Frank and the others sometimes show up early. We've been here a couple of days, and they showed up at dawn yesterday."

"Thanks Enrique. We'll do just that," Manuel answered.

"Manuel, while we're eating I want to show you some things in our survival manual," Hector said.

"Ok Hector, you read and I'll cook. Enrique, I'll cook enough for five. I don't do so bad."

"Thanks Manuel, I'll tell John and Sam."

About the time he got the food on the table, the three guys came up from the back. Introductions were made all around. The three were interested in Hector's serious reading of survival techniques. They all took

Enrique's suggestion and bunked down early just as the sun was setting.

"Guys, we got to get up. Frank just pulled up."

"Man, what time is it?" Hector asked.

"Around 4 am," Enrique said, "Get cleaned up, and come to the front just as soon as you can."

Since this was an old barracks it had a large wash room. The four were all there at one time trying their best to get woke up, shaved and dressed. When they came out front there was a man in a gray suit sitting at the table.

He said. "Guys, grab a chair."

He was tall with dark brown hair and piercing brown eyes.

"OK guys, this is it. At 5 am, a C-54 is going to land. You five jump in it as soon as the loadmaster gives you the thumbs up! Eat fast and have your belongings ready to go. This is the last load out of here. Things are moving!"

"You guys, listen up. Enrique is in charge, and he will answer to the load master. You all got it?"

"Yes sir!" they said.

It wasn't long before they could heard the drone of a large propeller driven aircraft.

Frank stuck his head in, "Enrique, I got the guys out with the lights. They will be down shortly. Get ready! You're going as soon as they taxi up, turn about, and the loadmaster gives you the high-sign."

They all filed out with their bags. They could see dark shapes of a car at each end of the runway. Next to each one was someone holding a blinking light, green at one end and red at the other.

Suddenly this huge black shape was coming down out of a dark sky. They then heard the screech of tires touching concrete and the sudden back-lash of feathered props. The huge shape came up towards them, spun around, the engines slowed down, and a side door opened up.

Frank said, "OK...Go!...Go! Straight for the open door. Look out for the props! Good luck!"

They all threw their bags to the loadmaster, grabbed ahold and climbed up. Each one helped the other get into the plane. The door slammed shut. There were jump seats dropped down on either side of the aircraft looking towards the center. As they got into their seats and were buckling up, the engines revved , they taxied a sort distance, the engines roared, and the plane leaped forward and raced down the dark runway. Before they knew it, they were airborne.

They all seemed to close their eyes at once and tried to resume their interrupted sleep. The drone of the props helped.

Manuel opened his eyes. Where was he? Then he remembered. He saw Enrique who was pulling back a small amount of the tape that was covering the windows.

"We're over a jungle. It appears to be Guatemala," he said.

The plane started to lose altitude.

The loadmaster said, " Buckle up guys. We're going in!"

The plane dropped down some, at the same time keeping horizontal, then down some more. They started to bank and went around losing some more altitude. It went in for its final approach, and you could hear the whine of the motors lowering the wheels. There was a squeal and a bump as the wheels touched the runway, then the sudden slowing and loud noise rush as the props were feathered and the air backwashed.

The plane taxied up, stopped, and the loadmaster opened the door. This time there was a portable step. They all grabbed their bags and headed down, Enrique in the lead.

There was a Cuban lieutenant at the bottom, "Who's in charge?" He asked.

"I guess I am," Enrique said.

"Is this all you have? Climb aboard that truck, men!"

They pulled up to a building. It appeared to be something that was thrown up somewhat hastily.

"Ok men, inside."

"Sir!" The lieutenant saluted a captain, "These five are all they brought."

"That's all right lieutenant. We'll take all we can get. These men are to be a heavy weapons platoon. Train them on the 57 mm recoilless rifle and bazooka. They will carry their own ammo and load. Get them up to the 6th and start training immediately. We don't have much time."

"Yes sir! Men, follow me."

They went back out to the truck and loaded up. The truck pulled out and drove along a road paralleling the runway. Manuel could see a lot of huge two and four-motor prop cargo transports lining the runway. There were also some smaller two-motor prop bombers lined up.

Enrique said, "Some of those big ones can drop paratroopers. There's some C-46's and C-54's.* The two engine bombers are Douglas A-26's.* I've been around them before."

"Where do you think they are taking us?" Manuel asked.

"I heard the captain say to get them up to the barracks…then 'heavy weapons' training. Something about, not much time, and to get that training done first. Did you see the guards on the perimeter of the airstrip? I recognized the uniforms, definitely Guatemalans!" Enrique exclaimed.

The truck bounced off the pavement and onto a small dirt road. They were gaining some elevation.

"You seem to know quite a lot," Hector said. "How do you do it?"

"Oh, I get around some," Enrique stated.

The truck pulled up to a gate. The guard lifted the crossbar and said, "Passé."

They drove up to what appeared to be another hastily constructed single-story wooden building. The truck came to a screeching stop. The lieutenant jumped out.

"Ok men, this is it. Your home until we get out of here. Line up right here, side by side. What I need to tell you is, you're in an army. You're to act and behave like recruits. The only problem is you've missed basic training! That is because you're the last of the Cuban Freedom Fighters who will be admitted. We're running out of time. Welcome to Brigade 2506. Be proud of it, and do your best."

Just then the screen door to the office building opened and slammed shut as two guys stepped out. The first was an Anglo, followed by a short muscular khaki-dressed Cuban with a military fatigue hat on. The first guy looked almost like Frank back at the deserted Opa-locka air base. He was tall. This guy had no dress suit, but he had tan long pants, a short-sleeved tan dress shirt, and the usual dark sunglasses.

The lieutenant stiffened and hollered, "Men, attennn-tion!"

All five of the guys stood up straight, arms at their sides. The guy with the sunglasses stepped off the porch followed by the uniformed guy. "Welcome, gentlemen. Welcome to Base Trax. My name is Joe, and that's all you need to know. This here is Sergeant Jimenez. He is going to train you in heavy weapons. You pay attention to him, and learn it fast and good! That will be all, Lieutenant. Sergeant Jimenez, they are all yours!"

Sergeant Jimenez stepped forward, "Gentlemen, at ease. I've got all your paper work here. Enrique, you're in charge of the heavy weapons platoon. You will be a corporal, the rest privates. Remember to salute all officers. Those are the ones with the shiny or gold cloth insignias on their collars or hats. Sound off with your first names from left to right. Loud!"

"John." "Sam." "Hector." "Manuel." "Enrique."

"Enrique, march these men down to the second building on the right. Pick out five bunks together, and stow your gear. Then march them over to the building directly across from it, the mess hall. Get something to eat. I'll see you back at the bunk house at 1300 sharp. Don't be late!"

"Yes Sir!" Endrique replied, "Men face right, forward march. Left... Left...left, right, left."

They got back to the barracks just before 1300. Sergeant Jimenez was there waiting for them.

"OK men, we're going to form up outside. We're going to start getting in shape, it's double time everywhere you go. Move out! Quickly! Endrique, we're going across the parade ground in front of the mess hall. HQ building on the far side with the brigade flag. Move 'em!"

Endrique shouted, "Ten-shut men, move out...forward march! Left...Left...Hup-two-three-four, double time...Go!"

They arrived huffing and puffing.

"All right men, move through that door." Sergeant "J" pointed, "The first guys will give you your boots, second guy at the counter...your gear, the third guy will give your shots! Then go left down the hall, first room on the right. A classroom, see you there."

They came into the room with sore shoulders and also realizing just how much out of shape they were. They were carrying packs filled with a couple of sets of t-shirts, fatigues, canteen, and toiletries.

"Men, have a seat. Take a few minutes to get settled. Your shoulders and leg muscles will ache for a few days. You will get over it. Pay attention. You're going to be a heavy weapons team," Sergeant Jimenez stated. "Pay very close attention. Your life and your buddy's life will depend upon it."

"We have two primary weapons: the bazooka and the 57 millimeter Recoilless Rifle. Each is a two-man operation, a weapons man and combination amo carrier-loader. John and Sam, Bazooka, Manuel, Hector, 57 millimeter. Corporal Enrique will be in charge. You will learn how to disassemble your weapons and put them back together, even in the dark! Today I will show you how to disassemble, clean and transport. You will practice this over and over and over, until you know it by heart! Tomorrow we will go to the range,* learn how to fire, and then fire and hit a target."

"We will be using high explosive armor piercing ammo. Each loader will carry at least six rounds, and Endrique three of each. When you're in the field, make sure that resupply always keeps up with you."

The next day it was full packs, K-rations, full load of ammo and a two-mile march up a steep narrow single-lane dirt road to the range. They hung red flags* at both ends of the range and at the entrance to the road leading in. Sergeant Jimenez and an Anglo guy dressed in the usual khaki pants, tan dress shirt, and dark glasses were already at the range. They could see a jeep parked near by.

"OK men, pay careful attention. It's important, life or death! Our life may depend upon your performance today, and your life when you are in Cuba. Both of these weapons load from the rear. The Bazooka is an anti-tank 3.5 inch rocket launcher. It has two wires on the round. This round is a rocket. It will accelerate as it heads to the target. The wires attach to the weapon like this. See two easy-on clips. Red to red and black to black. Then, for Heaven's sake, do not stand in back of it! Stand off to the side. The back blast will hurt you bad," Sergeant Jimenez instructed.

"Manuel, let's set up the .57 on its stand. It fires a modified high explosive artillery shell at reduced velocity. It is breach-loaded, that means from the rear. The tube is designed to allow some of the propellant gasses to escape out of the rear of the weapon. That is why it is called 'Recoilless' Rifle."

"Men, step off to the sides. John and Manuel, load, flip off the safety, aim down the barrel, and fire down range as you are ready."

Pow!...Swish! Bam!...Fooo...sh! Two tremendous explosions shook the ground down range.

This drill continued. Day after day. Hike in, load, fire, tear down, clean, and reassemble. Each time when they arrived at the range there was Sergeant Jimenez and one or two Anglo civilians in khaki pants, tan short-sleved shirt and wearing dark sunglasses. These guys, together with Sergeant Jimenez, showed them how to set up defensive positions along the roads.

"Who are these guys?" Hector asked Enrique.

"Either American CIA or Green Beret."

"Hey Enrique! How many guys on this base? By the number of barracks, it looks like a lot!" Manuel questioned.

"I'm guessing at least 1000. But as soon as they complete their weapons training, they move them down to the coastal plains. Paratroops have trained at another location with the C-46's and the tankers at Fort Knox, Kentucky."

"How do you know all this, Endrique?" Hector asked.

"Oh, you know, I get around."

Every day as they neared the base, they would double time with a para-troop shuffle* and sing out as they came into the camp;

     Left...Left...Left-right, Le...ft...
     We are going to Ha...va...na, Honey...
     We are going to Ha...va...na, Babe...
     We are going to Ha...va...na...
     To kick Cast...troo...o...oa...
     O...O...Honey…Oh...Ba...a...bee...Mine...
     Go to your Left...Your Right...Your Left...

Next, they would secure their weapons, go to the mess hall, eat, clean up, and crash in their bunks.

Then it happened, a couple of weeks after they arrived. Sergeant Jimenez came through the barracks door after supper.

"OK, men, this is it. When you get up tomorrow morning, pack it up. We're moving out. You won't see this place again, unless you come back as a tourist!"

It was April 10th. They filed outside the barrack's with all of their equipment, including side-arms, rifles, heavy weapons, and ammo in car-riers. There was some hustle and bustle about the base, but there were sur-prisingly few troops. A big army truck pulled up. Sergeant Jimenez came out of the barracks.

"All right men, load up. We're going back down to the airfield you came in at. Then we're off to *Trampoline*, the jumping off place. The 2506 is on the move!"

They bounced down the mountain to the base, pulled through a guarded gate and up onto the flight line. Sergeant Jimenez got out, ran into the of-fice and came right back out.

"OK men, get over to that C-54, the one with its engines idling. It's waiting for us, and it's ready to go!"

They got on the plane, stowed their gear and buckled up. The plane tax-ied out to the end of the runway, did a 180, revved its engines and headed down the runway in a rush of speed, propellers screaming.

Manuel looked around. There was a lot of gear in the rear and another fifteen or so fatigued-clothed men. These guys had already pulled the black tape from the windows. They all settled in and in different positions, either sleeping or starring off into space, lost to reality, each fighting his own fears.

They were awakened to reality when the plane began to bank and lose altitude. Enrique, was looking out his window, and said, "It's Puerto Cabezas! I saw the long pier going out into the Gulf."

The plane touched down, the tires squealed, the pilot reversed the air flow, the plane slowed and then taxied over to the tower.

"Pile out men!" Sergeant Jimenez roared, "Don't leave anything! Form up on the tarmac. I'll be right back."

He bounced out of the plane, went over to the administration building, and came right out just as the men got into formation.

"That truck will take us right out to the docks. We're loading just as soon as we get there and find Brigade 6."

They first saw it from the army truck. A rusty, dirty old cargo ship, the Rio Escondido.

Sergeant Jimenez proclaimed, "This is it men. It doesn't look like we'll be having any room service. I just talked to the Brigade commander. We're leaving early. This ship can only travel max six knots. The rest will rendezvous with us."

"Tell you what, men. Grab these four empty fifty-five gallon drums, and get them on the back of this cruise ship. I'll be right back with some rope. Stow your gear, and talk it up with the rest of the Brigade 6's men. See what's happening."

Enrique came back discouraged. "They scrapped the *Trinidad plan.*"

"What was that?" Hector asked.

"It was the original plan. We were going in to the city of Trinidad next to the mountains. If the invasion failed we could run into the mountains and join up with other rebels. Instead we're going into a swamp. Called the Bay of Pigs. No way out! Well, ours is not the reason why. Only do or die!" he said.

"How did you find this out?" Hector asked.

"Well, I told you, I get around. One of the 6th guys overheard some brass talking."

The Rio Escondido's motors started. It began shaking and complaining and then pushed off from the long pier passing the other boats. The ship traveled all night. The men had to sleep on the rusty old deck. It was cold food because there were barrels of aviation gas and ammo crates on the deck, and therefore, no fires allowed, even by the crew.

In the light of the morning, Sergeant Jimenez said, "All right, men, it's time for light weapons training and firing. Let's get a rope on one of those fifty-five gallon drums, and throw the drum over the side. We are going to have a class on firing a handgun and an automatic weapon."

They spent the morning learning to disassemble, clean, load, and fire a .45 pistol and a submachine gun. They ultimately sank all four fifty-five gallon drums. That was the extent of light weapons training, and all five of the sergeant's men passed with flying colors.

They arrived at the rendezvous point late that evening and found the other five ships were already there. All had come in from different directions to avoid any suspicion. They all entered the Bay of Pigs, the Rio Escondido last. Most of them went straight for the Blue Beach at the start of the bay. Two of the ships continued on to the Red Beach which was the farthest inland part of the bay.

The sun was rising as Castro's planes appeared, a Sea Fury and a B-26. They dived at and attacked two of the boats at the Red Beach. After the one pass they then went on to shoot at the boats at the Blue Beach.

These two planes were met with a continuous fire from all of the boats with .50 caliber machine guns. This concentrated fire brought down the B -26.

The guys could see one of their C-54's go over with the paratroopers. At that time a Cuban T-33 came in for a strafing* run on the boats and again the concentrated .50 caliber fire brought that plane down.

Sergeant Jimenez came over. "I don't know if you guys are accustomed to praying. But whether you are or aren't, this might be a good time. See those two landing craft heading our way. We're going in just as soon as they get here…Manuel?"

Manuel thought to himself, the Sarge means for me to pray. I've never done this before. I wish I had paid more attention at the Masses I attended with Mama.

"Manuel?" the Sarge said again, suggesting.

Miguel cleared his throat and started, "Jesus, please be with us, guide and protect us. *Vaya con Dios.* * Amen."

The two LCUS (landing Craft) came along side the Rio Escondido.

All the leaders yelled. "Get your gear, and get into those boats."

All five of the guys did just that together with the rest of the men. They already had their heavy and light weapons and ammo loaded up. Before they knew it they were on the shore, courtesy of the Brigade frogmen who had cleared and marked the way earlier. While they were unloading to the beach from the UCUS, a Sea Fury attacked the Rio Escondido, and a rocket hit the 55 gallon drums of aviation fuel. The hold had 20 tons of of explosives in it. The Rio Escondido exploded in a huge fireball, shaking the entire area.

Sergeant Jimenez yelled, "Get off the beach! Move inland. Hold it, you guys, they want us to help on Red Beach. Load up on that truck, and go with it along the beach road to the Red Zone. They need a heavy weapons team. The paratroops over there were dropped all over the swamp. I have to stay here. Good luck, men!"

All five guys threw their gear in and climbed up into the back of one of the armored 2 1/2 ton trucks. As they headed down the beach they could see the 4th Battalion heading inland to San Blass.

It was a bumpy and grinding trip up the beach road, at first a mile or so of a wide asphalt single-lane and then a mix of sand and crushed coral. It seemed more like eighty miles. Every time a Castro plane, or any plane for that matter dived at a boat or flew overhead, they pulled off the road to look inconspicuous. They came up to a group of men.

Enrique said, "These are 2nd Battalion guys, mostly infantry."

"Boy, are we glad to see you guys," their commander said. "We are having some trouble getting our guys and equipment in. We're heading inland trying to link up with the paratroops. But I'm afraid they were dropped off target. They're all over the swamp. That means we're on our own. Go on up the road inland with the truck and equipment. Check with my men setting up defensive positions. They are all strung out. But go up about a mile. Look for a First Lieutenant. He will set you up."

"Yes sir!" Enrique said as he saluted.

"Son, you can dispense with saluting officers. Might be snipers about."

"Yes sir!" Enrique got back into the truck. They headed up the rough one-lane, asphalt road. Occasionally they passed men moving up on the sides. Manuel noted that the swamp grew right up to the road. It was very thick with large trees.

The guys in the back heard Enrique say, "There he is, the tall guy right there, talking to those men. Stop here, and I'll run over."

The lieutenant was showing some men a map and pointing up towards the bend in the road.

"Excuse me sir," Enrique started to salute but stopped short.

"Yes corporal."

"The commander, the major at the beach, told me to report to you with my heavy weapons team. A bazooka and a 57 mm Recoilless, Sir."

"Great! We were just going to protect this bend in the road. Now I can move up with my men. Call your team over."

Enrique waved to his team, and they hurried over.

"Listen up men," the lieutenant said, "You guys will stay put here as an ambush if we have to retreat. You're our anchor. We'll call you forward if we get too far ahead and need for you to move up and then reset. Right now there should be paratroopers up ahead. But we can't find any."

"Corporal, set up the .57 on the outside of the curve. It will be point-blank if Castro's machines come around the curve. Bazooka inside of the curve, this side. Aim for the tank treads. We're counting on you guys to stop them if they get by us or push us back."

"Yes sir!" they all said.

He waved for the truck to pull up and jumped up on the running board, and the truck eased forward. The staff members who were with the lieutenant climbed in the back together with some men who had come up. They disappeared around the bend.

Enrique said, "Men dig in, set up right there. Aim for the center of the road at the curve, and get everything organized."

"Yes sir!" the four said as the dirt began to fly.

Enrique walked up to the bend in the road to have a look. It wandered kind of straight with a slight rise. Then the large swamp trees hid the road. He noticed that it was getting dark.

Enrique walked back to where the guys were setting up. "Men, eat something, and rest. Every two hours wake up the next man and he will take my place at the bend in the road. Hector, Manuel, John and Sam."

It was after 24 hours (12 at night). "Hector, I hear something in the swamp," Manuel said softly.

"Hun? Shhh listen, hear it?" he slowly rolled over for his .45.

There was a loud snap...rustle

"What is the password?" Manuel asked.

Hector answered. "Each number of the Brigade, separately."

Manuel said out loud. "2,5,0,6."

They both listened.

Hector said very quietly, "They must answer, Havana."

"Havana!" a voice was heard from the dark of the swamp.

Manuel hollered out, "Advance, and be recognized."

They saw two dark shapes.

"They're paratroopers," Hector said.

"Hey guys, over here. What happened? You're supposed to be up front."

The two hobbled forward. One had his arm in a sling, tommy gun slung over his shoulder.

"Are we glad to see you guys!" they said. "They dropped us in the swamp. Way off target. We couldn't find or haven't seen any of our group."

"We're about a mile from the Red Beach, HQ," Enrique heard the commotion and came over.

"You guys can rest up here," Enrique suggested.

"We will, but as soon as it gets light, we'll head up the road," one paratrooper said.

They all got back in their fox holes and the paratroopers laid down on the ground, and before they knew it they were snoring.

It was early morning. "We're rested up and it's getting light enough," one of the two paratroopers informed them. "So, we're headed up the road to Havana."

"OK guys. Good luck," Hector said.

The two paratroopers disappeared around the bend.

That was when they started to hear firing way to the rear and east.

"It's started, must be over at Blue Beach," Enrique said.

From behind them they heard the sound of a couple of engines and the grind of transmissions. A jeep and truck came into view. They pulled up and stopped. It was the commander from the Red Beach.

"Looks good, men! We're going forward. Hold this place. We may need you."

Off they went in a shower of gravel and sand. The truck was loaded with a bunch of Battalion 2 guys. They all waved.

"They didn't look very happy. I guess they had a hard time on the beach," Sam remarked.

Back at the Red Beach they could hear the diving whine of planes and the exploding of rockets. The explosions and firing away to the east on Blue Beach were constant now. A bunch of explosions and machine gun firing was heard to their front. Closer now. Suddenly a B-26 flew over their position. It was following the road.

"Was that ours or theirs?" John asked. "It's hard to tell."

"I don't know," Endrique hollered.

The B-26 had turned with the road and headed toward where all of their men had gone. They then heard bombs dropping and exploding, a plane diving, and aircraft 50-caliber machine guns firing. The B-26 came back over their position, much higher this time. It was heading towards the beach. Out of nowhere a prop–driven Sea Fury dove and fired at the

B-26. They couldn't see what happened because the big trees of the swamp towered above them.

There were explosions, firing, and the noise of planes diving around them to the front, behind in the bay, and way off at Blue Beach.

"What do you think?" Hector said, "We hear all of this shooting, but all we know is what is happening at our position! War is strange. We don't have the big picture. I wish we knew what is going on!"

This went on all day until it was late afternoon, and getting dark. They heard the grind of engines.

"There are some of our troops!" Enrique yelled from his position at the curve.

B-26 Invader bomber

Suddenly a jeep and two trucks loaded with men came around the curve and screeched to a halt. Enrique ran over.

It was the commander, "Men, we killed hundreds of them! But thousands more are coming! We're pulling back to the beach. We're low on ammo. We've got to get going. We've got injured in the back! I'm leaving a couple of men. I'll send you some reinforcements as soon as we get set up. Hold them!"

Off they went with dust and sand flying.

Enrique said to the men left behind, "One of each of you men with our weapons team."

"Ok corporal," they said.

It was dark now. No moon, no stars. Quiet and eerie.

"It's spooky," Hector said, "What's that?"

"What?" Manuel asked, "Wait, I feel it. The ground is shaking!"

Enrique ran over, "Something's coming and it's not one of ours! Get ready!"

Everything was shaking violently. A deep rumble filled the air. Suddenly a huge dark monster of a shape spun around the curve.

Hector hollered out, "What's that?"

Enrique exclaimed, "A Russian T–34 tank!"

Hector cried, "God save us!"

Manuel took one look at the gigantic shape before him. He started to freeze up. He thought to himself, maybe I should have listened to Mama.

She told me to not let those Freedom Fighters talk me into joining up. No, it was his own fault! He had to do something, and do it quick. What had seemed like an eternity while he was thinking was just a couple of seconds.

Manuel ordered, "Hector, load this .57. You keep on praying, and I'll fire this thing!"

He took aim and thought, "It's point blank, but what should I aim at?" Then he saw it...the seam between the main body and the turret. Just then he heard Sam and John's bazooka go off. Blam! Whosh. It hit the side of the treads with a roar, and the tank stopped dead in its tracks.

Manuel fired the .57... Pow! It hit the seam and exploded. The turret quit moving.

"Load me up, Hector, and keep praying. We stopped them!"

Then a huge hulk of another tank came into view. It was trying to move around the first one. The side with lighter armor was now exposed to Manuel. Bam! Whosh. On the other side the bazooka fired twice at its fully-exposed treads. Again another damaged tread and a stopped tank. Manuel fired point blank at the tank body just below the turret again. This time it bounced off.

Manuel yelled, "Quick Hector! Reload!" Blam! There was a terrific explosion...the smoke cleared. Not much damage but no movement anywhere.

"What's happening, Manuel?" Hector asked.

"I don't know, but there must have been the concussions, nothing's moving," he answered.

"Look there's another tank!" Enrique screamed.

"Quick! Load me, Hector."

Both the bazooka and the .57 fired in unison. They exploded on the third tank's

The Russian T-34 tank literally spun around the curve. It was coming straight for them.

front corner.

"They're going back up the road and taking the infantry with them!"

They both fired twice at the retreating tank. It stopped, and some men climbed out of the turret and ran up the road after their fast-disappearing infantry.

"Let's eat, and get some rest," Enrique commanded, "They'll be back. We'll put two men in my position at the curve and change every two hours. Bazooka team first, then .57."

They woke up in the early morning hours. The ground was shaking again, even more this time!

"Here they come again! Tanks as far back as we can see!"

"Get in your positions, men!" Enrique commanded. Here are the other two rounds I've been carrying. How many more have you guys got?"

Manuel said, "We're out. We shot six."

"Make them count."

"Ok, Corporal," they all said.

Just then the two dead tanks in front of them exploded as the tank coming up shot round after round into them. This made somewhat of an opening. All of the men dropped down and hugged the bottom of their fox holes. Then two tanks came through the smoke as they started to push down some large trees on either side.

Hector loading and Manuel firing the 57 mm Recoilless Rifle.

Enrique hollered, "Take the one on the right first, then the left. Fire right! Fire left!" Ok, pick up your gear, and let's get out of here!"

They all seven grabbed their weapons, ammo and packs and ran back the way they had come in. No one looked back. Suddenly there were explosions all around.

"It's incoming artillery!" Enrique yelled.

The rounds were dropping in the swamp, on either side, ahead of them and even behind the tanks they had just faced. It seemed that the safest place was on the narrow road they were on!

"They don't have any forward observers," Enrique said as they slowed down and walked to catch their breath.

We'll set up on the other side of that bend ahead," Enrique commanded.

"Corporal, what are we going to shoot? We've got weapons but no shells. We used up all we had and weren't resupplied," Sam asked.

"Set up just like we've got ammo. Remember the major said he was going to send us reinforcements when he got ready. Let's pray he does!" Enrique said.

As they were digging in, the whine of a motor was heard approaching from behind.

"Is it us?" Hector asked.

"Hope so," a couple of them said.

Just then a jeep with the major roared up.

"Corporal, I've got a machine gun, grenades, ammo, and a few men. Set up guys!"

"Any shells or rockets for a .57 or bazooka?" Enrique asked hopefully.

"No, nothing back at the beach. It all went up with the Rio Escondido."

The ground began to shake.

"Here they come!" Sam yelled.

They could see a line of Russian T-34s approaching.

"Give me a couple of grenades, Sir, I'll hit them from the side. Jump out from the swamp," one of the major's men said.

The tanks were just about upon them. They had not seen the men dug in.

"Hold your fire!" The major yelled, "Wait just a bit more. On my word!"

Just then from behind them the Freedom Fighters heard, POW! POW!

The Russian tank in front of them burst into flames. Another tank started to push by, POW! POW! The second tank stopped, and it too burst into flames. The entire road and some nearby trees were burning. It was all a raging fire with lots of black smoke.

They all looked behind them. An American M41 tank* had pulled up and taken out both of the Russian T-34s.

The M41's turret hatch opened up. A man with a cloth helmet jumped down and ran up. "That's it, Major. No more shells! I've got just enough fuel to get back part of the way to the beach! I've got bad news. The Red Beach is just about to give it up."

"All right men, gather around," the major said, "I'm authorized to tell you this. You have a few options; You can surrender or head back with us to the Blue Beach. We're going to either get out by water or go past the

Red Beach, and head to the mountains. But that is going to be difficult. It's more than 80 miles!"

"What about the swamp, sir?" Hector asked.

"It's OK with me if you think you can do it. Here." He ripped off part of a map and gave it to Hector.

"Good luck, guys. Now let's get out of here!"

The tank driver got back up into the idling tank, spun it around, and roared off, with Sam and David on top of it. The major's jeep kicked up sand and shot off.

There they were, three, standing in the center of the road, a bunch of burning tanks behind them. "Hector, what now?" Manuel asked.

"I guess you are going with us?" Hector said, looking at Enrique.

"You bet! Let's get into the swamp here. Go easy, and try not to leave a trail," Enrique suggested.

"Sounds good! They will think we went back to the beach," Hector added.

They went into the thick underbrush. The swamp was dark with the trees' canopy far up out of sight. For some reason, it must have been seasonal, the ground was strangely dry. Some of the brush was prickly. It was slow going. They plodded along and hooked and scratched themselves as they struggled to get some distance between them and the road.

Hector said, "We've been going due west for about two hours."

"How you know?" Enrique asked.

"I've got my reliable compass," Hector said proudly.

"That's the one the guy at No Name gave you!" Manuel exclaimed.

"That's not all he gave me," as Hector showed them a bottle of chlorine water purification tablets.

"Let's rest and make machetes with our bayonets," Hector said.

They cut stout sticks, trimmed them off smooth and bounded the bayonets to the sticks with some cord Hector produced as if by magic.

"We need some water and something to eat," Manuel said.

"Don't worry, this Zapata Swamp* is a grazer's paradise. I see lots of food," Hector exclaimed.

"How do you know all this? "Enrique questioned

Hector proudly said, "Oh, I get around! Let's stay here and leave first thing in the morning. We'll set up places to sleep." As for the water, he reached far up a vine and cut a notch. Then he cut it off near the ground and tested the drops coming out of it.

"It's not milky, it's ok," he said. He put it into his canteen. "When it fills we'll drop a couple of chlorine tablets into each canteen. You do the same to those vines," he pointed, "Now for some food. I'm going to look around. If you hear a whistle like a bird, whistle back so I can find you."

Endrique and Manuel cleared three small areas and cut some palm fronds to lie on.

Then they heard a "Wee...da, wee...da."

They answered back, "Wee...da, wee...da."

Hector came through the brush and into the camp area. It was getting dark, and they could barely see now.

"Look what I've got," he said as he proudly showed them three eggs.

"Where did you get these?" they asked.

"I saw the bird's nest empty with five eggs. You don't take them all. Then she may lay more. We'll check in the morning. Here," he showed them his hat full of leaves, flowers and pods.

"The Acacia tree. All of this is edible. We can't make a fire. I say poke a hole in the bird's egg shell, slurp it out and chew this other stuff."

Enrique said, "We had better bed down."

The morning came with a bang, in fact with a bombardment.

"They must be hitting Giron, the Blue Beach," Manuel said.

Hector said, "It's barely light, but let's pick it up. Make sure you make it look as natural as possible, so they can't find our camp and our tracks. Here are two chlorine tablets for each canteen. Follow me, I'm going to check the bird's nest again."

"Sure enough!" Hector said. A female bird hastily flew out of the nest as he put his hand into it and came out with three eggs.

"Eat up, pick a few more of these leaves and flowers from this tree, and follow me!" Hector commanded.

"We're going to go slightly south-southwest. We've got to swing around the Red Beach at Playa Larga."

They traveled about four hours. Off in the distance they could hear the explosions and shooting. Then it stopped.

Hector said, "Hold up! It's a clearing. No it's a small road. In fact a small dirt road. Let's see." He looked at the part of the map the Major had given him. "I started to turn our route to the south-southwest about an hour ago, and according to this map and my compass this is the first road heading into the Zapata Peninsula."

"We'll cross it. One by one. I'll go first, cover me!" Hector moved slowly across. Then he took a position and signaled. The other two came across one at a time.

"You can't see very far either way," Manuel noted.

"Just a minute before we go," Hector exclaimed as he went over and pulled some plantains from a tree-like plant with large leaves. Then he pulled all of the rest off and threw them to the other two guys. "Here's lunch," he said.

"Good work, Hector," Enrique complimented.

"Let's get going," Hector motioned ahead. "In a mile at our present course, we should hit a dirt trail. Then four miles farther we should come to the beach road."

They took turns leading and clearing the way with their makeshift bayonet machetes.

Hector kept on track by constantly looking at his compass and saying, "left some," "a little right," or "straight," as they slowly moved along.

Just as planned they came to the dirt trail. It was a wide trail, passable only by 4-wheel or on foot. Within a couple of hours they started coming to occasional brackish wet spots in the trail and then, sure enough, the beach road. It was a wide dirt road with a hint of crushed coral on it. They stopped and looked both ways.

"What's that sound? Manuel asked.

"It's a helicopter," Enrique said, "Castro's! I know it by the sound. Quick! Back in the brush. Spread out, and hide behind a tree."

The helicopter was following the road, looking. They could hear the men in the helicopter hollering. As it went overhead they could see a machine gun hanging out the side.

"We'll cross before they come back, then we've only a mile to the beach," Hector suggested. "What do you think, Enrique?"

"Sounds good!"

Hector commented, "We'd better get going. Along the way keep a lookout for pools of water in old stumps or coral rock formations."

"There's a large stump and some water pooled in it. There must have been some logging here," Hector motioned.

Enrique exclaimed, "There used to be a lot of virgin mahogany timber here. Yep, they logged all of the big trees."

"It doesn't look like much," Hector exclaimed. "But if you put these two chlorine tablets in your canteens and shake it up, in a half of an hour it will be all right to drink."

"There's the water," Manuel pointed.

They could faintly see the far shore about four miles across the bay through the mangroves. Enrique waded through the mangroves and exclaimed, "I see the *Houston* beached and to the south way out there the smoke from Grion. (Blue Beach)"

He waded back. "Guys, here is what I think we should do. Go back to where it's dry. Move farther down another mile, eat our plantains and sleep. First thing in the morning we'll go out past the mangroves, and look for a boat to save us."

At first light they waded out past the mangroves.

"Look! Out there!" Hector said. "A big boat!"

"It's a destroyer, an American," Enrique said enthusiastically, "Let's see if we can wade out to those reefs, and wave our shirts."

The sun broke out through the clouds. The three men kept wading and waving their shirts. From the destroyer, a boat started to head their way.

They got to the small coral reefs sticking out of the water. They climbed up on the rocks. The boat came closer. They started to leave the rocks and wade towards the small boat fast approaching. As it drew closer they could see two of their Cuban frogmen. Then a guy with a short-sleeved tan shirt and sunglasses started to stand up.

"Thank you Lord!" Hector exclaimed.

Manuel was aroused from his daydreaming stupor by a sudden jerk on his pole. He yanked it to set the hook and pulled hard. His pole bent double. He could see as he fought the monster that it was a clunker of a Red Snapper. As far back as he could remember it was the largest fish he had ever hooked off this dock. He started to get the better of the snapper, and as it got close to him he slipped his net under and brought it up.

As he proudly surveyed his upcoming meal, he suddenly got recall. He remembered. There was a guy sketching me. I thought he was a phantom from the past. I guess he must have been just an artist tourist. At least he only sketched me from the back. Well, he's gone. Thank the good Lord!

Author:

This story is purely fictitious. Any resemblance to any person living or dead is purely coincidental. The Bay of Pigs invasion, environment and activities are referenced by the books in the glossary.*

In no way is this story meant to take anything away from the Cuban Freedom Fighters of Brigade 2506. They fought bravely against tremendously overwhelming odds and put up a fantastic showing. They surrendered when they ran out of ammunition. They were fighting for democracy and freedom for their country. What they did not know is that unfortunately, the action was doomed before it started. If you read the books referenced, you will see that there is enough blame to go around for the government planners and people in control. You can draw your own conclusions. I pray that the men who died in this action did not die in vain, and some day the Cuban people will be truly free.

Brown Pelican just off the Key West city docks.

4

The Brown Pelican

Here I am, on my favorite dockside perch. You know it is just off Key West's Mallory docks, the old town's center of activity. I love to fly over here early in the morning. It is so invigorating. I fly low, skimming along the crests of the waves. I'm using a scientific term called "ground effect," whereby as the air compresses between me and the water, it increases lift and easily supports me. That way I use very little energy. It is one of my favorite pastimes.

I nest every evening on a small uninhabited (at least by humans) mangrove island. It is located between the mainland and this fantastic chain of Keys. There is a small colony of us brown pelicans located there. We just love it because it's so quiet and peaceful. But you should see it in breeding season, and when we raise our young. One can hardly move!

Wait! What is going on? That young man coming up the dock is a tourist, I suspect. What is he up to? Let's see, he has a two-wheel contraption, they call it a bicycle. Now he is taking some materials out of the front basket. It looks like he is going to sketch me. Why, he must be an artist.

He has brushes and tubes of color. It looks like I'm going to be a watercolor painting! I will hold this pose. Look, he is finished and packing up already. That didn't take long. I guess watercolor is a fast process, nothing like the time it takes for the oil colorists to paint. There he goes, pedaling his transportation.

Humans just don't have the capabilities we have. In fact, he has my image, but he doesn't know my soul. He doesn't know the great and dynamic history of the brown pelicans. I would like to enlighten you. Come along and I'll show you our environment, our home, our destiny.

I would like to start by taking you up. Let's use the thermals to soar. Let's take the Atlantic side of this string of keys running east northeast to south-southwest. Let's go up...up...up. There, I am leveling off at six thousand feet, even though some of my peers have gone up as high as ten thousand feet!

From up here we can see the long arc of these islands. If you look closer you can see the chain of shallow coral reefs running parallel to this arc. They are just under the beautiful turquoise water and occasionally rise slightly above. On the outside of the reef is the famous Gulf Stream and on the inside is the narrow Hawk Channel.

The Hawk Channel washes against the many coconut-studded sand beaches and mangrove shores. Both the Hawk Channel and the Gulf Stream are water highways, with treacherous reefs separating them. These reefs just sit there waiting a misstep by an unsuspecting ship.

This majestic environment is much over one hundred and fifty miles long. We consider it ours! We, brown pelicans traverse its entire length. It is our environment. Now we are one of the only two species of pelicans that reside in the United States. In the winter, one may see an occasional white pelican here, but their primary breeding ground is in western Canada and the northwestern US.

Even though I hate to admit it, the white pelican is much larger than us browns. They have a wingspan of up to nine and one half feet, where ours is six. They don't feed as spectacularly as we do. They float, and scoop up fish and we, well I'll show you, dive for our fish.

Let's drop on down, soar some, and then drop down again. I can spot a fish from as high as sixty-five feet, but I like to be closer to the ocean. I glide above the crest of a wave, not even flapping a wing. When I spot a fish I dive straight in, leaning to the left to protect my throat from the impact. Then I open my pouch to let in the fish. I may also get a couple of gallons of water which I drain out as I float there. Then I just swallow the fish whole. Mm...Mmm, Good!

Oh, did I tell you about floating? I'm very buoyant. I float easily because I have air sacks in both my skin and bones. I can also swim very proficiently. Well, enough about me. As I may have mentioned, we brown pelicans have been here in the Keys from the beginning of time. As everyone knows, God made us, and Adam named us.

Let's now go back in time, many years ago. Imagine a sparkling sand beach somewhere along this island chain. A dugout canoe, a boat made from a hollowed out log, is turning inward from the Hawk Channel. It is being paddled by three male natives. There are also two female passengers riding in it. They have come down in the Hawk Channel from the southeast Florida mainland. The waves carry them in towards the beach. They stop paddling and rest as they steady the canoe with their paddles. Suddenly a large wave picks them up, and they ride it up onto the sand. The three men drop their paddles in the boat, and jump out. The next wave pushes the boat farther up on the beach. The two women get out, with the help of the next wave they all pull the canoe up as far as they can.

The two older men take their weapons, one a spear and the other a bow with arrows, and head up into the vegetation. The remaining young man watches as the two women walk along the shore with a basket. They are gathering particular sizes and shapes of colored shells. These may be used for decorations, for tools to cut and clean the skins of animals, or even the end of a hoe for planting maize.

It seems the two men are the mates of the women and the third man

200 AD, Calusa Indians arriving in the Florida Keys

watching over the women is the son of one. Their brown bodies glisten in the sunlight.

Suddenly the two men emerge from the tree line. Believe it or not, there are some very large mahogany trees growing on this key. They signal, and the two women put their woven basket of shells in the canoe. Each takes a bundle of items, and all three head towards where the two men had appeared.

On the inside of the mahogany forest, in a sizable clearing, is a mound. It is about fifty feet in diameter and three to four feet high. In fact, there are many more such mounds scattered through these Keys. They are either shell middens* burial mounds, or ceremonial locations. The Indians have been visiting, camping, and living in these Keys since two hundred years after the birth of Christ.

How do I know all this? Because we were there; in fact, we were there much earlier than the Indians.

Our next visitors came along much later, sometime in the fifteen hundreds. They were supposedly much more educated and advanced. But they were a ruthless group of explorers.

Now we see a three-masted ship, a galleon. It has two raised decks above the main deck in both the front and rear. It is about one hundred and forty feet long and thirty five feet wide. Somehow it has found a way through the reef. It now sits at anchor in the Hawk Channel right off the shore of the same beach our Indian visitors had landed on at least six hundred years prior.

They have launched the ship's two longboats and are rowing in to the shore. There are at least twelve to fourteen men in each one. They too are thrown up on the beach by the same kind of waves that assisted our earlier native Americans.

They scramble out and pull the boats up onto the sand. They are not as graceful as our Indian friends were. There appears to be a leader. He walks up on the land and plants a yellow and red flag onto the sand. He is dressed in ornate clothing. Flowing pantaloons hang around his waist and down to his upper knees and tights cover his legs. His followers gather around him. They wear fancy hats and clothing. Some are wearing metal breast plates, and a couple have blunderbusses,* some have pikes and all

1500 AD, Spanish Explorers claiming the Keys for Spain

have straight-style swords.

These are the conquistadors or explorers who conquered Mexico. What are they here for? They will claim this land for the king and queen of Spain. However, basically, they are here for gold, silver, and jewels. They will find none here. Let's listen a moment to them.

The leader: "I, Don Juan Diego de Escanpar do claim this entire land in the name of their Royal Majesties, the King and Queen of Spain for all eternity. Men look around, see what is here. I would like gold, but if you can capture some natives, we can take them back to Cuba to work our sugar plantations."

One of the men, "Look, Don Diego, at the very large mahogany trees."

Don Diego says, "Very nice. When we return, we will log those trees, and send the lumber back to Spain. Their Majesties will be very proud, and it will bring us fame, favor, and fortune."

Now we pelicans had to be a bit wary around these men. They would have shot us and had us for dinner.

It is now a couple of hundred years later. This time in a small cove just around the corner from our beach is a boat at anchor. It is of a different look and design than the Spanish galleon. This ship is somewhat smaller and much more streamlined. It has triangular sails on two masts instead of the square sails of the galleon. It has no quarter or raised decks and has only three cannons on each side, their barrels pointing out of raised hatches on the ready.

There is a flag flying from the top of the tallest mast. It is all black and is emblazoned on each side with a skull on top and crossed-bones right below. There are two longboats drawn up on a small beach opening between the mangroves. In the distance is this end of a very small mahogany and pine forest. This is proof that our Spanish explorers have been visiting this area for quite some time and made good of their promise to log the forest.

On this beach are a mish mash of men, running, sitting, and lying about. Some appear to be drinking. They are almost all bare-chested and most barefooted. Some have gold earrings and gold nose rings. They have bandannas about their heads, single pigtails behind, and combination of beards of all colors, types, and sizes. They are all armed with pistols and swords.

These men are the pirates of the Caribbean. What are they here for? They could be looking for water. They will find little here, if any. There might be some in the old Calusa Indian well. But mainly they are here

1700 AD, Pirates anchored in a cove in the Florida Keys

waiting for a Spanish treasure galleon returning to Spain from Mexico to come sailing by in the Gulf Stream. They mean to procure the gold and valuables for themselves.

We pelicans did not fear these men. They were too busy with other matters to pay us any mind. We did observe.

What's next, you say? It's now the 1800's. The pirates have been bothersome and dangerous. The Spanish gold bullion treasure ships have been long gone so now the pirates are attacking United States ships of commerce. The United States of America is a growing country and people demand protection from, and an end to, the pirates. Enter the U. S. Navy.

We are now off our same beach. Some of our first pirates' ancestors have been visiting the mentioned cove just around the corner from our beach. A pirate lookout has just seen a tall ship's sails on the horizon. All bedlam breaks out. The pirates run for their longboats and hurriedly row out to their schooner. Already some on board the schooner have begun to unfurl the sails.

There is a mad scramble to get aboard, load their longboats, and assist their compatriots in the goal to get away from the tall ship which is fast bearing down on them. The sails catch a good breeze and as they are picking up speed the first warning shot flies across their bow.

The tall ship is flying from its masthead the red, white, and blue of the United States of America. Right below it, waving in the breeze is a blue

1800 AD, The U S Navy chasing a Pirate schooner

U. S. Navy pennant.

The pirate ship rushes to evade its pursuers, as the two bow chaser canons of the Navy ship continue to fire. We pelicans aren't hanging around to watch the fireworks. We make a beeline for the protection of the trees on the sound side of the Key.

Since the first quarter of this century, after the U. S. Navy took over Key West, Florida, the pirates began to look for other parts of the Caribbean to take their activities. They were quickly becoming unwelcome anywhere near the United States shores.

My next tale is a story of the Keys' wreckers. We pelicans notice, from our place in the protection of the remaining forest, a ship floundering right off our beach. The weather has been very nasty, a great storm. It is beginning to subside now, but not soon enough, for a great sailing ship, a three-masted cargo ship is hung up on the reef.

Somewhere a cry goes up, "Ship on the rocks!" and as if by divine guidance, two small ships, a sloop and a schooner appear. Their crews are a mixture of Bahamian, Cayman Islanders, and Key West Conchs.

These fearless men have come, first, to save souls, and second, to salvage cargo. If the captain of the ship in distress gives permission, these "wreckers," as they are called, will lend a hand. They look danger

1800 AD, A wrecking schooner and a sloop race
to help a stranded cargo ship on the reef.

straight in the eye! Not fearing for their lives, they will first get the passengers off to a safe place, and then unload the cargo. They will then move it in to the shore or closest safe location.

Next they will attempt to get the ship off the rocks. They have the tools and know-how to do this job. Many times other boats will appear and join in a team effort. When all is completed, the salvaged cargo and ship, if possible, is moved to Key West. There, a salvage court will assess payment for all parties.

Naturally, we pelicans prefer to sit this one out in the safety of our trees. The final major visitor who was the forerunner of the great surge of population and so-called progress, was a man called Flagler with his dream.

Of course we pelicans could see it coming. We saw Flagler's railroad building its way down the entire Florida East Coast. This was early in the 1900's. Then he stretched out from Miami into the Everglades, through Homestead and built "The Railroad That Went To Sea."

It was the engineering feat of the times. He accomplished what many had said was impossible, a railroad that ran through the Keys and linked Key West to the mainland! In that one hundred and twenty five miles of Keys, he constructed forty-four bridges. After that the visitors came, who

1900 AD, dream come true,
a railroad from the Florida mainland to Key West

told others, and then the highways.

You say, what next? We pelicans cannot foretell the future. But we have survived and observed. We were here before it all began, and God willing, will be here when it all ends.

The Brown Pelican

'57 era Nash Metropolitan (Met)

5

The Met

I bet you don't know anything about me…I was the first entirely designed in America, owned by an American company, marketed in America, but built entirely in Europe…automobile. I was sold under the "Nash" and "American Motors" name, even under the "Hudson" name.

My designer was Detroit Michigan's famous W. J. Flajole. My unibody was by England's Fisher & Ludlow, and I was assembled at the Austin Motor's plant in Birmingham, England. My 4-cylinder, in-line, Austin engine was linked to a 3-speed manual transmission.

"Not bad, huh, for a little guy?"

Many things have been said about my kind. These are just a few: "A good thing in a small package," "Performance far better than expected," "Felt very safe," "Ride is more than expected," "Fun to drive," "Ideal for a second car," and " Best handling car."

Well, enough of this mystery. If you haven't guessed by now…I am a Nash Metropolitan. Fortunately, I am one of the third series, and I like to think it was the best.

I was built in mid-1957. There were two models, hard-top and convertible. But I think I'm the best, a hardtop. My two-tone paint scheme, blue and white, is a very sharp contrast. It also makes me look much lower and streamlined. My engine size has been increased to about 91 cubic inches. I now have a whopping 50 horsepower.

I am sitting here at "Key West Motors," a car lot in Key West, Florida. The good news is that I'm a one-owner. Yep, my only owner was a little old lady from Key West. Nash Metropolitan's advertising was targeted to ladies when it first came out.

I sure hope my next owner is as easy on me as she was. All I need is a hot-rodder who wants to drop a Chevy V8 in me. Heaven forbid! Dear Lord please don't let that happen.

Well, let's take a look around at "Key West Motors." This is really not such a bad place. It is near the Navy base right downtown. It's a good place to attract business, and also on a corner so it can be seen from more than two streets. I'm out front by the sidewalk. Typical Key West palm trees on either side of me. I hope they're not coconut palms…I don't need any dents. I guess she wanted a bigger car, something to carry her grandkids in. She drove me in yesterday and drove out with a new Nash Rambler. As a consolation, I guess I can say she stayed with the brand. Everyone knows that Nash is the very best!

The shop foreman did run me through the shop yesterday afternoon. I feel exhilarated. New oil, greased, vacuumed and shined.

Oh, here comes a couple of guys now! Let's listen in, I'm going to be looking my best.

The tall man with a slight Bahamian accent is talking, "We have a lot of very nice vehicles in, Mr. Kranich. May I call you Norman?"

"Yes sir, no problem. Just call me Norman, That is correct sir. I need something that can get me around the island, back and fourth to the Navy base and occasionally up the keys to a bridge to fish."

"Well Norman, I'm sure we can fix you up. We've got a lot of nice cars at Key West Motors. I'm sure you would be interested in at least one."

Norman wasn't too short himself, just under six feet, average build, lean and a full head of black hair. His hair was wavy and combed back as was the style of his youth in the 30's. He also had piercing black eyes and a faint shadow of a mustache above his upper lip.

"I also like to be conservative. In fact, I want a car that is good on gas and reasonably priced," Norman declared.

"Well Norman, here's a nice Volkswagen, only a couple of years old. As I'm sure you know the VW's get good gas mileage, in the 20-30's."

"What's the price for it?"

"Well Mr. Kranich the sticker here says $1,200. I can let you have it for $1,150."

"What else do you have? What is the blue and white hardtop here?"

"That Norman is a "Met", actually a Nash Metropolitan. Let's see, it is a '57', only 10 years old. You know, that for miles per gallon, it gets in

the '30's. In fact, *Motor Trend* magazine even took a car like this to the top of Pikes Peak, 14,000 feet above sea level."

"One more thing, Norman, it will go from zero to sixty in less than twenty three-seconds! Now that's a lot faster than a VW."

"What is the price on it?"

"Norman, it is listed at $800, but I can let you have it for $750. Also, take a look, it's got the famous Nash weather eye heater and AM radio in it, factory stock."

"Ok, I'll take it."

"Don't you want to drive it first?"

"No don't have to. I trust your judgment."

"Oh well then, Mr. Kranich, let's go to the office, and write it up."

"Wow, that happened pretty fast! It looks like I have a new owner."

Here comes an attendant. In fact, he is the guy who serviced me yesterday afternoon.

Ah…Ah... Roar. How do you like the sound? The Austin four is a nice sound in a little package. We backed out and pulled up to Key West Motor's office. The salesman and my new owner were standing out front. Norman had a key in one hand and papers in the other.

Norman and the salesman shook hands, the attendant gave him the other key, and he got in.

As Norman pulled out, "The sales man yelled, it's a three–speed, Mr. Kranich. Have fun!"

We eased out of the lot, turned right, went a few blocks and turned right again, heading south. Then I heard him say under his breath,

"On to Roosevelt Blvd, and let's see what she'll do!"

"Uh oh!" I thought.

We came to a stop sign. The street sign read Roosevelt Blvd. We turned left paralleling the Atlantic Ocean on the right. The waves were caressing the bright sandy beach, and dazzling white seagulls were gliding about.

I could feel his foot come down on my accelerator.

Burr- Ah shift

Burr– Ah..Ah..Ah.. Shift

Burr– Burr

Norm was running me through all three speeds. I could feel the carbon blowing out of my 4 cylinders. My past owner, the little old lady, never went over 45, and did it slowly.

We were cruising along rather briskly. If I could have, I would have said, "Norm, we're at 65, and the speed limit is 45 along here." But I didn't have to. That is, he realized it when the red lights and siren suddenly came on behind us. I heard Norman say under his breath, "Oh, oh!"

We pulled over to the side, the cruiser right behind us. The officer got out of his vehicle, adjusted his hat, and came up. Norman was getting out his driver's license.

"Sir, could I see your driver's license, registration, and insurance?"

"Yes sir, here it is."

"Norman, is that you? I didn't recognize you in this buggy. I figured you were just another hot shot tourist."

"Hi Sam. I'm sorry, I just bought this car and was trying it out."

"More like, blowing it out!...Norm," Sam said as he handed Norman's paperwork back.

"You know speeding can get you a ticket! What is this thing? I've never seen one before like it. Probably the only one on this island."

"Me neither," Norman said. "It's a Nash Metropolitan. I was probably at top speed anyway. It only has an English 4-cylinder under the hood and three on the floor. I bought it to go back and forth to the Navy yard."

"Open the hood, and let's take a look."
Norm pulled the latch, got out, and lifted up the hood.

"There it is."

"You're right Norm, an Austin 4-cylinder. It was moving pretty good when you came by me! Well, Norm, I've got to get going. Keep a light pace, take care, and I'll see you around. Maybe at the Officer's Club this weekend. Will you be playing with your orchestra?"

"You bet we will! See you then, Sam…and thanks."

"Well, we were sure lucky," I thought, as my new owner started up and pulled out. Instead of racing around Roosevelt Blvd, he turned left at 1st street, right before the salt ponds, headed north to Fogarty, and then turned right after a couple of blocks, to my new home. A big four-door Pontiac was parked in the drive next to the house and a small camper trailer in front of it. I was given a small gravel side space out front. It was nice because I could see everything that came up and down the street.

As time went on I learned some things about my new owner. I took him to the downtown naval station and submarine base every work day. "Naturally he didn't talk to me, at least not directly. Occasionally he talked to himself, a short exclamation of sorts. But the afternoon he took the captain from his work at the Naval Station to the Boca Chica Naval Air Station I learned a lot. If I had been a human I would have needed a security clearance. Norm and a uniformed guy came out, a guy in a bright, smart, crisp navy white uniform. They got in, and started me up.

"Thanks for giving me a lift, Norm. Car's in the shop, and all the motor pool jeeps are either out or getting serviced. I need to get over to that meeting."

"Think nothing of it, Captain. It's nice to get out."

"Where did you get this buggy, Norm?"

"I picked it up a month ago at Key West Motors. It's been doing real good."

"What is it?"

"A Nash Metropolitan...it gets about 30 miles per gallon on this island. Not bad, huh?"

"I like it. Small but comfortable. A little bit perky also!" the commander said.

"Norm, are you going to get those submariners their hazardous duty pay?"

"Yes sir, I'm on it," Norm answered.

"I can't say where they're off to, but I think you can guess."

"Yes sir, it seems the world is never at peace."

"If any of them need an advance it's ok," the commander said.

"I'll take care of it, Sir."

We pulled up to the main gate at the Boca Chica Naval Air Station. The guard did a smart salute and waved us through. There I was on a secure installation. I felt so proud! I was putting two and two together. My owner, Norman was involved in some real heavy stuff!

I think I will have time for one more story. It's a fish story. Since I'm living in Key West, I'm sure it is appropriate. It was early on a Saturday morning. Norm came out of the house and before he shut the door I heard him say, "Bye Sweetie, I'm going to see what's biting off the old dock up by *No Name Key*."

Well, we set off, rod and reel in the back seat, out of Key West on Highway 1, past Boca Chica Naval Air Station. There weren't many cars on the road. Norm's black hair was blowing in the wind. I noticed we kept just under the speed limit. These highway patrol would not be as sympathetic as Sam, the patrolman was!

It wasn't too long before we turned left onto a small asphalt-paved road. The sign read as we were crossing the last bridge, "Big Pine Key." The pines weren't big here-as a matter of fact they look stunted! What was that? It looked like a deer. But it was only the size of a large dog!

We went back through an intermittent forest and field, and turned right past a sign that read, "Deer Key Refuge." We came up to a dead end. There was an old dilapidated wood pier going out into the water.

Norman got out, put on his cap, grabbed the fishing gear, and headed out onto the pier, whistling as he went. The pier was moving from side-to-side as he walked out onto it. I'll just rest. I surely need it after that ride. I could see Norm out at the end of the pier casting out. He had one foot up on the rail and was intently looking over at his line. All of a sudden there was a commotion. Norm was reeling in, the rod was bent double, and he was heading this way towards shore. I could see something big jump up and the flash of a white body. Norm kept pulling the fish in towards shore. He didn't have a net or a gaff. He reeled in standing on the shore and dragged it up on the beach. The fish was huge and thrashing about.

After some time it stopped flipping, and Norm carried it to the car.

He said to himself, "Going to take this home. I need a picture."

He got this old plastic out of my trunk and wrapped the fish up and threw it and the gear in my back seat...ugh.

We drove back home, kind of in a happy mood. Norm was whistling all the way home to the AM radio.

We pulled up into our drive, and Norm hurried in the front door. Dolores, his wife, came out the front carrying a

Norman walking out on the old wooden No Name Key bridge.

camera.

"What you going to do with that? You're not going to eat it."

"Take my picture holding this goliath, and then I'm going to take it over to Manuel's. He will know how to cook it."

That said, that done, and that's my fish story. Now you know something about me. Tell your friends.

Norman with his huge barracuda

Unloading, hosing down the catch of shrimp, and sending them into the packing house.

6

The Sponge Adventure

"Let'er rip Capt'n. I'm ready for another batch."

David had been hosing down the shrimp in the hopper, and then hit the switch that turned on the conveyor which took the catch into the packing house. The men were unloading their catch on the Key West city docks. The packer and processor was the Singleton Fish and Ice Plant. In an hour or so their shrimp would have their heads removed, packed in wooden crates, and iced for shipment. At one time the Singleton Plant was the largest in the world.

David was a 27-year-old Afro-American. He had a close hair cut, was five foot nine inches, and was thin but muscular from the hard work required on a shrimp trawler.

They had been out for three days in the Gulf on Captain Bob's ocean-going trawler "Sea Breeze." Talk about a haul! This morning they had stumbled into a mess of shrimp. It was the pink shrimp. They had been "Midwater Trawling"* just offshore near the Dry Tortugas Key.

Their hold was full, and they had come right in to get it unloaded, cleaned and packed. It had taken a couple of hours so far, of shoveling the shrimp into the large stainless steel unloading bucket and winching it to the hopper where David was working.

"Here it comes." Captain Bob held the unloading dump rope as his other mate, Amos
was operating the unloading winch and boom.

Amos, was a 42-year-old Afro-American
who had been with the Captain since he bought
the "Sea Breeze." In fact they had worked together before on another trawler. Amos was 6
feet 2 inches tall and well built.

The stainless steel bucket swung out and
over the boat and stopped right above where
David was working.

"Dump it, Capt'n," David hollered. The 80
pounds of shrimp tumbled into the hopper.

Pink shrimp* is what is harvested mostly in
the Florida waters. There are three other species found in the Gulf of

Mexico and South Atlantic waters: Brown, White and Royal Red.* Shrimp replenish themselves fairly fast. Their life cycle is 13 months. That is a rapid reproduction rate.

Captain Bob was 54 and about five foot nine inches. He was filled out but not fat. He had a round face with a full black beard showing faint signs of becoming grey. He was an Anglo of German descent.

David hollered, "The packer wants to know how much more Capt'n?"

"Tell him a couple more loads," Bob said. "As soon as I get the last to you, Davey, come on board, and we'll get the boat cleaned up."

The Sea Breeze was a sea-going trawler.* It was 60 feet in length. This boat was built with the lines of the Greek shrimp boats. Instead of the V-shaped hull it had a rounded cross–section. The bow was high with a deck house located forward. This left the stern for hauling in the nets. The rounded hull shape made a deep and slow roll at sea and a boat that could take rough seas. It was built in 1960 by the Diesel Engine Sales Company (DESC)* of St Augustine, Florida, one of the largest shrimp boat builders in the USA.

Captain Bob's boat was a traditionally built boat, with a pine keel, white oak frames, and cypress planking. One item to note: when the cypress planking became too expensive, the boatyards shifted to yellow pine. But Bob felt fortunate his boat had the cypress.

Captain Bob Mitchel had this boat for the last five years, since 1964. He was in the fishing business since he graduated from high school in 1933. His fishing was temporarily postponed in 1941 when he joined the US Navy. Bob saw service on a destroyer until the war's end in 1945. He then bounced right back here to Key West and resumed his love of the sea.

After that Bob saved every penny he could. He was fortunate to find

some silent backers that let him run the show. Now Captain Bob was 51% owner of his own fishing boat and business.

"We finally got it cleaned. Thank you guys. It was a lot of hard work, but we made some cash," Bob exclaimed. "Start her up, Amos, and let's get her over to our slip."

The 300 HP Detroit Diesel engine sputtered, coughed, and caught... and the heart and soul of this boat roared! They pulled away from Singleton's docks and went out into the channel and then to the marina the "Sea Breeze" called home. The marina had three sections: commercial, fishing excursions, and private. Amos shut her down. They tied up to the dock posts and jumped onto the pier.

As the three walked out to the parking lot, Captain Bob said, "Tell you what guys…give me some time to get the paperwork done. Stop by the house tomorrow morning, and I will have your checks ready." He just didn't know how long they would be out, so consequently Bob never could have the guys' checks made out ahead of time.

"Here's my car. See you tomorrow...about 9 am Capt'n?"

"Sounds good, Amos. See you then."

"You guys want a ride?" Amos asked.

"No thanks, Amos," Bob and Dave said in unison.

They both lived within walking distance of the marina, six to eight blocks.

"Well, I'm glad it's Friday, David. I'm tired, What're you going to do this weekend?" Bob said as they walked along.

"I'm going to be working on the skipjack," David replied.

"How's that boat coming along? You still thinking about sponging, David?"

"Yep, to answer your questions. The boat is looking good! I'm working on the canvas right now, and I'll be sponge fishing in due time."

"Tell you what, David, I'll be by to check on your progress on that boat tomorrow morning. I'll bring your check by after I pay Amos."

"Sounds good, Captain Bob. See you then."

Knock! Knock!

"Will you get that, Bob?" His wife hollered down from upstairs.

"Ok, Honey, I'm expecting someone," Bob responded as he headed towards the front door.

"Oh…Hi Amos. Come on in. Let me get your check."

"When are we going back out Capt'n?"

"Amos, I figure we'll take a day for maintenance. How about whenever you want to on Monday. Go on over to the boat, and check out the nets. I know that there's some mending to do, and I know you'll be first class with that project."

"Sounds good Capt'n. See you Monday."

"The wife and I may see you sooner. We're going to come by your church Sunday. What time is the service?"

"Sounds real fine Capt'n, that will be 10:30. See you both then."

Captain Bob walked Amos to the front door and said his good bye's, turned and walked back in.

Bang! The screen door slammed shut.

"Honey, There's that door again, can you adjust it?" Bob's wife requested.

"Sure, Sweetheart, I'm going over to David's. I'll be helping him with his boat," Bob replied.

"Ok Dear," she replied, "Please don't forget the door, see you at lunch."

Slam!

It was only four long blocks to where David lived. Bob enjoyed the walk. Something was unusual about where David's parents' house was. It was located at the end of a small inlet. In fact the property was connected to the water. The basic house was an original Bahamian cottage. Down close to the water was an old boat house. This property had been in David's family for several generations. Their great grandfather had built the cottage in the Bahamas and then dismantled, shipped, and reassembled it here in Key West.

The property was long and narrow. If it was any wider it would be sought after by the developers. As it was, it was still extremely valuable, but David's parents were just content to stay there in the old home place.

He walked past the cottage and went back to the boat house. The skipjack sat there on the outside. In fact it was propped up and sitting on the ways.* David's ways were a double wooden track leading down to and into the water. Bob could see that it

would be easy to launch her. He walked around to the back of the boat house. There David was, canvas all around him, a big needle in his hand.

"Hi David," Bob said.

"Hi Captain, what do you think?" David asked. "The boats looking good, huh?"

"The boat looks ready. I see you've got her painted," Bob exclaimed.

"Yep, did that a couple of weeks ago. I used a fiberglass paint," said David.

"It looks like you could use a hand with the sail," Captain Bob exclaimed.

"Sure could, Capt'n."

The skipjack* was flat-sided with the sides above the floor about 12 inches. The beam was 9 feet, 4 inches. Overall she was 22 feet long. There was a deck house over the cabin, and this had about 5 feet, 6 inches of head room. The cabin was about 10 feet long, and 7 feet wide. It was divided fore and aft by a center board trunk. This came up about 2 feet from the floor. There was room under the fore deck to stow gear, and there were two narrow bunks one on either side. The cockpit was in the rear. It was on the same floor as the cabin. The boat was steered by a tiller out the back, no wheel. With the center board down, she drafted 4 feet 6 inches. She had about 400 pounds of ballast.

The rigging was simple: two sails, jib and main. They were both laced to booms on one mast. The overhang of the booms, both front and rear, put out a lot of canvas.

"This is sure big! It's a lot of canvas," Bob remarked.

"That's right

Skipjack on the ways before launching.

Capt'n. But this is the jib. I finished the mainsail last week," David said proudly. "This little boat will spread a lot of canvas and catch a lot of wind! Here, help me hold this and I will stitch the seam."

He was using an awl to punch a hole through the canvas in the center of a grommet and then run the heavy cord through it with a large needle.

"I see, it appears you have all the grommets in," Bob remarked.

"Yep...I also did that last week. I've been getting excited to take her out."

They worked the rest of the morning.

"David, I had better get home for lunch. But I'll come back after I eat and we'll hang these sails."

"Capt'n, you could eat here with us," David offered.

"I'd like to, but I can't disappoint the missus She'll have lunch ready. Thanks though."

"Hey! Honey, I'm home."

Bang!...The screen door slammed shut.

"I thought you adjusted that door?"

"I did, I thought," Bob apologized.

"What's David up to?" she asked.

"He's coming along with that boat. I'm going back after lunch to help him."

"You sure do love boats, Honey. You're on them 24 hours a day sometimes, and then on your time off, you rest by working on them! I'll never understand you...but I love you!"

David and Bob finished the jib sail. They then attached it to the jib boom and roped all the grommets to the fore jib rope. The hoisting ropes then went up to the top of the mast through pulleys and then back down to the deck.

"She's a good looker, Dave. What are your plans for taking her out?" Bob asked.

"You know Capt'n, it's been a long time. I've been working on this boat for a year and a half or more. I'm straining at the leash. I think I will throw some provisions on her, get the sponge boat prepared for towing with my sponging equipment, and head out early next Saturday. Cap'n, you could come out with me."

"I would like to David. But if I do...You'll be the Captain, and I'll be the First Mate."

"But Capt'n, that doesn't seem to be right."

"Nope, it's your boat, and that's the only way I'd do it. On my boat I'm the Captain, and on your boat, you're the man!"

"Ok, thanks, Captain Bob."

Monday always has a way of coming around, and Bob was moving slow.

"Honey, after I eat this toast and drink my coffee, I'm going to go over to the boat. Amos was going to go over this morning. I've got him mending the nets. I've got to pull some maintenance on the engine and some general clean-up. I guess I'll get David to service the booms."

Sea-Breeze being loaded up with supplies to go out trawling.

"When you going back out?" she asked.

"I figure we'll head back out tomorrow. We'll go past Tortuga and then into the Bay. We should be back in no later than Friday. Pray we run into another mess of shrimp like we did last week!"

"See you, Honey."

Bang!

Captain Bob loved where he lived. This walk to his boat he relished. He loved seeing the coconut palms, bright flowers year-round, old brightly painted wooden Bahamian and Key West houses. He was happy. He turned into the marina.

"Morning, Amos, how're the nets looking?"

Not too bad, Capt'n. But you were right. They needed some work."

"Seen David?"

"Up here, Capt'n," David hollered, "You never did look up."

Captain Bob looked up. David was up on the mast.

"Getting those cables checked?" Bob asked.

"Yes sir, I've got a few preventative maintenance repairs to make."

Amos said, "I'll take the other boom, David, and we'll get done faster. Then I'll rustle up some lunch."

"David, when you get to it, let's lower the outriggers.* It will be smart to check and grease all those pulleys and inspect everything related to

them."

"Ay, aye, Sir."

After a few hours of work…

"Amos, I'll make the coffee if you do the honors of preparing that food you promised us."

"Well Capt'n, looks like all this refrigerator is going to do for us is bacon and eggs."

"We'll take it!" David and Bob said in unison.

"Tastes good! Thanks Amos. Guys, I thought that we'd go out tomorrow for a couple-three days."

NET
MENDING

REK

"Sounds good, Capt'n. We thought you'd never ask," David joked.

"About 6:30? Amos, come by with your pickup truck to the house. While we're getting provisions and from what you said, we need some, David will fuel and ice up. I checked on the weather, and it seems like it will hold for our trip."

"We're with you, Capt'n," they both said.

It was about 8:30 AM. "Not a bad start for a shrimp trawler," Captain Bob exclaimed.

He was aft* looking at the wake.* David was at the helm,* and Amos was stowing the provisions in the galley.* There was a faint diesel odor in

the air, but this didn't bother him. After all, this was his choice and living. He could see the tour and fishing excursions getting ready for the tourists and sport fishermen.

He waved as he was occasionally hailed by a captain or crewmember on these boats. Captain Bob was well known and liked. He had a lot of seamen friends. They left Garrison Bight behind and turned to the left, entering the Man of War Harbor and went past the 'Inner Harbor.' This was also known as the Key West Bight. This natural, large deep water harbor had been a very nice stopping place for seamen and their sailing ships for as long as man was sailing these Caribbean waters.

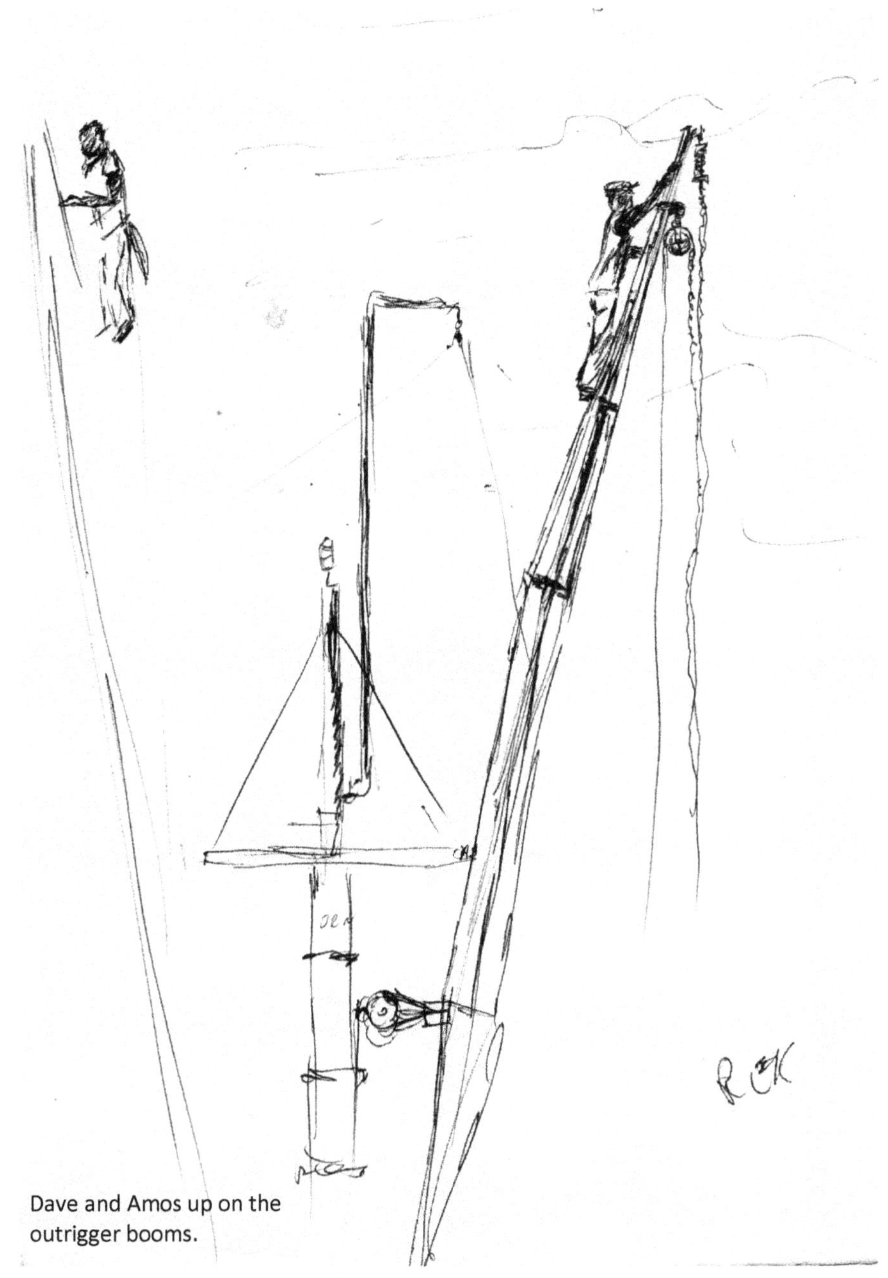

Dave and Amos up on the outrigger booms.

It was also a safe stopping place and had water from local wells. As time went on, it became the center of activity of old Key West for the sponge, turtle, fish, and shrimping industries.

David was moving the throttle forward. Where he was in the rear Bob could feel the surge of power. He loved that, it gave him a great feeling both inside and out. He finished coiling some rope, made sure all the lines were secure, and took a last look at the two boom lifting tackles. The booms were up vertical and snug against the mast. Bob went up front along the side rail and into one of the side doors to the wheel house.

"How's it going, David?"

"Feels fine, Capt'n."

"Just as soon as we get past the sub base…pour it to her!"

"Aye aye, Sir!" David answered.

As they cruised by the west side of Key West, they could see the Sub-Tender, U.S.S. Bushnell,* together with two subs tethered alongside. The subs looked like toys next to the huge mother ship. Then a couple of Navy two-motor patrol planes out of Boca Chica Naval Air Station flew by overhead gaining altitude. Boca Chica was just two Keys up from Key West and became very important and grew during the Second World War.

Amos hollered up from the galley, "How about some coffee and donuts guys?"

"Be right down, Amos. Thanks. I'll be right back, David, then I'll take a turn at the wheel, so you can go down and eat."

"Cap'n, I figure if you're going out a ways and then trawl, I'll make some sandwiches, and put them in the fridge. Then we can eat as we work."

"You read my mind, Amos. Thanks for the coffee and donuts."

"Well David, Amos read my mind, you probably heard. While you are in the galley with Amos, I'll go out twenty miles. Then just this side of the Continental Shelf we'll rig for fish, mid-trawl.* I want to try at the edge of the drop-off."

"Then we'll head due west for another 20 miles along the edge of the shelf. Possibly we'll get some tuna or mackerel. If that doesn't work we'll head north towards Tortugas. Tonight we'll either anchor off the island there or dock."

David took over the wheel from the captain. The seas were not heavy, just gentle swells. They were making about 8 knots (9 miles per hour). A few clouds floated lazily along.

"We're getting close Capt'n," David said bringing Bob out of his thoughts.

"Ok, David, I'll take over. You and Amos get the net adjusted, and winch the otter boards* over the side."

"Nets and boards out Capt'n," David yelled.

Sea Breeze with the outrigger booms extended holding the otter boards.

Bob had both wheel house doors open. He could also see out the back window of the enclosure. He left the wheel momentarily and looked out. He then went back in and adjusted the engine for a boat speed of about 3 knots. (2.5-3 knots equaling about 3 1/2 to 4 1/2 miles per hour is a good speed for trawling. Not too fast but enough to keep the net open. They used flotation on the upper edge and weight on the lower edge of the net. This and the speed controlled the vertical opening.)

They cruised along due west with the swell hitting them from the left (south). Dave was at the transom (rear) watching the net. Amos was locking the winch which controlled the modified "T" boom superstructure. This had the cable and hook which lifted the catch in the net when it was pulled in. The towing booms or outriggers were horizontal out both sides pulling on the net.

"Amos, how about those sandwiches? I'll take a Coke," the Captain said.

"Sounds good," David hollered.

As he ate his sandwich Bob looked about. He thought, we're all alone out here except for that one sport fishing boat heading out way behind us. Probably going for marlin. Of course there are the gulls perched on the rigging of this ship. They are just waiting for us to pull the net up. They are looking for fish just as we are!

"It's been a couple of hours. Let's bring it up guys." Captain Bob cut the engine way back and went out and to the rear to help.

Amos worked the winch. First the net was pulled up. Then he lifted both booms. This brought the net over the rear of the trawler. David hooked the net up, and then up went the boom superstructure. Now the net was over the rear, aft of the hold's* hatch.

"Looks like we've got some mackerel. There is some by-catch* in there too."

"Throw them over as fast as you can," The captain said. "They may not die."

They had about 20 mackerel, legal size. The rest were undersize mackerel and assorted non-commercial fish. They opened the hatch and threw the mackerel into empty boxes and shoveled some ice on top. The hatch was insulated, and so was the hold. The ice would keep five to seven days depending on just how hot the weather was. They also had a refrigeration unit that would freeze a small part of the hold. They would only use it if needed.

Bob went back to the wheel house, stopped, turned, and hollered, "Tell you what guys…Clean her up some, and I'm going to cruise for about half an hour. Then we'll drop the nets for another half an hour and after that, we'll turn North and head for the Tortugas."

"Aye Capt'n! We're on it!" Amos said.

"Captain!" David knocked on the wheel house door, "Sea turtles, two...no there's three of them."

"We can't catch'em David, they're protected."

"Yep, Capt'n. But I've got a hunch."

"What's that David?"

"Calico scallops.* They might be feeding on the Calico larva. I thought I detected signs on some fish we just brought in."

"Tell you what David, I'm going to flip around 180 and then get the net out. We'll move in off the shelf a bit and hit bottom. Just a short run, 15 minutes or so."

"She's out, Capt'n!" David yelled.

"That's 20 minutes, guys, bring her up."

They went through the same motions. Nets up and in, booms up and then the modified boom superstructure pulling the net with the catch over the rear.

"Look Capt'n, I was right!" David exclaimed with glee.

Amos was dumping out the nets. A huge pile of Calico Scallops poured out on the deck.

"Well guys, it's a good catch! That's the good news. Now for the bad. We're going to anchor, and shuck them out here. I want to get those shells back on the bed so the juveniles have a chance to live and grow."

"Ooooh, Captain!" they both said.

"It's a good catch," Amos reminded David and he started up the freezing compartment.

"We'll pack them in there. Now let's get going. I'll help." Bob said, "This is going to make this trip worthwhile, guys. Think about that."

Later…

"Sun's going down. Amos rustle us up some grub, and we'll eat, and rest up," Bob said yawning.

Middle of the night…

Captain Bob woke up, sat up on the bunk. He could hear David and Amos forward breathing heavy, almost snoring. He thought, something's strange, something's up. The boat was rocking quite a lot and the wind was blowing a lot more than when they bunked down. He slipped on his clothes and boots and went out through the lower area to the rear deck.

The full moon was up there, but the clouds were racing by. The wind was blowing in gusts and the swells were long and deep…and becoming large choppy waves.

He hurried back through the galley and hollered, "Hey guys, Amos! David! Something's up! I think we got a storm on the way!"

The two men started to move. Bob went up the steps to the wheel house. He flipped on the radio…nothing but static.

Just then Dave came up. "What's up, Capt'n?"

"Make sure everything is tied down, and batten down the hatches. Let's get the anchor up."

"Amos is on it, Capt'n. I'll help him."

By this time the moon was gone, the wind was screaming through the booms and rigging. Waves were up, and the boat was rocking violently… from left to right and front to rear. "Anchors up, Capt'n." David came through the door, hanging on to steady himself.

"You guys watch the gear aft. I'm going to head for the Tortugas."

"Watch out, and don't do anything crazy! You guys are worth more to me than this boat!"

The motor roared into life. Bob checked the compass and pointed the boat north-northwest. Even though Tortugas was due north, the wind and waves were hitting them from the west. He had to oversteer, partially into the wind. The big and high outrigger booms were banging left and right.

He was going to holler to the guys when he heard the winch tighten up the topping tackle which lowered and lifted the booms. Amos had tied a rope around his waist and David was holding and watching as Amos jumped out and momentarily engaged the winch.

Bob could barely see back through the inside of the wheelhouse through the rear quarters. Amos was crawling back through the rear door. David was holding on and reeling him in, hand-over-hand as he pulled on the rope.

Bob put his attention back out front. He couldn't see very far, just up to the bow. All he could do was point the boat with the shaking compass. Rain was coming down in torrents and blasting across from port (left) to starboard (right). This combined with the ups and downs as they climbed one huge wave and then went crashing down into the trough with mountains of water all around.

The higher center of gravity caused by the two booms and the rear boom superstructure didn't help any. They made the boat lean way over...first one side and then the other. Waves were awash over the deck.

Bob thought, sure this is an ocean-going trawler...but not an ocean-going storm trawler! We should be in port now, not trying to fight a storm...at least not one so violent as this!

Just then the boat climbed up and over a giant wave...Bob heard the motor race as the prop came out of the water. Then they went rushing down hitting the bottom of the wave. Another wave hit them from the side, totally engulfing the boat. They came out of it, and as they climbed another wave, huge sheets of water were pouring off the deck.

Then, as quick as it started, the wind slowed, and the waves eased off into huge swells. The rain was still coming down, but now Bob could see past the bow. It was getting faintly light.

Bob opened the interior door to the lower deck. "You guys still there?"

"Yep, Boss, what was that?" Amos asked.

Bob could see both Amos and David getting up off the floor.

"Don't know, but I have a guess. Look away off to the southeast. I think we had just the outside touch of a giant waterspout."

"You think just a part of it?" David asked. "I wouldn't want to see all of it! Thank the Lord, we're all in one piece!"

Just then the radio cracked out, "Warning! Warning! Huge water spout spotted 50 miles south of Tortugas in the Florida Straights. Moving east. All boats keep a watch out and steer clear!"

"Thanks a lot!" Amos said, "They're a little late!"

"How does the gear look, guys?"

"Ok, Capt'n. There's a lot of loose lines, but we made it," Amos answered, "It was good we stowed the nets this evening after they dried."

"Well guys, check everything, and give me a report. Then rest up. I'm going an hour or two toward the Tortugas. I'll get you up and we'll have breakfast. If nothing is broke, we'll try for some more shrimp on our way back home."

Morning...

"Amos, thanks for that breakfast. We'll rig up one 55 foot net. I just don't like pulling two. This is about where we hit 'em last week. So let's do it! The depth finder says about 1,200 feet to the bottom, so let's half that. If we hit 'em we'll unload and then double back toward Tougas."

Bob pushed the throttle forward as he felt the drag of the net and the Pelagic (mid-water) trawl doors. Captain Bob tried to stay off the ocean floor to minimize the damage to the environment.

Hours later,

"Well, it worked again. We hit them, unloaded and doubled back, unloaded and then got a third load on the way home. Thanks guys. We'll get in about four and go straight to Steadmans and unload. Check the cooler and hang on, we're heading in!"

Leaving Steadman's...

"Well men, over a thousand pounds of Royal Red shrimp, some tuna and a nice haul of Calico scallops. What do you think, not a bad catch! Some money for each of us, and some for the backers. Tell you what, let's come back tomorrow, check out the boat, do a good cleaning, some maintenance, and then take a break. We'll come back next Monday."

"Sounds good, Capt'n," they both agreed.

After a full day of maintenance, things were all put back in place in the lower quarters, nets cleaned and mended, and rope and cables repaired. The storm had taken some toll.

Everyone they talked to were surprised and interested in their storm adventure, families, dock workers, and the captains. It seemed they were the only ones out in it.

Next morning...

"Well guys, here's your checks. We did real good, so there's some extra in them." (Captain Bob always added a bonus if the catch total was more than expected. It kept his men happy and dedicated. He knew that good, enthusiastic, and talented workers were hard to find. He had two of them and he aimed to keep them!)

"Captain, I'm going to launch the skipjack tomorrow. Can you help?"

"Sure can. How about a shake-down cruise?"

"How did you guess? I've got provisions loaded for three days, and the sponge gear is stowed," David said proudly.

"Ok it's a deal, how about you Amos?" Captain Bob asked.

"I'd like to David, but the wife's got plans. But count me in on another trip. You heading up Big Pine Key way?"

"Yes, the area I was telling you about, the old sponge fishing area. See you tomorrow, Capt'n."

Next morning at David's boat dock...

Hey Cap'n! How you doing?"

"I'm all set, wife says ok, and I got my gear in this overnight satchel. The boat sure looks good, especially with those two sails we set up. What's the plan?" Bob asked.

"Well, you see, it's going to be easy. We just hook the winch to the front of the boat, and then pull it forward just a bit. Then we take the chocks out from under the rear and winch her down.

"Well, David, I'll make sure the "ways" is clear. How about the water depth? I'm sure it's been years since anything has been launched from here."

"Thanks for reminding me, Capt'n, but I'm ahead of you. I waded out and shoveled off the track last evening. It drops off real quick."

They hooked the winch cable to the front of the boat.

"Crank...ah, crank...ah, crank...ah."

"You didn't tell me that this was a manual crank, David," Bob exclaimed.

"*You* know Capt'n, I don't make enough money to go first class!" He laughed.

"You don't? What happened to your bonus?"

"That is invested in the food we're going to eat on this expedition!" David stated.

"Well, this winch does have a safety, and it locks both ways. That helps."

The boat winched down slowly and then floated.

"Hold her there, Capt'n. I'm going to row the sponge skiff over, and tie it to the rear of the skipjack."

"Ok Capt'n, come on in, and we'll unhook her, and catch a breeze."

"Aye, aye! Captain David."

"Let's get the centerboard* down...There's enough clearance in this inlet," David ordered meekly. "Just turn that crank, and then pop in those two stops. They'll keep the board down. You can see those other adjustments."

"It's nice and cozy inside," Bob exclaimed. "You just have to watch out for your head at times."

"Up sails, Bob! You get the fore and I'll take the aft," David said.

They sailed down the channel and out into the harbor. The two sails began to fill out nicely. David was in the rear on the tiller.

"Bob, you just have to watch out for this main-sail's boom when it crosses over from side to side. We'll each say something when the man at the tiller has to tack."*

"All right, Captain David, I'm starting to get the hang of operating the sails. That upper boom on the main sail sure spreads a lot of canvas!"

"We'll go around Dredgers Key right there," David said as he pointed. "Into Garrison Bight channel, and then northeast up the sound side. It's about 15 miles up to the north side of Big Torch Key. I figure up there we'd do a sponge fishing dry run. I would like to try the Niles Channel if we can get into it. We ought to be up there around lunchtime."

"David, we'll have to keep in mind the water hues. I'm sure you know all of them. Black water is rocks or grass clumps, and white water is a shallow or coral bottom. Red is a sand bar, no-crossing-steer-clear, and yellow or light green is a narrow channel good only for a boat that draws only a couple of feet. And last, dark-green and blue are deep water."

"Thanks, Bob, It's a good review. I'll keep a sharp lookout."

They began to enter the many small keys and mangrove islands north of Big Coppitt Key.

"Let's see your charts, David," Bob said with a question in his voice.

"They are inside the cabin on that shelf on the right."

"Pretty good charts. We can use the channel markers, land marks, compass and dead reckoning to plot our position. Actually we'll have to keep our wits about us with all these mangrove islands, sand flats, and sea grass. Of course we don't have to worry about tying up the propeller with sea grass. There's no prop!"

They were fortunate the wind was from the south and west. It was pushing them fine. A few times the centerboard scraped, and they scrambled to raise it up some so it would clear the bottom.

"Hey Dave, I looked in the bilge.* It looks like we've taken in a little water. But I think the planks are swelling and it is slowing down."

"Bob, If you will take the tiller, I will work the hand pump, and you can see where it is for your turn. Keep a watch on the main boom. Don't let it hit your head, especially if it tacks to the other side. I'm also going to inspect all parts of the boat."

"Aye! Aye! Captain David."

"Its been about three hours. We've just past Sugarloaf Key. We'll be turning to the south-southeast in about three miles. Everything looks good around the boat from stem to stern," David exclaimed proudly.

"Captain David, how about taking the tiller, and I'll dig up some sandwiches from the ice chest," Bob remarked.

"Sounds good, Bob," Dave replied.

"There are the channel markers, Captain David," Bob pointed.

"We'll tack here. Watch the boom!" David warned. "There's the bridge up ahead."

"Here's your sandwich and a Coke. Captain, what you thinking of do-

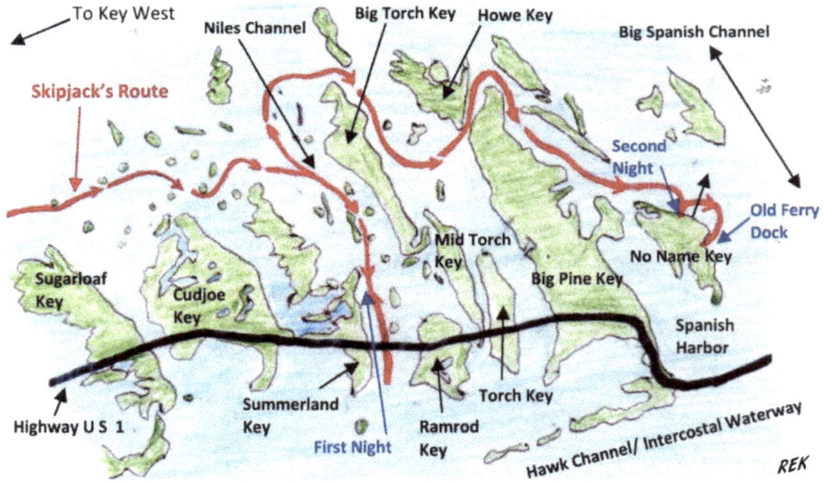

ing?"

"How about going west of Big Torch Key in the Niles channel getting close, but not too close, to the bridge and anchoring? It's about 5-6 feet according to the charts. We'll finish our sandwiches. Then we'll take the skiff under the bridge into the 9 foot water on the other side, and have a look at the bottom."

They pulled the skiff up to the rear of the skipjack.

"This is a neat skiff, David. I guess the pole with the three long hooks

Is to snatch up the sponges from the bottom."

"Yep," Dave answered.

"What is this ladder arrangement?" Bob asked.

"Well, Bob, you can lean on it as you scull the oar, and we'll hang the sponge pole across it. The hooked end goes between the two uprights in the front of the skiff."

"Bob, you can take the aft and stand or sit, hook the oar into the transom (rear) and scull us. That side-to-side movement will propel us. I'm going to take my grandfather's wooden bucket with the glass in the bottom and look underwater for sponges, gold doubloons... or whatever."

"That bucket looks old, but it's in very good shape. How is that?" Bob asked.

"It was in the attic of the house. I had to patch a few cracks and put in new glass," David said proudly.

"This pole is really long!" Bob exclaimed.

"This one is only 25 feet. Granddad had one in the attic twice that long! David stated. "I figure I'm not yet ready for that!"

"Bob sculled while standing and holding onto the vertical ladder. It was about 8 feet head clearance at the bridge. This bridge was one of the old Flagler railroad bridges. The highway had been built on the top by the state after the railroad was devastated by the 1935 hurricane. Off in the distance he could see Summerland Key to the west and Ramrod Key to the east.

Bob looked forward and saw that David was hanging over the side. "Whatcha see?" Bob asked.

"Scull her to a stop, Bob, and lean over here and take a look."

Bob took the bucket, pushed it down into the water and looked in. Some fish were swimming about. Not too large, but he did see one grouper. There was a little pink and green coral, and lots of sea grass. David was sculling the boat and trying to keep it in one place.

"Now, Bob look way down next to the coral. See that slimy mass. The round mass next to the large one. The big one is a logger head sponge. It's no good! The fiber is too coarse. But the small one next to it is either sheep's-wool or a grass sponge ."

"They look about the same to me," Bob said.

"I know just what you mean," David replied. "But the loggerheads grow large. So if it's large, suspect it. The smaller one is slightly different. I have been reading my grandfather's notes."

"You going to get it?" Bob asked.

"Might as well start. Here take the oar," Dave offered.

David picked up the pole, got on his knees and thrust down the hook end, while looking in the bucket. There was about 15 feet of pole above the water.

"It's hard to aim the hooks with the refraction*...Got it!" David exclaimed.

Up it came.

"I'm going to put any sponge I find in that net, and let it drag along in the water. When the sponge is out of water and it starts to rot, it will smell! You don't want to be around it."

They stayed in the area, Bob sculling and David plucking sponges from the bottom.

"Ok, Bob, I'll scull and you ride. We'll go back to the skipjack. It's time for supper."

"How about we pull anchor and move back the way we came up the channel and away from this bridge?" Bob suggested. "Also while you get supper I'm going to see if there are any fish in these waters that will take my lure."

"Wow! Will you look at this!" Bob yelled as his rod bent double.

He reeled it in. "A red snapper. I'm going to break in this boat right and clean it in the back. We'll have it tomorrow." He put the fish in the ice chest.

Morning already, thought Bob, as he rolled over in his sleeping bag in the wooden bunk and ended up with his face in the mosquito net.

"That coffee smells good, David. Next trip I'm going to bring some foam padding for this bunk!"

"Sorry, Bob. It's the one thing I forgot."

They weighed anchor.* The morning breeze ruffled the sails, and the skipjack started to move up the Niles Channel.

"We'll swing up and around Big Torch Key, then thread our way over to Pine Channel," Dave suggested as he worked the tiller. "Bob, would you look at the charts? Can we squeeze between the north end of Big Pine Key and Howe Key?"

Bob went up into the cabin and brought back the charts. "Well, David, it will be close. We'll have to let the center board scrape as needed. What about the sponging?"

"Bob, I would like to get to the east side of Big Pine, sponge some there till I get the other net I've got filled. Of course that's being optimistic! Then we'll go to the east side of No Name Key...the Big Spanish Channel side. Well land on a beach and prepare a hidden storage place for the animal matter in these sponges to rot, smell and dry."

It happened just like they planned. Bob stayed up on the bow, keeping watch on the bottom, looking for the green-yellow and dark-green water that was passable for the skipjack. As they threaded their way amongst the dark green mangrove island clumps they were constantly disturbing all kinds of sea birds nesting there. The sudden beating of wings and flash of their white plumes sometimes startled them. They saw fish jumping and darting below as they fed and tried to not become food.

"There's the north end of No Name," Bob stated and pointed. "Look at that expanse ahead. You could get some sailing out there in the big Spanish Channel. It's definitely deep blue! Must be at least 20 to 30 feet deep!"

"Bob, look, is that a kind of cove with an opening in the mangroves?"

"Sure looks like it."

"I'm going to go in there as far as possible. What about the tide?" David asked.

"It looks like it's out," Bob answered. "So we won't get grounded."

With a splash, they dropped anchor.

"We've better drop them both, Captain Dave," Bob said. "It will keep the boat stable."

"Sure enough, Bob. Let's take your fish in and some fixings, and we'll have a fish bake."

"Wow! Those sponges are getting ripe!" Bob exclaimed.

"Tell you what, Bob. I'll take the sponges away from here, and hide them. You start on the campfire and the fish. It shouldn't take me more than 30 to 45 minutes. They need to dry out. I'll come back next week, retrieve and process them.

They threw everything into the skiff and rowed to the shore. There was a small spit of sandy beach. They pulled the skiff up a bit on the sand and tied it fast to a sturdy mangrove. David dragged the net full of sponges out of sight towards some bushes and a small pine tree.

Bob exclaimed out loud, "Thank you David, and good riddance to those smelly sponges," as he worked on the small camp fire.

David came back shortly. "There, I've got them hid and spread out to dry. They won't smell after that. Then all you do is beat them with a flat paddle to get all the dry animal matter out. I went a round-about to cover my tracks."

"I don't think anyone would ever come near those smelly things," Bob exclaimed, "much less steal them! I've got a good fire and the fish are in the coals. It won't be long."

"The breeze should keep the mosquitos away. Isn't it a little strong, Bob?"

"Yes. I've been watching the weather. We may get a squall…see that way out over the Gulf. We've got plenty of time…could be two, maybe three hours."

It was just getting dark, "Sure is good fish," Dave exclaimed as he smacked his lips. "It was a big one. Snapper's one of the best. What's that noise?" Dave asked.

SCRITCH, SCRATCH, SCRAPE!

Suddenly two large sea turtles appeared…moving up from the small beach. David jumped up.

Bob took to his knees, "They're Loggerheads!" Bob exclaimed. "Must be a couple feet across their shells! They're big!"

The two turtles headed right towards the camp fire…crawling fast! Then just missing the fire, they went around it and past both men. They then disappeared into the interior darkness amongst the pines.

"It's a turtle stampede!"* Bob yelled, "The storm has scared them in. I've heard about it but never saw one. Must have come up on the beach to lay eggs."

"Well we've seen one now!" David said. "Sure scared me at first!"

"The wind is picking up…starting to blow. Let's extinguish the fire and head out to the skipjack. We'll ride it out," Bob commanded.

They hurriedly gathered their gear, poured water and sand on the fire and rowed the short distance to the skipjack. The water was choppy, the wind blowing in gusts, and rain beginning to fall.

"Batten down the hatches, and let's get inside, Bob," David hollered.

Next morning…"How did you sleep Bob?" David asked.

David was up and cooking breakfast on the bottle gas stove.

"Well, at first it was like trying to sleep on a rocking horse! But after the storm passed, it was great! Just like the night before in the Nile Channel. I do like sleeping on a boat, but our big trawler makes it a lot easier.

Not as choppy."

"What're we up to this morning, Captain David?"

"Well, first mate Bob, how about we take the skipjack out in the Big Spanish Channel for a couple of hours, and see what she'll do?"

"That's a good idea," Bob agreed. "How abou, let's drop the sponge skiff at the next inlet towards the bridge. It's where the old highway ferry used to dock. There's a bigger sand strip there, and it's protected from the waves and wind."

"Good idea Bob. Let's do it!"

They pulled the anchors, wound the ropes, and raised the sails. They were down at the next inlet in nothing flat.

"The skiff will be safe here on the beach and double safe with the anchor out," David stated.

They waded out waist deep and climbed back into the skipjack. Then they pulled up the anchor, raised sails and immediately were heading out towards the Big Spanish Channel.

"What's that heading towards us from the Bahia Honda Bridge?" David asked as he pointed.

"Looks like a pretty fancy cruiser, possibly a Chris-Craft. Now that boat costs a lot! It's sure streamlined. Must be at least 70 feet."

It was heading straight towards them, but then it turned left and headed in towards the cove Bob and David had just left. There were three guys on the deck and the captain on the flying bridge. One guy had binoculars trained on them. David waved. All four just starred, as they headed towards the beach…fast!

"Not very friendly," Bob said.

"Think the skiff will be ok? David questioned.

"Yes, no problem. Now think, just why would they want our skiff? Take a look at that motorized runabout they have on the back of their boat!"

They sailed for about an hour. Each taking a turn at the tiller as the other fished…actually trolled.

"Well, we put her through her paces, and got a couple of snapper. Let's go back, and pick up the skiff," David suggested.

"If you want to, David, we can go under the bridge, jump on the Intercostal Waterway along the Hawk Channel, Atlantic side. We'll be back home in Key West by evening!"

"You really think she'll do ok in the Atlantic?" Dave questioned.

"Yep. I've been checking her out, and the old skipjack should do real good!" Bob replied seriously.

The brisk wind was pushing them in towards the cove at a steady pace.

"She is doing real fine. In a few minutes we'll hook on the skiff and head towards the bridge," Dave said proudly.

Bang! Thump! Thump! The left side of the boat picked up and leaned to the right about 30 degrees from 90. It was everything they could do to keep from being thrown overboard.

Then another Thump! The teller was yanked out of David's hand and the rudder slammed against the rear of the boat, all of this in almost instant succession.

"What happened, Bob?" David yelled.

Bob was down on the deck and slowly starting to move. He scooted across the deck and looked back.

"I bet we hit a submerged piling. I'm sorry I missed it. I didn't think we were close to the old ferry pier. They also should have taken them all out!"

"Bob, the rudder is stuck, it's jammed." David shouted.

"Let me have a look," Bob suggested, "You're right. So we don't go around in circles. Let's counter act it with the sails. We're almost to the skiff. Got any tools? We need a hammer and a adjustable wrench, possibly a punch and some bolts.

"Oh, Oh…Of all things I forgot them. I had a tool box at the boathouse but forgot to put it in," David apologized.

"Maybe our friends with the cruiser will lend us some of their tools. Here we are. We're close enough. We'll drop anchor and wade in. They walked out of the water and headed up towards the old beach house.

There were three guys on some folding chairs. A fourth chair was vacant. They were arranged in a circle. A couple of shovels leaned against the side of the old shack. The men were so intent on four piles of shiny round yellow objects on the ground in front of them that David and Bob were right there before they were noticed.

"Excuse us," Bob said.

All three looked up at once. Surprise registered in their eyes.

"We hit a submerged piling with our sailboat and jammed the rudder. We need to borrow some tools," Bob asked.

"Wow! Are those gold doubloons?" David asked. "A real treasure!"

All they got was silence and stares.

"What's going on?"

David and Bob turned around. The fourth guy was behind them.

"Vince, these guys need some tools. They jammed their rudder on that sailboat," One of the three guys sitting down answered.

"Listen, you two. I need for you to sit down there near that tree. We don't have time to visit," Vince commanded.

David said, "We've got to get our boat repaired, and get on for home."

"Oh, you've got plenty of time," he said as he pulled his unbuttoned shirt open to expose a shoulder holster packing a .38 revolver.

"Yes sir," Bob said, "Come on, David, let's sit."

"What should we do with them, Vince? They've already seen too much," one of the three said.

"Here's what…You two get this stuff bagged up and in the run-about. Joe and I are going to take care of these two guys."

"Gonna plug them, Vince?" Joe asked.

"Na, we'll tie them to a couple of trees in the forest back there.

"Tie 'em real good! We'll let the snakes and the gators take care of 'em. When they're found, it will only be bones."

"You two guys turn around, on your knees. Hands behind. Joe, tie their hands real good. There's some rope in the shack," Vince was issuing orders. "On your feet, guys. Now march straight back towards those pines."

Vince had his gun out of the holster and in his hand, waving it about.

"Now don't run or try any funny stuff or I will have to use this."

"No sir," Bob said.

"Just shut up and walk! There are two good trees. They're out sight of the water and the shack."

"You want to gag them, Vince?" Joe asked.

"No, no one ever comes to this all forsaken island. Ok guys, say hello to the snakes and gators for me," Vince smirked.

David and Bob heard the runabout start up and go out to the cruiser. A few minutes later the cruiser's big engines burst into action, and the boat headed out into the channel full blast.

"They went towards the Atlantic," David said.

"Hey David, this is sure an interesting sponging adventure." Bob said as he chuckled, "That guy sure can tie a knot, I don't have any slack back there."

"What do you think was going on Bob?" David asked.

"Well it sure has something to do with those gold doubloons. Must have found them on someone else's property and are trying to keep the state from confiscating them or avoiding taxes. Who knows?"

"What's that?" David asked. "Listen."

"I don't hear anything," Bob answered.

"There it is," David whispered. "I hope it's not the gators!"

"I hear it!" Bob said, "Let's be quiet."

Then a small brown face with a white nose looked out of some brush at them.

"What's that?" Bob exclaimed very softly.

"It's a Key deer." David whispered, "I've never seen one close up."

"It looks too small. It's full grown and is only three feet high!" Bob said.

The small deer came out of the bushes and started to graze on some grass in the small clearing.

"Suddenly the deer's ears and tail stood straight up. Then with tail twitching…it leaped across the small clearing with a bound, jumped over a bush and was gone, leaving only the sound of cracking twigs in the far distance.

"Now, what scared him? I didn't hear anything," David both asked and stated.

Then just as fast as the deer disappeared, a guy appeared in the same bush the deer first entered from. This guy was dressed all in green camouflage fatigues, had his face blackened, and was carrying an M1 carbine.

Bob and David were surprised speechless. The guy looked at them, crouched down and looked through the brush towards the beach. Then, a second guy came in from the same direction. He was dressed the same as the first, and was carrying a large army backpack and M1.

Bob and Dave remained stunned.

The second guy kneeled down, looked at them and then looked back the way he had come in, "Lieutenant! Come take a look at this!" he stated and shook his head in amazement.

A third guy appeared. He had a side arm, a forty five, no rifle, and was also dressed in camouflage.

"What are you guys doing here?" the lieutenant asked.

"I guess we could ask the same. Are you friend or foe? Will you cut us loose?" Bob asked.

"Sarge, cut them loose. I'm going to check on the point."
The second guy whipped out a bayonet from the scabbard on his belt, and swish...swish, the two guy's ropes were cut.

Bob and Dave stood there, both rubbing their hands and arms. "Thank the Lord! You guys are like a miracle!" David exclaimed.

The Lieutenant and the point man came back. "Just a sailboat and skiff out there," the point said.

The Lieutenant questioned, "Ok guys, what happened?"

"Well, our boat hit a submerged piling and jammed the rudder. We came in to ask four guys who had a big cruiser anchored out there if we could borrow any tools. They were sitting by the house. They had a pile of gold doubloons, and I guess they didn't like what we saw...they tied us up and left."

"There is a rumor about a treasure being found last year. They must have hid it here," the sarge said.

"We heard the cruiser when it first came in and decided to investigate. We took our time and just got here," The lieutenant explained.

"What are you guys doing?" Bob asked.

The three military guys looked at each other, not saying a thing.

The lieutenant finally said, "Guys I'm going to trust you. We're training, possibly for Cuba. Please forget all of this, you didn't see us."

"We will," Bob and David said in unison.

Just then they heard the deep sound of a diesel engine. "That's our trawler! I know its sound...It must be Amos," Bob exclaimed.

Bob and David scrambled over to the bushes to look out.

"It sure is our boat," David responded.

They both looked back to thank the three military guys, but they weren't there. It was just like they never were.

They ran down to the beach. The small motor-driven boat from their trawler was heading in from the Sea Breeze. Bob's wife was standing waving, David's dad was sitting, and Amos was driving. They pulled right up onto the beach.

"What's happening, guys?" the three in the boat asked.

"You will never believe us!" David and Bob both answered.

REK

7
The Girl On The Bridge

Robin, Sandy and I were seated at the table for breakfast. Aunt Dolores was just about to finish in the kitchen and start serving, when Uncle Norman appeared.

"Good morning, Sweetie," he said as he kissed her on the cheek.

"Why, good morning to you, Honey," she said.

Then with his usual fanfare, he came down the steps proclaiming, "Today Bob and I are going to go fishing!"

"We'll go," Sandra exclaimed.

"Take us too!" Robin echoed.

"No, you girls have homework to do. Clean your rooms, and then we will do some shopping." Aunt Dolores announced.

"Oh no!" they both exclaimed in unison.

Then Aunt Dolores set heaping plates of scrambled eggs, bacon and powder dough biscuits on the center of the table.

Everyone was helping themselves, and Uncle Norman began to explain, "Sorry, girls, but this morning Bob and I are going out to the bridge to No Name Key and catch some Snapper for supper, and you girls will be able to go fishing soon enough."

"Right after breakfast, Bob, meet me by the Metropolitan out front. I'm going to get some fishing gear from the trailer."

I hurried and brushed my teeth and went out front. There was Uncle Norman's petite turquoise and white Metropolitan. Uncle Norman had bought this little Metropolitan used in the early 60's. It seated two adults and had a small fold-down seat behind. This seat could only be used for small children and Uncle Norman's fishing rods. This car was made by Nash in the late 50's. It was a gas saver, as much as 40 miles per gallon, when fuel economy wasn't even appreciated. However, Uncle Norman drove it like a sports car. The little Austin engine with the three-speed got him around at a good pace.

"Well, Bob, we're ready to go," he said as he placed a couple of fishing rods in the back jump seats together with an ice chest.

"I've got our lunch in the ice chest. We'll pick up some ice and bait on the way. You had better run back to the camper, and get that floppy hat you wore on your hike across Florida. It can get real hot on the bridge."

I hurried back to the camper and came right back.

"We're off for a great day of fishing. We'll go by Garrison Bight, and get our ice and bait," Uncle Norman said very cheerfully.

We zipped down Fogarty Ave, then took a right out to North Roosevelt Boulevard and crossed over to a store and bait shack adjacent to the Key West Yacht Club.

"I like to come in here to get my ice. This is where all us local conchs shop for our fishing supplies. You know what a conch is Bob?

"I think it is someone who lives here in the Keys," I guessed.

"Almost right. Of course a conch is really a seashell. But conchs are people either born in the Keys or who have lived here a long time and have taken up the Keys' ways. I'm the latter."

"Let's get going!" he said.

We pulled back out onto North Roosevelt Boulevard and moved along at a fast pace to the East end of Key West.

"What a beautiful street!" I thought.

There were coconut palms lining the street on both sides and some in the middle. Getting the green light at our turn at US 1, off we went! The little Metropolitan just purred along as Uncle Norman went through the three gears. We were through Cow Key before I knew it.

"We'll go a little slower through this next Key. It's got the big Naval Air Station on it. There it is, Boca Chica Naval Air Station. It would be a bit embarrassing if the paymaster of the Key West sub base got a ticket!"

I could see three big blimps on the runway next to very large hangers. There was a lumbering prop naval transport plane struggling to get air borne.

We left the Naval Air Station, and the little car picked up speed. Saddlebunch, Sugarloaf, Cudjoe, Summerland, Ramrod and then Big Pine Key. We did those 30 miles in less than 45 minutes! It had taken me a couple of days when I was walking.

Uncle Norman began his gearing down, and we turned off US 1 to the left heading north on 4A. What a beautiful day it was. I was enthralled as we crossed all the bridges connecting the Keys. I could see the clear turquoise green water now as we traveled. When I walked these bridges I was constantly looking out for the oncoming cars, and consequently I had little time to enjoy the view.

"How you doing, Bob? We're going to take this newly paved road to the right here. It goes out to the brand new concrete bridge to No Name."

Big Pine Key was true to its name. There were plenty of big pine trees. But they were big only in contrast to those of the other Keys. They were very small in comparison to the pine trees on the mainland that I was familiar with.

"Since this is a two-lane bridge, and it goes out to a dead end, we'll drive out a ways. We can always move if we have to. Look, there's a convertible out on the bridge. We'll just park near to it, and see what's biting," Uncle Norman stated.

We passed and parked a couple of car lengths in front of the convertible. As we went by I noticed a lady fishing. She was leaning on the concrete rail and had on a large sun hat. We got out, and Uncle Norman grabbed the rods and his tackle box.

He whispered, "Bobby that's a good looking girl about your age. Maybe you could strike up a conversation."

As we walked up to within a car's length of her, I could now see my Uncle was right-on. She was a knock-out! She turned to look at us…a beauty! Wow! I was in love!

"Hi, young lady. What's biting? I'm from Key West. My name's Norman…Norman Kranich. This is my nephew, Bob Kranich. He's down visiting from Tampa. He just walked the backcountry…in fact the entire way from Georgia to Key West!"

"Oh, I didn't give you a chance to answer. How's fishing?"

She answered, "I haven't caught anything. Maybe I had a bite. It took all of my bait. Oh, nice to meet you both. My name's Pat. I'm down from Miami visiting my Aunt and Uncle. They live in Marathon."

I found myself staring…that voice, it was so sweet, and those eyes… deep blue!

"Well Pat, Bob and I are going to try to catch some bait."

Norman opened up his tackle box, "Here Bobby, put this on, and throw it out like this."

Uncle Norman positioned himself between Pat and me. He cast out. It took me a couple of casting tries. By this time my mind was off fishing. I made like I was fishing, looking out and turning my reel a time or two, then locking the drag. Now and then I tried to sneak a look past Uncle Norman, who was unexpectantly and expertly blocking the view.

She had let her sun hat drop back off her head, and it was held by a chin strap against her back. I could now see her long brown hair. It was beautiful!

"Well, young lady, how long will you be down here visiting?" Uncle Norman asked.

"A couple more days, Mr. Kranich. I've got to go back to work Monday."

"Just call me Norm. What do you do for a living?"

"I'm a secretary for an airline," she answered.

She kind of looked past Uncle Norman, "What do you do Bob?"

"I..."

"Oh, he is an engineering designer. He works at contracting," Uncle Norman offered before I could get started.

"That sounds interesting," she said.

"I'm sure it is," Uncle Norman answered. "He is also a college guy, and just got out of the U.S. Army."

"I got a bite, Bob. It's hooked. Yep, a shiner. Good bait," he said as he reeled it in.

Just then my rod jerked. "Got something, Uncle Norman," I pulled it in.

"Good Bobby, now we both got some bait. Hook yours on like this. Now throw it out, and maybe we'll catch a snapper. You know they run under this bridge when the tide is flowing."

"What are you using for bait, young lady? Bring your line in, and try this lure to catch a shiner. That will change your luck. The snapper will bite on live bait," Uncle Norman suggested.

She brought hers in, hooked on the lure, and threw it out. It didn't go very far.

"Bring it back, and I'll throw it out for you. Here, Bob, hold my rod,"

She reeled it in, and Uncle Norman cast it way out for her. He was now out of my way. I got a great view of her, and my heart leaped.

Before we could say anything, she pulled in a shiner.

"Here, let me show you how to hook it on," Uncle Norman handed me his rod, and he proceeded to hook the shiner on her rig.

He then positioned himself back between us, "Now we all are ready to catch a Red Snapper. See the tide is flowing."

She was the first one to get a hit, "I've got one!"

"Reel it in!" Uncle Norman yelled.

She pulled it in over the rail. It flopped on the road, "How do I get it off?" she asked.

"I'll help," I started to say.

"Here, hold my rod, Bobby," Uncle Norman handed me the pole, grabbed the large fish by the gills, and wrestled the hook free. "You got an ice chest?"

"It's in the car." She came right back, and he dropped it on the ice.

"Uncle Norman! Something is playing around on both of ours," I hollered.

He rushed over and took ahold of his rig, just in time. We both got hits and both got big snappers. We got them off the hooks and on the ice.

Then my world changed.

"Well, Norman, Bob, it was nice talking to you both, and thank you for the help fishing. But I've got to go. My aunt said I need to be back for lunch by noon. It's past eleven. I had better be on my way," Pat said as she picked up her fishing rod and the ice chest.

There went my chances, I thought as she turned around and waved as she got in her convertible and drove off.

That evening, we were all eating red snapper prepared by my Aunt Dolores, a great cook.

Uncle Norman said, "You know we met a beautiful girl on the bridge at No Name Key today. In fact we fished with her, and guess what, Bobby didn't even get her phone number!"

Key West, Queen Anne style, Victorian era house, *Island Flavor*.
Built sometime between 1880 and 1900.

8

Island Flavor

The old house had been vacant for a few years. The once meticulously manicured yard now had a variety of knee-high non-grass plants. The faded green island's hurricane shutters were closed, but they were still trying to do their best to protect the interior. Here and there a shutter hung crooked, a screw holding a brass hinge gave up. The stately date palms and flowering bushes continued to bear and flower. Nature seems to always take care of its own.

The yard was spacious. This house was far enough away from the center of Key West and ancient enough to have been constructed when the land was reasonably priced. Therefore, it sat conveniently in the center of two lots.

The fence was still in good condition because its builders had the foresight to use Key mahogany wood which is known for its resistance to weathering, rot, and decay. This wood was from Big Pine Key. Those trees were the small trees that remained after the early Spanish explorers had cut all of the large and valuable virgin mahogany trees down in the 1500's.

"There's one, dear!"

"There's no for sale sign, Al."

"That's why it's available, Janie," he said.

"But it looks so abandoned," she sighed.

"Janie, we just have to find out who owns it, and make an offer," Al exclaimed.

Al and Jane Krenshaw were visitors to the island. They were looking for an investment property. It was now just a couple of years after the Second World War, 1947. People were beginning to move around again.

"Here it is on the map, Al, the Monroe County Court House. It's down at Southard and Whitehead streets."

"Thank you, Jane, Honey. Let's get on down there, and see just who owns our future Key West home!"

"That's strange," the clerk said. "We have no record since December, 1945. What is really strange is that even the tax roll stopped! Tell you what I'm going to do, check with my supervisor, and also dig deeper in the files once again. In fact, what I found wasn't even in the correct place! Tell you what, you may want to have a seat. There are Coke and coffee machines in the hall."

"She sure looked perplexed. What do you think, Al?"

"Yep, she sure did. Want some coffee?"

"Here we sit, Dear, drinking coffee and munching peanut butter crackers both out of a machine. I should be sitting down and being served in a fancy Key West restaurant, enjoying some shrimp or snapper," Jane exclaimed jokingly.

"You're correct, Honey, but we're on a quest to find our quaint Key West domicile."

They saw the clerk motion to them.

"Well, here's what you folks have to do. This is the information on the last owners. Of course it's been three years since the taxes were paid. That interest will be accrued as part of the cost. Try to contact them, and good luck with that! Then you will have to advertise in at least three national newspapers. I would also recommend you obtain the services of an attorney for the final closing."

"If you are serious about going ahead with this, we will hold off on doing our own advertising. We'll give you some time to take care of this. If so, you can fill out this form of *Intent to Purchase for Taxes.* "

"We'll get this form filled out, and get on our way," Al said.

"Please keep in touch with us, and keep us informed. You will have two months to complete. That will be until August 27th," the clerk stated.

"Thank you, Ma'am. Let's get started, Janie."

"Sounds good, Al. Now how about that shrimp and lobster!" Jane smiled.

"Well, Honey, what do you think? We might have a Key West house!" Al said in an excited voice.

"Do you think it will cost much?" Jane asked.

"Let's see, the back taxes are for about 3 years, plus interest. It depends what the county's tax rate per $100 is. It will be interesting to see what we find out when we attempt to find the last owners!"

"What about a lawyer, Al?"

"I'm going to have a talk with my friend, Mike back in Miami."

"Honey, I have found out some historic things about our new house in Key West."

"Yes, dear," Jane said with a question in her voice.

"I talked to that architect and showed him the photos we took. He says that it is a Victorian-era house, built sometime between 1880 and 1900s. The style is Queen Ann. This can be seen by the turret, steep-pitched roofs, and large porch. Even though it is characteristic of the Queen Ann style, it is plain in comparison to the large Queen-Anne houses found elsewhere in the United States. The owners didn't have the funding to both build and maintain a large stately Queen Anne in the tropics of Key West."

We now go back in time: Date: April 18, 1942, at 1:30 AM.

A German U-boat, type VIIC,* Number U302 is at 50 meters (approximately 150 feet) below the surface of the Atlantic, approximately one mile off the coast of Miami Beach, Florida.

This boat was the main ship of the German U-boat (submarine) force. There were 568 of them manufactured between 1940 to 1945. They had a range of 8,500 nautical miles and had active sonar. For propulsion, they had two supercharged 6 cylinder, 4-stroke diesel engines. For underwater propulsion they had two electric motors. The armament consisted of four front and one rear torpedo tube. There was also a 88 mm automatic deck gun and an 20mm antiaircraft gun.

Note: The following German language has been translated into English.

"Throttle-1/4…Set of rise, to periscope depth," ordered the U-boat Captain.

"Sir!..50 meters…40 meters...30 meters…20 meters…10 meters," answered one of the sailors on the diving controls.

"Steady...Up periscope!" announced the U-boat captain.

The commander brought the two handles of the periscope down... looked in...focused…swung it around 360 degrees as his hands turned the handles which focused it.

"See the lights, Second. They don't even enforce a black-out. They're all lit up! Have a look, Vermeer. Then move the boat in towards shore another 1/4 kilometer.* Keep a lookout. If all clear... bring her up. Get the men to put out the 2-man raft with Herr Schmidt's equipment, and secure it. I'm going to get him."

"Yes, Sir!" said Second in command, Vermeer.

Knock...Knock..."Herr Schmidt, it's about time to depart."

"Thank you, Commander," Peter said.

[Peter Schmidt, 38 years old, black hair, slight build, but muscular. Born in 1903 in Milwaukee, Wisconsin of German immigrants. Educated at Milwaukee Business College. Degree in finance. Moved back to Germany in 1933 to work for Krupp Armaments. Drafted in 1935. After basic military training, assigned to the Abwehr. (This was a German military intelligence organization.)]

"How about the equipment?"

"We've already got it loaded. Both the Enigma code machine and transmitter are in their suitcase, and in turn, it is in the rubber liner. The book with our coded schedule is in with the transmitter. We've got the liner strapped to the two-man raft."

"Yes, thank you. I have the dollars in the waterproof container strapped under my clothes, together with my knife."

[For his espionage mission: Peter Schmidt is to be inserted by a U-boat of the Reichsmarine (German Navy) into the Miami, Florida area. There, he is to observe the U.S. Army Air Force activities at the 36th Street Airport.*]

[His Enigma Electro-mechanical Rotor Cypher machine is a four-rotor German Naval model.* In addition, the transmitter is a captured British unit.* It has a limited frequency and reduced power. The transmitter is suitable for Morse key only. Together they both fit into a small suitcase and weigh no more than 35 pounds.]

"This way, Herr Schmidt. We're going out on deck," the captain announced.

There was a slight breeze. The U-302 was rocking gently. Even though it was February, the air was balmy.

"Herr Schmidt, just sit in the raft and we'll slide you down. Good mission."

"Thank you Captain…and thank you for the excellent trip. Good hunting."

The raft hit the water, splashed, rocked violently and then steadied. Peter slipped the ropes off the raft and rowed away from the sub. He heard the diesel engines shut down and the whine of the electric motors. He looked back then and saw the sub diving. The commander saluted and disappeared into the conning tower, the hatch shutting above him.

The U-302 slipped silently out of sight, and all that remained were bubbles on the surface and more boiling to the surface.

He looked towards the Miami Beach lights and rowed backwards so he could see where he was going. He checked his British waterproof watch. It was 2:15 AM. His handlers had made sure he had no German clothing or accessories, except of course the Enigma Code Machine. The insignia was taken off of it together with any identifying markings. To unknowing persons it might pass as a strange typewriter. He rowed towards the brightest lights. There was a slight drift by the current and wave action north.

That will be ok, he thought. It will take me off the main section of the Miami Beach area. Even though there were long steady waves he noticed the rowing was still not so easy in this round rubber two-man raft.

Even this raft was non-German. It was captured U.S. Army Air force. If he needed to he could just leave it on the beach, and hopefully, the authorities would think it was from a training exercise.

He was in the breakers now. He could see the beach, a light color just beyond the sparkle of the waves. The raft picked up on a wave, rode over the top as it broke, came rushing down, and hit the sand. Besides soaking him, it then slid the raft up on the sand, and the raft came to a stop.

He got out, found his knife, slit open the rubber liner, reached in and grabbed the suitcase. He saw a couple walking arm-in-arm down the beach. They were farther up than he was . He sat down facing the ocean, his back to them, suitcase on his lap so they could not see it.

"Look, Dear, someone else is on the beach."

"Yes, Honey, it is so lovely out here. He looks so content. Just like us."

As soon as they passed by, he got up and headed straight up the beach. He walked past a small hotel, and out in front he saw he was on a paved two-lane road, Collins Ave. Then, he noticed there was a bus stop on the other side of the road. I'm in luck, he thought. He crossed over and saw that a bus was coming his way. As it drew near he could see its lit up route sign, 36th St. Airport.

"What luck," he murmured to himself.

He reached for his money pouch, pulled out a couple of ones and a five. The bus pulled up, and he got on.

"How much?" he asked.

"25 cents," the driver said, "You need the exact change."

"I'm sorry Sir, I don't have it. Can I give you this dollar? You keep the change?"

"Not supposd to do it, but it's late. Ok."

He sat down on a seat up front. He looked around. Not many people were on the bus at 5:30 AM. The total was a couple AAF (Army Air Force) guys, and an old lady with a shopping bag.

"Driver, any hotels near the airport?" Peter asked.

"You won't find any hotels there. They're all back at the beach. But there are a few motor inns."

"Here we are now. You will see them on the right."

"Thank you," Peter said as he stepped off the bus.

There was a faint morning glow just coming from behind the skyline off the Atlantic. It was back lighting the city skyline. He saw a single story structure and a big sign that read, Howard Johnson's. There was a small building with a picture window next to it. A neon sign read, office, VACANCY.

"You got the last one. With all these Army Air Force guys coming to this airport, we're full almost every night!" the young male desk clerk exclaimed. "Got any ID…drivers license?" he asked.

"Yes Sir, I've got my driver's license. It's New York."

"Ok, Mr. Smith. That will be $8.50, out of $20. Number 12, third door on the right. Have a good day. Oh, check out time is 10 AM. But you will get some extra time this morning. The room is ready now."

"I appreciate it, Sir. Thanks," Peter said.

He walked outside the office and down the sidewalk to room 12. Peter unlocked the door and went in, double locking it behind him. There was a dresser, double bed, single chair, and a lamp. He put his suitcase against the wall next to the bed. He sat down on the bed, took off his shoes, laid back and fell deep asleep.

He was started awake by a lot of noise. Where am I, he thought, as he sat up. Then it came back to him. Peter went over to the window, pulled the drape just so. The traffic was intense on 36th street in front of the motor lodge. "I'll get cleaned up, and then I need to find some clothes and some toiletries. I need a shave, but that will have to wait," he said out loud to himself.

"Where can I find a place to shop? I need some clothes and toiletries," Peter asked the motor inn desk clerk. It was a different person, a much older man. His name tag said "Manager."

"I'm staying in room 12, came in early this morning."

"Got a car?"

"No, Sir."

"You catch the bus out front here, heading west towards the airport… marked Hialeah. It will go up Royal Poinciana Boulevard and will come to Miami Springs. That is near the golf course. There are a lot of shops there."

"Thanks a lot, Sir."

Peter came out of the office and saw the restaurant across the parking lot. The sign said, Howard Johnson's. He suddenly realized he was famished and went over.

Back in his room he hid the suitcase under the bed. He then transferred some money to his pocket from his waterproof container strapped to his body. They had provided him with a lot of money. All U.S. bills. He had about $15,000 in all manner of bills, about $10,000 in $500s, and the rest in assorted denominations. None of it was new or crisp.

It didn't take long for the bus to arrive. He got on, and this time he had the correct change. After a few stops it turned towards the airport. Then it headed up 42nd and turned on South Royal Poinciana Boulevard. He got up and sat in a window seat just in time to see a two-motor Army Air Force C-47 transport climbing up and over the airport in the far distance. He had studied photos of the enemy's planes profusely. He made a mental note.

He soon saw the shops and got off the bus. A sign read, Miami Springs. Peter was surprised by the assortment and price of clothing. He thought, Things are difficult to come by back in the homeland and very expensive. You need to have money, and then have to know where to go to buy.

He walked out wearing a full suit for $32, shirt $2, dress shoes and socks $5, and a $2 fedora (hat).* Peter Smith did not look like the same person. Next door was a "five & dime" department store. There he bought a small suitcase to carry his old clothes and the toiletries, spare shirts, socks and undergarments he had purchased.

Back at the motor lodge he realized that he needed to extend his stay a couple of more days. He needed some time to find and purchase a house close to the airport. Part of his mission was to set up a base of operations. He would have to broadcast in two weeks to a U-boat that would be on station in his vicinity.

The next morning found Peter searching through the Yellow Pages:

Here's one,   **Real Estate Agents**
Mary Evans
Realtor for Miami Springs, Hialeah area.

He dialed from the room phone.

"Mary Evans speaking."

"Mary, this is Peter Smith. I arrived in Miami yesterday on the train from New York. I sold my house up there and wish to find one down here. I need to be in the 36th street, Miami Springs area."

"Mr. Smith, I only have one small bungalow just off Palm Avenue on 9th. It's not too far from Miami Springs."

"Ms. Evans, I don't have a vehicle."

"That's all right, it's on a bus line. If you want to see it I could pick you up right after lunch. Where are you staying?"

"The Howard Johnson's on 36th Street."

"I know just where that is. See you about 1:00 then. I''ll be driving a blue Plymouth Coupe."

"Thank you, Ms. Evans."

Peter didn't know just what a Plymouth Coupe looked like, but he knew blue!

He was sitting looking out of the window of the Howard Johnson's. He saw a shiny blue two-door car being driven by a lady pull up. He had already paid for his lunch and was sipping his coffee. He dropped a 25 cent tip on the table and went out. She had parked, got out, and was looking about.

He waved and said, "Ms. Evans! Ms. Evans!"

As he hurried up to her, she said, "Mr. Peter Smith?"

"Yes, sorry I wasn't standing out front. I just finished my lunch."

He noticed she was a nice looking woman of about 30. She was wearing a two-piece suit, which fit her very well. He also noticed there was no wedding ring.

"Oh, are you ready to go then?"

"Yes."

"Please get in and we'll look at that bungalow I mentioned. It's only a short drive." We'll go the most direct route, Mr. Smith. This is also the way the bus travels."

They turned right on Highway 27.

"This is Highway 27 or Okeechobee road. It does head out of town to Lake Okeechobee," she said. "But we'll turn right here on Palm Avenue. You know it goes north through Hialeah a mile or so to the Hialeah Park Race Track. Buses will also come out of Miami Springs up this way."

"Ms. Evans, I already have been to Miami Springs. I did some shopping there yesterday."

"Mr. Smith, you can call me Mary."

"Thank you, Mary. My first name is Peter."

"Here is East 9th street. The house is just a few blocks off Palm Avenue."

They were in what appeared to be a quiet neighborhood, small one-story houses. He was surprised by the palm trees and bright flowers. She pulled the Plymouth into the drive and stopped.

"Let's take a look," she said.

"Ok," Peter answered, and they both got out.

He noticed the houses were brightly colored.

Mary said, "Of course, Peter, you should know there are no basements here, in contrast to your city of New York. Our water table here is very high."

"That's ok. I don't need a lot of room."

She went up the front porch, unlocked the door and went in. He followed.

"It's two bedroom, a bath and one-half," she said as they looked around.

"Why are there some furnishings still here?" he asked.

"It was owned by a couple of Army Air Force officers, and they got reassigned even before the wives could get down. If you want, the furnishings go with the house."

"That will be great! What is the price?"

"Well normally it would be about $4,000. But I have to tell you… because of the War, demand right next to the Army Air Force base and the Hialeah Race Track, the asking price is $5,500. I think I could get it down to $5,300 if you're interested.

"I am, and I want it. What do I do? I brought the cash from my house down with me."

"Oh, I'm afraid I can't take cash. Tell you what, I'll drop you off at the bank in Miami Springs. You start an account. I will run over to the office, and bring back the paper work. The bank's certified casher's check made out to Mary Evans Real Estate will do just fine."

"Here's the bank, Peter. I'll be back in an hour."

"You just sign here, Peter. Now, here is you're receipt and the keys. I will take care of the title and all of the necessary paper work for you. I will drop everything by in a week. Just give me a call next Wednesday."

They shook hands, and she drove him back to his motor inn. Peter didn't waste any time. He visited the Miami Springs Golf Course, and he checked it out. The Nineteenth Hole, the bar, restaurant and lounge there would be a perfect location to hang out. He noticed a lot of Army Air Force officers frequented it. Next, he went to the Hialeah Park race track. It had the lounge and restaurant areas he was looking for. He then rode the bus around Hialeah and Miami Springs using 36th Street to keep him in the air base area.

He spent his time moving about these places until he found out the best times to be there. These times were naturally when the military were present. He sat around, appearing to read newspapers, horse racing literature, golf magazines, but he was always listening.

At the two-week deadline he had his Enigma machine and transmitter set up in the spare bedroom. This Enigma was a German Navy "G" model. It had four code rotors. The German Navy code book gave him the settings to be used at the predetermined times. Every date required different rotor settings. The U-Boat had the identical information. This allowed him to communicate with it. This code book was printed in red, water-soluble ink on pink paper so it could be easily destroyed if need be.

He was required to keep his message to only a few hundred characters. This reduced duplication of characters to complicate the process of the enemy breaking the coded messages.

It was 11:30 AM. He tapped the call sign out on his key using Morse Code. He waited…suddenly his key sounded an answer. The U-Boat was on station. He commenced typing on the Enigma's keyboard:

    "All well, base operations in place_

    USAAF Air Transport Command using C-47_

    Original 21st Recon Squadron Search & Rescue active_

    PS out_

He waited.

His key started clicking. Four letters, U Out_

Peter thought to himself. Success! I will be back at the time in two weeks, transmitting. The enemy are dumkoffs!

Peter was constantly on the go: race track, golf course, bars, in the grocery line, even on the bus, constantly listening for that one word or phrase. He would then put it all together.

Right after December 7th, the attack on Pearl Harbor by the Japanese and the formal entry of the US into the war, activity at the base suddenly increased. He then started hearing words like 26th Antisubmarine Command, U-Boats, B-18 Bolo, and B-24 Liberator Bombers. He could see these additional aircraft. Even his bungalow was at times flown over.

He transmitted all this information. Then he started to hear new

B-24 Liberator Bomber

information: Miami Beach Training Center and Officer Candidate schools of the Army Air Corps. It sounded real big. He wondered...just what's going on? Then he had an idea. Mary Evans, she should know something.

"Hi, Mary. Remember me? Peter Smith."

"Oh hi, Peter. How have you been doing?"

"Real fine. I'm working selling equipment to both the golf course and the race track, then training in its use and installation. I was wondering if you would do me the honor of dining out this Friday, Saturday or whenever you are free. I saw a nice restaurant in Miami Springs."

"Well, thank you, Peter. Friday would be fine."

"Now, Mary, I can't pick you up. I can't buy a car...you know the war and all that. How about picking me up at 7:00 PM at my bungalow?"

"I understand, Peter, I'll be there. See you then."

At the restaurant: "This is a very nice restaurant, Peter. I've seen it before but never been here. These prices are kind of high. Is it ok?"

"Mary, it's a night to just enjoy! Oh by the way, I've been hearing a lot lately about Miami Beach. I wonder what's going on?"

"Haven't you heard, Peter? The US Army Air Force has turned the entire Miami Beach into a training center.* They've leased all hotels, apartments and theaters. They're training both basic and officers. In fact, they are using the entire, actual beach!"

"Wow, sounds fantastic, in fact almost unbelievable. Mary, it won't be long, and we will lick those Nazis!"

A couple of evenings later found Peter Smith at the prescribed time at his Enigma machine, all rotor settings up to date. He used the key to type his call sign and received an immediate answer. He proceeded to type on the Enigma machine.

Miami Beach new training center_
    Using all buildings & beach area_
    Base & USAF OCS_
    PS out_

His Enigma machine started typing. The U-Boat was sending him a message. He quickly grabbed his pencil and paper:
    Orders for PS_
    Proceed at once, Key West_
    Observe Naval sub facility_
    Leave base key front door_
    No change in transmit schedule_
    U out_

Peter typed a reply:
    Instructions received_
    PS out_

Peter thought, someone's going to take my place. I've only got two weeks to get to Key West, get set up, and transmit. I'll have to leave tomorrow morning.

Seven am the next morning saw Peter with two suitcases. One was filled with all the clothes he could pack into it. The other one was the same one with the same equipment he arrived with. This time he went to the other side of the street and caught a bus marked Miami.

Now it was just a few minutes past 12 noon and the big Greyhound bus was up on Highway Number 1 heading south. In less than a couple of hours time they were through Homestead, then Florida City and heading out the causeway towards the Florida Keys.

He was impressed by the road. In fact he found out later that it had been completed just a few years earlier. After the 1935 hurricane had wiped out the Florida East Coast railroad, the state bought the right-of-way and railroad bridges. The bridges were all intact, and the highway was built right on top of the widened railroad grade.

Peter saw the US Navy was in the process of laying 12 inch water pipes along the highway and attaching them to the bridges. Key West must not have its own water, he thought.

He also noticed the beautiful clear turquoise water. He made a mental note, it would be hard for a submarine to hide in these waters. He said to himself, "This may be a nice new highway, but it doesn't compare to our high-speed autobahns back home!"

The hum of the bus's huge tires and the tranquil scenery made Peter grow sleepy. Nevertheless, he forced himself to stay awake and make mental notes: number of bridges, military activity, and the lay of the land. But he really perked up when he saw the Boca Chica Naval Air Station.

The bus slowed in that congested area, and Peter got his eyes full! Then it was only one more Key and they were on Roosevelt Boulevard in Key West. This road ran right through the old section of the city. The bus slowed down and pulled into the station.

"Key West," the driver announced over the intercom, as the bus came to a stop.

Peter grabbed his equipment suitcase from the overhead. He had to give his ticket stub to the driver outside to get his clothes' suitcase. He wasn't going to let the equipment suitcase out of his sight.

He looked around. This was a temporary bus station. It was using a building right across from the US Naval Station. He thought, this is excellent. Now let's look around in this area. He was amazed by the island architecture as he walked around a couple of blocks. They were all strange wooden houses painted in bright colors.

Then he saw it…A two-story house with storm shutters. The most important part was it had a six-sided turret on a corner of the second floor. There were windows on each side. But what caught his eye was the "For Sale" sign tacked to the front fence. He went up, wrote down the phone number, and then forcefully pulled the sign off the fence. He laid it
face down in the high grass on the opposite side of the fence.

Since it was now late afternoon, Peter decided it would be best to go the few blocks back to the bus station, and ask directions for a place to stay the night.

The ticket agent told him a place a couple of blocks up Southard Street was respectable and did not cater to sailors. He walked the two blocks and saw the sign, "Boarding House."

He rang the door bell.

An old lady came to the door, "Yes, may I help you?"

"Why Ma'am, I'm hoping you can. I just got in from Miami on the bus. I need a place to stay for a few days."

"You're not Navy are you?"

"No Ma'am."

"Well I've got one room. It's upstairs. I serve supper in an hour, at five sharp…and Sir, no girls in the room!"

"Yes Ma'am."

"Step inside," she ordered. "I'll get you to sign the register. It's two nights deposit. Tomorrow you can tell me how long you need to stay. What's your name?"

"Peter, Ma'am. Peter Smith."

"Smith. Hmm. I'm Bessie McCall. Right this way, young fella."

Peter was relieved to be able to put his two suitcases down. He sat down in the chair and looked around. The room was small but very clean. There was a closet. He got up, opened the door and hid his equipment suitcase on the top shelf under the spare blanket.

In the morning, after a hearty breakfast, he inquired where to find a bank. Bessie told him to go to Simonton Street, and turn right. A couple of blocks would bring him to the post office and a bank.

Peter hated to lug it, but he took his equipment suitcase. That Bessie would likely be snooping. He walked downtown. He had two things to do: First, open a bank account, and second, make a phone call to the realtor. He used the same story, selling a piece of property in New York and coming down to Key West to work.

"What kind of work do you do?" the bank agent asked him.

"Accounting and records," Peter replied.

"I heard the county has a couple of openings. You know, the war and the draft are taking a lot of men."

"Thanks for the information," Peter replied.

He thought, that's a good lead. It would be a real cover. I think it would be good to go to the county first. It was only four blocks back to Southward and Whitehead Streets.

"Wow!" he said out loud.

Then he caught himself and thought. Look at this, the county courthouse is right across the street from the main entrance to the Naval Sub Base.

He went inside and looked at the register to find out where the personnel department was.

"Hi, may I help you?" the clerk asked.

"Yes, Ma'am. I would like to apply for employment."

"What is your occupation?" she asked.

"Either accounting or records," Peter replied.

"How uncanny. We just now have a opening for property records. Please fill out this form."

He had no past employment records. But his college records in his home town of Milwaukee would help if he was checked. He put down working for himself in New York, finance and investing, a house in Miami, and his degree from Milwaukee Business College.

"Ma'am, I don't have a work record. I have been working for myself in finance and investing. However, I have the degree, and a house in Miami."

"Sir, Mr. Frederickson will take that all into consideration," she explained. "He will see you now."

"You have an unusual work record, Mr. Smith. But, you seem like an honest fellow. We need the help. When can you start? We're so short of qualified men down here. They're all drafted, and they're taking more every day."

"Well, Mr. Frederickson, thank you. In a couple of days. I need to find a place to stay."

"Ok. How about first thing Monday? Mable will get all of your paperwork taken care of."

Peter walked out to the office. He saw a phone booth in the hall.

"Yes, this is Peter Smith. I'm interested in the house you have for sale. The one with the turret."

With his new job, the Key West bank account and his Miami house for collateral, he was now the new owner of the house he saw the day before.

Peter immediately went about getting things in order at his house. He went down to Duval Furniture and bought a few things: bed, dresser, chair, and lamp for the bedroom. A couch, chair, end table and two lamps for the living room. Small kitchen table and two chairs. But his special purchases were a medium size chair and small end table for the turret and a small rectangular table. He had a special use for this table.

Next, on a recommendation from the furniture salesman, he found a carpenter. He wanted someone who was self-employed.

Saturday, there was a knock on his door. "Hello, I'm John West. Sam James at Duval Furniture said you needed a carpenter."

"Yes, come in. I'm Peter, Peter Smith. I have a special job for you. It may seem a little bit unusual, but trust me, I need it. I want you to enclose this area below the stairs. I'm going to build a dark room. I need for you to use the same wood for paneling as you see in this house and I need a door. It must have hidden hinges and opener."

"That is kind of strange, Mr. Smith."

"Yes, it is, but I want to keep my supplies safe. If you can do it, I will pay you for your time."

"Yes I can. I can start today."

When it was done, Peter gave the carpenter a little extra for a tip and asked for his confidentiality. It was in this small room under the stairs that Peter put the small rectangular table and one of the kitchen chairs. Luckily the wood walls enclosed an electric receptacle on the wall. Peter now had his transmitting room. He set up his Enigma machine and transmitter. He brought in a lamp, and he was in business!

He wasted no time doing his spying job. He went to work and kept his eye on the comings and goings through the main gate of the Navy Base. Evenings found him eating at the bars and restaurants on Duval Street. He was continuing picking up bits and pieces of military conversation. Mornings saw him sitting on his chair in the tower, shutters open and watching the Navy Base. Weekends found him prowling all of the poplar places up and down Duval Street. He could be seen any place there was a civic gathering.

On the appointed day and time, exactly two weeks since he had left Miami, he was sitting in his transmitter room under the stairs. He had the

Enigma rotors to the correct settings.

He typed out his call sign on his key.

His key sounded an answer.

    Set up_

    All in place_

    Sonar training_

    Base occupancy, 5-7,000_

    Subs-5, Tender-1_

    PS out_

His key responded:

    U out_

He smiled and said to himself, we're in business!

Jane and Al's house in Miami:

"Well, Janie, let's go up, and check on that address the Monroe County Court House clerk gave us."

"You mean the owners of the Key West Victorian house, Al?"

"Yep. Let's go. I got the address here. It's on East Ninth Street, a couple blocks east of Palm Avenue. I was looking at the map, and it looks like we should take 42nd Ave up past the airport from Coral Gables. We will almost run right into it. We'll just turn left on Ninth."

"Al, there it is! The small bungalow on the right," Janie pointed.

They pulled up and parked curb side. The place looked a little messy and unkempt. They walked up the sidewalk. Al stepped up on the porch and knocked on the door. There were a few old flyers in the mail box and one or two on the porch floor. No answer. Al knocked much harder.

"Let's walk around back, and take a look."

"Do you think it will be all right, Al?" Janie asked.

"Who's going to complain?" Al answered.

They went around back. "Not much back here," Al murmured.

They walked back out front. There was an older guy sitting on the front porch of the house next door. Al walked up to the guy.

"Hey old timer, know anything about the house and its occupants?"

"Morning. I know a little."

He was sitting on an old overstuffed chair. An undershirt barely covered his chest, and white hairs were sticking out. He had a glass of iced tea in his hand. He looked like he was enjoying his day.

"I haven't seen anyone for about a year. Although I sometimes feel someone is over there. If you want to go back a few years, a real estate lady brought a guy there in '42. I've lived here at this house the last thirty years. The guy must have bought it, because he would come out early every day, catch a bus for Miami Springs and return late at night. I would see him before I went to work and late after I came home. He did that for a couple of months and then disappeared. A few weeks later a guy, who looked just like his brother started leaving early and returning just like the first guy.

Then in '46 I saw both of them together one time. But neither one after that. This last year it's been real quiet."

"The place looks desolate. But the grass is kind of ok?" Al questioned.

The old man answered, "Well, a kid comes by about once a month and cuts the grass. Kind of high when he does. I once asked him about it, and he said some guy contracted him to take care of it."

"That's interesting," Al mused.

"Oh, by the away, you're not the first ones to be asking about that house. A couple of guys came by last month. Knocked on the front door. Then they went around back and looked in the windows. They came over to talk to me. Said they were salesmen. Ha, salesmen my foot! I know CIC* guys when I see them."

"CIC, what does that mean?" Al asked.

"Counter Intelligence Corps. I worked around a couple of these guys at the Miami Beach Training Center in '44. They were a US Army special unit. They worked with the FBI doing background checks on military personnel. Special investigation of people of foreign ancestry. I told them the same thing I just told you."

"Sir, we appreciate you talking to us. Thanks a lot."

"Take care, and good luck looking for them. Ma'am," he nodded to them both.

Al and Janie drove off.

"What are we going to do, Al?"

"We'll just run those ads, get Mike our lawyer on stand-by, and buy that house," Al stated forcefully.

Peter kept up both his spying and work routine. He was picking up a lot of tidbits of information. He transmitted on schedule every two weeks.

Naval District HQ K Y_
Rear Admiral James Kauffman_
Administrative offices moved Miami_
Key West sub killer group_

Ships, Destroyers 3_
B-18s
Costal Bomber task force_
Colonel Louis Merrick_
Munitions dump Fleming Key_
Anti-sub vessel, Icarus 165 ft._
Key West sub pens-3, subs-5_
Military population, 10,000+

There were times in 1943, when the U-boat did not rendezvous. Peter was reading in the newspapers that in 1942 the German U-boats were ravaging the Atlantic Coast, and Gulf, sinking 400 ships. At least 35 were off the Florida coast. In 1943 the US improved their anti-sub defense by using convoys and destroyer escort.

Then it happened. In 1944, Peter had no more contacts and no more orders. However, he continued to spy, keep records and tried to contact the U-boat at the prescribed times. But no luck.

One day in May 1945, it was a month after the surrender of Nazi Ger-

many, Peter noticed a green Army, 1941 four-door Ford sedan driving through his neighborhood. The next day it was parked on his block just a few houses down from his. Peter hurriedly packed his suitcase. He looked out his window and saw two guys in business suits walking up the drive. He ran down the stairs and went quietly out the back door. As they were knocking on the front door he eased over the back fence and walked hurriedly through the neighbor's yard and over to Duval Street. He was down the street and buying a bus ticket to Miami as the two guys were getting back in their car.

"Well, Janie, it's all done. Here is the deed to the house, our dream home in Key West. Mike did a great job with the ads and working with the Monroe County tax office. Not a bad price for a few years' back taxes, plus interest. Let's go down next week for a few days."

"Sounds good, Al," Janie exclaimed with a squeal.

They pulled up to their Key West house.

Janie said, "Let's name it *Island Flavor.*"

"That sounds ok to me. Let's use this key the county clerk gave us," Al agreed.

"That was real nice. The county had the locks changed, both front and rear for us, Al."

"Yep, there, we're in like Flynn!" Al said proudly.

"Look, Al, there is a little bit of furniture. There is one easy chair in the living room. Look in the kitchen, only one chair at the kitchen table. Just a few pots and pans. It looks like a bachelor pad."

"Let's take a look upstairs, Jane."

They went up. One bedroom was bare. In the other room they found a bed and dresser.

"This was definitely a one man's abode," Al exclaimed, "Hey, Janie, look in this turret room."

There was one chair in the center and a small end table next to it. Laying on the end table was a pair of binoculars.

"This guy must have been spying on his neighbors!" Al exclaimed.

"No neighbors Al. Look out of this tower window. It's looking towards the naval base!"

"Well, who knows? Let's go downstairs and bring in the things we brought."

"Now that we're set up, let's go grocery shopping," Janie suggested.

"Good idea, Honey. I'm getting hungry, and let's buy one more kitchen chair!"

Coming in from shopping Al said, "We've got the groceries and the chair. Now let's eat!"

"That was good! Thank you, Dear. Now I'll put the rest of these groceries up. You know I've been thinking, there would be a lot more storage in this house if they had built a pantry under these stairs. Instead they just closed it up," he said as he slammed his hand against the stairwell wall.

"Hey, it moved!"

"What moved dear?" Jane asked.

"The stair wall. No honey look it's a door! Look you can open it. It's a door disguised as a wall."

They both peered inside. It was dark. Al went part of the way in. His eyes became accustomed to the dark.

"There is a lamp on a small table," he said as he clicked it on.

"Look, there's a typewriter," Janie said.

"Well Janie, if it is a typewriter, it's a pretty weird one! No, I think we're on to something here. If I'm not mistaken, what we have here is a transmit and receive station. See, here is a Morse Code typing key and this I'm sure is a radio transmitter. Now let's look at this strange typewriter. It does have a keyboard with 26 letters of the alphabet. But these four rotors, they, too, have the 26 letters of the alphabet on each one. I bet it's a code machine! Let's look on the bottom. There's a small metal tag. It says, **Kriegsmarine Engima.** Marine is naturally water. I bet it's the German Navy's Engima code machine! You know, Janie, it is only three years after the war."

"What are we going to do, Al?"

"We'll go back up to Miami. I want to put in a call to the U.S. Army CIC Branch."

Just as soon as they got back to Miami, Al put in his call.

"US Army, Miami information," the Army operator said.

"I would like to be connected to the CIC Branch please," Al said kind of forceful.

"Sir, there is no CIC Branch."

Al repeated getting slightly impatient, "I mean, Counter Intelligence Corps."

"Sir, that group was disbanded after the war."

"Well, possibly you could tell this disbanded group, I found a hidden broadcasting station with a Kriegsmarine Engima machine in the house I just bought in Key West!"

"Sir, who am I taking to?"

"Al Krenshaw."

"Just one minute sir."

Al switched on the lamp. The light showed a strange looking typewriter with wires running to a small box with dials and switches

Someone came on the line, "Mr Krenshaw, this is Bob Jones speaking. Please tell me once more what you just told the operator."

Al proceeded to repeat what he had told the operator, and what he and Jane had found.

"Al, please listen carefully. We're on this. Do not go back to your home in Key West until I call you back. Please give me some time. Also do not visit the house on 9th Street either. Do you understand?"

"Yes, but..."

"Al, I will get back to you. Just trust me. Thanks, Al. We'll be in touch."

Al told Janie what took place on the phone. They went about their business in Miami. But they waited…and waited. A couple of weeks later they got the call, "Al Krenshaw."

"Yes, this is Al Krenshaw."

"Al, this is Bob Jones, CIC remember."

"Yes Mr. Jones."

"Al it's ok to go back to your Key West home now. We caught him! Peter Schmidt, Alias Peter Smith. We picked him up when he broke into your Key West home and was carrying out the Enigma machine and the other equipment. He must have realized in order to cover his tracks he needed to dispose of the items. He was a German spy, came in off a U-boat in '42. We're on the trail of his Miami counterpart, and we'll have him shortly."

"Bob, uh, Mr. Jones, thank you for all of this," Al said.

"Al, you must remember...actually you must forget. You never called me, and I never talked to you!"

Author:

This story is fictional. Any resemblance to any person or place is purely coincidental. The historic sources are in the Author's Notes of Definitions and References in the rear of the book.

(However, Jane and Al Krenshaw's speech and mannerisms bear some resemblance to my Mom and Dad, Al and Jane Kranich. God rest their souls.)

9

The Storm

The semi-tropical island sat like a precious jewel at the end of a long string of pearls. It floated between two great bodies of water, the sparkling Gulf of Mexico on the north and the mighty Atlantic on its south.

In the natural harbor on the west and open side of this Island of the Sun, a female dolphin and its two young swim, dive, and frolic in the early morning mist. It was still and dark, only a hint of light in the east.

Suddenly the female let out a high-pitched sound. Her two offspring immediately gave her their undivided attention. She turned and headed out towards the Atlantic. The siblings followed after their parent. All three were moving fast, diving and then rolling up to the top to breathe.

As this family disappeared towards the dark ocean, suddenly the sun on the far horizon burst forth in a shaft of light. It was bright yellow at first.

Then it moved up and into a very low and ominous dark hanging mass. This collection of clouds suddenly burned with a brilliant orange-red.

At this particular moment, sea gulls, sandpipers, terns, and pelicans could be seen flying from the Atlantic side over this jewel to the far side of the island. They then landed on the far beach amongst the pine, the exquisite coconut palms, and the tall stately palmetto trees.

The barometer was dropping, the humidity was building, and the air pressure was changing. On the Atlantic beach the breakers were beginning to build and pound the surf and shore. Sand crabs were leaving their holes as the water slowly gained ground and headed up the beach towards the dunes. Many of these sand crabs were moving inland and making as best they could for the high ground on the dunes or for that matter, the Gulf waters on the lea side of the island.

On one of the quiet city streets at ground level, a busy ant colony was shifting its stores, eggs, and members to a higher location. They were moving in a straight line from a crack in the sidewalk over to a brick wall. One could see this line of march was straight up along the top of the wall and into a brick structure attached to it.

A cat, and right behind it, a city street dog, came running by. Both animals scattered the ant's organized marching line. These two creatures, alerted by a change in the air pressure knew a drastic weather change was coming on. They were looking for a safe and secure hideaway. Some say animals can feel the vibration and smell the ozone from far away lightning.

It became very still. Then it started, slightly at first, small short puffs of a breeze. Then stronger bursts, turning into a strong wind. Plap!...Plap!.. Plap! Plap! Plap! Raindrops were hitting the wall, the pavement and the sandy dry dust. At first the large drops slamming into the powdery earth made what appeared to be small smoke pockets. Shortly the hard downpour saturated everything. The wind was now blowing violently, the rain tearing into the earth in torrential waves.

The coconut palms were waving frantically to and fro. Then one by one the dried frons were torn from their hold on the tree's trunk and sent reeling into the wind. The streets were fast filling with puddles, which were linking with each other. As the water over powered the drainage it rose, forming small lakes.

Unexpectantly there was a Clang!... Clang!... Clang! Clang! Clang! as perfect round balls of ice fell straight down from the sky. It seemed the wind halted momentarily just for this performance. The hail came as a sampling at first, but then a barrage of ice balls plummeted everything. Just as fast as it started...it stopped. The last few, not to be left out, dropped one by one. This was followed by increased gusts of wind bearing ferocious pelting rain.

Inland a thirty-foot palmetto tree bent and swayed as all of its green frons hanging on precariously were bent and pushed to its far side. It was losing its dried frons just like the coconut palms.

Loud cracks of thunder were followed by electric flashes zigzagging

across the sky. One of these actually touched down finding a grounding path through a stately oak. This left a burnt scar on the base of the tree and a scent of scorched wood lingering in the air.

Almost as quick and surprising as it started, the wind ceased, and the rain turned to a slow drizzle. Then both gave up. The sun, now high in the sky found an opening in the clouds, and sent its golden rays to illuminate the entire scene.

Somewhere in a distant pine, a seemingly content and cheerful mockingbird breaks the silence in joyful song to celebrate and welcome the new day.

A Three-Bay Classic Revival Temple house with a Captain's Walk on top.

10

Wrecker's Tale

Captain Dan Benson came down from his Captain's Walk or copula as some called it. This was a lookout on the top of his house. He told his wife Jennie that he just saw the signal flag from his schooner that his first mate had run up. This meant all of the provisions were loaded. He had to make a run with his crew up to Key Largo where his pineapple plantation was located.

He kissed and hugged his two teenage daughters, Anne and Clare, and then Jennie, and went outside. He took the usual walk around his house before he went down the street. He was very proud of this house, the original three-bay Classic Revival Temple house he purchased right after the Civil War. It was because he had been successful as a Bahamian seaman and wrecker that he was able to buy both his pineapple plantation in the Upper Keys, and then this house in Key West. Not bad for a man born in 1830!

He had extended the porches to the side and then put the main entrance there. A dining room and connecting parlor were added a couple of years later. The crowning jewel was the Captain's Walk on the top. This was where he could watch the harbor and the ships coming and going.

The original structure was built of heart pine and Honduran mahogany. It made use of wooden pegs, mortise-and-tendon joints,* and an internal structure of fine-squared timbers. He had made sure the addition kept up this quality of construction.

Captain Dan started his six block stroll to the Key West docks. He could have hired one of the drivers to take him in a buggy, but he wasn't in a hurry.

He enjoyed this walk. First, he went past the new stone Methodist church which he attended when he was ashore. This church was one of the few structures built from coral stone quarried on the island. It was an outstanding sight, especially with the tall Spanish laurel tree growing right next to it.

After going past his church he turned north through the town section. There were small shops, inns, and houses of spirits, and there were dock workers and the usual US Navy sailors about. Key West has always had its complement of Navy personnel on the island. This has been since Commodore David Porter* first sailed into Key West harbor.

In April, 1823 the commodore arrived with a squadron to establish a depot, to end piracy and stop slave ships. Because it had a natural deep water harbor, Key West had been the primary port between New Orleans and Jacksonville during the Civil War.

Dan passed through the merchants' warehouses and then came to the wharves and piers. He liked to make a mental note of what boats were in port. What he especially liked to see was his schooner. He rounded the corner and there it was, his two-masted schooner, the Jenney Mae. She was of a good size, 80 feet from the bowsprit* to the stern. It was 18 feet wide amidships, had a shallow draft of five feet max, and was built for speed.

The schooner had windward ability (close sailing to the wind). It was deep built behind, light in the front and gaff rigged.* The raked* masts supported much canvas. The rear mast was 68 feet to the extreme top, and the front mast about eight feet shorter. There were two quarter boats,* one on each side in the rear.

This boat was built in Key West. They had used a native wood, mahogany, which was called madeira by the locals. This wood would outlast many other woods. It was strong and light. A special trait was that it would not rot, and Teredo worms* wouldn't touch it.

Dan had bought it two years earlier when it was completed and was put up for sale. He wanted to use it to carry his pineapples to market. The Jenney Mae would complement the small 40 foot single-masted sloop* he kept at his pineapple plantation at Plantation Key. His wish for it was to use it as a wrecker when the opportunity presented itself.

Consequently, he had set it up with all the necessary equipment he would need. The boat had two spare 750-pound anchors, and he had the two longboats stowed aft for moving the anchors or ship's cargo as needed during a wrecking salvage operation. He also had hooks, blocks, tackles, lines, axes, saws, and carpenter's tools.

His first mate, John, saw him and waved. He crossed the gangplank and up onto the deck of his ship.

"How goes it, John?"

"We're loaded and ready to cast off, Captain," John answered.

"Did you have any luck finding men?" Dan asked.

"Yes Sir. Only two, but they're fine men," John exclaimed. "You know, Capt'n it's hard to find seamen who don't mind farming, but since you pay good, they're ready."

"Just one minute, Capt'n. Ok, mates, gangplank in and cast off."

The four regular crew members and the two new men ran about getting the boat loose from its tyings.

"Captain, as you can see and feel, the wind is right to pull us out from the dock. We'll be out in the channel in no time."

"Right, John. Carry on."

"Aye aye, Sir!"

It seemed this Key West port had, for most of the time, a cooperative breeze. If there wasn't one, they would have to man the two quarter boats with a couple of hired hands to tow the ship away from the pier, and get her out into the harbor.

Dan thought, it was summer and only eight 'clock early morning. That was good, for they would get up to the Key Largo harbor, and it would still be light when they went into the channel. He would never chance it in the dark unless it was an emergency or a wreck was in progress.

The usual method they used, if they weren't taking on a lot of supplies, was, they would anchor in the harbor and go back and forth in the quarter boats.

"There, we're underway sir. Yonder, there is one of the new men, Roberts. He is a new Englander and Benjamin, the dark Bahamian there, is a salvage diver. We're in luck. He's got experience diving on at least three wrecks and grows fruit back home. Looks like a double helping, Sir."

"Good work, John," Captain Dan commented. "Let's tak'er out into the Southwest channel, then east up the Hawk Channel along the Keys."

It was a long trip of sailing, about 75 nautical miles east-northeast and then northeast another 15 miles to Key Largo. John loved this trip. It took about ten hours. Key Largo was the largest and longest of the Keys. Their course took them as much as five miles out from the chain of Keys and as little as a half of a mile.

The water was turquoise. Farther out was the deep blue of the straits of Florida. You could see large flocks of ibis and gulls with the occasional line of fishing pelicans skimming the tops of the waves. Porpoise abounded in these waters and raced playfully alongside the Jenney Mae as she traveled up the Keys. It was a beautiful day, and the first mate "heaved the log."*

"It looks good, Sir. We're traveling along at ten knots," John exclaimed.

"It's looking shipshape, John. At this rate we'll be there on time. Since we have six shipmates now, in two hours, let two men be relieved for an hour, then two more, and the last two after the noon meal. We should be there around five this evening with plenty of sun to guide us in through the channel."

"Aye aye, Sir."

Captain Dan had one of the first pineapple plantations on Plantation Key, hence the name. He had taken a few thousand pineapple suckers from a boat he had helped get off a reef after a storm. This was his payment for his wrecking fee. It had been a kind of out-of-court settlement among the captain of the boat, the owners, and Captain Dan. He then needed some land, so he went up to Plantation Key. Now he was expanding his operations to the southwest end of Key Largo.

Dan had applied to homestead 140 acres on that key. He had told his farmer-sailors from Plantation Key to go on up to that parcel. They were to start building a couple of buildings to be the nucleus of his farm operations there. The captain liked to think wrecking was his main business, but it was unpredictable. This pineapple farming would help his bottom line.

There were a couple of reasons why he choose Key Largo for his second pineapple farm. The Upper Keys had good limestone soil and were blessed by 20 more inches of rain than the Lower Keys. But his deep down real reason was that just offshore were two deadly reefs, the Molasses and the Carysfort. He could plant pineapples and watch these reefs for floundering ships for his wrecking business.

"There it is, Sir. I can see the sloop in the harbor," John interrupted Dan's thoughts.

You could see the white of a stowed sail and mast on the other side of a spit of land.

"Let me borrow your glass," Dan asked.

"Here Sir," he handed the Captain the spyglass.

They rounded the north side of Rodriquez Key and headed straight for the harbor.

John yelled, "Keep a sharp eye up front, Carlos, and guide me in."

Carlos was already up front hanging out over the rail. Captain Dan kept his eye on Carlos for John. That way he could relay signals. The location of the wheel had both masts in the line of sight, and it was hard for the pilot to see to the front of the vessel. John needed to keep both hands on wheel. The schooner ploughed right on into the center of the channel, and they were soon gliding into the small harbor right next to the sloop.

"We'll anchor over there in the middle, and take the boats in," Dan commanded.

"Aye aye, Sir," John answered.

There was a small wagon, horse, and his farm manager there to meet them. "Hi Jonathan. I see you've got some transportation," Dan hailed as he stepped from the quarter-boat.

"Yes, Sir. Our neighbors up the Key didn't mind parting with them. I offered what you said."

"Good work Jonathan," Dan complemented. "Well men, climb aboard! We've got about one-half of a mile to go."

"How's it going?" Captain Dan asked Jonathan.

"We've got a cook shack and are almost finished with a small bunk house. You know we've been at it about a week and a half!" Jonathan said proudly. "You can see we've got lots of good wood here."

The Gulf shore was very rocky. There were some fair sized mahogany trees seventy feet or so high. They must have been left over as saplings when the Spanish explorers cut all of the virgin trees down in the late 1600's. These were mixed with pines and coconut. The soil was naturally sandy with limestone and coral.

"Looks great, Jonathan," Captain Dan complimented. "With the four of you, and us four from the schooner, and the two new men John picked up, tomorrow we can get to work on finishing this house."

They cooked their supper on the fireplace that was built in the bunk-house. Since all of them were sailors, they all had their hammocks to hang on posts that had been put up in there just for that use. Mosquito netting had been installed on the window openings and some men had the same over their hammocks.

"That was a good breakfast, men. Jonathan, how about you and I look over the land once more to see just where we're going to put the new pineapples?"

"John, you keep the men busy. How about Benjamin? You said he farmed in the Bahamas. Let's see if he knows anything that will help us grow pineapples on this land."

"Hi, Benjamin, you know I'm Captain Dan. John says you farmed in the Bahamas. Can you tell us anything we should know about farming pineapples on this land?"

"I'll try, Sir," Benjamin answered.

"Jonathan and Benjamin let's look around. See you later, John, keep em' busy!"

"Aye aye, Sir."

They walked inland towards the sound. It was only about a fourth of a mile. As they walked, Dan said, "I have a couple of acres planted in pineapples on Plantation Key. They're looking good. Should be ready to cut and ship in a month or so."

Benjamin started to talk. "Sir, if I may, the pineapples like sandy and well-drained soil. You've got it here, and of course, plenty of sun. They can survive with low rainfall. It's because their leaves spiral out from the center, and that way any moisture collects in the center over the flower area. Of course, it's those flowers that fuse together to make the one fruit in each plant."

"More about soil, Sir, see these 20 to 30 feet in diameter red-spotted soil areas? They are called Red Holes.* There won't be any rocks below the surface. It's a special place to grow bananas or other fruit trees."

"Benjamin, you're plenty knowledgeable. How long were you farming?" the Captain asked.

"It was in my family, Sir. I learned from my grandfather and father. Although I did want some adventure. That's how I got down to the Keys. I went sailing."

"What about replanting here from my fields in Plantation Key?" Captain Dan asked.

"Well, Sir, the seeds are no good. Because the pineapple is from the family bromeliad,* it takes ten years to reproduce from the seed. I recommend some new suckers or slips from another source. You could get them from Cuba. It's only 90 miles, a day's good sailing. Those new cuttings will last a couple of years. I've been there and could help you find a donor. If we're fortunate, we may find *Smooth Cayenne,** which makes an excellent deep yellow fruit. Then it will take from 12 to 24 months to make fruit. We will need about six to ten thousand plantings per acre. You then should get from four to seven thousand fruit."

"One more thing, Sir, I would like to perform an easy test on the soil. We'll pick up a handful of soil from different locations where you wish to plant. We'll of course mark the place and the soil sample. Then we'll stir the soil up with three to four times the water. The time it takes to clear, well tell us what we want to know. One hour is a very good well-drained soil. You don't want to go over much more than three to four hours."

"Thank you, Benjamin, I've really had a lesson in pineapple growing," Captain Dan exclaimed. "We will work one more day here, and then we'll take our sailing crew of four and Benjamin and go and find those pineapple slips."

"I'm going to leave Roberts with your farm crew, Jonathan. We're going to leave all the provisions we brought. We will stop briefly back in Key West, resupply, and then off to Cuba! I hope to be back in less than a week. Finish clearing that acre and half."

"Aye aye, Sir,"

"Benjamin, let's check that soil."

"Sir, it took only one and one half hours for all four jars to clear. It's well-drained soil," Benjamin said proudly.

They spent just enough time in Key West for Captain Dan to briefly enjoy his family. John and the men replenished the supplies for a seven-day round-trip to Cuba. They rowed the goods out to their schooner anchored in the harbor. That night the men made the rounds in Key West.

Early morning…

"John, sir," Benjamin said. "We should tell the captain the best way to get to Cuba is sail in the night because the winds are light then. In the daytime the winds can make a wind-over-the-tide effect. I was in it once. It could be very rough."

John and Benjamin took one of the boats in, docked, and walked to Captain Dan's house. Jonathan waited on the walk as John went up to the door and knocked.

"John, are you sure this is correct? Or are you just buying time for the men to recoup from last night?" the captain asked.

"Sir, they could use some recouping time. But Benjamin was adamant and sober when he told me this."

"Look, John, be ready to cast off a couple hours before sunset. I'll be down then."

"Aye aye, Sir!" John touched his forehead and went down the stairs from the house.

That evening, about three hours before sunset, John had a couple of the men and a long boat waiting at the docks to ferry Captain Dan out to his schooner. They were out of the Key West harbor and into the Florida Straights before they knew it, thanks to a light northerly wind. A red fireball sun was touching the Gulf waters off to their right. It was creating a red-orange glow on the high clouds and waves.

"Sir, according to the charts it's right at ninety miles to Havana. If you please Sir, I've got a basic course set for south-southwest 203 degrees. We may have to make an adjustment or two."

"Very good, John, carry on."

"Thank you, Captain."

Captain Dan could see the Jenney Mae was cutting a fine wake. The sails were filled and billowing. He sure did love his schooner. John didn't have the two upper gaff topsails out yet. Even then he guessed they were traveling at about nine knots.

"Sir, we should reach the axis of the Gulf Stream fifty miles from homeport. The roughest part will be about ten miles before and ten miles after," John remarked. "It would be nice if this northerly wind would shift easterly for the easiest passage."

"Where did you get all that information, John, If I may ask?" the captain questioned.

"Well sir, I've been talking to a couple of the men, Benjamin included. They have made this trip before."

"Well done, John," Captain Dan exclaimed.

Almost all of Captain Dan's sailing was the Keys and up the East Coast. He never had a need to go to Cuba.

"John, since there's seven of us, let's work you and two men the next five hours. I'll take the second watch. Have the odd man up two and one-half hours before and after the apex. I'm turning in. Call if you need me."

"Aye aye, Sir!" John hollered, "Benjamin and Sam up in five hours with the captain, Smith down in two and one-half and up five hours later."

"Aye aye, First Mate," they said, as they went to their stations and bunks.

Just as John had predicted, along about twelve, the waves became slightly rougher. Then the winds shifted easterly, and the Jenney Mae tacked, leaned to the east and continued to do nine knots.

The captain came up, "I'll take her, John. Get some rest."

"Thank you Sir," and he headed below.

It seemed the sun had rushed around the earth. When John came back up on deck it was now peeking through a morning cloud in the east. The captain came up from the galley holding a cup of coffee. Sam was at the wheel.

"Morning, John, I trust you slept well."

"Thank you, Sir. We should be sighting Havana soon. That is, if my course was correct."

"Land Ho!" Benjamin sang out. "There's also a light. It's faint, but it's there."

"Where is that, Benjamin?" Captain Dan asked.

"Sir, it wasn't there when I last visited but I heard the Spanish built a light tower right next to the Morro Castle. There it is. You can see the rock base and the castle now."

"John, we'll sail into the harbor, drop anchor, and take one of our boats in to check with the harbor master and authorities."

As they slipped by under the massive walls, they could see the guns sticking out of the gunports on the castle ramparts. They furled sails and dropped anchor in an open area in the harbor. They could see a couple of Spanish frigates.* There were also three large commercial vessels anchored nearby.

Before they could even start lowering their long boat, John said, "Captain, we've got company."

A longboat was on a straight course for them. It was being rowed by uniformed Spanish seamen with their bright blue and white uniforms.

"John, have a couple of men set up a table and something to sit on. Have the cook put on some coffee and sweets."

"Aye aye, Sir."

Captain Dan went to the rail opening. He waved and hollered, "Bienvenido a bordo."*

He could see the officer say something, and all eight oars came up in the air. They did a perfect maneuver and brought their boat right up alongside the Jenney Mae. A couple of the men threw them lines so they could tie up. The officer came aboard first and saluted. He then said in very perfect English, "I am Captain Juarez of his Majesty Alfonso the Twelfth's Spanish forces. May I introduce Juan Diego, our harbormaster."

Juan Diego stepped forward, bowed, and said, "At your service."

Captain Dan pointed towards where the cook had set up the table and chairs, and said, "Would you gentlemen like to sit a minute for some refreshments? Then we can discuss my visit to your country. I am Captain Dan Benson of Key West, Florida. You two gentlemen speak excellent English. May I ask where you obtained it?"

"Yes, Captain, both Juan Diego and I were stationed in New Orleans."

"A rather busy location," the First Mate John stated.

"Gentlemen, this is my First Mate, John."

The cook had put on his sailing jacket and was serving coffee and sweets.

The harbormaster spoke up, "Gentlemen I just have to ask you questions for my report, then you are welcome to visit. Please state your business in Cuba. Also there's the consideration of a harbor fee. It's only twenty-five American dollars. It can be in silver or any other suitable hard currency."

Captain Dan said, "We need some plantings for our pineapple plantation back in the Keys."

"So it's pineapple slips you desire. We've got lots of them. There are plenty of plantations. I recommend a trip down the coast to the Bahia de Cardenas. I know the harbormaster there. This paperwork will also suffice for your visiting fee at Cardenas. Tell Carlos de Santiago that you had a nice talk with Juan Diego. For a small persuasion, I'm sure he will put you in contact with the persons you will need to talk to."

Captain Dan was prepared for the harbor fee, and he placed seven silver five dollar pieces in front of the harbormaster.

"It's fine U.S. minted silver, Juan Diego," Captain Dan said.

"It's good. Thank you, Captain. Well, we must go. We have a lot of pressing business. Captain Dan, John, thank you for your great hospitality. Please enjoy your stay in our country de Cuba. Buena suerte."

"Well, Captain, there they go," John said. "I didn't know you were fluent in Spanish, Sir."

"I used to trade a lot around St. Augustine, John. It becomes very useful on the Florida East Coast."

"John, what do you think? Do we try Havana or go on to Cardenas?"

"Let me call Benjamin, Captain. Let's see what he knows about Cardenas."

He didn't have to call very loud because the men had been watching and listening to the events taking place. He motioned to Benjamin, who came up to John and the captain.

"Benjamin, the harbormaster suggests Cardenas for finding a pineapple plantation. What do you think?"

"Sir, it would be the best route. If we stayed in Havana tonight...well I hate to admit it, but the men may not be in too good condition on the 'morrow. Please don't tell them I said so. As far as Cardenas, I heard that it has a lot of pineapple estates."

"Thanks, Benjamin," John said. "Captain, I'll check our charts, but I think we can be there by late afternoon."

"Thanks, John, let's set the sails."

"Aye aye, Captain." John touched his forehead in a civilian salute.

There was a nice breeze in the harbor and a good wind outside. The schooner's sails caught this wind as they got aways out from land. John took over the wheel, as the men scurried around loosening this rope and tightening another. They carefully kept their eyes on the breakers. Sam was in the bow keeping a careful lookout.

John said, "We should be just about there," pointing.

Benjamin was near by. "John, there are outer banks, but see that opening. The channel goes right through the center. It did at least when I was here three years ago."

"Keep a sharp eye there, Sam," John commanded. "We're going in."

They slipped in dead center between the rocks of the two outer banks.

"There's Cardenas over center right," Benjamin pointed.

They were in the bay. There was no harbor as such. They could see the orange tile roofs of the city with the palm trees swaying in the breeze. They dropped both anchors.

"We'll leave some men here, John," Captain Dan said. "Issue them side arms."

John commanded, "Sam, take charge while we're gone. Let's get one of the long boats launched."

This time they were able to get in before the Cardenas harbormaster came out to meet them. There was a long pier with some sloops and small fishing boats tied up. They came alongside the pier, and a short chunky man with one assistant was standing there waiting for them.

As he stepped onto the pier, Captain Dan took a chance and said, "Carlos de Santiago," as he reached forth his hand to shake. The short chunky man broke into a smile showing a bright gold front tooth.

"At your service, Captain, You must have been in the presence of my honorable cousin in Havana."

"Yes, I have had the pleasure of meeting him. I'm Captain Dan Benson of Key West."

"Well Sir, walk with me and my assistant to my office. I have some delicious Cuban coffee, con leche* just waiting to be tasted."

In the office, "So you need many pineapple slips. I may be able to help you."

" I would like to offer some U.S. silver for your trouble," Captain Dan slid two silver coins over to Carlos de Santiago.

"You are very gracious, Senior," Carlos said, "Meet with me mid-morning tomorrow, say ten o'clock, and I will have a plantation representative present."

"Thank you very much, Carlos de Santiago."

They shook hands and left the office as the assistant opened the door for them.

"Before we go back to the boat, John, let's stop at the market," Captain Dan announced.

They bought some fruit, sweets and a nice cut of meat.

At the boat: "How goes it, men?" Captain Dan asked of the crew he had left on the longboat. "Men, our cook is going to put on a feast, and then you all can go into town and have a rip-roaring time. But we've got to keep our wits about us. Get back in before twelve and get some rest, because we've all got a big day tomorrow."

The morning found the men, Captain Dan, John, and Benjamin back at the harbormaster's office. They noticed three handsome horses tied up outside. A man with a big sombrero was sitting on one of them.

John knocked. "Come in." They recognized Carlos de Santiago's voice.

Two men were in the process of standing up. Carlos de Santiago and his assistant were already standing, "Ah, my good amigo, Captain Dan Benson and his First Mate John. I would like for you to meet Don Juan Monterego and his brother Don Carlos Monterego. They have a very nice pineapple plantation," Carlos said with a flourish.

They shook hands all around, with Captain Dan introducing Benjamin.

Don Juan said, "Gentlemen I can show you our plantation, today if you wish. It is only eight miles inland. We can hire you a coach, and be there in less than one hour."

"Very good. We would grateful if you showed us your plantation," Captain Dan said.

"Let us go outside. Thank you Carlos," Don Juan said.

They went outside. The man waiting with the horses looked at them and Don Juan commanded, "Hector, coach."

The man rode off only to return in a few minutes followed by a closed coach pulled by two horses with a driver on top.

"If you don't mind, Captain Dan, you three may ride in the coach. My brother and I will keep our horses, and follow behind," Don Juan said.

The coach set off through the very narrow streets of Cardenas. Occasionally they would come to and go through a square. That's when the traffic of coaches and people increased.

At one square, Benjamin remarked, "That's the *Plaza de Colon*. See the statue of Columbus. It was erected by Queen Isabella II of Spain in

1862. That elegant cathedral behind it is the *Cathedral de la Concepcion Immaculada.* It was built in 1846.”

They passed another notable landmark. A small steam engine sat in front of a railroad station.

Benjamin said, “That railroad is instrumental in working the sugarcane fields. It’s been around more than 30 years, I’ve been told.”

“You sure are familiar with Cuba, Benjamin,” John said.

“I’ve been on a couple of trips, both trading and pineapples.”

“That is to our benefit,” Captain Dan remarked.

They were soon out of the city and on a narrow dirt road. There were sugarcane fields on both sides. Captain Dan noticed workers and people nodding and showing recognition to their coach and group. He decided Don Juan must be well-known and respected in these parts. The coach pulled off the road and came to a halt.

Don Carlos opened the door, “Gentlemen, please come down, and watch your step.”

Don Juan was looping his horse’s reins around a hitching post right next to his brother’s steed. There was a small adobe brick hut with a lean-to of wood attached. They were surrounded by all kinds of palm trees, coconuts included. There were some very large leaf plants with bananas in bunches hanging down.

Stretching out in front was a huge pineapple field. The plant’s spikes were sticking up with the round pineapples growing in the center. It all was bright green and lush. There were some workers in and around the hut and a few in the field.

Don Juan broke the silent spell, “How do you like this field? We could get you about 6000 slips off it.”

Benjamin looked first at the captain and then at Don Juan, “Could I take a look?”

“Yes, be my guest,” Don Juan spread his arm and hand in a gesture towards the field.

Benjamin walked out into the field. He bent down on his haunches and touched a plant and then moved out farther in the field inspecting as he went. Everyone stood by and watched him. He then came back in, looked at Captain Dan, and then said to Don Juan, “It is a very nice field with good growing fruit. They appear to be about three years old. I mean no insult, but would you have any fields with one year-old plants growing?”

Don Juan appeared to be slightly set back, “Yes it is a three-year field. I accept your knowledge. We do have a couple of fields with one-year old plants. You realize those slips would be more costly."

Captain Dan injected himself into the conversation, "We would very much prefer the one year-old slips if you could part with them, Don Juan."

"Ye, we will ride over to that field. It is not far."

They proceeded to venture farther down the road. After stopping they went through the same procedure. When Benjamin came back from his inspection, this time he nodded his head and smiled. "Excellent!" he stated.

"Very good, gentlemen. If you will mount back up we will go just a very short distance farther on this road and will have some refreshments at my simple hacienda."

They rolled to a stop after leaving the road and driving down a lane lined with Royal Poinciana palms on both sides. Then they drove through an entrance in a stone wall. Don Juan's simple hacienda looked like a governor's palace. A couple of hired hands or servants came out, took the horses, and opened the coach's doors.

"Right this way, gentlemen," Don Juan gestured, as he pointed towards the entrance to the house.

Inside they were ushered by a servant to a large room with an immense table. Servants came in bearing cool drinks and sweet breads.

"Well, gentlemen, Captain Dan, we'll get this business over soon so we can relax. The slips from the three year field would be one hundred dollars per thousand. The one year field will be a premium of two hundred extra for the six thousand pineapple slips. That would be a total of eight hundred dollars in silver. What do you think, Captain Dan?"

"Thank you, Don Juan. You are very gracious," Captain Dan said, "to part with your plants. I could give you a down payment and the balance when you deliver to the water."

"A down payment will not be necessary. A gentlemen's handshake shall suffice," he said as he stood up and extended his hand.

Dan took it in a firm grip. "Gracias, Don Juan."

"Your man Benjamin may be our guest and help or just observe our cutting. They will start arriving at the docks tomorrow afternoon. Do you have means to transport them to your boat?"

"Yes, we have two longboats to go back and forth," Captain Dan replied.

The captain gave Benjamin a look, and Benjamin nodded.

"We will get back to our ship and prepare to start receiving shipment tomorrow," the captain said.

Don Juan motioned and said, "I will see you to your carriage."

The next day the pineapple slips started arriving by wagon from the fields by noon. Juan Diego, the harbormaster had produced four men to help with the wagon unloading and boat loading. Sometime after noon of the second day, a wagon drove up to the docks with Benjamin riding up on the seat next to the driver.

Don Juan, his brother, and four additional riders, armed, were following along behind.

"Hello, Captain. Salutations. This here is the last load, as your good, hard working man, Benjamin, can ascertain to. Would you allow me to hire him? He is a one-man crew!" Don Juan said smiling.

"Thank you for the compliment, Don Juan. But I can't lose him. He is invaluable. If it be your pleasure, we could all ride out in the longboat, and we can complete our transaction."

They got in the boat, Captain Dan, John, Benjamin and the two brothers. John and Benjamin rowed the short distance out to the boat.

"Please excuse my armed men. But they will guarantee me getting the silver you will pay me to the bank," Don Juan stated.

"Nothing wrong with taking precautions," Captain Dan replied.

"A very excellent schooner, Captain. You say you can use it to save wrecks? It must be a dangerous endeavor."

"Yes, Don Juan, exciting, dangerous, and sometimes financially rewarding."

The next morning saw the crew of the Jenney Mae rested and lofting sails. Captain Dan had given his respects to the harbormaster, Juan Diego yesterday. He had ridden the boat back with Juan Diego and his brother to the dock and shaken hands all around.

Now their sails were filling with a soft tropical breeze. Before they knew it, they were slipping away from Cardenas heading towards the opening between the outer banks that both formed and protected the Bay de Cardenas.

"Well, John, once we get through the gap, I'm sure you know we'll proceed northwest. We'll parallel the shore. When we get adjacent to Havana's light tower we'll head north-northeast straight for Key West. Even though we'll be leaving in the morning, the winds appear to be southerly," Captain Dan said. He was just thinking out loud because he knew John the First Mate could take them back to Key West.

Even so, John said, "Aye aye, Sir."

"Havana Ho!" one of the men called down from the small look-out platform high on the rear or main mast. This platform was a perch for just one man at the bottom of the main gaff topsail. They used it when this sail was not in use.

"There's the light tower now!" the man sung out again.

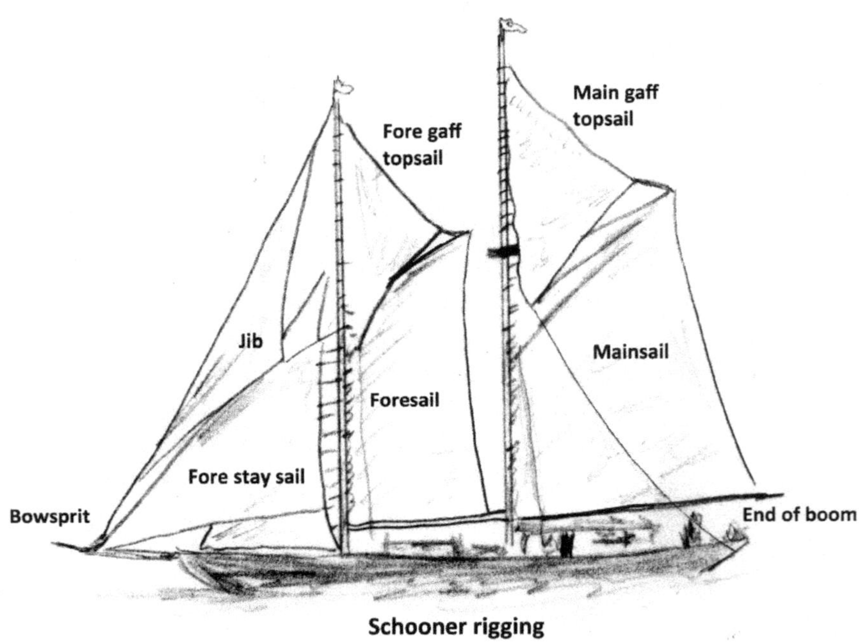

Schooner rigging

Unknown to our schooner and its crew, when they slipped out through the channel opening of the Bahia de Cardenas, a sloop had rounded the headlands from the Bahia de Santa Clara (which was another bay farther inside the Bahia de Cardenas) and proceeded to stalk them.

Sloops are single-masted sailing ships. They are on the same lines as a schooner, but they are usually smaller. They are very fast in pursuit or being pursued. They are easiy to operate because the sails are worked from the deck, no climbing up. A schooner uses the same method of controlling the sails. Because they are easy to operate, it takes only a small crew. That leaves the rest of the men to operate the guns. They are also of a shallow draft, depending on the size and weight. They only need approximately four to six feet of water to operate in, much less than a schooner.

This sloop had a few more men than were needed. There was a reason: It was to man the single lightweight four-pounder cannons on each side. The ports for these guns were disguised by paint and decorations. This boat also had front and rear swivel-cannons that shot a one-pound ball or a handful of grape.* These four swivel-cannons were permanently mounted on the rails, two per side. The actual swivel grips, small cannon balls, grape shot, and power were stored in an arms chest just below the rails.

One man could fire a swivel-cannon, and the layout allowed two swivel-cannon and one four pounder to bear on either side at any time.

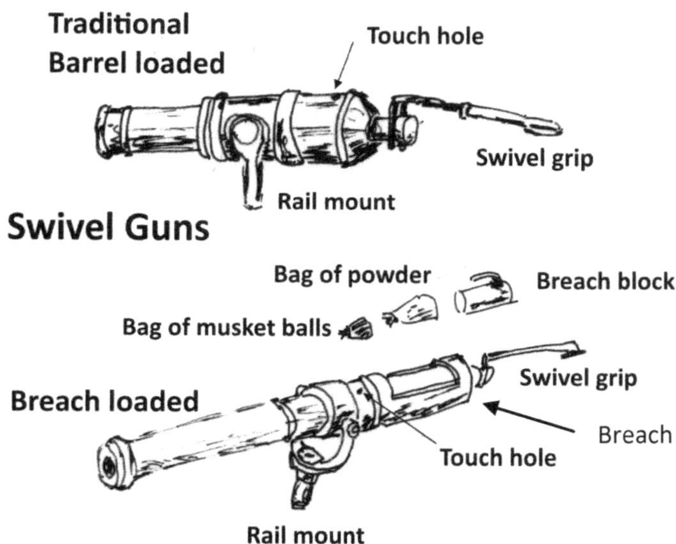

On the pirate's ship:

"She's going through the channel, Captain," the First Mate said.

"Keep yer eye on 'er Carlos," Captain Gomez ordered.

"Where we gonna do her in, Captain?" Carlos asked.

"Not on this crossing. We'll follow her. I'm sure there's more silver where they got what they bought those pineapple sticks with. No, we're out for bigger fish! Now don't lose'er. But stay back so she doesn't suspect us."

"Aye aye, Captain!"

"Now look lively you swabs! Trim those sails! Tighten up the main stays!" Captain Gomez hollered at his men.

It was a motley crew. These thirteen men had been on Gomez's sloop the last two years. Even though most of the pirates were obsolete by the late 1850's, Gomez and his men refused to believe it. There hunting grounds were the entire Cuban island. After all there were 3,750 miles of coastline and over 200 bays and harbors. Plenty of places to hide. They would pick on smaller boats and rob them. Then they would sail the small ship somewhere they could sell it or if not they would burn it. After all, the old pirate motto is, "Dead men tell no tales."

It was well into the afternoon. The sun was bright, and fluffy clouds were drifting overhead. The captain came out from his cabin below.

"We're more than halfway, Sir," John said to the captain. "See the color of the water. It is almost deep purple."

"Sure is pretty, John. We haven't got our north wind and the rough seas. But you can see and feel the Gulf Stream. It's taking us, we won't need the gaff sails."

John commanded, "Men, we can lower both the Gaff sails."

They dropped both sails and one of the men climbed to the small top perch on the main mast, "Sail Ho!" he hollered.

"Who's that?" the captain asked John.

"It's Roberts, Sir. He wanted to look around, and I let him."

"What do you see, Roberts?" John asked as he and the captain both looked up.

Roberts came down, a small telescope hung about his neck. "Sir, I thought I saw something this morning. So soon as I could I clum up there and shure enough I saw'er. Sir, she is fifteen degrees off the starboard stern. She is a sloop. If I'm not mistaken she's been at that position since we left the Havana light. She can see us better than we can see her. We're taller."

"Let me borrow your glass, Roberts. I'm going up to take a look."

John climbed up the shrouds which were on the sides of the schooner supporting the masts. When he got to the perch he put his arm around the mast to steady himself as he looked through Robert's telescope. After a few minutes he scurried down.

"Just like Roberts says, Sir. She's back there. About a fifty-foot sloop. Good size!"

"Well John, let's see if she's really following us. Put on every sail, the fore and main gaff and the jib. We'll give her a run for the money!"

"Carlos, what's going on?"

"Captain they must 'ave put on some more sail. She is pullin' away from us. I wonder if they're up to us?"

"Hey you there, Smithe."

"Yes sir, Captain."

"Have the men unfurl the square rigging.* Carlos, we've got to stay up with the schooner. She's all out!"

"Let's go men! You heard the capt'n," Carlos commanded.

Late afternoon turned into dark evening with both ships racing into the void.

"Morning, Sir. We're approaching Key West harbor," John said as pleasantly as he could as he woke the Captain.

"Thank you, John. I'll be right on deck."

The captain splashed some water on his face, put on his cap and went up to the deck.

"John, we'll anchor in the harbor. We'll just be overnight. Tell the men they can have leave just as soon as we're shipshape. But remind them we're leaving early in the morning and for them to be in good condition. We've got a lot of pineapple slip planting to do. John, if I can find what I'm going-a-looking for, I'll send it out to the boat late this afternoon."

"Have a couple of men row me in, John, and take care."

"Benjamin! Roberts! Longboat for the captain. If you please."

"Thank you, Benjamin, Roberts. I appreciate the ride."

The captain stepped up onto the wharf. He went straight over to a door in the nearest warehouse. Then he went into the office where there was a wooden well-used counter. Ropes and block and tackles hung about with every other type of ship's hardware.

May I help yea, Sir?" the clerk asked.

"Yes, I'm inquiring about my good friend, Master James. Is he in?"

"Just one minute Sir. Whom shall I say is calling?"

"Captain Dan...Dan Benson."

The clerk knocked on a door, then respectfully put his head in, "A Captain Dan Benson to see you, Sir."

A boisterous voice came from within. "Captain Dan, send him in."

Captain Dan stepped past the clerk, "Thank you kindly," he went inside. "Hello good Master James. How are you faring? You look shipshape!"

"I'm faring very well, Dan, It's been a while. If I remember correctly I saw you last when you brought in the wrecking merchandise from the last ship that hit the rocks on up the Keys. That's been about five months ago. What can I do for you? How can I help you?"

"James, this is kind of an unusual request. I know that with the Navy around we shouldn't have to be arming ourselves. But we were followed out of Cuba. It may have been Cuban pirates. "Do you have any swivel guns? I want four, the grape and powder and what ever else I need."

"Good Grief, Man! Do you think that they may be lurking about?" James asked.

"Don't know. We may have lost them last night. But I'm going to be ready for them."

"Well, Dan, I've still got a few back in the warehouse. I'll clean them up and get you everything you need. If I've got them I'll also give you the chests to store them, the grape, and powder on deck."

"Thanks, James. My First Mate John can be found at the Key West Inn."

"Don't you worry, Dan. I'll take care of it for you. I pray you don't need to use them."

Captain Dan literally skipped the short distance to his home. As he was coming up the walk his two girls and wife Jenney Mae, were outside to greet him.

"Hello, Dear, we saw your boat come into the harbor this morning. The girls have been going up to the captain's walk a lot the last few days looking for you," she said as she embraced him.

"This is so lovely, Dear," the captain said as he put his arms out to hug the two girls who ran up to him.

The next morning came too soon.

"I'll be a week or two, Jenney May. We have to plant the six thousand pineapple slips. It will take about an acre of land. We've got it ready. Then we have to harvest the old field on Plantation Key and immediately transport the pineapples up the East Coast as far as New York. I will send word by my field manager Jonathan as to my schedule."

He said his goodbyes and hugs and went down the street. When he got to the dock one of his longboats was waiting for him.

"Good morning, John. You too, Benjamin and Roberts," the captain said.

John announced, "Cap'n we've got the swivel guns secured. It kind of feels like we're sailing a Man-of-War,"* he said jokingly,

"Sir. Benjamin and me'self went by Master James' warehouse after the evening meal, and he gave us the guns, shot, and powder. They was all loaded in chests. Right smartly, I must say. We stowed them on deck and I've took the liberty to get the swivel mounts installed. You know Matthew is the best carpenter we've got. He said he knows just where to place and mount them. He's working on it now, Sir," he said proudly.

"One more item Cap'n. Jonathan will show it to you as I row out," John stated. "Go to it, Benjamin."

"Well Captain Dan, this here is the best tool to use to plant those pineapple slips. It's a narrow bladed hoe.* We've bought four of them," he said as he showed one of them to Captain Dan.

"Why is it so short, Benjamin?" the Captain asked.

"Sir, it needs to be short. You use it with one hand and grab a slip with the other. We only have to dig down three and one half to four inches. Since the hoe's handle is twelve inches long, that is the distance between plantings. We don't have to measure. One other thing, we should use double rows, if you please. Two foot between rows and well-staged will yield the most for the space."

"Well done, men," the Captain said.

Captain Dan climbed up on the schooner's deck. He looked back at First Mate John and Benjamin and said, "Now, men, let's get this Man-of-War up to Key Largo."

On the way to Key Largo, the Captain and John looked over Matthew's work on the swivel gun mounts.

Matthew explained, "Sir, even though we have only four cannons, I've built six mount locations. These swivel guns are lightweight. They're only about seventy pounds apiece. Why, one man can pick 'em up, and place 'em from one side to other. Usually you're only fir'n off one side. I've placed mounts, port, and starboard in front, two midd'lin and two aft. I feel that it should do it"

"Looks good, Matthew. Thank ye kindly," the Captain said, "Now John, let's look in these chests and see those guns."

They opened a chest, "Capt'n I've already did some looking," John said. "Two are like this. But two are strange looking. See over here."

John opened the second chest, "Why, John," the captain said. "These two are breach* loaders. You take this breach block out of the trough at the back of the gun, then throw in this pre-measured bag of grape. Put this bag of gun power behind the balls and push the breach block forward and lock it in place, like this. You can fire this gun twice as fast as the other muzzle* loaders."

"Very good, Sir," John exclaimed.

"John, we'll wait till mid-morning. When we are away from any Key Wester's hearing, we'll have a class and then do some live firing. It looks like Master James got us up with plenty of powder and shot."

"Ok, men, listen up and pay attention. The Captain's going to give us a class on firing these here *'big guns'*," he said, kind of smiling. "Any one got any experience?"

"Yep. Simon and I were in the U S Navy," one of the men, Amos said. "We fired big bore guns, not those pop guns!"

"Well, Sir if it is ok with you," another man, Clyde spoke up, "Confederate Navy, out of Mobile."

Captain Dan stated, "It don't matter what navy you were in. You're manning the Jenney May now. We're all Americans! Now listen up. You three experienced men will command and fire the guns. The rest of you are co-loaders. That leaves me at the wheel and John running the ship's ropes. So let's go through the mounting process, loading, aiming, and firing. Now remember to look to me to fire all at once. Do your best. Man the guns on the sea side."

Captain yelled, "Fire!"...Blam! Blam! Blam! The smoke covered the deck on the starboard side.

Captain yelled again, "Reload!"… Fire!... Blam! Blam! Blam!

"OK, men," the captain yelled. "Swab them out, and when they are cool, real cool, we'll stow them back in their chests."

"There's the Key Largo harbor Capt'n," the First Mate announced, "I see the sloop, Sir."

As they sailed into the harbor and were lowering a longboat the wagon appeared on the beach. It pulled right up to the pier.

"Jonathan seen us, and come to give us a ride, Capt'n."

The Captain gave the order to drop the anchors, and load up. They pulled their longboat up to the small dock.

"Hello, Captain, good to see you. I trust your trip was favorable," Jonathan said with a welcome.

"Yes, Jonathan, we've got six thousand slips. We'll get a good rest, and see what we can do in the morning."

"Well, Sir, I think you will be pleased. The men have got the field cleared and ready to plant those slips," Jonathan said proudly.

"Very good, Jonathan. Let's get on to the plantation house. We're famished."

"The cook's working on it, Sir. Let's load up, men."

When you're tired and have a lot of work to do, the morning comes along very fast.

"Captain... Jonathan and I were talking," First Mate John said as they were finishing their breakfast, "We can cut our time in half. We can take

Benjamin and our crew and plant the slips up here in the new ground with those twelve inch hoes. While we're doing that, Jonathan can take the schooner after we unload the slips, and he and his crew can start cutting pineapples."

Jonathan added, "Sir, both crews should be finished in a couple of days."

"A great idea, men!" The captain paused thinking...then said, "We'll have to plan. Just as soon as the pineapples are put in the hold they will begin to ripen. We'll have to leave for the East Coast immediately! John make sure we have provisions for a week."

"Aye aye, Sir."

"Men, let's get going!" Captain Dan said enthusiastically.

As soon as the slips were unloaded, the boat crew started planting and the land crew went down to Plantation Key to harvest pineapples.

At the end of the second day, Captain Dan asked, "What do you think, John, we've about got it all planted."

"Yes, Sir. Benjamin has got a couple men on the last two rows. It's looking good. Here they come now, Sir. They're a tired looking crew."

Captain Dan stepped towards the men and waved. "Men, you've done real fine. Climb up on the wagon, and let's get back to the cabin. We'll clean up and eat. I hope the cook is ready!"

While eating, John said to the Captain, "The schooner should be arriving soon. Sir, do you want me to make the wagon ready?"

"Yes John, and tell you what. Have our boat crew get any belongings they may need. Tell them that we'll sleep on board this evening and leave at first light. I appreciate the fact that they have worked hard. But they know as well as I do we've got to move those pineapples to market."

"Aye aye, Sir! We'll be ready to leave on the half hour!"

The horse, wagon, and boat crew pulled up to the dock.

John said, "Look Sir, the schooner's already in, and there be the sloop coming through the channel."

One of the schooner's longboats was just pulling off. They could see Jonathan standing up in the boat. His men were dipping the oars. They guided up to the dock and tied up.

Jonathan said, "Hello, Captain, John. Hi, men." His men grabbed their duffels and headed towards the wagon.

"How's it look, Jonathan?" Dan said.

"Very fine, Sir. A right good-looking batch of pineapples," Jonathan exclaimed, "I do hope the cook has a bit of grub for us."

John said, "He's holding up for you. It was a real fine meal!"

"One thing, Captain. Did you and the crew just arrive? I mean did you have anyone up here before you just arrived on the wagon?"

"The reason I ask is as we were coming through the channel, Roberts there had his glass trained on the harbor and thought he saw two figures on the pier."

"That's right, Sir. Two of 'em, they was. You know I got a good glass. Just like I saw that sloop," Roberts piped in. "Beg your pardon, Sir."

"Thanks, Roberts," Captain Dan said, "Jonathan, as soon as Roberts gets his eating and cleaning done, bring him back. We're going to need him to go a'sailin' with us."

"Thank ye kindly, Sir," Roberts said with a grin.

"Jonathan, keep a sharp eye. We will too. Could be those pirates that followed us out of Cuba. I'll post a watch tonight. You do the same. After we leave make sure a couple of men are out here on the boats keeping a good lookout. Better arm them. Now we best get out to the boat, and you get your men up to the cook shack."

As the long boat pulled up to the schooner they hailed the sloops crew. They were heading towards the pier, a waiting wagon, and a well-deserved supper.

As they climbed on board they could smell the aroma of fresh fruit. It was a quiet night. The schooner rocked in gentle swells. Dan had the men take a ship's watch, two men every two hours. It was an uneventful night.

About five a. m., Captain Dan said to John, "How about we rustle the men out. Get the cook to making some coffee, and we'll get some wind in these here sails."

"We'll use the jib, foresail, and the mainsail through the channel. After we get out into the deep water then put them all on and we'll get to cracking!"

"Aye aye, Sir!" John acknowledged.

It was about an hour into their trip, "Sail, Sir!" Roberts hollered down from the perch on the main mast. "She's up ahead. Just came out of the harbor on portside. There's another, it's smaller. If I'm not mistaken, Sir, the larger one is the same Cuban sloop."

They could see the two white triangles in contrast to the green palms in their rear on the shore.

"Looks like they are aiming to head us off. Planning to cross our bow, Sir," John said.

"John, put everything we got up, the forestay sail and gaff, top and main. We'll try to outrun them."

"Everything is up and out, Sir."

"Make sure all the lines are taunt. We'll need all we can get. Now I want the two breach-loading swivel guns at the two bow positions. Preload them and keep them out of sight in the chests."

"Sir," Roberts pointed out, "See the smallest sloop has crossed our stern. They're trying to come at us from both sides. She's much smaller and slower."

John said, "Look, Captain, the big sloop on the land side is using their square rigging top side. She's pretty fast."

Cuban pirate ship:

"Captain Gomez, she's fast!" Carlos pointed out.

"Don't you worry. We've got 'em. Have the men stand by the four pounder on starboard side. Now get those ropes tightened on the jib! And be quick about it!"

They were converging on a point just forward of the schooner.

"Look Captain Dan. They're flying the skull and crossbones!" John said as he pointed.

"Hold her steady, John," Dan said.

"Fire!...Blam! The pirate's four pounder released its cannon ball in a shower of sparks, flame, and smoke. It plunked into the water just forward of the Jenney Mae.

Captain Dan ordered, "John, put the two men and loaders forward. Tell them no swivel guns in view and no mounting until I give the order. Just as soon as they're in place start to bring our flag down,* so they'll think we're heaving to."*

The two boats were both racing along parallel to each other at nine knots, both at full sails. The pirate sloop eased closer.

The pirate captain, Gomez, cupped his hands. "Heave to! Or we'll blow you out of the water!"

At that point Captain Dan spun the wheel, and the schooner leaned far out to starboard, and then straightened up, heading right towards the pirate ship, aiming mid-ships.

"Men, swivel guns up and fire all you can!" Captain Dan ordered.

The pirates were taken by surprise. The two bow swivel guns of the Jenney Mae fired. Blam! Blam! Grapeshot bounced and raced across the deck of the pirate sloop. Blam! Blam! More grape. The pirate gunners ducked down forgetting to fire. They were just trying to save their skins.

"Fire! Fire you swabs!" was the last thing Captain Gomez ordered as the Jenney May hit the pirate sloop, not straight because at the last minute Captain Dan turned the wheel to glance at a slight angle.

"Hold on, men! Cease fire!" Dan yelled.

The Jenney May came to a sudden crashing stop as it slammed into the sloop and rode up on it. The pirate sloop tipped way up as the hit side dipped down into the sea, water racing over the gunnels.

The Jenney May slid back. It was now at an angle to the sloop. Her men picked themselves up from the jolt and started working the sails' ropes. She pulled away as the sails filled. The pirate sloop was upright but dangerously low in the water. The pirates could be seen swimming or hanging on to parts of their ship. As the Jenney May pulled away, the smaller sloop gave up the chase and was last seen pulling up to the sinking sister ship.

The sails were billowing out, and the Jenney May was moving at a fair pace. All that could be seen behind them were the triangles from the smaller pirate sloop.

"John," Captain Dan called, "Let's get a damage report. Where's the carpenter, Matthew? Are we taking in any water?"

"Needn't worry Capt'n. Matthew's already down below. Benjamin is with him," John answered.

The two men came up from below. "Sir, one plank had some separation. We plugged the leak. She's a tough lady! Now if you wish we'll take a look up front." Both Dan and John nodded.

"Take the wheel, John," Dan said, "I'm going up front to see what they find."

As the captain came up, Benjamin was hanging over the bow looking down, Matthew holding on to him.

"What's it look like men?'

Matthew pulled Benjamin up, and said, "Sir, the bowspirit has a nasty crack and the support ropes of the foremast and jib sails are about gone. If you please Sir, we'll splint the cracked bowspirit and then replace the bad sections of rope."

Benjamin piped in, "Sir, if we could slow down to about three knots, we'll get that bowspirit spliced and wrapped. Then if we can go dead in the water for about an hour, together with all the men we can get those support ropes fixed."

"Very good, men, we'll do it. Carry on!"

"John, we're going to ease down to three knots while the men splint the spirit. Then we'll go dead in the water while all hands get our mast support and sail ropes repaired."

"Aye aye, Sir!"

John didn't even have to issue the orders. The men, upon hearing the captain's information being passed on, set to work trimming the sails. Matthew found a piece of splicing wood which is kept on all boats for such an emergency. Benjamin, Matthew, Roberts, and one other of the men laid the eight-foot piece of wood across the crack and parallel to the bowspirit as it jutted out in front of the ship. Then they took wet rope and lashed and wrapped it evenly around the bowspirit and the wood they were using for a splice, stretching the rope as they went.

They waved to John who then commanded the men to drop sails so the schooner would go dead in the water. This took the stress off all of the ropes that supported the masts. These ropes ran from the top of the foremast, holding the two jib sails down to the bow spirit, and then down to the bow of the ship where they were attached at the waterline.

All of the men then commenced splicing the now slack ropes. They had rigged up a kind of a breeches buoy.* It was hanging from the bowspirit over the water so a man could sit in it and work on the ropes where they attached near the waterline.

It had taken only a couple of hours for all of the repairs, and Matthew gave John the high sign. The men scurried about, sails went up, ropes were tightened, and the wind took over. The Jenney May was doing what she did best...flying in the wind!

"Sir, in thirty miles we'll be turning north and heading up the coast of the Florida mainland," John stated.

"Good work, John. I'm going below to my cabin, and look over the charts. We'll start an every four hours shift. See to the men's schedule."

Aye aye, Sir," John touched his forehead.

Four hours later the captain came up. "Has the cook got the men's food, John?"

"Yes Sir, here'e comes now with some coffee." John pointed, "Well, Sir, we left Hawk Channel and the Keys three hours ago. We're on a northwest bearing. Should sight St. Augustine by morning."

"Very good, John. We'll keep it up...as fast as the wind, sails and Jenney May will take us. Got to get these pineapples to market."

They were in the Atlantic, keeping the coast in sight but out where the land swells didn't affect the water.

Morning...

"There's Augustine, Sir, off the port bow."

"Thank ye kindly, John. We've been at it for a day and a half. What I want to do is bear slightly east of north. We'll be out of sight of land for a time, but should be back along the coast by this time tomorrow."

There were very few large cities or towns along the Georgia coast. If you were in close you might see an occasional small harbor with a few cabins and some fishing boats. But the main places of civilization were St. Augustine, Florida; Savanna, Georgia; and then Charleston, South Carolina.

Twenty four hours later they sited Charleston off the port bow on the distance shore. The bright early morning sun was just rising up out of the calm Atlantic.

Captain Dan was suddenly awakened by a strange inaction. There was no movement. He got up slipped on his boots and went topside. The sails were only slightly flapping...the schooner was dead in the water. The waves were heading in towards the shore. The boat was gently rocking to and fro.

"What's happening, John?"

"Don't know, Sir. We're going along at right smart pace, a sudden gust of wind hit, and then bam! No wind...no nothing!"

"John, let's fool around with the sails a bit. See if we can catch any breeze."

Nothing happened.

"John, we had better lower a quarter-boat. We'll put all six men in it. Put out a rope, and we'll try to take her in to Charleston.

"Aye aye, Sir."

"Well Sir, the men's rowing and the swells have brought us into the harbor. Look Capt'n, no ships moving about. The good news is the tide is beginning to turn, and it's heading in, helping us."

"John, bring the men in. Rest them, feed 'em and then we'll continue to tow the Jenney May into the harbor and anchor. Also, John, send me our Confederate Navy man. I think we may need to sell these pineapples in Charleston, and I'm going to need his southern accent. They are probably still fighting the Civil War here!"

They rowed and towed the Jenney May into the Charleston harbor and dropped anchor just a little bit past Fort Sumter and just out from the docks. An American flag was proudly flying from the fort's ramparts.

"You wanted to see me, Sir," the Confederate Navy Man reported to the Captain.

"Yes, Clyde. As you know we've no wind. Now we can't be stuck here any time. Our pineapples will spoil. We're going to town, and try to sell 'em to a broker in yon warehouse. What is needed is for you to kind of take the lead, and do the introductions. Might be your southern accent will soften things."

"I'll do my best, Sir."

"Thank ye kindly, Clyde. Change into your best, and four of us will take a quarter-boat in."

"John, if the quarter-boat's ready, then you, Clyde, Benjamin, and I will go on in, and see if we can dispose of this cargo."

"Yes Sir, very good, Sir," John replied.

They pulled up to the dock, tied up, and climbed out. There was a ship being loaded with pine timbers. A few loiterers about, (more-than-likely) looking for work.

A man came up, "Help you-all, Sirs?"

Clyde looked at Dan, and Dan nodded, "Yes, Sar. Can you-all direct us to the port war...house manager?"

"That a...would be Colonel Daw...son, Sar. That door in yon war...house there," as he pointed.

The four men walked up to and stopped in front of the door. A sign above read: "Charleston Port Sales."

Clyde knocked. "Come in."

Clyde opened the door, and they all filed in.

"May I help you-all, Sirs?" a clerk asked.

He was standing at a ledger desk facing them.

Clyde responded, "We just pulled into the harbor. We-uns are looking for Colonel Daw...son."

"Just one second, Sar. I'll ask if he can see you-all."

He knocked on a door on the opposite side of the room and went inside.

"Send them in," they could hear someone say.

The clerk came out, pointing into the room. "Colonel Daw...son can see you-all. Right this way, gentlemen."

The four men went into the office. "Gentlemen, what can I do for you-all?" Colonel Dawson said with a flourish.

Clyde responded. It appeared he was beginning to enjoy his job and position. "Colonel Daw..son, Sar! May I introduce Captain Dan Benson, First Mate John, Benjamin, and myself, Clyde, of the good ship Jenney May out of Key West. Now sitting in you-all's fine harbor."

They all shook hands with the Colonel and then Captain Dan started, "Colonel Dawson, our ship the Jenney May has a full hold of six thousand fantastic South Florida, Key Largo pineapples. We were on our way up the coast to market them. Of course the lack of a suitable breeze has brought us to your fine shore. We would like to strike a deal for you to purchase our cargo."

The Colonel responded, "Gentlemen, I got word of your arrival. Of course I didn't know what your cargo was. Well, fine sirs, let me explain about our condition here in Charleston. As you may know, we're still trying to recover and rebuild from the great war. In fact, Sherman came through here and thoroughly devastated us. As you look around I'm sure you can verify that. So, we're not very financially secure. The best I could do gentlemen is thirty cents on the dollar."

Captain Dan spoke up, "Well it certainly is something we should consider since we are stuck in this port."

"Gentlemen, I know you started off this discussion by using this fine southern gentleman from Mobile. I know the accent. Tell you what, on his accord, I will add an extra five cents. So, gentlemen, thirty five cents on the dollar is my best and final offer. That is depending upon inspection, quantity, and condition of your pineapples. If it is agreed upon, by day after tomorrow, Charleston, Savanna and every community tween will be eating your great fruit!"

Captain Dan said, "It's a deal. Sir, you have just bought yourself six thousand pineapples."

They all shook hands and the Colonel said, "I'll have my clerk draw up the agreement. If your men will help, we will get them off your schooner and onto the dock. We'll tally up, and I'll have you-all a draft on the bank of Charleston."

The pineapples came off the Jenney May unusually fast. The Colonel put his men and extra labors to work. The quarter and longboats were coming and going. Wagons pulled up to the dock, and the pineapples were on their way as fast as they were loaded in the wagons.

Captain Dan and John came out of the Bank of Charleston. "John, two thousand one hundred dollars isn't close to six thousand, but it's much better than a boat load of rotten pineapples! I think the Good Lord has been sailing with us. Tell you what, since "Mobile Clyde" got us an extra five cents on the dollar, I'm going to give each man a bonus of twenty dollars and tomorrow in Charleston."

"And a day to recuperate," John put in.

OK, John, dole out the bonuses, and tell them when they get the hold cleaned out, they have leave. But we're going just as soon as we get the wind.

"Aye aye, Sir!" John said enthusiastically.

"John, tell them to stay out of trouble. Don't want another Civil War started or have to bail them out of some Charleston jail!"

"You got that, Sir," John responded.

The third evening in Charleston harbor…The Jenney May was barely rocking to and fro floating on a calm sea. First Mate John was pulling watch topside. Captain Dan was sleeping in his cabin. He was more than likely dreaming about being home in Key West. Suddenly Dan sat upright in his bunk. The ship was rocking hard. He jumped up and slipped on his boots. Just then there was a hurried knocking on the door to his cabin, "Captain! Captain Dan! It's the wind!"

Captain Dan threw open his door, "What's it like, John? Let's go, and take a look."

They both went up top. The sails were moving about as the wind whistled through the rigging.

"It looks and sounds like a steady blow, John. It will be dawn in a couple of hours. If we don't start to see men by an hour later, we'll go-a-look'en."

"Aye, Sir."

The sun was trying to break through a mass of fast-moving, low-hanging clouds.

"Looks like I see the quarter-boat leaving the dock, Capt'n," John proclaimed.

"How many men we got, John?" the Captain asked.

John was looking through his glass, "I count six, Sir. No wait. There's a couple of heaps in the stern. If those two piles are men, we may have all eight!"

"I had better get the coffee started, seeing the cook was out with them. Hope he don't mind me messing with his gear. We'll go easy on them, John. They're a good crew," the Captain said as he stoked the fire for the coffee.

The entire complement of eight men appeared on deck, a couple being held up by the others. The cook saluted and headed straight for his area. He could be heard in the background, something about people messing around with his utensils.

John said, "Welcome aboard, men. I trust you-all have had a fine visit to the more historic and educational parts of Charleston. We will be getting under way soon! As you can see we have a fine breeze. Get yourselves shipshape either with food or lots of coffee. Or whatever suits your physical needs or disposition. I need men on the ropes and sails in thirty minutes! That is all!"

The Jenney May weighed anchor. Her sails caught the wind, and she pointed her bow out to sea. Her stern waved goodbye to Charleston as she picked up speed. Other boats throughout the harbor were following the Jenney May's example.

"Head for home, John," the captain said.

"Aye aye, Sir."

All day and night they continued along at a steady pace. The wind was strong, and so was the sea.

Early morning the third day…

"Sir we're making good time, but I don't like the look of the sunrise or of the clouds up ahead," John stated.

"I've been noticing that, John. I think we've got a blow a'coming."

That afternoon…

"We'll be off Miami shortly, but we won't be able to see a thing. It's

The Jenney May leaving Charleston and heading back to the Keys.

getting dark, and we're fighting the waves," John commented.

"It's a storm for sure, John. I checked the barometer. It's dropping."

"I've had the men batten down the hatches." John said, just as the first rain drops were flung into his face.

A few minutes later the rain was pelting them hard. Then it was hail, bouncing loud and fast off all parts of the boat and covering all parts of the deck making it hard for the men to work. Then as suddenly as it started, it stopped.

"Quick, men drop the jib sails!" the captain commanded.

It was dark as night and twelve noon! The waves were crashing over the sides and onto the deck. The Jenney May was rising high up on one wave and plunging down into the trough of another.

John yelled, "Roberts, help me hold the wheel!"

Captain Dan was down below with the charts plotting a course because they were making the turn into the Hawk Channel approaching the Keys. They needed to keep moving but they must avoid the shoals and the reefs.

Captain Dan struggled up to topside. The ship was careening at all angles. He grabbed a safety line and worked his way to the wheel.

Cupping his hands, he yelled, "Due South men. Just as soon as we see the Cape Florida Light on the starboard. Then we continue to pray the lightship Florida is still at her moorings at Carysfort Reef, and the light is on. If it is we can be sure we'll keep off it."

"She is dying down some, Sir!" Roberts reported.

The wind was slowing.

There's Cape Florida light!" John pointed forward off the starboard side.

"Where, John? I don't see it," the captain questioned.

"It was just a flash through the rain." John answered.

Just then a lookout posted on the bow sang out, "Light on the starboard!"

The waves cut back a bit, but the Jenney May was still jumping like a hooked fish.

"Thank the Good Lord," the captain exclaimed, "Ok, men, keep our bearings due south and have that man up front continue looking for the next light."

The storm had abated somewhat. It could now be called a squall. Winds were gusting at sixty miles per hour, with rain continuing to pelt the ship and men. The waves were still ferocious, only the Jenney May didn't have to climb mountains of water higher than herself.

Carysfort light dead ahead!” the lookout cried out from the bow.

“John!” Captain Dan called, “Ease to port! We're heading straight for the reef!”

“That should do it, Capt’n. I can see the waves hitting it.”

“Wreck ashore!” came the call from the bow lookout. “She’s on the rocks at the far end of the reef!”

John said, “Capt’n she’s a three master. We goin’ into action?”

“You bet, John! Tak’er just past the reef. Get as close as you can, but see that we don’t get pushed into the rocks. Then we’ll drop our two anchors.”

“The wind has slowed some, but it’s still dangerous! The tide’s running in, and that should help us.” The captain added.

They went in just past the three-masted cargo sailing ship. She was definitely up on the rocks but still floating. They then carefully eased closer and dropped their two anchors, front and rear. By letting out anchor chain they got even closer to the flailing ship. The wind, waves and tide kept them in the position they wanted to be in.

“I need one quarter-boat made ready. Launch on the lee side* of our boat. Five men for rowers, I’m the sixth. John, when you see us coming back, if I give the high sign prepare to launch the other quarter-boat. We’ll need one of the extra anchors and chain. We’ll drop it out against the wind in front of the wreck.”

“Aye, Sir!”

“Push off, men. We’ll get close,” The captain commanded just as soon as he stepped into the long boat.

It was hard rowing in the running seas and wind. As they got close, Dan could see some men lining the rail. There was also an older man with his long white beard blowing in the wind.

“That must be the captain,” Dan exclaimed, “Bring me in close.”

Dan half stood up and hollered, “Dan Benson, licensed Key West wrecker of the schooner Jenney May. Do you accept assistance?”

“Ahoy, Dan Benson. Captain James of the ship Victoria. Yes, we need help.”

Cupping his hands Dan yelled, “We’re going to come back with an anchor. Prepare a hawser* from your capstan* for our anchor. We want to stop you from going any further on the rocks. All right men, pull back to the Jenney. I’ll give John the sign. I need two volunteers to help John with the anchor,” as all hands went up. “Thanks, men. Just two, Roberts and Clyde. The rest of us will prepare to go back with the tools loaded.”

As they pulled up to the Jenney May they could see John and his men had the other quarter-boat ready to launch. A huge extra anchor was draped over the stern of the quarter-boat. As they got close, John's men lowered the second quarter-boat. Both Clyde and Roberts jumped in it. Dan's men tied their boat tight to the Jenney May and climbed aboard. John was the last to go over the side.

Just before they pulled away John said, "Capt'n, I just saw our sloop leaving Key Largo. Jonathan must have spotted us and the wreck!"

"Good, We'll need him. John, swing in to the wreck. Captain James is

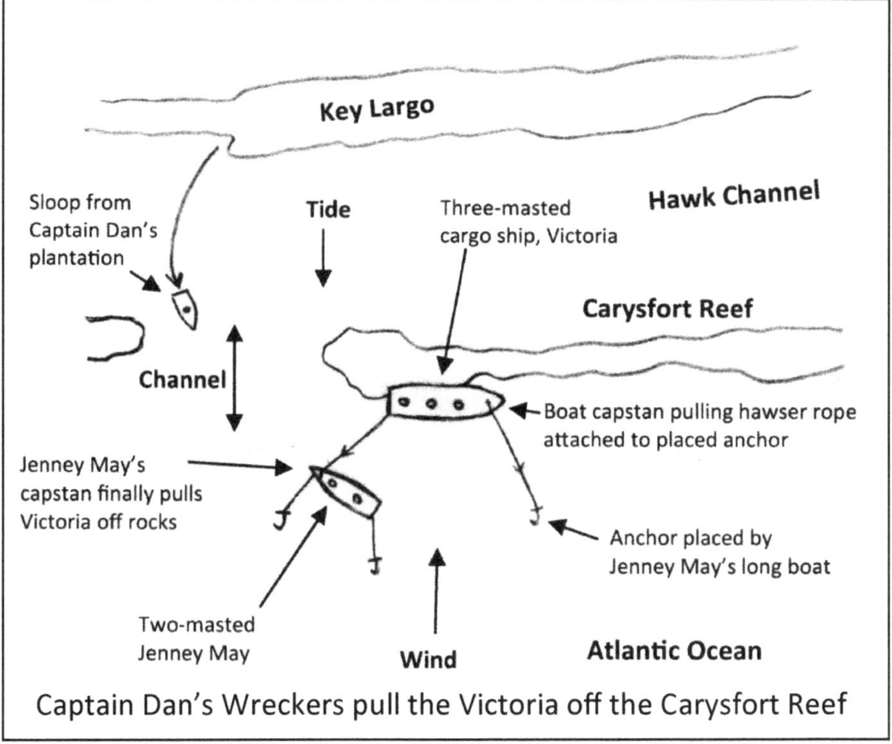

Captain Dan's Wreckers pull the Victoria off the Carysfort Reef

going to have you a hawser line to attach to our anchor. When you get that anchor dropped, pull back to the wreck. I'll come in with the sloop."

John's Aye! Aye! blew away with the wind and spray. Before he could grab a seat, the five men, not waiting for a command, dug in their oars.

"Ahoy! Jenney May!" It was Jonathan with the sloop.

"Come around lee side, Jonathan," Dan yelled as he motioned.

The sloop came around the Jenney May right up to the quarter boat.

"You two men stay and prepare for cargo coming aboard." Captain Dan said to the men from the long boat. "Lets get in the sloop Benjamin."

They jumped up and climbed into the sloop.

"Good to see you and the men, Jonathan. You ready to go over to the wreck and pick up some cargo?"

"Ready, Sir. We've been watching. Saw the ship go aground, but couldn't get out. The weather was too bad. Finally got out as you came up."

"Jonathan, I figure we'll relay, fill you up two or three times and bring it over to the Jenney May. Then we'll both go in to the dock to off load, and come right back."

"I've got the bumpers on the sides, Sir. Figure they may cushion the bumps and grinds," Jonathan said.

All this was being discussed as Jonathan skillfully maneuvered the sloop right up close to the wreck.

"Anchor's out, Sir!" One of Jonathan's men called out.

"Thank you, Smith," Jonathan acknowledged.

John's quarter-boat came up alongside the sloop. "Jump in, men, and we'll take you up to the wreck," John yelled.

They all climbed out of the lashed and pitching quarter-boat up onto the Victoria.

Captain James and his crewmen were right there helping the Jenney May's seamen on board.

"Glad for your assistance, Captain Dan," he said as he extended his hand, "We're ready to tighten up the hawser to your anchor. It would help if we had all hands."

"Ok, men, follow Captain James to the capstan. Everyone grab a bar," Captain Dan commanded.

There were ten capstan bars nine foot in length. Two men got on each bar. The hawser rope went out the front side of the Victoria and to the anchor John had deployed.

"John, do the honors," Dan said.

"All right, men, Heave ho! We're going to go!"

All of the men at the sound of "Heave" pushed hard. In the base of the capstan were notches, and the pawls dropped into notches so the capstan wouldn't unwind. It turned easy at first, then the rope tightened on the anchor. It loosened suddenly. The anchor must have slipped. But then it dug in.

"Heave! Ho! Heave Ho!" John sang as the men strained.

Then the boat moved slightly...then a lot, then no more.

"That's it!" John said, "We need to lighten her."

Captain James said, "You men did good! You ready for some cargo transfer, Captain Dan? We've got the hold hatches open and the winch ready."

"Jonathan, take your men and bring up the sloop. We'll lash her to the Victoria and offload cargo. Just one second. Captain James, do you have any passengers who have to leave?"

"Sir, please take my daughter and her cousin."

"They will be safe on the Jenney May, Captain James."
Captain Dan said, "John, take a couple of men and the quarter-boat, and transfer the two ladies to the Jenney May. Make sure they are safe and comfortable. Return just as soon as you can."

"Aye aye, Sir."

"Captain James, what are you carrying, Sir?" Captain Dan asked.

"Well, Sir we have a lot of foodstuffs. Bottles and cans. We were going to New Orleans, out of New York."

"Good, that stuff is heavy, the water won't hurt it. If we could get two or three loads on the sloop, then loaded on the schooner, possibly at high tide we might be able to float and pull 'er off," Captain Dan suggested.

They worked hard and way into the night. The seas became just rough, and the wind steadied, a far cry from the height of the storm.

It was a weary Captain Dan talking to a very tired Captain James. "We've got the sloop and the schooner loaded. Let the men rest and eat. The tide will be ready to turn in a couple of hours, then we'll man the capstan again."

"Sounds like a reasonable idea, Sir," Captain James agreed.

Both captains said to a rugged worn out group, "Get some rest, men. We'll try the capstan at high tide in two hours."

It was very early morning. There was a faint crack of light showing in the eastern horizon.

John shook Captain Dan. "Tide's just stopped, Sir. It'll be turning soon."

"Thank ye kindly, John," he answered.

They all had slept on the upper deck under oil cloths,* no one wanting to venture below decks, the ship being in such a precarious position. Their earlier work on the capstan had pulled the ship slightly off the rocks. The wind, rain, and waves were now being merciful so they could put their attention to the work at hand.

Both the sloop and the schooner were still in their places. Dan had thought it best to have them available in case of an emergency.

Captain James came up to Captain Dan with two cups of coffee, "Our cook has performed a miracle! Here's some coffee, Dan."

"I'll take it, in fact, need it!" Dan exclaimed, "Let's get to it!" Dan commanded his men, "Let's get this capstan turning!"

The men from both boats took up their positions on the capstan. John took up the cadence, "Heave Ho!...Heave Ho! This ships go'n to go!"

The tide had turned and was pushing against the waves and the Victoria. The hawser rope took up its slack. The pawl clicked as the men pushed to John's cadence, slowly reeling in. The boat suddenly lurched and then settled.

"I've got an idea, Captain James," Dan said. "I'm going to take my men over to the Jenney May. We'll take another hawser with us from your stern. We'll then try to winch your stern some with the Jenney May's hawser."

"Sounds good. Whatever you say, Captain Dan," Captain James acknowledged.

"You men," Captain James signaled as he pointed, "Lets' get a hawser long enough to get over to the schooner. Let 'er out the stern to the quarter boat."

With the seas subsiding and the tide running out, the quarter-boat was quickly at the Jenney May. They tied the anchor chain off and freed up their capstan. Captain Dan only had eight men to turn his capstan. However his unit had longer bars and was geared much lower. Eight men, eight long bars. Click...Clack...the pawl went as it took up the slack and the rope tightened. Then it suddenly became easy.

"She's broke free!" John yelled, "Take up the slack, men. It'll move the Victoria away from the rocks."

"Four men remain here. Get the ship ready to sail. Benjamin, John, Roberts and Clyde, let's get the quarter-boat back to the Victoria," Dan commanded.

"Well all we need fixed now is to get our rudder repaired," Captain James stated. "Got any divers?"

"Strange you should ask, Captain James. Meet Benjamin, one of the best Bahamian divers in these here waters," Captain Dan said proudly.

"You build me up too much, Sir," Benjamin said.

"Benjamin, you will have your chance to prove it! Let's go to the

Stern," the captain commanded.

They looked over the rail. The seas were now long swells going inland fighting the outrunning tide.

"I think something has come loose on the outside. We'll check everything below as we're heading towards the reef. The good news is we're manning the pumps, and we don't have very much water in the bilge."

"I'm going to need to dive off the quarter-boat, Capt'n Dan," Benjamin said.

"You've got whatever you need, if we got it," Dan exclaimed "John take whatever men you need to go with Benjamin."

"Here John take these chain, bolts, wrenches, master link, and a safety rope," Captain James handed over the parts to John.

"Thank you, Sir," John said, "I need a couple more men to hold her steady."

Jonathan pointed, and a couple of the sloop's men went with John. They maneuvered the quarter-boat close to the stern of the Victoria, dropped anchors, and that together with the rowers kept her steady.

Benjamin stripped down, and overboard he went. He swam to the lee side of the Victoria, took a good breath and dived. He couldn't see any farther than his hands, the storm had so stirred up the water. He found the rudder, felt around, needed some air, and went shooting back up to the surface. He saw that the quarter-boat had maneuvered close to where he had dived down. They were expert rowers and seamen. This was perfect. He grabbed on the gunnels and breathed hard. They were watching him. No one said anything. They knew he was catching his breath. He took another deep breath and went back down. This time he knew just where the rudder was. He felt and then, that was it! A chain was hanging loose. It was one of the control chains that connected to the rudder. He felt around and found where it had broken off.

Back up he went. The boat was still there, the men holding it steady. This time he said, "I need that safety link. I think I got it!"

John said, "She snaps in like this. No bolt needed."

Down he went. He found the chain and where it went on the rudder. He forced himself to stay down, put his face right next to the rudder, opened his eyes, and snapped the safety link into both the chain and rudder. He immediately pushed off and up, his lungs pounding in his chest. He shot up and broke the surface. John and Clyde grabbed him and pulled him into the quarter-boat.

They came back around to where the sloop was lashed to the Victoria.

They gave a wave to both Captains.

Captain James was smiling, "It worked! The wheel works!"

He turned to Captain Dan, "If your two boats with the cargo can follow me to Key West, we'll settle up. The Wrecking Court will be awarding you charges. We won't be contesting, and we shouldn't be held up very long."

Captain Dan said, "Sounds good, Captain James. We're with you, and we'll make sure you get in safely. It's been good working with you. Take her into the wind, and we'll be following. I'm going to put the sloop out front."

"That's a pleasant sight, John. Key West harbor," Captain Dan exclaimed.

They pulled into the harbor and dropped anchor. Three quarter boats converged at the dock, one from each boat. Captain Dan had the pleasure to convey the two ladies back to Captain James.

"How did you two ladies fare?" Captain James asked.

"The Jenney May is a pleasant ship, Daddy."

"Well, Captain Dan, I'm going to get these ladies checked into some lodgings. I'll meet you at the Wrecker's Court in one hour."

"If you could make that three hours, I've got to check in first with my family," Captain Dan said.

Dan turned to John, "John, if you would, please see that the Wrecker's Court people are getting along with the inventory and then see that the men are fed and rested. I am going to run on home and will return in three hours.'

"Aye aye, Sir," John answered.

This was the first time that he could remember, but Captain Dan was so worn out that he hailed a buggy.

"Hi Sam," Dan said to the driver, "you know where I'm heading."

"Yes, Sir! We're on our way," the driver said as he snapped his buggy whip in the air over his horse's head.

Crack! "Now get along, Betsey!"

"Hope you had a good sail'n Mister Dan."

"Sure did. Thank you, Sam."

"Well here you is, Mister Dan."

"Thank ye kindly, Sam."

As he turned to go up the stairs to his house both of his girls ran down the steps and grabbed him with big hugs. As they let go, his wife Jenney May came up and greeted him with a kiss.

"We've been missing you, dear. How was your trip?" she asked.

"Well, Honey, except for a pirate attack, no wind, dealing with the Confederate South, a hurricane and then getting a wrecked three-master off the reef… just normal," Dan said with a smile.

A. M. Adams two-masted turtle schooner in the Key West docks.

11

The Cayman Turtle Schooner

In this story, the first two watercolors and sketch are of the A. M. Adams Turtle Schooner. I was privileged to be able to see, sketch, and watercolor this boat as it was docked at the Key West Turtle Crawls in May of 1969. This was to be only a few years from environmental laws being passed to prohibit the trading of green sea turtles. These laws naturally finished the turtle food business for the A. M. Adams, Thompson Enterprises, and Key West.

The A. M. Adams was a two-masted turtle schooner. She was commissioned by Norberg Thompson of Thompson Enterprises, Key West, Florida, and built in 1936 by the James Arch and Son's Ship Yard in Georgetown, Grand Cayman. The Adams was one hundred and thirty feet long, with Cayman mahogany frames and Florida long-leaf yellow pine heartwood planking over these frames.

In the two watercolors, the Adams heyday is past. Its once proud sailing history is now left with reduced height masts, minimum sail surface, and the primary power of a diesel engine. The A. M. Adams has been lost to history. It was last seen on the Maroni River in French Guiana in the 1970's.*

The following story is fictional. It is not about the A. M. Adams. Any resemblance to any person or a particular place is coincidental. Some history of turtle fishing is brought into this story. You will learn about the green turtle habits and lifestyle, the building of a dugout canoe, a Cayman lightweight turtle boat and the proud sailing of a Caribbean schooner. (History, and topography of the Cayman Islands)*

Genesis 1:1 "In the beginning God created the heaven and the earth. Now the earth was formless and empty, darkness was over the surface of the deep."

Genesis 1: 9 "And God said, "Let the water under the sky be gathered to one place, and let dry ground appear…""

Suddenly the earth began to shudder. Huge plates of solid rock cracked and moved, sliding across one and another in an east-west line. A huge trench dropped down, and at the same time a mass rose above the water forming today's Cuban Sierra Maestro mountain range. Some earth

A. M. Adams, two-masted turtle schooner in the Key West docks flying both the Cayman Islands and U. S. flags.

between the oceans could not reach above the waters. However, one hundred and fifty miles south of what is today known as Cuba and one hundred and eighty miles west-northwest of today's Jamaica three small rocky tips appeared up out of the watery void.

The largest and furthest west was twenty-two miles long and four miles wide. Seventy-five miles to the east, the middle and tallest was twelve miles long, one to two miles wide, and one hundred and forty four feet high. Five miles farther east was the smallest, at ten miles long and one mile wide.

Today these are Grand Cayman, Cayman Brak, and Little Cayman consecutively. They are composed of two limestone formations, the core of bluff limestone and the surface of a younger porous formation.

Because the surface is so porous there are no rivers or streams, and consequently no runoff to cloud the surrounding sea. This leaves a dynamic visibility. These islands have sandy beaches, cliffs, caves, hardwood forests, lagoons, bays, ponds, and mangrove swamps and are surrounded by coral reefs. Past these reefs the bottom drops off for thousands of feet!

Genesis 1:10 "...and God saw that it was good."

Ship's record: May 10, 1503*
    "Believe storm has pushed us westerly off course.
    We are in the central Caribbean.
    Sighted two very small islands full of
    Tortoises as was the sea around them."

This was Christopher Columbus' last and fourth voyage to the Americas. He was heading back to Spain in his two small ships and was blown off course. He marked his map with two islands which today are the Lesser Caymans. He called them "Las Tortugas," The Turtles.

Ship's log: 1586, May, the fifth:*
    Back to sea after successful sacking of Cartagena
    and Santo Domingo. Getting low on fresh food
    and water. Keeping a lookout for islands or major land.

A knock on his cabin door. "Sir! Sir Francis."
He opens it. The excited first mate. "Sir, we've just sighted land. Possibly two islands."

"I'll be right up."

This was Sir Francis Drake, an explorer and military marine captain, famous for sailing around the globe. In this particular expedition he was in charge of a large fleet of 23 English ships. They had left England in 1585. Their mission from Queen Elizabeth the Second was to harass and plunder the Spanish in the West Indies. (Caribbean)

Ships Log: 1586, May, the Sixth
    Sighted two islands. Dropped anchor and went ashore.
    These may be the Caymans or as some are known, the
    "Las Tortugas."
    Found much food of both species. The tortoise and the
    the Spanish name, Caimans. We call Alligartas.*
    We used both for nourishment.

Even though Columbus named these three islands "Las Tortugas" in 1503, by 1580 they were appearing on maps as Cayman Magnus, (Grand Cayman today) and, Caymanes (Lesser Caymans).

Over the years these islands became a place for ships to stop to get water from the few wells, obtain fresh turtle, crocodile and alligator meat, and careen* their boats.

It is thought the first inhabitants, two Welshmen named Bodden and Walters arrived sometime in 1658. They may have come from Jamaica after serving in the English army of Oliver Cromwell. Effectively the Caymans were under the control of Jamaica after Cromwell captured Jamaica from the Spanish in 1655. By 1670 they were officially recognized even by Spain as British. Visitors to the islands came and went, and the islands slowly acquired settlers.

It is early morning, the first of the month of June, 1856. Long ocean swells are reflecting the light from a huge full circle of the moon. Lying on top of one of those swells is a shape. It is a dark teardrop shape with some reflection from the sheen of water glistening from its top.

This shape will float there for some time and then disappear under with slight splashes from its two front flippers that it uses like paddles. Then it will rise again a little further in. This large female green sea turtle is returning to the same island and the same beach she was born on. It was also the same beach on the same island her mother was born on. She is repeating the eternal life cycle. She has been carrying these eggs the last couple of weeks, and it is time to bring them to this beach.

Her destination is the middle island in the Cayman Chain, Cayman Brac. She floats in on a swell that suddenly turns into a huge breaker. It pushes her up on a smooth sandy beach, and she momentarily pauses as the water rushes back to its source, pulling hard against her. The water attempts to force, but can't budge the two hundred and fifty pound, three and one half foot long turtle lying in the fast firming up sand. As the water returns to the sea, she continues on with her mission.

Moving ever so slowly, the turtle literally inches herself along, pulling

Female green turtle returning to the sea after laying her eggs.

with her front and rear flippers and moving from six to twelve inches at each pull. Moving up the beach, her goal is the sand above the high tide line. When she arrives at a place that is to her liking, she digs a body hole by rotating her body as she moves sand with the four flippers. Many times this is very near the exact location where she herself was born. Next with her rear flippers she excavates another hole about twelve inches deep down in the original body hole.

Between seventy-five and one hundred and eighty eggs are laid. These eggs are round, soft, and white. Because they are soft they don't break as they drop out. Then the sea turtle uses her rear flippers to cover the eggs. Finally she packs the sand down over the eggs and fills the large body hole. A throwing of sand all over camouflages the nest. This all takes about one to two hours to complete. Then she begins the reach-pull, reach-pull, slow process of returning to the sea.

Her eggs are now going to lie there and incubate about sixty days. They will make it to hatching if predators don't discover them. Another factor is also at work. If the sand becomes very hot the nest will produce more females than males.

For our story we are particularly interested in one egg. It came out first. It fell the farthest. On the bottom it is the coolest. This egg is going to be a male. The sixty days are completed and all over and above this egg the other turtles are breaking their shells and digging towards the surface.

Crack! The egg breaks open. A male turtle's head pops out, then two flippers. It is dark and sandy. The turtles above him have loosened the sand, and he has an easier time than the ones that have gone ahead. For some reason they all wait until it is night. It has taken them a day to get ready. The cool air above lets them know that it is night, and suddenly these hatchlings burst forth from the nest. They take a few seconds to get their instinctive bearings, and then head towards the brightest horizon, which is naturally the sea.

This is a very dangerous time in a green sea turtle's life. Predators abound: seagulls, crabs, foxes and raccoons, then once in the sea, more birds and fish. Only about five percent make it to the water and swim out to be relatively safe.

"Hey, where did everyone go?" this special turtle says to himself as he climbs out of the nest hole.

He looks around. He sees the lighter horizon and a few small dark shapes disappearing in the waves on the beach.

"Hey, wait for me!" His little flippers take off, churning up the sand.

There is a faint light just barely illuminating the horizon. Birds are starting to fly about. The turtle is halfway across the beach. Suddenly a flap of wings is heard above him and a faint shadow drops down covering him up.

"Get! Go bird!" A young boy reaches down and picks him up by his shell. His four flippers continue to move about.

"I've got me a baby sea turtle!" Parker says out loud.

He then picks up his long stout walking stick in one hand and the little turtle in the other and hurries up the beach, back the way he had come. Parker was a trim, heavily tanned boy of fourteen years with a mop of black-brown hair. Heritage wise he was a mix of the seafaring peoples who have been arriving on the Cayman Islands for centuries. Parker was composed of Spanish, French, and English pirates, privateers, military people, and African islanders.

Parker sprinted down the beach a short distance. He then left the beach. Just over the dunes past some coconut palms was his house. It was made of palmetto logs, mud bricks, and a mix of sawed cedar and mahogany wood. There was an abundance of these materials on the interior of this island.

"Grandfather! Grandfather! Look what I have!"

"Did you find some large turtles, Parker?"

"No Sir, look!"

"Why, it's a baby turtle. It isn't a mouthful!" Parker's Grandfather stated.

"No, we're not going to eat it. I would like to keep it for a pet."

The baby turtle's little flappers were still going, flailing about.

"Look, Mother," Grandfather said as he pointed at Parker. "I sent him out to find and turn over a large turtle to sell or eat, and he comes home with this!"

"My, my, what should I make of this?" Grandmother said sympathetically.

"Well, Parker, you had better get him in some seawater. Go fetch that big bait tub from the shed, and fill it with seawater and seaweed," Grandfather instructed. "He is so little he needs to be in the water, and he will eat that seaweed we've got floating in the lagoon. Also, bring a coral rock to put in there to give him some land."

"There, Grandpa, I've done what you said. But why is he just floating in the center of that seaweed?"

"Well, Sonny, that is what they usually do anyways. If you hadn't picked him up, and he had made it to the ocean he would have swum out a ways until he found some of this seaweed. You know the first couple of days are the most dangerous for a green sea turtle. They have to get off the beach and into the water before the birds and critters get them. You know that most of 'em don't make it!"

"Grandpa, if he is a green sea turtle, why isn't he green?"

"Well, Parker, first of all he is young, a baby. What you see is his baby coloring. But when he gets big he will be all kinds of colors: brown, yellow, white, and blue-green. But he is called a green sea turtle from the color of the fat beneath his shell. Some think it is from all the sea grass he eats. As he grows up, let's watch his markings on his shell. No two are alike."

"Come on in here you two! Quit gibbering! It's time for lunch," Grandma yelled from the house.

"What are you going to call your turtle, young fella?" Grandma asked as she was cleaning up after lunch.

"Well Grandma, remember Uncle Sebastian? You know he likes the water. He is a sailor. I'm going to call him Sebastian!"

"You know if that rambler ever gets back to shore, he'll be proud."

"Grandma, I'm going out to the shed and see what Grandpa is doing."

"What are you working on, Grandpa?"

"I'm sharpening up all my saws, axes, and tools for cutting wood."

"Do you need some help?"

"I want you to just watch, and I'll show you how each tool gets sharpened with different files, grinders, and sharpening stones. Then you can give it a try. Also I've got a job for you early tomorrow."

"What's that Grandpa?"

"We are going to build a Cayman dugout canoe. It's not going to be like the original Cayman dugouts. In fact, some of those were twenty-five to fifty feet long. No, we two couldn't handle one of those. Ours is going to be around fourteen feet. What I need for you to do is head up to the highland behind the house...take the trail. Then look for a mahogany tree, not too tall, real straight, and this diameter. Go get your walking staff, and I'll put a mark on it. You can also use the walking stick for estimating the length. It will be about four times its length."

"Sonny, if you don't find anything, we'll both try the other trail the next day," Grandpa said.

Bright and early the next morning Parker went out to the covering close to the shed. Sebastian was nestled in his sea grass. Parker was sure he was growing some. He had placed some minnows in the tank to keep Sebastian company.

"Now you be careful Parker...and be back in time for lunch," Grandma hollered as he started down the trail.

"Pa, do you think it's safe for him to go alone?" Grandma asked.

"Sure, what can hurt him? He has already been beachcombing and turning turtles for me! This is just up the trail to the woods. Besides he and I have been there many times before."

"Ok, dear," she said. "I guess he needs to grow and learn."

The trail left the costal mangroves and went past the edge of a small salt water lagoon. There were a few sea birds about. Parker liked to watch the long-legged ones. They would stand in the water, spear fish with their beak, and then gulp them down whole.

Next, the trail wound along a marsh fringed by bushes and small trees, kind of jungle-like. There were orchids attached to many of the branches and tree trunks.

Parker had come this way many times before with his grandpa. He was hoping he would find a tree along the trail as it slowly wound its way up toward the highlands.

This island, Cayman Brac was the highest of all three islands. At one hundred and forty-four feet it was one hundred feet higher than Little Cayman, and Grand Cayman was lower still. This island was flat on top, like a plateau. It dropped down from the east end to the sea on the west.

He passed a small well which was near a place called Pirates Cave. There were lots of caves along the perimeter of the island and in the hardwood forest. Some said they had been used by pirates to hide their booty and loot. However, so far no one had reported finding any treasure.

The wells were useful. In fact he and Grandpa had drunk from this one many times. There were no permanent streams or rivers on the islands because the soil was so porous. Consequently, there was no runoff. That made the waters very clear around the beaches.

Parker came to a switchback* in the trail. It was a flat spot that made an abrupt 180 degree turn to the right. He stopped briefly to rest and then spotted, off to the left about fifteen yards, a tree that appeared to meet his Grandpa's measurements.

"I need to get over there to check the diameter," he said out loud.

The brush was very thick along the trail. He pushed himself through, receiving a few scratches in the process. Once past this natural barrier, he suddenly realized the ground did not slope off sharply but was a level, overgrown, old trail. Of course there were bushes and vines growing on it. But it was much easier than walking along a sloping mountain side.

He took his bearings and headed towards his mahogany target. He got up to it and laid his walking stick alongside to check the diameter. It was exact! He looked up, and the tree top was strange. Something like lightening or a hurricane must have broken or blown off the major part of the top. A few limbs had been left, and they were still growing. The tree had a thick straight trunk but it was unusually short.

Parker could see the straight part of the tree was just long enough, at least eighteen feet. He made a sudden turn to return to the trail, and caught his foot on something. He came crashing to the ground. His knee was hurting a bit when he got up.

But he said to himself again out loud, "I'm glad no one saw me perform that foolish maneuver! What tripped me?"

He looked down. There was a strange rusted metal loop about the size of a man's hand sticking out of the ground. It was protruding about three inches above the earth. He bent down and touched it. Parker pulled out the knife his grandfather had given him at his last birthday and began to dig around this object. It was the handle of a cutlass with only a short stub of a rusty blade attached.

"Wow!" he said, "Grandpa will be interested in this!"

He made his way back to the trail and down the path. As he approached the lagoon, he stopped. There across the trail was what appeared to be a large log.

"That wasn't there before," he said.

Parker approached slowly. As he got closer he realized, this dark thing didn't look like a log. Then he saw what appeared to be green scales. Suddenly there was a sharp crack! He had stepped on a dry stick. Part of the thing turned, and Parker realized that he was looking at the snout of a Cayman crocodile! The crocodile raised up on its legs, turned towards Parker and started moving towards him. He had never seen one of these before, only the fossil remains of a skull. In fact, they were thought to have been extinct! At one time the island swarmed with them, and then stranded mariners supposedly ate them all.

Parker hurriedly looked left and right for an escape route. It was too far back to where the trail gained elevation. In fact it was too late for him! The Cayman crocodile suddenly rushed him! In desperation Parker dropped his cutlass handle and made a full swing of his walking stick from his back and over his head. The beast was five feet in front of him, opening is teeth-filled jaws when slam! The knot on the end of Parker's walking stick came down on the top of the crocodile's head, right between both of the beady eyes. The croc' stopped as suddenly as it had started, and Parker followed it up with two more such blows. The reptile lay there in a quiet heap.

Parker picked up his cutlass handle and rushed around the dead pile. He ran and ran, and didn't stop until he got in sight of his home. His grandfather was working outside under the covering next to the shed.

Parker came rushing up, "Grandfather! Grandfather! A crocodile! A crocodile! I found a cutlass! I found our tree!"

"Now just settle down, Parker. Catch your breath and tell me just what happened, slowly."

"So you tell me there is a dead Cayman crocodile on the trail by the lagoon, and you killed it. Let's grab a sandwich that Grandma has made for us, and go up the trail, and take a look."

"You're right Parker. How about that? This Cayman croc' is at least eight feet long. You say you did him in? How?"

"Well, Grandpa he was charging at me and I just swung my walking stick. Out of self defense."

"Sonny, It looks like the Good Lord was watching out for you. People haven't seen one of these on this island for years. We need to go down to the village, and tell the authorities. I think they will be interested in this. First thing tomorrow you and I will go down the beach to our neighbors. John will take us with his big sail'n dugout canoe to the far end of the island. There at Channel Bay we can inform whoever we should."

"There he lays." Grandpa pointed out the crocodile to the two men, Peter and Daniel, who had sailed back in John's boat with Grandpa and Parker.

"He is a big un'," Daniel said. "We'll sketch, and measure him up. Keep your eyes peeled for any more. Parker, if you should come across any more, try not to kill them."

"Yes, Sir," Parker answered.

They all laughed. Parker looked confused.

Grandpa said, "They're just jesting Parker. You had to defend yourself."

On the way back to the beach Grandpa told John, "I mean to bring in a fair-sized mahogany log. Goin' to build us a dugout canoe. It'll be somewhat smaller than yours, John."

"You need some help getting that log out? Let me know when," John offered.

"In a couple of weeks," Grandpa said. "We've got to get the tree cut down, the log sized, and then we'll give you a call. Maybe that mule of your'n can pull it back to the beach for us."

"He sure can, Gramps. Dynamite can do it! We'll be seeing you then,"

John said.

"Thanks a' lot for the information, Gramps," Peter and Daniel said as John's dugout put out from the beach with Grandpa and Parker pushing it into the surf.

"What we goin' to do next, Grandpa?" Parker asked.

"Well, fearless hunter, tomorrow morning we're going to skin a croc! The hide should be worth something. Someone in town will buy it after we cure it."

"Parker, here's the overall plan. We can only do a few of the steps at this time. First, we're going to flip it over. Get your knife out. We will cut it from the chin to the end of the tail. There now we'll remove the head and feet. Next we will clean out bones and all, and leave the hide."

"Wow Grandpa, this is a lot of messy work."

"Don't fret. We will take this hide, and head back to the shed."

"Grandpa, how did you learn to do this?"

"My father taught me how. But it's been a long time."

"What you going to do with the head, Grandpa?"

"We're going to nail it to that far tree. Where grandma won't see it."

"Parker, help me take this salt I've been saving and sprinkle it on the inside of the hide. Next we'll roll the hide, and put it in this tub. Now you fill this tub up with salt water from the beach until it covers the hide. We'll let it soak there for a week."*

"Now Parker, that finishes the gator project temporarily. Tomorrow morning we'll take our ax and go and take a look at that tree you found. You say it's just a little ways past the gator fight?"

"Yes Grandpa, I think you will like it. Not too high, but the exact distance around."

"How's that green turtle coming along? What's his name?"

"Sebastian, Grandpa. He's gotten bigger. About the size of one of grandma's pots," Parker said excitedly.

"When he gets about one-half bigger, I think we'll have to build a turtle crawl. He will out grow that big tub he is in very soon."

"What's a turtle crawl, Grandpa?"

"Oh, you will see when you help me build it. But basically it's a sea-side pen your turtle can grow up in. We'll use some of the branches of the mahogany log we're going to bring in."

The next morning at the mahogany tree location, "You were right Parker, it's perfect. That tree is excellent. You did a good job. We're fortunate to find one that has a large trunk but is not too tall. Some of these mahogany trees can grow over one hundred feet tall. In fact they can live more than three hundred years!"

"Thanks, Grandpa. Look, right there is where I found the sword handle," Parker pointed.

"Oh yes. I can see where you dug it out. Now let's get on with this tree felling. It looks like the tree grew up a good size, and then a big part of the top came out. Must've been from a big storm. After that it kind of stopped growing higher. What we need to do first is plan our cut. I mean which way to make it fall. We need an escape route. Because when the tree starts to fall, sometimes it will jump off the stump."

"You know a lot, Grandpa."

"Well not everything, but my job is to teach you everything I know. Then you can be smarter than me someday."

"I don't know if that will ever happen, Grandpa."

"It will, Sonny. It will!"

"Ok, I'm going to make it fall that way, downhill towards the trail going home. We'll just have to clear some brush and small saplings. Our emergency escape route is along the path we came in on."

They cleared both ways, for the tree to land and the escape route. They were in luck, because there wasn't too much in the way, and that was because Grandpa had planned well.

"Let's take a break. I'm tired and we haven't even started on the tree. Pass me some water and a snack from that sack, young'un."

"Now that we're rested, I'm going to let you start on the felling direction. Here is where we will cut a large "V" into the tree over half the way in. Give me the ax. Now stand over there, on the opposite of me. Watch as I chop. Watch my stand, my swing and the pull out."

Chop! Chop! Chop! "There now you try."

"Ok Grandpa. Like this?" Chip. Chip. Chip.

"Parker, that's a good start. You're through the bark."

They took turns. Soon there was a large "V" about one half to two thirds of the way into the tree trunk about a foot off the ground.

"Ok Parker, you need to get over to the trail on the escape route. You never know just when she will go."

Grandpa went to the other side of the tree opposite the large "V" cut. The tree was starting to lean, the correct way, towards the lower trail and their cleared area. Grandfather cautiously cut a small "V" on the opposite side of the tree from the large "V."

"Stay back, and keep a watch," he said as he swung a hard Chop!

There was a sudden...Crack! The tree started to move above the large 'V'. Grandpa jumped, ax in hand, turned and ran!

Snap! The tree started to fall. Then suddenly at forty-five degrees it paused momentarily.

A center of the tree's cut that didn't want to break held briefly and a huge ball of roots, rocks, and rotten logs jumped upward with the base of the tree.

Finally the tree landed with a crashing of trunk and limbs, and came to a sudden stop. All was quiet.

"Well, I never saw that happen before. They usually just fall over with a bang. Look at that ball of earth and roots."

"Grandpa, look up against the side of the trail. Right by the tree roots. Is that a cave?"

"I think you're right, Sonny."

They climbed down under the tree roots and into the depression in the earth.

"It looks like a limestone cave opening. Let's dig it out."

They crawled down into the depression next to the exposed opening. They kneeled and began scooping the loose earth out with their hands. When they got done, the opening was just big enough for a man to crawl through. They peered in.

"Parker, run get me the rucksack. I've got some candles and flints in it."

Grandpa eased in with his lit candle leading the way. Inside you could sit up. It was about as wide as a man stretched out and twice as deep. Inside strange shadows shown about in the flickering light against the limestone walls.

"Grandpa, what's that over there, and what's that smell?"

They could barely see the grinning mouth of a Cayman crocodile's skull.

"Oh, Sonny, that is what your crocodile is going to look like very soon. As far as the smell, this smell is just stale and damp limestone air. Now look past the crocodile skull. Look over there!"

There were rusted blades and handles of three cutlasses and the rusted metal part of a flint-lock pistol. The flint was still in it.

"Looks like the rest of your cutlasses, Parker."

Parker scrambled over, wax dripping from his candle, with grandpa right behind.

"Ouch! My knee," Parker cried out.

"Be careful, Sonny."

"Look, Grandpa, what I bumped my knee on."

It was a small chest about six by nine inches sticking up out of the floor of the cave.

"What have we here, Sonny? It looks like a pirate chest. It's buried in the floor of the cave. It couldn't be more than six inches high. I'm going to get the ax, and we'll dig it out. You stay right here."

Grandpa crawled back in with his ax. He chopped into the hard packed floor right next to the small chest. Since it was small, it dug out fairly easy. They went back out into the sunlight. The chest was made of mahogany wood with rusted metal corners and a lock piece in the cover on a long side.

"We've done enough, Parker, you can bring the cutlasses."

They rolled a couple of rocks over against the entrance. Then they threw some dirt and brush on it.

"We'll come back tomorrow and cut the length of trunk for our canoe. Then we'll size up and cut limbs for our turtle crawl. Any left over timber we'll get ready to move to the house...don't want to waste anything. Now let's get this chest to the shed, and open it."

Bam! Bam! Grandpa swung his hammer hitting the lock. The lock's side bent in, and the lid sprang open spilling out tarnished gold coins on the bench. Grandpa took one in his palm and rubbed it with an old cloth.

"Best I can see there are some Spanish markings. It's hard to make out, and the coin is not very round. These may be from the shipments from Mexico in 1600. This chest is full! Must be close to a hundred of them!"

"Parker, we're not going to tell anyone. We're going to hide this. Once we start turtling and exploring with our dugout canoe, occasionally we will find one or two coins on a beach somewhere. That way we can sell them in Channel Bay, and no one will think they came from around here."

"Ok, Grandpa."

"Remember, no one! Otherwise the authorities may want to confiscate the treasure."

"Not even grandma? What does confiscate mean?"

"Hold on Sonny, not so fast! Let me tell grandma, and confiscate means, take it away with the power of the law! Some day the gold coins will help you."

"Parker, what do you think about this tree trunk? It's straight and the perfect diameter. We've just got it cut to length. You did a great job today. Thank you for helping me cut it. You also did a great job finding it. Tomorrow we'll cut the rest of the tree up and then make a skid to carry the limbs for the turtle crawl."

"That was a lot of work, Grandpa!"

"Yep, Sonny, and now we're ready for John and his mule."

"Grandpa, what about the crocodile?"

"Ok, Sonny, you're right. It's been a week and we've got a date with a croc's hide."

"What we go'in to do, Grandpa?"

"First we're going to take this salted hide out of this saltwater tub. Then let's carry it down to the water and rinse all of the salt out of it. Next we're going to rub the flesh side with this oil I have. Hold it up there. We're going to nail it to the sunny side of our shed with these small sharpened hardwood sticks we've made. Can't use metal. It'll rust and mark the hide. Pull on it. I want to stretch it out as we tack it. Now we'll rub oil on this scale side."

"What do we do next, Grandpa?" Parker questioned.

"Parker, we just wait a month or two and pray the wind, sun, and the oil tan it."

"Well, John, what can we do to help you and your mule Dynamite get this mahogany log and limbs to our beach front?"

"That's a mighty nice log you'uns got there. He can sure pull it, but let's help him some. Dig down under the front of it and put a straight round log under it. We'll debark it first. Then as we pull the big'un we'll keep putting more logs under it, and we'll easily pull it to your place. Once we get started it will roll right along. Dynamite can just coast."

They moved slowly down the trail. Parker brought the roller logs up to the front of the big moving, mahogany trunk. He handed them to Grandpa. Then Grandpa laid them in front of the big log. Meanwhile up front John and Dynamite plodded slowly along.

"That is a mighty fine skid you made with those smaller logs, Grandpa. Sonny, your Gramps is mighty handy. Won't take us long to get it pulled to your house," John said admiringly.

"Well, John, what do I owe you?" Grandpa asked.

"Nary a thing," John replied. "But I could us a few of those bigger skid logs. In fact, I could use a skid back home."

"John, let's move these smaller limbs off the skid. You help too, Parker. Parker and I need these to make a turtle crawl for his pet turtle. Then,

John, you can have the whole skid. You can pull it to your place right after you sit a spell, and eat some lunch with us."

"I can't turn that down," John replied.

"Parker, run get some water for Dynamite. Use that bucket hanging up in the shed."

"Ok, Grandpa." He ran over towards the shed.

"Let's go inside. Grandma is getting something ready for us to snack on."

"How do, John? Is the Missus well? Have a seat. I will bring out some food," Grandma said.

"Thank'ee ma'm. She sure is do'n fine," John answered.

"Hi, Grandma!" Parker rushed in. "What's for lunch?"

"Don't you fret, young'un. Run along, and wash up. You look a mess. What have these men had you ado 'in?"

"I've been working, Grandma."

"You look like you've been mess'en!"

"Now Grandma, go easy on the boy. He's been working hard! We've got all of that timber in with John and Dynamite's help."

"I'll bet Dynamite did it all," she exclaimed jokingly.

"We couldn't have done it without Dynamite's help," Grandpa put in.

Grandma came out with a steaming plate of fried fish. She then served baked yams.

"You men finish that and I have a dessert of sugared bananas. Now eat up!"

"Parker, it's a new day. We've got a sail'n dugout canoe to build," Grandpa stated.

"Is it going to be a big job?" asked Parker.

"Yep. But you will learn a lot, and when it's done were going to sail the sea!"

"Wow! Grandpa. I'm ready."

"You will notice we left the log on the rollers. It's like a table. We can turn it using a large pole for a lever, and when it's finished, we can roll it out to the sea to launch. Let's get started."

"What we go'in to do first, Grandpa?"

"Parker, first we will shave off all the bark. Now this tool is an adze. As you can see, it's like a hoe on one end and an axe on the other. We will use this to strip off all the bark. It's good that we have started soon. If you leave the bark on too long the sap will rise, and the bark will stick to the inner skin of the tree trunk. After that exercise we will use a straight pole for a lever and roll the log over until we find the part of the log that will be best for the bottom. We want to flatten out the part of the log that we will use for the bottom. Then we will turn the log over onto the flat bottom.

Just removing the bark and flattening out the bottom took them almost a week. Of course this team took many breaks. Grandpa and Parker walked the beach to look for turtles. They had to occasionally help Grandma with the garden. It was also essential to visit Sebastian. There they added water to his large tub and found some choice seaweed from the lagoon for him to eat.

"What do you think, Parker? You know I like all this dugout canoe work, but the most fun is setting on it and drinking Grandma's lemonade."

"Oh Grandpa, you're sure crazy!"

"Yep, but I'm sure happy," he exclaimed.

"What's next on our canoe, Grandpa?"

"Believe it or not, we have to flatten out the top so we can begin hollowing it out. But before we hollow it out, we will bring the front and rear to points."

"Why points in both the front and rear, Grandpa?"

"That way we will be able to go both forward and backward easily. By just turning around in the canoe the rear will become the front."

Another two weeks went by, and they were now ready to begin hollowing out.

"Sonny, today we're going to mark the outline of the sides of our canoe. Parker, run and get me some of that charcoal I have in the shed."

"Be right back, Grandpa," he said as he ran off.

"There, we've marked the outline of the sides of our dugout canoe. Next you will find out just why it is called a dugout. We are going to cut a grove on the top where I marked. We'll cut straight down on the line with the adze and chip out towards the center. Then we'll cut a trough down the center."

"Grandpa."

"What Parker?"

"I noticed it is much easier to say what we're going to do than do it!"

"Now you're being crazy, Parker. But you're right. First I'd like to talk about what I'm going to do. It's called planning."

"Now we're going to build a fire right here on the ground, not too far away from the canoe. Get my flints and tinder. There, the fire is starting. Come along and we'll get those three cannon balls we found a long time ago from the shed."

"Grandpa, the ones we found on the other side of the lagoon?"

"Yep, the're only six pounders, but they will do just fine. Now try to lay them on top of the fire. The coals will heat them red hot. Let's get lunch, and then come back."

"They're ready! See Parker, red hot. Now we're going to put them in the center notch we cut out."

"How we go'in to pick them up, Grandpa?"

"Easy Sonny, we will each hold on to these two sticks. Then we'll straddle the cannon balls with them. Push in and pick up. Keep just far enough apart to have the cannon balls in our grasp. Just like this. Easy Sonny. Now set the ball down in the groove, and take your stick away."

Sizzle! Snap! The hot cannon balls sank down into the groove and proceeded to burn a circle recess.

"What's happening, Grandpa?"

"The ball is softening the trunk wood as it burns in. Next we'll roll the cannon balls over in the groove a 'ways. While they're still hot and burning the new wood, I'm going to cut or dig out some of this wood. Get it? Dugout!"

"Oh Grandpa, I get it!"

"Now we're lucky to have these iron tools. The early natives in Jamaica, Cuba, and other places had to use hot rocks, stone axes, and shells to scrape the wood out."

"How long will it take us to dig the dugout?"

"Now you are getting poetic, Parker. We will get about an inch deeper every time we work along the groove. Since we're not in a hurry, we'll get down to a bottom in a week. We'll have to do some other chores or Grandma will think we're just playing out here on the beach."

"Can't we go net fishing and looking for turtles?"

"I think that comes under the topic of hunting for food. That is an acceptable pastime. First let's see if Grandma needs any help with the garden."

"There's our dugout canoe, Parker. All we have to do is a couple more things. We'll scrape and polish the insides with shells and sand rocks. Then we will seal and waterproof it with some grease I've made from turtle fat.”

“I’m ready, Grandpa!” Parker exclaimed.

“I’m glad for that because you are my greatest helper and worker. But tomorrow we are going on a short expedition. We will go inland around the lagoon and to the other side. We need to find three very special accessories for our canoe. We need a mast about the size of my upper arm and fifteen feet long. We need a ten-foot spar about the same size to hold the bottom of our sail. We also need an out-rigger log, not too dense but strong, and some poles to attach it.”

“What’s an outrigger, Grandpa?”

“Parker, it must be a very straight log about six inches in diameter. We will attach it parallel to our canoe about four feet from the side. It will keep us from tipping when we sail.”

“We’re going to sail! Yah!” Parker yelled.

“Easy, Sonny. Now let’s go for supper.”

Next morning: “OK, let’s see, you’ve got the lunch and water canteen, Parker?”

“Yes, Grandpa.”

“Good, I’ve got the ax. We’re off on our expedition.”

“Bye, men,” Grandma yelled.

“Bye, Grandma,” Parker answered.

They took the inland trail. Shortly they broke off of it and skirted the lagoon. In some places it was clear, and they could see the lagoon, and in other places the dense and tangled branches and dark green leaves of the mangroves blocked the view.

Parker was bringing up the rear. He could tell grandpa had been along this way before because it seemed like he was following a trail even though Parker couldn’t see one. They broke out into an open area. Parker could see way up toward the beach. He looked across the lagoon and could see their beach on the other side.

“There is the place where I found those cannon balls. Right next to that big bump. See those rocks sticking out. They're ballast rocks. This here area is known as a careening place, Parker.”

“What is a careening place, Grandpa?”

“Careening is when a ship’s bottom is scraped and repaired. Wood boats have to have this done occasionally. They attach ropes to the mast, and pull the ship up on its side. Then they scrape the barnacles off. Then a ship can go much faster because the bottom is smoother.”

"What are barnacles, Grandpa?"

"Those are small sea worms that attach to the bottom of the wood on a ship, and then make small shells around their body."

"Now what they would do is bring the ship in the lagoon here, then throw out all the ballast rocks over there on that big pile."

"What are ballast rocks for, Grandpa?"

"They put lots of rocks in the bottom of a sailing ship to keep it heavier on the bottom, and keep it from tipping over."

"Do they throw out the cannon balls too, Grandpa?"

"Why yes, anything that was heavy, even the guns. Then they would hook ropes and pulleys to the top of the mast and pull the ship over on its side. They probably used the big trees right over there to hook their ropes to. In fact, that's where we are going to get our mast, spar, and outrigger poles."

"Look, Grandpa! I found a piece of pottery."

"That's so. If we were to dig around in this area we would find stuff that has been discarded for centuries!"

"Let's go into these trees and find our wood."

"Grandpa, we've got our mast and spar. How about the outrigger?"

"Sonny, I've got an idea. Let's go over to the beach."

They walked along the lagoon's edge towards the beach. This was all an open area except for an occasional mangrove. They could see where the water was flowing into the lagoon across the coral reefs as the tide rose. It was smooth out in the center.

"There's the channel for the lagoon, Parker. See it? It's that part that's smooth flowing and not bubbling over the coral."

"I see it, Grandpa."

They came over a dune and out onto the beach. The breeze off the Caribbean Sea caressed their bodies. They could smell the sea.

"It sure smells fresh, Grandpa. I like the sea."

"I'm with you, Parker. Let's walk along the beach for a ways. There's what I'm looking for," he said as he pointed to a long piece of drift wood. Grandpa lifted it up. "It's light, but strong," he exclaimed.

"Finding that was good luck. Hun Grandpa?"

"Yep, we'll shoulder this and take it back to the careening place, leave it, and take our mast and spar home. We'll come back tomorrow for it."

The mast was installed way forward into the canoe, about two feet back from the front. It fit through a hole in the center of a board (which went from the top of one side to the top of the other) and attached to the inside bottom of the boat. The spar attached to the mast right above the board and ran a little past the back end.

"Well, Grandpa, what are we going to use for a sail? Our bed blankets?"

"No, Sonny, your Grandma would exile us to the very top of the island! You know that John has a sail'n dugout canoe. Well he said that he was going to make a new sail. He told me we can have his old 'un. Tomorrow we're going to hike the mile down to his place and get that sail. Of course we've got to take him something to swap. What about that old croc' hide?"

"That would be ok, Grandpa."

"Before we go to John's, let's look at Sebastian."

They went out to the shed.

"He's getting big! You've been feeding him real good, Parker. You know what? After our first sail canoe ride, we'll build him his very own turtle crawl."

It didn't take them very long to get to John's place, only about a half hour. It was a little slower going on the sand trail. John's house was about three times larger than Grandpa's. With that mule he cultivated a much bigger garden. Also, because he had a canoe he was more productive with his turtle harvesting.

"Hi, John. Came to get that sail."

"Hi, Gramps. You and Parker are looking fine."

"We brung you that cured croc' hide. It will make some fine belts."

"You didn't have to do that, Gramps. Come 'round back to my shop and we'll get that sail. You may have to cut her down a little. What's your boat's length?"

"Around twelve feet. "

"Yep, mine's eighteen. Tell you what. Let me help you cut it down right now. That way you won't have to carry all that extra. You can take some for patching."

"That's right kind of you, John. Let's get started."

It was just a simple triangle with loops to go up the mast and support rope on the edging. They cut it down, overlapped the edge with the rope inside and stitched it up.

"We'll load it up on my mule, and I'll take it back for you. But first the missus has us some lunch."

"Thanks for bringing the sail, John."

They waved as John and Dynamite headed back up the sand trail.

"John's missus sure does cook good! That was a good lunch!"

"Careful, Parker, not so loud. Remember Grandma's cooking is the best."

"Oh that's right, I almost forgot."

They slipped the sail loops over the mast. Then they tied a loop of rope to the top of the mast to run the rope through and pull the sail up.

"Now, Parker, help me lift this mast over the board. There, drop it through the hole in the board."

Grandpa then pinned the mast to the bottom of the canoe. Next the spar hooked to the bottom of the mast just above the sides of the canoe. They did this just after they ran it through the loops on the bottom of the sail.

"Now just pull that rope, Parker."

As he pulled the sail, it ran up the mast. They then tied it to the board. The wind caught the sail, filled it, and billowed out.

"Parker, in the morning we're going back to the careening place and bring back that outrigger pole.

"There she is, Parker. Ready to go!"

"Looks good, Grandpa."

"Well, just what are we waiting for? You place these poles in front of the dugout. We'll roll it down into the water. It's good that we have a gradual slope down towards the water."

Grandpa used a long pole as a lever, and the canoe moved slightly and then started a slow descent to the water. The front hit a wave coming in which floated the front half of the canoe. The second wave followed right behind, floating the entire vessel.

"Jump in, Parker!"

Grandpa did a belly-flop over the canoe's side and flipped over sprawling out on the bottom. When Grandpa looked up, Parker was seated and holding one of the paddles they had carved out of a light but strong wood they had found growing up on the bluff on the higher part of the island.

"You beat me to a seat, Parker. I'll have to be faster next time. Tell you what, you sit up front, and I'll man the back. Now let's paddle out."

It didn't take them long to paddle out from the surf. There the water was a deep blue, and the waves were passing under them with gentle swells.

"Up with the sail, Parker."

"Yes, Sir! Captain Grandpa."

He pulled on the rope, and the sail climbed the mast.

"Tie it right there on the board. Let me show you this one time. He moved forward in the canoe and tied the rope to the board holding the mast.

"See how steady she is. That outrigger is balancing us."

The sail caught a breeze and filled.

"I'd better get to the back. We steer this sail outrigger canoe with this larger paddle off the stern, like this. I use it just like a rudder."

"What is a rudder, Grandpa?"

"Parker, it steers the boat, like this. See if I put it out to the right the boat turns to the right, and if I put it out to the left the boat turns to the left."

"How do you know all that, Grandpa?"

"Well round-about 1820, before you were born in 1846, I worked on a turtle schooner. We worked around Cuba, Nicaragua, and even on the other side of Cuba to Key West in the USA.

"Wow, Grandpa, I'd like to go to all of those places!"

"Some day you can. Now let's take this dugout canoe down to John's."

They washed right up on the beach.

"Drop the sail, Parker. Look, someone's waving from John's house. Why it's John. He must have seen us."

"It looks mighty good," John exclaimed, "I wondered who that was, and then I recognized my sail!"

"We thank you kindly, John. We won't be bothering you very long, but we just had to try her out."

Back at Grandpa and Parker's house. Grandma said, "How you sailors do'n? I saw you sail away. Didn't know if I'd ever see you again. Figured you two would just drop off the face of the earth!"

"Oh, Grandma, you're just joking!"

"Now you both get washed up. How'd you two know it was time for supper?"

"Parker, I promised you we would build a turtle crawl. Today is the day. Remember all those sticks we brought from the mahogany tree? We'll need the ax for me and a hatchet for you. We'll grab a few sticks and walk over to the lagoon."

"Will this be a good place, Grandpa?"

"Yep, because it's not very far from our house. Let's get our shoes off. First we'll sharpen these stakes. Then we will start right here where the water is knee deep."

He pounded a stake in, leaving it to stick up a couple of feet.

"Now, we'll go out to where it is waist deep and pounded in another stake. Next, we will put in the other two corners. Now, Parker, what we have here is a square about fifteen by fifteen feet. Next we'll put the gate we can access by foot here in the middle of the shore side."

On the deeper side he put in two additional stakes.

"What are those two stakes for, Grandpa?"

"This will be for a gate so we can bring the dugout canoe in. If we get some turtles that we want to save until we take them to market, we can bring them in and out through this gate."

"Next we need to put additional stakes in between each corner. They will have to be about six inches apart and three feet above the high tide water. We'll then tie them together with rope, and put a cross-piece over each gate."

"Wow, Grandpa, I just figured it up. Fifteen feet times four equals sixty times two per foot equals one hundred and twenty stakes. We've got a lot of work to do!"

"That's correct, Parker, and two lashed-together gates. See those mangroves over there. We're going to use a lot of those long saplings after we run out of the mahogany lumber. It's going to take us the rest of the week to build this turtle crawl."

"Well Sonny, we're going to get Sebastian, and see if he likes his turtle crawl home."

"Grandpa, look, he sure has gotten big! He is about the size of grandma's frying pan," Parker exclaimed.

"It looks like we made that turtle crawl none-too-soon. Let me grab him by the sides of his shell and we'll take him to his new home."

"Grandpa, look at Sebastian's shell. I just noticed that it's kind of heart shaped."

"That's right, Sonny."

"Grandpa, look at the many colors. They are brown, dark green, some grey and black. But look there in the middle there is also some yellow. It looks like a cross!"

"So it is, Parker. We may have a holy turtle!

"Oh, Grandpa, I don't know about that, but he sure is special."

"Here we are, Sebastian. Let's see if you like the turtle crawl," Grandpa said as Parker opened the shore gate.

They waded in and Grandpa set Sebastian in the water. There was a sudden splash as the turtle's flippers grabbed the water and he dived. Grandpa and Parker went out, closed the gate and sat down on an old knurled driftwood log. They watched Sebastian. He would come back up to the top and with a single explosive breath expel all the old air. He would then do a rapid inhalation which replaced the air in his lungs and then dive down again.

"I never heard him do that before, Grandpa."

"He couldn't dive very far in that tub he was in, so he didn't have to take a fast breath, hold it, and come back up for air. Now that we've got Sebastian taken care of, tomorrow we're going turtle hunting."

Parker said, "I'm ready."

They were a little over a quarter mile out from their house, which was about an eighth of a mile past the coral reefs. They had been turtling and fishing whenever time had allowed them this last year. Every now and then they would find a turtle but the fishing was good! The water out here was deep blue, and deep it was! The Cayman islands lay adjacent to the Cayman Trench. The Cayman Trench was very deep water, over four miles deep, and for that reason Grandpa did not venture too far out.

"There's one, Grandpa! Over to the right."

"I see it," Grandpa said, as he dipped his paddle and headed towards it. Drop the sail and grab your paddle. Just like before, we'll ease up to him, drop the weighted rope over his head, catch his flippers, and pull him in."

The turtle dived.

"We'll have to guess where he'll come up."

They paddled along on their present trajectory. The turtle came up, blew out, breathed in, and started to dive. Parker looped the rope over the turtle, and it sank over in front of its head.

"I've got him!" Parker yelled.

Grandpa and Parker both pulled hard on the rope. It was hooked around both flippers. The turtle rolled up and over the sides of the dugout canoe and bounced upside down in the bottom, all four flippers moving wildly in the air.

"Leave him on his back. It's the best way to transfer him," Grandpa said. "Let's head in, Parker. Up sail! It looks like Sebastian will have another friend to keep him company. That will make two extra turtles in the crawl."

"Grandma, tomorrow Parker and I will sail down to Channel Bay to sell those two turtles. We should be back by evening. Can you please pack us a lunch?"

"Sure can. Anything for my two best men."

They had about eight miles to sail to the west. They were paralleling the shore. The wind was at their back, blowing east to west. They would have to tack* going back. They reached the end of the island and had to swing to the south. When they got to the lee side, they headed in towards the bluff. There were a few houses, a pier, and a few sails in the mere hint of a harbor. They approached the pier, and right next to some local dugout canoes, there was a sloop. As they got close, someone hailed them.

"Ahoy, I'm Captain James Green of the sloop Mable Jane. Who be you?"

They came along side. "I'm Grandpa and this is Parker, my grandson."

"Tie up and come aboard. Are those turtles for sale?"

Grandpa threw James the line. "Yes," he said.

"I'll give ye wholesale for them," the captain offered.

"Wholesale and ten percent," Grandpa answered.

"Deal it is then!" Captain James replied, "My first mate will bring them aboard. Come with me."

"This is Richard, my first mate. Richard, we've got a couple of turtles. Have the hands stow them."

They all shook hands.

James took them down inside the boat to a room with a table, "I'll be right back. Smith, get these men, a drink, and a biscuit."

A fellow, more-than-likely the Captain's steward, appeared wearing a coarse sailcloth apron and bearing some punch and some pastries.

"Thank ye kindly, Sir," Grandpa said.

"You're more-n welcome. Made them fresh this mar'n."

"Here's your pay, Grandpa." Captain James came back into the cabin.

"Parker said, "Mr. James, Captain, Sir, can we look around at your ship?"

"Why yes, you can. Come along. She is a sloop. Single-masted. We can put up four sails if need be. We usually use the two you see. She is sixty-two feet and the fastest sloop, I'll bet, in the Caribbean. We just stopped here to take on some water. We were told that the base of that limestone bluff has a sweet spring, and it sure has."

"We're headed to Cuba, to'ther side, to Havana harbor. Going to pick up some pineapples and then make a run to Key West."

"Wow!" Parker exclaimed.

"As you can see, this here is where we steer our sloop," Captain James continued. "That there, in the middle, is our long boat. It has long oars for six men. It's pretty heavy, but we can launch it with that davit tackle right here."

"Look, Grandpa. This boat is not made of a log, it's all boards."

"They're called planks, young fella, lot easier to build with 'em," Captain James said.

Parker looked all over the long boat. It intrigued him.

"That youngster is inquisitive," Captain James said to Grandpa.

"Yes, Sir he is a bright boy. He helped me build that dugout canoe."

"And a fine boat it is, Sir. I watched you two come around the tip there. A fine bit of seamanship."

"Thank you, Captain James," Grandpa said. "Come on, Parker, we'd best be on our way."

Back in their dugout, Captain James threw them their line and waved as they paddled away from the sloop.

"We already sold our turtles. We go'n home, Grandpa?"

"Not so fast, Sonny. We've got some money. Let's go to the little store on shore there. We'll get some coffee, some sugar for Grandma, and they might even have a treat for you!"

"Let's go. Thanks, Gramps."

After some shopping they paddled away from the small dock, put up their sail, and left Channel Bay fast disappearing in the distance behind them. As soon as they rounded the end of Cayman Brac, the wind hit them.

"Now, Parker, you're going to learn how to tack," Grandpa hollered. "We'll have to stay little farther offshore because we have to go side-ways left and then side-ways right against the wind. That way the sail will catch the wind, and we'll be able to move forward against it."

They were tacking back and forth and about half of the way home when the wind suddenly shifted from the northeast blowing towards the southwest to the southeast blowing strong gusts towards the northwest.

The winds have shifted, Parker. We won't have to tack, but I don't like it. Look over our island towards the south," Grandpa pointed.

The sky was dark with a green tint.

"I thought it looked a little bit strange this morning," Grandpa said. "It's also real humid."

"What is it, Grandpa?"

"It's a bad storm a'comin. We got to get home!"

The wind was blowing in strong gusts. It felt like it would start raining. Then they saw a lightning flash far off over the island to the southeast. It was getting dark. Grandpa was fighting to keep the canoe on course. The sail was bellowing out. It was a good thing they had an outrigger to keep them from tipping.

"We'll go right past our place and run into the lagoon!"

They turned and headed for the lagoon. The waves and water were up so high that they didn't even have to worry about finding the channel. They literally flew right in with the waves and tide.

"Drop sail, Parker, and grab your paddle. We'll go to the back on our side of the lagoon. Head for that near tree. We'll go up into the mangroves and tie up to them."

They jumped out.

"Let's go to the house!" Grandpa said, clutching the coffee and the sugar. "Run, Parker!"

As they ran towards the house the rain let loose with pelting torrents. They could hear the waves crashing on the beach.

Grandma was at the door. "I've put some things in the main stone part of the house, Hon. I've got a bag of food, a pot, and a jug of water ready, also a sack with some blankets."

"Good. Thank you! Here's some coffee and sugar. Secure and water-tight it. Wait for a minute, while Parker and I tie things down in the shed."

Grandpa and Parker ran out to the shop. They threw the loose tools in a heavy metal chest. Back they ran to the house. The palm trees on the beach were bending and swaying with the wind gusts. Rain was pelting the metal roof of the house.

They ate some food Grandma had prepared. "I think it's a small cyclone. If we survive to the lull we need to get to high ground. Parker and I have a cave about fifty feet above sea level half way up the bluff. When this wind changes and blows from the sea towards us, we'll have a surge!"

Suddenly it became quiet. The rain stopped. "Now let's go! We'll take the kerosene lantern. No running. Grandma behind me, and Parker stay close. Each of us gets a bag."

Out the back of the house they went. It was pitch black, except for the yellow of the lantern. Down the trail, past the marsh, past the place where

Parker met the crocodile, and then up the trail.

"Here it is. Parker, help me move these branches, rocks, and dirt."

Just then the wind and rain started back up. Then all three crawled in.

Grandma said, "You always said you were going to take me to a fancy lodging some day. You sure know all the real fine places, Grandpa."

They put their things out, spread the blankets, and turned out the lantern. Inside it was a little cool but dry.

Sebastian noticed there was a lot of movement of the water. When he came up to breathe the waves would throw him around the crawl. Sometimes they would throw him into the beach posts of the crawl. He also noticed it was raining. Shucks, rain didn't bother him, but he didn't like the up and down and being knocked about.

He held his breath and swam down to the bottom. It was only four feet deep, but with the tide and wind he now had water at times almost over the crawl posts. One of the times he was on top he saw a dark shape with a white flapping object shoot by. He had never seen it before but in the front was that human who had brought him sea grass. He couldn't see it any more because it had gone to the rear of the lagoon.

He noticed the waves were becoming more violent and bigger as the time wore on. He came up for air and a tremendous wave raised him high up. It then came crashing down on the mangroves and trees at the edge of the lagoon. As fast as the first wave started to return to the lagoon a much bigger wave sent Sebastian high up and then sucked him up over the crawl posts and into the center of the lagoon. Sebastian immediately exhaled and did a rapid inhalation. He dived down, and down, paddling hard with all four of his flippers.

He then shot back up, blew out and in, and again down he went. Then he realized, "I'm free!"

He headed straight out to sea. He would dive, stay under as he paddled and come up one to three seconds and dive again. He kept this up. This is exactly what he would have done a couple of years before when he was just a hatchling and running to the sea but now he was two feet long and about seventy pounds.

He was swimming at his maximum, about one and one half to two miles per hour. He didn't know exactly where he was going, but he knew where he was. Turtles navigate by wave direction, sunlight, and temperature. They have an internal magnetic compass. They have a magnetic crystal in their brain which can sense the earth's magnetic field. Sebastian kept paddling and paddling.

They awoke to a bit of light shining in through the small entrance they had crawled in. Grandpa sat up, reached over, and used a valuable match to light the lantern. A black sooty flame cast shadows inside the cave. Grandpa adjusted the wick, and the flame cleaned itself.

The flickering light shined on a sitting-up Parker rubbing the sleep out of his eyes, yawning, and stretching.

Grandpa started to rise, "Hold it right there, Grandpa! Eat a little bite first," as she reached in her bag, I know if you two get started, you'll never stop to eat some energy! Here, it's cold but it will help."

"Thank you dear. Here, Parker. You heard your Grandma."

"Yes, Ma'm, Yes, Sir. Thank you."

"I'm going to take a look outside to see if it's safe. Parker, stay with Grandma a minute till I'm back."

"Oh...Grandpa," Parker complained.

Grandpa crawled out. There were sudden gusts of occasional wind carrying some pelting rain. It was light but many dark clouds were moving about. He could see some downed trees, but no water-surge damage. Basically they had been high and dry.

He put his head back up to the cave entrance, "Hand me out the bags as you get them packed."

Grandma and Parker came out. They loaded up and started down the trail back towards the house. Along the way they had to climb over some downed trees that had fallen across the trail.

"Well we're blessed, thank the Good Lord," Grandpa said as their home came into view, "We're all three in good shape. But the shed is damaged, and the front room of the house has some problems. It looks like it is from wind and rain. See where the water came up over the dune down by the beach. It knocked over these trees and came up to our front but not inside."

"Grandma said, " You'll be able to fix it?"

"Yes, Dear, I made it, and I can do it again! Parker, help me clear this mess so Grandma can get in her kitchen. I see the front room has missing siding and roof panels and water damage. But look, the kitchen and the rest of the house is ok! We're going out to the shed and get some tools. Come on, Parker"

A lot of the shed roof panels had been blown off, and it was leaning precariously. Grandpa looked in, "It looks bad but it won't fall. I'm going in and drag out the metal box of tools. Stay here, Parker.”

“There, that wasn’t too bad.” He opened the box and took out hammers, nails, a crow bar, and a saw. “We’ll use the shed roof tin to repair the house roof, and the shed boards to fix the sides of the house.”

“Parker, now that we’ve got the house in shape and our shed is half what it was, it’s time to go looking for our dugout canoe.”

“Yes, Grandpa, I was wondering when we we’re going to check on it.”

“Sonny, you know, first things first! Grandma had to have her house, and we needed our shed for our tools. We were fortunate it only took two weeks. Now let’s go see what we can see.”

The lagoon was as calm as usual. There were fallen trees, broken mangrove bushes, and lots of driftwood floating about.

“Look, Grandpa, the turtle crawl is gone!”

There were a few posts protruding at many different angles, and over in a mangrove was one of the gates.

“Do you think Sebastian is gone, Grandpa?”

“Well Sonny, it sure looks like it. You know you shouldn’t feel bad. Your turtle is in his environment. He is a sea turtle, and turtles love the sea and live in it. It’s their home. He is pretty big now and he doesn’t have many enemies. After all what fish would like to eat a big turtle shell? You know he has that unusual marking, a cross on his shell. If we ever catch him, we’ll take care of him.”

“I know Grandpa, but I’m sad.”

“Let’s go check on our canoe. We tied it up about here. But the tree has been knocked over!”

“Look over there, Grandpa. It’s our sail!”

“It sure is. It’s on the other side of those mangroves.”

They went around and worked their way up to the sail. There it was. The sail had come loose from the mast and boom and was draped over the mangroves. Below it was their canoe.

“Oh look Grandpa, one side of our canoe is broken in!”

“I see it, Parker. We may be able to fix I, but we’ll need John and Dynamite to drag it out of here. We can trim out a path but we’ll need mule power to move it! Let’s head back to the house, and take a break. We’ll see if we can help Grandma and ‘morrow we’ll go down to John’s. First thought, I want to roll up the sail. We can patch it with the extra sail cloth John gave us. Look, we’re in luck, there’s our two oars!”

“That was a nice dinner, Grandma.”

"Thankee kindly, Parker."

"Grandpa, I need some paper and a pen. I have an idea I want to draw, and I'll show it to you when I get finished."

"Sure, Parker, on that shelf over there."

"Thanks, Grandpa."

"Now just what do you think has gotten into that young'un, Sir?" Grandma asked.

"Don't rightly know, Hon, but I guess we'll see shortly."

Later on that evening...

"Here it is Grandpa!"

"Let's see what you have here. Why it appears to be a boat. But it's not a dugout canoe. Parker, what a good drawing! Where did you get this idea? You've drawn it very well. What are we going to do with this?"

"Grandpa, I've been thinking about it for a long time. Ever since I saw that long boat on Captain James's sloop in Channel Bay. Grandpa, this boat will be lighter, faster, and maybe easier to build! I'm going to call it a Turtle boat."

"Parker, I'm interested. First, we'll need a scale model. We can carve it out of cedar, because it's softwood. Now for our scale model we'll make it at a one to twelve scale. You know twelve inches on the real boat will equal one inch on the model. Since your boat is fourteen feet we'll need a fourteen-inch wood block."

Grandpa started carving, "How does this look Parker?"

"Good, Grandpa, just like my drawing. How did you know about a scale model, Grandpa?"

"Remember I sailed on a schooner when I was in my twenties. I was around when some were built here in the Caymans. Now see we can cut this model crossways to get the station curves.* We're going to need some flat wood boards to build this boat."

"How will we get those, Grandpa?"

"Parker, I think it's about time we found some of those gold coins."

John took the three gold coins in his hand, "You say that you found these on the beach? Must have washed up from the storm, or been uncovered by it. You say you need some mahogany planks...do you? You know just what we should do, go to Channel Bay, convert these three coins to some Cayman money, and then we'll find you those planks."

They went down to Channel Bay in John's sail'n canoe, converted the coins, bought the planks, and transported them to Grandpa's house.

Parker and Grandpa waved to John as he sailed off.

"Well, Parker, here we have our pile of planks. John was sure right, those three gold coins would buy us what we needed. He pointed to the pile of mahogany boards they had unloaded from John's dugout canoe.

"We'll move these planks up to the shed and stack them. Then tomorrow morning we have to go out to the swamp. We will need to find some naturally curved roots of the mahogany tree. Those roots will work for our front and rear wood timbers for the stem and stern. Of course we'll have to carve them some to fit our needs."

Next morning…

"Parker, prepare to get moist. We'll have to dig around this root and then dam around it so we can chop it out. It looks like it will be perfect."

"I see another one over there!" Parker exclaimed.

"Hold your excitement, Parker. Let's get this one cut, and then we'll get yours over there. These two curved mahogany roots will work real fine. Of course we will have to use the draw shave* to flatten them out and form them."

On their way back to the house Grandpa continued planning. "We'll use that thicker plank for the keel.* The planks we have are real wide. We'll be able to cut out the ribs and then splice them together at the keel. We're going to have twelve stations plus the stem and stern will equal fourteen feet."

They carved down both front stem and rear stern posts to be flat with a smooth curve and slightly pointed on the outsides of the curves. Everything was spliced, fitted, glued with animal glue,* drilled out, and held together with tree nails.*

"Grandpa, now our boat looks like a skeleton."

"Well, Parker, the next step is to bend these thinner planks around the ribs from stem to stern. It will take a lot of fitting but we will have it done in less than one fourth the time it took us to build the dugout canoe. You had a great idea."

A week later…

"The planking took us a lot of fitting, Grandpa."

"Yes, but that is what will keep it from leaking. That, and the glue, and pitch sealer. All we've got left is to put a couple of cross planks to sit on and a real stiff plank out front with a hole in it to accept the mast. We'll have go back to find and cut a mast and a boom."

"Also, Grandpa, we'll have to make us two more paddles. Do we need an outrigger?"

"Parker, this boat is wider than the dugout canoe, let's try without it."

"There it is, Parker, all finished. What were you going to call it?"

"A turtle boat, Grandpa. Now I'd like to paint it."

"What color and why?"

"Well blue, naturally, Grandpa. It will look real nice and will camouflage the bottom of the boat so the fish and turtles won't see us when they look up."

"Makes sense. Tell you what, when we go to town and try it out, we'll buy some. What color did you say?"

"Blue, Grandpa, turtle boat blue."

Out on the sea…

"She sure sails great! What do you think, Parker?"

"Yes, Grandpa. I love it!"

Sebastian had been free for a whole month now. He had paddled fast and furious for a couple of days and then slowed down. He had headed north, paddling leisurely at his own comfortable speed. Occasionally he would run into patches of seaweed floating on the top of the water. This gave him some nourishment, but he longed for some of that tender sweet sea grass that was just off shore.

He knew he had been swimming in real deep water, because when he had dived down, he couldn't find a bottom. That never really bothered him because he could just float whenever he tired. He did want to find that sea grass, but he needed shallows off shore for that. Sebastian was rewarded when he ran into a large land mass. Of course he didn't know that it was south central Cuba.

He had gone into the shallows and found the food he was looking for. He then saw some other green turtles. Since he was wary and kind of a loner, he kept his distance. He did notice that some turtles would congregate together.

One day he saw two boats put out from shore and head towards the turtles. He didn't like the look of things, and he headed out. He then saw men in the boats throw nets over some of the turtles. He took a deep breath and dove. Sebastian decided to go down to the bottom and stay. He thought, I'll just lodge my shell under a rock and slow down, maybe just sleep. It worked, and his heartbeat slowed down to once every nine minutes.

After a couple of hours he came up to the surface. It was dark. He paddled around and grazed on that sweet tender sea grass he loved so. His serrated jaw was made especially to cut sea grass and other sea plants. Occasionally he also ate algae. In fact all adult green sea turtles are herbivores.*

When it got light he saw a couple of green sea turtles. They had come up from a dive close to him. He saw they were females. He paid them no mind. He would not be interested in female green sea turtles for at least another ten years. Males don't breed until they are fifteen to twenty years old.

Sebastian decided to move farther west along the coast. Using his very keen sense of smell he knew he would find the sea grass up that way also. He also didn't want to see any more of those small boats.

At Channel Bay, Grandpa and Parker found some of that turtle boat blue paint they wanted, as Parker had named it. When they came out of the small combination food, clothing, and hardware store they saw a group of people were on the dock admiring their turtle boat. One of the men was Captain James Green of the sloop *Mable Jane*.

"Hi, Grandpa. Hi, Parker, Is this your boat? It looks sturdy but light. Where did you get it?" Captain James asked.

"Why, my grandson here designed it, and we built it," Grandpa answered.

"This young fella is very intelligent and a good idea man. I saw you two come into the harbor. It sails right smart! Would you want to sell it?"

"Grandpa answered, "No, but we'll build you one."

Then the owner of the store who had followed them out said, "Hey, make me one!"

A turtle fisherman standing by said, "Me too! I mean one for me also!"

Grandpa said, "Whoa...we'll make each of yours in the order you asked. But we need a month apiece. Don't want to kill ourselves. Besides we want to sail this boat some too!"

On the way out of the bay, Parker said to Grandpa, "How we going to make all of those boats, Grandpa?"

"Well, Sonny, it looks like we got a boat building business started, thanks to you. I guess John and his friend will be busy getting us mahogany boards. With the down payment each of those three gave us we can build the first one and when we get paid for it we'll be able to build the other two. Wait until Grandma hears about this!"

As they were rounding the part of the island a two-masted sailing ship came into view. It was out farther and passing them, heading in the general direction they were going.

"What's that ship, Grandpa?"

"It's called a schooner, Parker. Remember, Captain James' ship is a sloop, one-masted. That there ship has two masts, two main jib sails, and booms. Now in front is an additional sail just like the sloop has.

"I like that boat, Grandpa. The next time I build a different kind boat it will be one of those! Where did it come from and where is it going?"

"That schooner is probably a turtle schooner out of George Town in the Grand Cayman island. It's two islands west of here, about seventy-five miles. It is probably going to the turtle grounds off Cuba or Nicaragua. If they go up to Cuba they will have to watch out. You never know just how the Spanish who run that island will react. They're starting to restrict turtling around their island."

"Grandpa, sometime can we go to George Town and see some schooners?"

"You bet, Parker. But first we've got some boats to build."

Grandpa and Parker went back home. They took their boat out of the water and when it dried they painted it, turtle boat blue. Then shortly, with John, Dynamite, and a wagon their lumber began to arrive. John had decided he would extend some credit to Grandpa and Parker. He said, "Might as well bring in enough to make three boats as long as I got Dynamite hooked up."

So "Grandpa's Boat Yard" was started. Parker and Grandpa sailed some, turtled some, fished some, and built boats. After they built and delivered the first three boats it seemed someone always wanted a turtle boat. Even so, they didn't rush. They still enjoyed life.

"Grandpa, let's go look at some schooners in George Town."

"Well, Sonny, first we'll need to get Grandma's permission. Then we'll do one better. If I recall, there are a couple of boat builders on Grand Cayman. We'll see if we can visit one of them if they have a schooner under construction.

"I just love sailing, Grandpa. Is that Little Cayman there?"

"Sure is, Sonny."

They had been sailing a little over an hour and had just lost sight of Cayman Brac.

"It is slightly smaller than our island of Cayman Brac. About two miles less in length. As soon as we pass it, in ten miles we've got about forty miles of open ocean. We'll pray for good weather coming and goin'."

It was uneventful except for a couple of flying fish that jumped over their boat.

"Land ho! Grandpa," Parker hollered.

"Good work, Parker. You've got sharp eyes. Now we'll keep our eyes open for a schooner being built on the beach. I'm going to steer parallel to the coast, and we'll keep a lookout."

As they rounded the northwest corner of the island, Grandpa saw what he was looking for.

"Look over there in that small bay. It's a schooner. I kind of figured we would find something on the lee side."

They turned in. Fortunately they could see the channel, and the way was open and clear.

"Look, Parker, it's a nice place to launch a big boat. I'm sure that's why they chose it."

They pulled up on the beach and secured their boat. There were about fifteen or twenty people moving about up by the dunes. There was also a collection of sheds there. They were probably the office, sleeping quarters, and workshops of the boat builders. They could see the schooner looked finished.

"It looks like they're about set to launch, Parker," Grandpa observe.

Parker was taking it all in. As they got closer to the structures a man approached them.

"Hi, friends. You come to partake of the celebration, and help us launch? It's going to be first thing tomorrow morning."

"Thanks for the invite. I think we will do just that," Grandpa answered.

"Well, Sir, and my fine young man," the man said, "go up and help yourself to refreshments and introduce yourselves. Most of us will sleep on the beach tonight. Tomorrow we'll see if the *Grand Cayman II* schooner will float."

"Thank ye kindly, Sir," Grandpa answered.

"Parker, let's see if they will let us on the schooner, so you can see how it's constructed."

"I'd like that, Grandpa," Parker said.

When they got up to the schooner they could see that some people were being shown around, so they climbed up the ladder everyone was using and looked about.

A fella came up to them. "Welcome aboard. I'm Captain Walter, or at least hope to be. We've been working on the *Grand Cayman II* here the last seven months. We finished a little ahead of schedule, and tomorrow we'll see if she floats."

"I'm Grandpa and this is my grandson, Parker. Could we look around a bit? Parker is very interested in schooners."

"Sure. Go ahead young fella. Look around," the captain said, "Your Grandpa and I will visit a spell. Sir, you look familiar. Do I know you?"

"You sure do!" Grandpa said, "I just recognize you. You served as a new hand on my last schooner voyage."

"Will I'll be swamped! You're First Mate Samuel!"

Grandpa interrupted, "Just call me Grandpa."

"I sure will, Grandpa. Let me shake your hand. By the way forgive me for spying on you two, but I had my handy telescope on you two coming in. That's a fine boat you sailed in on. What's it called?"

"We call it a turtle boat," Grandpa answered.

"So you're the fellas building these boats on Cayman Brac?"

"Yep. That's us," Grandpa said proudly.

"Well, Grandpa, I need two. We're going turtling just as soon as we get a'float'n and outfitted."

"Come up, and see us. I'll try to get you a couple," Grandpa said.

"Grandpa, I looked around, and I got the boat in my mind," Parker said as he came back from touring the schooner.

"Parker, let's go up, and get ourselves some food. I'm famished! I could eat one of those flying fish we saw today, raw!"

They woke up early the next morning as the bright rays of the sun first announced the day. They could see some wagons had just come in, and people of all sorts and sizes were piling out.

"Let's wash up, and get some breakfast, Parker," Grandpa said to a sleepy-eyed young man peering out of a blanket on the beach.

"Look what they have done already. They have that cable from the schooner to that coral that's jutting out there. Then it's blocked and tackled* back to the beach. Everyone is going to pull that line, and it will pull the boat off the beach and launch her into the water."

Right after breakfast everyone went down to the beach, and a long line of people, kids, men, and women grabbed the line. The custom was to have women pull because it was good luck. The workers had cut away the shoring under the hull. The schooner had round logs placed under it for rollers.

The signal was given. Everyone pulled on the rope, and the boat slowly rolled down into the water. They all gave out yells, hollers, and screams.

Grandpa said, "Parker, let's get some snacks, and we'll see if we can go down towards Georgetown to find a schooner under construction."

They said their goodbyes and launched their turtle boat south past Sandy Bay.

"Parker, that long stretch of sandy beach we're looking at over there is where hundreds of green turtles will come in to lay their eggs."

"Wow, Grandpa, It sure is a lot of beach! Is it a couple of miles long? It's as far as I can see."

"Sure is. Next there is Long Bay. It's right there. It sets back in, and there's what we're looking for. See, they're in the early stages of building a schooner. They have a launching ramp* cut into the costal rock."

There was a skeleton of a schooner up on the beach next to the ramp. They headed in.

"It looks like it's about forty-five tons," Grandpa surmised.

"What does that mean Grandpa?"

"That's total weight, Parker. It's a way to measure ship size."

The schooner had the entire keel with stem and stern post. It appeared all of the ribs were attached.

"See the frames and knees, Parker. They make the ribs. Everything we're looking at is made from mahogany. We've got plenty of that on Cayman Brac."

"What do they call the outside boards, Grandpa?"

"Those are stringers from stem to stern. They will attach the outsides planking to that. The deck will be attached after that. You know that yellow pine is best for the planking. Unfortunately it doesn't grow in these here parts. It has to be imported from Tampa, Florida or Mobile, Alabama from the United States of America!"

"How do they watertight it?"

"What they do is drive oakum* in all the seams. It will swell and bond to the wood planks."

They walked over to the schooner and approached a man who appeared to be directing the work.

"Sir, we're traveling from Cayman Brac to George Town. Could we look at your fine boat from a distance? We won't be a bother. My grandson wants to build one of these some day."

"What's the name?" the man asked.

"Just call me Grandpa."

"Ok, tell you what, the men will be taking lunch, so you won't be a bother. Come with me, and we'll have a look inside. By the way, I'm Mel Prater, the foreman on the job."

"Good to meet you," Grandpa said.

"Now, young feller, what do you know about boats?"

"Well, Sir, Grandpa and I built that one we sailed in on. We improved it from the dugout we first built."

"My, my. Right after I show you the *Sunsetter* schooner, we'll have a look at your boat."

"Thank you for letting us have a look at your schooner under construction, Sir. It appears it will be a fine one!"

"You're welcome. Now let's have that look at your craft."

The three of them walked over to where they had their turtle boat pulled up on the beach. The foreman looked the boat over.

"Why it sure is a fine boat. You two say you're out of Cayman Brac? I bet you're the ones I've heard about. Tell you what, I need some of these boats. Build me two of them, and I'll sail the *Sunsetter* up to see you in about five months...the Good Lord willing."

"We'll keep an eye out for your sails," Grandpa replied.

"Parker, there's George Town. We could have walked there from the last schooner, the *Sunsetter*. Let's get in there, and buy a few items we can't find back home. But don't forget, we've got to buy Grandma a fine surprise present."

They stayed overnight in George Town. Compared to the Channel Bay town on their island, this was about five times larger. It had one large dock and a couple of small ones, shops, and even a small hotel.

The next morning saw their turtle boat loaded and our two adventurers leaving the George Town docks.

"Well, Parker, we're going to make a run for home. It's about ninety miles, but feel that breeze, and the weather is pleasant. I bet I know just what you're going to do with that new sketch pad you bought."

"Grandpa by the time we get home, I'm going to have my schooner all put down on this paper. I was thinking, could we start our schooner soon and go slow? We could take twice as much time, and just a few of us could build it in a year and a half."

"Parker, it looks like we will have to find a few more of those gold coins. We'll say we found them on a beach on Grand Cayman."

It was a sunny day. Sebastian had let the current take him all the way west to the western extreme of Cuba. He was getting close to his full size. He now weighed about two hundred and seventy five pounds, and his shell was four feet long.

He was crossing from western Cuba to the closest point of Mexico. He was riding up and down with the swells, and in the distance on the horizon was a bank of white, fluffy clouds.

Sebastian was paddling leisurely when he saw the fin. It was off to his left and plotting a zig-zag pattern, first left and then right. Sebastian's instinct had warned him. He would have preferred the fin going up in a roll and then down, because then the fin would have been a porpoise. But he knew instinctively, a level fin was a shark, and this fin was large. Besides man, the shark is the next dangerous threat to a green turtle, especially if it was a Great White or a Tiger shark. This one was big enough to take a bite out of Sebastian.

He took a deep breath and dove under. Now he could see it was a large shark, and it was heading straight for him. This tiger shark's extraordinary sense, his electro sense, had told him something he could eat was far ahead. He headed towards Sebastian as fast as his propulsion could move him. As he got closer his sense of smell and hearing verified food...a turtle.

Sebastian came up, and took a deep fast breath. He dove under, saw the shark heading towards him, and turned his shell back sideways facing the shark. The shark's nose glanced off Sebastian's shell. The full width of his shell was much too big for the shark to bite. He then turned to face the shark. The shark was about nine feet long, a real big one. The shark was trying to turn to face Sebastian, but because Sebastian was shorter than the shark by half, he could turn a tighter radius. Sebastian would lunge at the side of the tiger shark with his hard sharp bill. One time Sebastian actually bit him slightly.

That's when the shark fled back aways. Sebastian made some powerful strokes with his large front flippers. He was paddling for all he was worth. Glancing over his side he saw the shark circling around, and the fin going under as the shark made his charge.

Sebastian hit the green mass, almost climbing up onto it. It was a large seaweed pile floating along on top of the sea. In fact, Sebastian partially walked and floated on it. The shark hit it and got a mouthful of sea grass. He tried to go under it. He could see the shadow of Sebastian, but since the green mass was three to five feet thick the shark couldn't get at the green sea turtle. He then went off continuing his search for prey.

Sebastian just lay there eating sea grass and seaweed, and watching the fin disappear off in the distance. Whee! That was close.

They had started building their schooner just as soon as they returned from George Town. Everyone had believed the story of the beach, Grand Cayman, and the gold coins. But this time they had found a handful. Grandma had given them a strange look, but seemed to go along with the story. John thought they had the Midas Touch, but Grandpa gave thanks to the Good Lord.

It had been about six months. The keel, stem and stern, framing, and knees were completed. John and his cousin were coming over to start the stringers. They would come over once a week and stay overnight. Of course that depended on just what they had to do at home. Sometimes they would miss a week. It seemed John was always busy farming and helping people with his mule Dynamite.

When John came over to work, then Grandpa and Parker would work on another turtle boat. The days passed and the schooner grew. John had located a lumber schooner who had docked in Channel Bay with a load of White Pine from Mobile, Alabama, USA. They bought the whole load for the planking and decking. The lumber schooner's captain had promised to return in about a month with the sail-cloth, fasteners, and other various parts they would need.

The captain of the *Sunsetter,* when he came by for his two turtle boats, made a contract with Grandpa to bring two yellow pine masts and spars on his next trip.

"Things are beginning to look good. We've got a thirty-five ton, sixty-foot schooner beginning to take shape here. We're working on the decks, and the masts and spars are on their way. John thinks he can get the chains and anchor from an old wreck he has located. So now, what are you going to call her?"

"I've been thinking about that, Grandpa. How about *Saint Sebastian*?"

"Well, that sounds real fine, then *Saint Sebastian* it is!"

True to his word the captain of the *Sunsetter* arrived with the masts. Then he even helped with his crew to install them. The schooner was nearing completion. As they too had promised, the lumber schooner appeared with almost perfect timing, arriving with the sail cloth and accessories.

"Parker, we've got all this installed, and soon we will need to launch this boat!" Grandpa exclaimed. "Then we'll have to get us a crew!"

Parker said, "Well, let's see, you, me, John and his cousin. How many more will we need?"

"We could sail her with just us four. But first we'll have to have a big celebration and get the whole island to help us launch the *Saint Sebastian*."

As word was going out about the gala celebration and launching of the *Saint Sebastian*, the men made the final mechanical preparations. First they attached a substantial roping to the ship. Then they rowed out to a nearby coral reef and attached a heavy pulley. The rope from the ship was run through the pulley and back up to the beach.

The next morning wagons and boats loaded with men, women, and children began arriving. The boats' supports had been removed that evening, and it was sitting with a slight lean with palm logs under it. Just after lunch all the people took hold of the rope, with Grandma first in the very front. The few men who had built her watched for safety's sake, and Parker gave the command, "Pull away!"

The rope's slack was taken up, as over one hundred persons easily pulled the *Saint Sebastian* into the sea. As it slipped into the water, it stood straight up. A great cheer went up from the throng, and they then went back to the food and festivities. A few just stood there in awe looking at the floating, majestic ship. Parker, Grandpa, John, and the builders pulled the boat over to the small dock and tied her off. They still had some week's work of sail-making and ropes and fittings to assemble.

"Parker, Grandma has agreed to our Nicaragua turtling voyage. But she said, no more than one month! She is going to have one of John's older daughters come over to be with her while we're gone. John and his cousin are going to go, and they found two experienced hands to sail with us."

"At first I wanted to go to the southern coast of Cuba, but the Spanish have stopped all foreign ships from turtling. It's something about the Cuban Independence war going on. It seems a Cuban planter named Carlos Manuel De C'espedes has started this war. The Spanish are afraid of turtle boats bringing in filibusters to aid in the insurrection."

"What's a filibuster, Grandpa?"

"Parker, it's a person who goes to a country that he is not a citizen of and helps the revolution to overthrow that government."

"Well Grandpa I guess we are going to Nicaragua. When are we leaving?"

"Just as soon as John and the men get here. More'n likely day after

The *Saint Sebastian* was almost completed and ready for its test run.

'morrow. There's two things: we want to get the boat stocked up with food and water, and to get gone before Grandma changes her mind!"

The early morning breeze filled their sails just as soon as they unfurled them. It was an uneventful cruise through the channel with the tide.

"Parker, this will be your first trip. You need to learn all you can from all the hands. Pay attention and help in all tasks. I will be the captain, John the first mate, and the three men the hands. You will be all positions so you learn," Grandpa instructed. "Now let me show you how to chart a course. See on this map, we're going across the Caribbean, southwest. Now look at this ship's compass in front of John."

"How's she do'n John?"

"She's sail'n pretty," John was at the wheel.

A schooner has a single top deck with the wheel in the middle of the rear.

"Now, Parker, come with me, and we'll check ropes and sails."

It was a beautiful trip, good weather, sunny skies, and fair winds. Their destination was the Miskito Bank off the extreme northeast coast of Nicaragua's fishing grounds. When they arrived, what they did first was sail along the shoals.* They were looking for coral outcroppings. These were places where turtles would spend the evening.

When they found a good location they went into shore and built a small turtle crawl with mangrove poles. They then went out just before sunset in the two small turtle boats. They put out nets that they anchored at one end and supported with floats at the other. The turtles would come up to breathe and get tangled in the nets. Then in early morning the turtle crews would return, pull the turtles into the small boats and take a boat load of turtles to the turtle crawl. This went on for two and one half weeks.

"Well, men," Grandpa said early one morning, "we've got enough turtles. I've never got a load of turtles in such a short time. Let's go over to the crawl and load up."

They sailed over to the turtle crawl. The small boats went back and forth carrying the turtles. It was a sight, the men trying to recapture the turtles. They put the turtles on their backs with wooden blocks under their heads for support and wedges against their shells to keep them from sliding around.

"Well, men our deck is full. We've got eighty turtles. It's all our small schooner will hold. In the old days the big schooners I sailed on needed a couple of hundred to call it a day. Also instead of the fifty percent usually kept by the captain and boat, Parker and I have decided one third will be our share. That way you mates can share equally the rest."

A cheer went up from the crew.

"Let's head for home," Grandpa said cheerfully. "John, head towards the Grand Cayman."

"Aye, Grandpa, are we heading towards George Town?"

"Yes, we should be able to get more there for our turtles."

"I'm sure you're correct. It's a good plan. That way we'll get rid of these turtles. I'm sure we'll all keep at least one for home. They're good eating. I can taste that turtle soup now," John said as he smacked his lips.

They were not mistaken. The George Town people and merchants were happy to see them. The entire load sold in a few hours. While they were still tied up at the small dock preparing to sail, one of the two hands who had gone with them came up to Grandpa and Parker.

"Hi, Thomas," Grandpa said. "I guess you and Benji will be saying goodbye since this is your island."

"Yep, Grandpa, but I wanted to ask, if you go out again, Benji and I want to go, if you'll let us. Also we found three mates who'll come, if it's just Parker and us. See them men standing at the start of the pier. It's James, George and Edward. They're good men. I'll vouch for them. They've had a lot of experience like Benji and me."

"Thank you, kindly, Thomas. We'll be giving you a call, and take care. God bless you," Grandpa replied.

"Thank you, Sir, God be with you also."

Grandma was overjoyed to see them. John and his cousin had left the wagon and dynamite at Grandpa's just in case the ladies needed transportation, so Parker, Grandpa, and Grandma waved as the wagon passed out of sight down the old sandy Cayman Brac trail.

"Well, when are you'n going out by yourself, Parker?" Grandpa asked.

"Do you really think I can go by myself, Grandpa? Parker asked.

"Sure enough! You are into your twenties. That's old enough," Grandpa replied.

"Now just a minute, you two," Grandma interjected, "Think things over."

"Now Grandma, hold your horses. Parker wouldn't go by himself. He would need a good first mate like Thomas who came along with us this last time. Also he would need a good crew. Thomas knows some good men and says they're ready. Besides I just trained him, taught him everything I know."

"Well, Grandpa, let's take a month or so. Then I'll be ready," Parker answered.

Parker thought a lot about his upcoming trip. He was a little apprehensive, but he knew that he needed to get through his first experience as a captain.

"Well, Sonny, we went turtling at the start of the season, in January. It's been almost a month. You know you have only a good month or two of the season left. What's your plan?" Grandpa asked.

"Grandpa, I was just thinking, we need to get word to Thomas and his crew. Then we can get on our way."

"Let's sail one of the turtle boats down to Johns. He will be taking his

Under full sail the *Saint Sebastian* is on its way to the turtle grounds of Nicaragua.

big dugout down to George Town soon and can bring back Thomas and the crew. Meanwhile, we'll stock up the *Saint Sebastian* for five or six weeks."

It took about a week, but John showed up with his boat loaded with Thomas and his crew.

"Thomas, men, we're stocked up. We just need to fill the casks with water. Thomas will be my first mate if it's ok with you men," Parker tried to sound captain like, but he was shaky inside.

"Yes, Sir," the men all answered.

This made Parker feel much better, and Grandpa beamed. Parker waved to both Grandpa and Grandma as the *Saint Sebastian* with Thomas at the helm* slipped out through the channel with the tide.

"Captain, I took the liberty to glance at the charts. It's due southwest if I may suggest," Thomas spoke up.

"Thanks, Thomas, that's fine. I guess I will have to get used to the Captain bit," Parker replied. "Due southwest it is!"

"Aye aye, Sir," Thomas said beaming.

This trip was uneventful, just like the one with Grandpa. The turtling seasons were two, January to March and July to September. According to Cayman tradition, there were no hurricanes during those months. The weather was normally real fine, sunny with a good breeze and only occasional squalls. A good schooner with a fair wind could make the three-hundred-mile trip to northeast Nicaragua in two to three days. A sailboat will keep on twenty-four hours a day with the men changing shift every six hours. As long as the wind blows, they keep going.

They got to the Nicaragua Miskitos Cayos Reef area and promptly set out doing the same thing they had done on the last trip. In fact the men were so enthusiastic Parker didn't have to give many orders. The two weeks went by fast for Parker because they were so busy. It seemed the turtles were more plentiful than the last time.

"Men, it looks like we're ready to load."

"Captain, if I may, George has a suggestion," Thomas said timidly.

"Speak up, George," Parker said.

"Captain, you might consider taking our turtles up to Key West."

"Key West! You mean the USA," Parker asked.

"Yes, Sir, They've got a big crawl up there on the city docks and will pay two to three times the amount you can get in George Town," George stated.

"What about it, Thomas?" Parker asked.

"Yes Sir, Captain. He's right. However, we've got a lot of sailing to get there. You go three hundred miles up between Mexico and Cuba, and then it's two hundred from there into Key West. There's good winds that way this time of year. We could make it in three to four days. But Sir, you're the captain, we'll all support your likes."

"Ok, men, let's load up, and I'll think about it," Parker answered.

The men loaded in unusual enthusiasm and were finished by the end of the day. They were anchored eating their evening meal cooked by Edward, the designated ship's cook.

"Men, I've never been to the USA. In fact this is the farthest I've ever been from the good old Caymans. Tell you what, let's get on to Key West, and sell these turtles!" Parker said enthusiastically.

A cheer went up, and the men sprang into action. The sails were unfurled, and the anchors weighed.

"Men, we'll do the usual shift schedule, Thomas's shift first, and mine in six hours."

Parker lingered reviewing the charts with Thomas so he understood the route. Then he turned in. That night they made one hundred miles. They were clipping along between seven to nine knots.

"Captain, two more mornings and we'll be inbetween Mexico and Cuba. We'll head right for the center if you wish. We'uns don't want to have a run-in with those Spanish. They're bad. They're trying to hang on to their possessions in the Caribbean. I've heard that a planter in Cuba just rose up and declared freedom for Cuba. No Sir, we want to stay away from those ones!" Thomas stated.

Two days later, in the morning:

"Captain, we can't see them, but we should be equal distance from Mexico on the starboard and Cuba off the port bow. If we go two more hours, I suggest we turn hard east-northeast. Then it's one good twenty-four hours, and we'll be looking at the Key West harbor," Thomas said beaming. "The wind has been good to us so far, and we should hit good wind on this last stretch."

"Thanks, Thomas. I've been checking our progress on the charts. The Good Lord has favored us with the wind and the weather."

"What's that key off to port, Thomas?" Parker asked.

"Sir that's Dry Tortugas. It use to be a pirate's hangout until the U. S. stationed the Navy in Key West," Thomas answered.

"Land Ho!" came a yell from Benji, who had climbed up on the main mast.

"Key West. We're here," Parker exclaimed. "Men, let's look sharp! We want them to know that Caymans are sailors."

"Aye aye, Sir," they all said.

"Drop the top sails," Parker yelled out.

The boat entered the harbor where a couple of U S Navy sailing ships were anchored.

"Captain, this harbor is so deep we don't need a pilot. The turtle crawl is on the far side. There it is. See the dock where those flags are flying," Thomas pointed.

They eased up to one side of the pier and dropped all sails.

"Sir, when we dock, the Port Master's Mate will come aboard, check us, and then let us step on their land," Thomas said.

They threw the lines to the men on the pier. As they tied up, two men walked out of a building at the end of the pier and came up to the schooner. Parker and Thomas were at the rails of the schooner.

"Port Master's representative here. State your ship's name, registry, and business," the short clerk-looking man of mid-fifties announced.

"Parker, Captain of the *Saint Sebastian* schooner of the Grand Cayman Islands, with turtles to sell."

"Have you had any sickness the last two weeks, Captain Parker?" the man rang out.

"No sir, we're all well," Parker answered.

"Permission to come aboard and inspect your cargo," the Port Master's representative asked.

"Permission granted," Parker confirmed.

The men stepped onto the boat and looked about, "Looks like a good bunch of green turtles," the Port Master's representative said, "I'll be bidding you good day, Sir. you may go about your business."

"Thank you, Sir," Parker responded.

He stepped off, and a man came up. "Captain, I'm Mr. Smithe. I'm ready to look at and purchase your cargo of turtles."

"Come aboard, Mr Smithe," Parker offered. "This is my First Mate, Thomas."

The man came aboard, shook hands and went right about his business, counting, looking close at some turtles, and writing on a notebook. Thomas and Parker looked on, watching the man.

"Captain, if you and your First Mate will stop over to the office, we'll transact our business. Nice looking bunch of greens."

They entered the office and went over to a counter. Mr Smithe came over.

"Captain, we don't haggle over price here. We know you and your men have worked hard to bring these turtles to us. We appreciate it, and we will give you a fair price." He opened his notebook. "We'll give you this price for one, times eighty four equals this final figure here," he pointed to a figure. "What do you say?"

Parker looked at the notebook. He motioned for Thomas to look. Thomas nodded.

Parker said, "That's fair, Mr. Smithe."

"Well, thank you, Captain, First Mate. Please have a seat over there, and our treasurer will get your payment. "We pay in cash, is that is ok? U. S. silver or dollars paper, your call."

Parker said, "Thank you, Sir. Silver will work best for us."

The treasurer went to a back room. Shortly he came out with a small pouch. He counted the silver out in front of the two men and put it back in the pouch. Mr. Smithe shook hands with Parker and Thomas and showed them to the door. He stepped out and waved to his men on the pier. Both Smithe's workers and Parker's men started pulling turtles out of the schooner and down the pier. They then let the turtles slide down a chute into a very large and substantialy built turtle crawl located alongside the pier.

Thomas said, "Captain, just as soon as we're unloaded, we'll have to undock the schooner, and we can anchor it right off here in the harbor. They keep the pier ready for any boat coming in. They may even load and unload fish here."

"Good idea, Thomas," Parker conferred.

It didn't take the experienced workers very long to empty the *Saint Sebastian*. They then cast off from the pier and with only the main sail unfurled, they eased out into the harbor and dropped anchor. Then Parker divided up the silver and paid the men.

Parker then cautioned, "You men were correct, we got three times the money. They seem to be unusually honest here. Now I'm going to give shore leave, but we'll head out in the mid-morning."

Thomas piped in, "If I may, Sir."

"Yes, go ahead, Thomas."

"Men, I don't want to tell you what to do with your money, but you would be smart to leave most of it here. Captain Parker and I are going to take turns being aboard, so it will be safe."

They all commented, that it was a good idea. Parker took his turn and walked around old Key West. He could tell it was a naval seaport with the large number of U. S. sailors carousing about. He marveled at the great number of stately houses. Many had a small structure on top with windows on all sides. Someone told him it was called a captain's walk.

Because of the Bahamian and Cuban influences there were lots of brightly colored houses, and many had porches with small columns and wood gingerbread decorations. He stopped at an inn and had a meal. He kept himself busy both looking at the pretty girls and listening to people's accents and language.

Morning came, and Parker and Thomas rowed in to pick up the men. Their four tired-looking men came up to the dock, and there were two additional men with them.

"Captain, Sir, these men wish to speak with you. We met them last evening at an inn."

"Well go ahead Sir, state your business," Parker said. "I'm Captain Parker, and this is my First Mate Thomas."

"Captain Parker, I'm Major Endrique Monce. I represent Carlos Manuel de C'espedes who is at this time fighting to free the Cuban people from the Spanish enslavers! This is my associate, Sergeant Salizar. We saw your fine schooner dock at the turtle crawls yesterday. Sir, what we propose, is to hire you, your crew, and your fine boat. We have men who wish to go to Cuba to fight with Carlos Manuel de C'espedes to free Cuba. We just need for you to go slightly out of your way up the Keys to "No Name Key" and pick up our volunteers, and their equipment, and transport them to the south side of Cuba."

Parker was taken aback, "Sir I don't know what to say. We hadn't planned on this. We need to return to the Cayman Islands."

"Captain, I appeal to your good honor, your sympathy, and the decency to free enslaved people. I beg you, Sir!"

"I would have to ask my men. They would all have to agree."

"Sir, it wouldn't be any more than one day out of your way. I'm sure you're heading back around the western side of Cuba. I will pay you very well per man you transport. "

"What do you think, Thomas? Men?"

Thomas questioned, "First, where do we pick up the men and equipment? Where do we drop off, and what's he paying? We don't like the Spanish government any more than he does."

"Gentlemen, first, 'No Name Key' is where the men are camped out. It is about a half day's sailing up the Keys. You turn up the Spanish Channel at Bahia Honda. We will load just as soon as you arrive. Drop-off is the middle south side of Cuba, at Trinidad. It's below the mountain range. There is a good beach for landing. I will pay three silver pieces per man at loading and three at our destination. That will be six times twenty-five which equals one hundred and fifty pieces of silver. What do you say? Do it for Cuba! Please gentlemen, I beg of you."

"Thomas said, "It looks like a filibuster* to me. I'm in, Captain, depending on your decision."

The others said, "Us too!"

Parker looked at his crew. They were all shaking their heads yes.

"Ok, we'll do it. When will you two men be ready?"

"Sir, Captain, men, thank you, thank you."

They both picked up their bags, and the Major said, "We go with you now, Captain."

The turtle boat rowed back out to the schooner with its full load of eight men.

"Thomas, just as soon as we get on board have the men weigh anchor and get this boat on board. While they are doing that we'll check the charts."

"Aye aye, Sir!"

"Major Monce, you and Sergeant Salizar may put your belongings by that hatch over there. Stay close, in case Thomas and I have any questions."

"Yes, Captain Parker."

Thomas and Parker laid out the chart for the Keys area. "Look Captain, it's about forty miles to the main Bahia Honda channel, but we could shave off some time by cutting through here at the Spanish Harbor."

"Major Monce, what do you know about the approaches to No Name Key? Can we go through the Spanish Harbor?"

Sergeant Salizar answered before the Major could answer, "Sir, if I may, I know."

"Yes, go on Sergeant," Monce answered.

"Si, Captain Parker, we came out that way on our way to Key West."

"Ok, Sergeant, if you will keep a sharp eye for any landmarks we should begin our turn on or near four hours," Parker answered.

The men already had all the main sails up, and they headed out leaving the Key West harbor.

Parker commanded, "Thomas, just as soon as we pass the southern most point, bear east-northeast. Have one of the men take soundings, and one heave the log. Also, if the wind is good we'll do with full sails."

"Aye aye, Sir."

Parker thought, I'm getting use to this captaining.

"Eight knots, Sir," the man on the line sung out.

"Very good, Benji," Parker answered.

Parker looked about. It was a balmy sunny morning, and a good breeze was carrying them along briskly. He noticed the water here was a beautiful turquoise color. There were a lot of sea birds. Cormorants, gulls, and pelicans were flying along searching the waves for their food. The shoreline was sometimes sandy and sometimes coral. All along the shore just back of the dunes there were coconut and other palm trees.

"Captain Parker!" Sergeant Salizar hollered as he pointed. "When we get to the end of those Keys we turn up that channel, this side of the far Key."

"Thank you, Sergeant. What do you think, Thomas."

"Well, Captain, it agrees with my plot."

"We best take it a little cautious, Thomas," Parker recommended.

Thomas yelled out, "We're going in here, men. Benji, on the lead line. George, keep a sharp lookout off the front!"

They came around the key and kept to the center of the channel on a due north bearing.

"Major Monce called out, "Captain Parker, straight on. I see the camp," as he pointed towards the island.

"Thomas, we'll go in as far as we can. There's no waves here like on the Atlantic," as they headed towards a small beach amongst the mangroves.

"It's getting shallow, Captain!" Benji called out.

"Very well, drop sails, drop anchor," Parker concurred.

"Major Monce, you two, myself and three of my men will take the two boats in. How much equipment do you have?"
"Captain Parker, each man has a bag of personal items, and we have three canvas tents, cooking gear, food and two crates, if I may add, of rifles, Sir."

The two boats rode up on the sand. Captain Monce and the Sergeant went hurriedly up the beach. They shook hands with a couple of the men. Then they could be heard giving orders. The twenty-five men were scurrying about. The three tents came down, and men came over to the boats carrying all sorts of items.

Parker took note, the Cuban freedom fighters looked like they were from all walks of life. There were dignified men in wrinkled suits, now carrying their jackets. Some men were just in trousers, barebacked. At least half of them looked Cuban, but the others were Anglo.

Captain Monce came over, his men gathering around the pile of tents and other items. "Gentlemen, this is Captain Parker. He has been kind enough to offer us transportation, so we can free Cuba. Please give him your attention and respect. Captain Parker, we are ready."

"Ok men, listen up! Four men to each boat, Two will row with us. We'll load those persons' personal gear and some equipment."

"Captain Parker," Monce spoke up. "Captain, if we could load one of those crates in each boat first."

"Yes, Major. Have your men load them. Keep the items down low and centered!"

They went back and forth four times with the two boats. Half way through, Parker and his three swapped jobs with Thomas and Benji. It was mid-afternoon when they weighed anchor.

"Thomas, it looks like due southwest will take us right off the west coast of Cuba, right where we were a couple of days back. God willing we shall make these two hundred and fifty miles in a little over a twenty-four hours," Parker commented.

"Aye aye, Sir," Thomas responded.

"What I want to do is four-hour shifts and only two men on a rest per shift."

"Aye aye, Sir."

"Captain Monce," Parker called,

"Yes, Captain."

"Do your men have food? We have enough water for us and them to get to Trinidad," Parker asked.

"Yes, Captain, I've got enough military rations to get us there and then for a couple of days. It's not fancy, but we'll live. We have to link up with Carlos Manuel de C'espedes' forces."

"Good, we'll sail as fast as the Good Lord will allow," Parker added.

"Captain Parker, please keep a safe distance from the west side of Cuba. We don't want to be picked up by a Spanish warship before we have a chance to fight!"

"Don't worry, Sir. We don't want that either!" Parker exclaimed.

They swung around western Cuba. It was a hundred miles on the circumference of a great circle.

Thomas informed Parker, "It's a straight shot east-northeast to Trinidad, Sir, and less that two hundred miles to go. We should be there tomorrow at this same time."

Parker could see that at least one-half of the volunteers who had been seasick were starting to recover. They really didn't need as much food as they first thought.

"Land Ho! Straight ahead," Benji sung out.

"It's my homeland at last!" Sergeant Salizar said with feeling. "Now I will be able to help the revolution. You know it's the poor Creoles born in Cuba against the Spanish merchants and the forces of the Spanish king."

"Captain Parker," Major Monce said. "There is a small harbor with a dock. There is a small village there, and Trinidad is farther back."

"Just one second, Major," Parker said as he motioned to Thomas. They stepped over to the rail in the rear. "Benji take the wheel," Thomas commanded.

"What do you think Thomas, dock or unload with the Turtle boats?" Parker asked.

"I've been pondering that very thought, Captain. If I could suggest, here's what I would do. Let Sergeant Salizar go first with four men to a boat and equipment. Kind of a reverse loading. Last trip, one boat with Major Monce, four of us, and his two crates of guns."

Parker added, "Sounds good. We don't want him to start a Navy with the *Saint Sebastian* as their first ship. Also he's to pay us before he leaves the ship."

Parker went over to Major Monce and told him the debarking procedures. He could see the Major wasn't too happy, but he had no recourse.

As they entered the harbor, they could see a grouping of small whitewashed mud brick houses with orange tile roofs. The Escambray Mountains loomed straight ahead towering over the small seaside village. The unloading went off uneventful. While on shore Sergeant Salizar was organizing his volunteers.

"Ok, Major Monce, we've got your guns loaded. We're going in," Parker said. As he was coming back from his cabin where he had hidden the pieces of silver Monce had paid him.

"Thomas, you and George stow the other Turtle boat. Prepare to sail just as soon as we get back."

"Aye aye, Sir."

Parker, Benji and their other two men rowed in and tied up to the dock. Sergeant Salizar had some men from the line he had formed come down and lift the crates out of the boat.

Parker said to his men, "Prepare to cast off men. I'll be right back."

As he shook hands with Major Monce, he said, "Major, good luck, and God go with you."

"Thank you, Captain Parker, and good sailing," He then turned and headed towards Sergeant Salizar who had opened both crates and was issuing rifles and bandoleers of ammunition. Parker could see a couple of new faces, men dressed in white, loose-fitting clothes with large brimmed hats. They had rifles slung over their shoulders and bandoleers of ammunition across their chests. They were talking to Major Monce.

Parker's men had the turtle boat untied. He stepped in and Benji followed, giving the boat a push off from the dock. It didn't take the four of them very long to row out to the schooner. As they we're hoisting up the turtle boat, Thomas said, "Weigh anchor! Sails up!"

"Good work, Thomas," Parker commented, "Let's get on home!"

"It looks like it's about two hundred miles south-southwest, Captain," Thomas reported, as he stood there with both hands on the wheel.

They headed straight out to sea from the Trinidad area. They had been sailing just for twenty or thirty minutes, when Benji cried out, "Sail Ho! Some smoke too! Off the starboard Captain."

Thomas gave Parker his telescope, and Parker went over to the rail. He saw a large two-masted ship, but it had a smoke stack in the center between the two masts. It was bearing straight for them. He handed the telescope to Thomas and took the wheel.

"What do you make of it, Thomas?" Parker asked.

"Doesn't look too good, Sir. Looks like a Spanish gunboat. I can see gunports lining the side and the Spanish flag. This one is both sail and steam power, and I can see the iron plate on her sides."

"Think we can outrun them?"

The Spanish gunboat had sails and steam power both.

Just then a puff of smoke came from a front gunport, and then a bang! There was a splash of a cannon ball just in front of their schooner.

"We could, Sir, but we can't out run that!" as he pointed to where the cannon balls ripples were still in sight.

"Drop sails, Thomas. That will let them know we are not running," Parker commanded.

"Aye aye, Sir. Drop sails men, real fast!" Thomas commanded.

The sails came down. The *Saint Sebastian* just sat there, rocking with the swells. The Spanish ship came into hailing distance.

"Ahoy there!" came a call from the Spanish ship, "Prepare to be boarded."

A large quarter boat rowed by eight men in Spanish naval uniforms and two officers, one in the front and one in the rear, was fast approaching. They came alongside. The two officers and four men came aboard. Thomas and Parker met them. The two officers stepped forward. The four men had rifles and were right behind by the rail in a row.

One officer, who appeared to be senior, asked, "Who is Captain?"

Parker said, "I am Captain Parker of the *Saint Sebastian*, out of the Cayman Islands."

"Senor, I am Major Dominique. I represent His Royal Majesty of Spain and the Spanish Governor of Cuba. You are trespassing in Spanish Cuban waters. What do you have to say for yourselves?"

"Sir," Parker offered, "We were just trying to catch some green turtles."

"A likely story," the Spanish officer said. "We saw you. You were too far into shore. You were dropping off filibusters? Yes?"

Parker said, "No sir, we were after green turtles."

The commanding officer turned to the officer behind him, "Lieutenant, you will take this prize capture to Havana. I will leave these four men with you. His men will sail the schooner and this man, Captain Parker, will be tied and locked up. His men will be impressed into the Spanish Navy. This captain will like Havana's Morro Castle. But it is a pity he will probably hang for delivering filibusters. We've got to cast off, so take over, we're already late for our visit to Santiago de Cuba."

"Si, Senior!" The Spanish Lieutenant saluted.

The ranking one went over the side into the longboat and they pushed off hastily heading back to their ship.

The Spanish lieutenant said to two of the Spanish sailors, "Carlos, Sanchez, take the captain below, tie him up and lock him in the cabin. Pedro, Domingo, watch these men. Who is the first mate?"

Thomas stepped forward, "Me, sir."

"Very good. Sails up and set a course for the western tip of Cuba. Due west and south of the Isle of Pines.

"Aye, Sir. Men, let's get the sails up," Thomas commanded. But there was a noticeable slowness in the men's response.

The two sailors were talking Spanish and motioned for Parker to lead. He opened the hatch and went down the ladder. The two men followed.

Parker said, "This is the way." That's when he realized they spoke no English.

He opened the door to his cabin. They followed him in, tied his hands behind him, and then motioned for him to lie in his cot. Next they tied his ankles together. They went out speaking Spanish. They closed the door and he could hear them gibbering in their language, which Parker couldn't understand. He guessed they were trying to find a way to lock the door from the outside. Then he could hear them leaving and climbing back up the ladder.

He thought, they must have improvised something.

He could feel the *Saint Sebastian* swinging around. He decided, that while they are getting accustomed to his ship he needed to act fast. He didn't want to hang in Havana or even visit the dreaded Morro Castle Prison.

He rolled around and got the hammock swinging...Bang! He fell out onto the floor. Ouch! That hurt, he thought.

He laid still for a moment to make sure no one had heard the sound. Then he scrunched and bent until he was sitting up. Then he tapewormed his way pushing with his two legs and sliding with his bottom. He came up to a couple of storage drawers, built into the side of the ship. He turned his back to them, took hold of a handle pull on the bottom one, and pulled with his fingers. The drawer came open. He got up on his knees and reached in until he found the knife. With his fingers he picked it up. He then held it with his hand and backed up and stuck it into a timber of the ship. After that he just put the rope on the blade and sawed through. Hands free, the leg ropes came off easy.

He looked around. Parker thought, what next? If I could slip off the boat and head for shore, I could join up with Major Monce's group. Anything is better than the alternative.

He looked around. There was a glass window port in the rear. It was large enough for him to slip through. He took down the hammock and cut the ropes from both ends. Then he tied them together It would be long enough. There was a small chair. He tied the rope to it and set it below the window port. He tied the rope to his belt, opened the port, slipped through, and did a somersault. The chair came up to the port, and stopped there with a slam, hanging against the window. Parker came to a sudden stop swinging there back and forth out the rear of the ship, in the air, just over the water. He held on to the rope with one hand, cut the rope with the knife he had taken with him, and quietly let himself down into the water.

Immediately the *Saint Sebastian* pulled away from him as he treaded water. He was fortunate the seas were calm with only slight swells. Par-

ker took one last look at the schooner, then he started to slowly swim toward the shore, far in the distance. It was then he realized there was something wrong with his shoulder. It was cramping. He must have injured it when he fell off the hammock. He stopped swimming and treaded water. He had to make it to shore somehow. He started to pull with his good arm.

Sebastian had just arrived from Nicaragua. He was diving down and eating some of the good sweet sea grass. He decided he had eaten enough and would dive down and swim out some. He took a deep breath and went down, down. He held his breath for quite a while, then pulling with strong front flippers he shot up to the surface.

Parker had been pulling with his good arm, then taking a deep breath and just floating. His one arm was hurting and cramping real bad. It looked like he hadn't gotten any closer to the shore. He set out again with his tiring good arm. He said out loud, "I don't think I'm going to make it...God, please help me!"

Suddenly a dark green hump came up right next to Parker. In fact, it actually bumped into him! Instinctively Parker grabbed for it. He didn't know at first what it was. Then he realized, it's a green turtle!

Sebastian felt a bump as he surfaced. He was about to take a deep and fast breath when he looked back. It's a human! How did he get here? Then he had a strange feeling, something in the deep dark confines of his mind. This human looked familiar. Sebastian wasn't fearful. He just floated there, the human hanging on.

Parker didn't know what to think, but he continued to hold onto his floating green turtle lifesaver. Then he saw it; on the top of the turtle's shell was the unusual cross marking.

He said out loud, "It's Sebastian! I can't believe it. Thank you Lord."

Just over the horizon, moving slowly towards this activity was an English Frigate, one of His Majesty's fighting ships.

"What's happening, John? Is the Spanish gunboat gone?" The first mate hollered to the man in the crow's nest who was looking through a large telescope.

"Aye, sir, The gunboat is out of sight. She's heading due east. That schooner with the Cayman flag was slow to start and still slow to go due west."

"First Mate, let's slip in behind the schooner. It looks like they took her as a prize, probably heading to Havana." The captain commented.

"Aye aye, Sir." It was a good thing, Sir that you had us drop the tops'ls. That way the Spanish gunboat didn't see us," the First Mate said.

"We're not ago'n to let them Spanish take one of our possession's ships, even if they're breaking the law. Poor devils, probably poaching green turtles, or even worse, dropping off filibusters. Let's get on with it!" The captain ordered.

"Aye aye, Sir!" the First Mate saluted the captain.

"Ok, men, up all sails. Get those tops'ls back up. Beat to quarters. Everyone on deck. Man your positions," The First Mate commanded.

They swung around and started on a path to intercept the Cayman schooner. Her Majesty's frigate the *Southerland*, 24 guns was patrolling the international waters of the Caribbean. Their primary mission was to apprehend any slaving ships trying to get their cargo to a Spanish port. Most of the nations had signed a 'No Slavery' pact, but Spain had not. However, accordingly to popular belief, she would soon.

From the crow's nest, "Sir, there's something in the water off the starboard beam. It looks like a man next to a green turtle,"

"There he is, Sir, I've got him in my sights," The First Mate said pointing.

"I see him, a man holding on to a large green turtle!" The captain answered. "Head for the man, First Mate. Launch a long boat!"

"Aye aye, Sir!"

Sebastian saw the large ship approaching. He wasn't going to stay around and be caught. He took a deep breath and dived.

Parker was treading water as the long boat pulled alongside. Strong arms pulled him up into the boat.

On the British frigate, the captain said, "Captain Parker, I don't want to know what you were up to, off the shore of Cuba. But we'll have your schooner back shortly."

Just then the First Mate said, "Captain, we're ready for your word, Sir."

"One across her bow, First Mate."

"Aye aye, Sir. Fire one from the bow chaser across her bow!" The First Mate hollered.

Blam! The gun carriage leaped back from the recoil and was then engulfed in smoke.

The *Saint Sebastian's* Spanish flag went down.

"First Mate, take Captain Parker and eight marines. Leave him, and bring those Spaniards back here. We'll drop them off later. Now as for Captain Parker, I command you to get on your boat, head due south, and back to the Cayman Islands. I don't want to see you around here again!"

"Yes Sir, and thank you, Sir!" Parker answered.

"You're welcome. Now Captain Parker, get out of here."

"Thomas, it's sure good to be back on the *Saint Sebastian*, "Let's head for home...again." Parker said.

"Aye aye, Sir," and Thomas said, "Men, full sails!"

As the sails took hold and filled, Parker said under his breath, "I don't think I'll go green turtle hunting any more. The *Saint Sebastian* will have to haul lumber or other goods."

"What did you say, Sir?" Thomas asked.

"Oh nothing, Thomas. I'll tell you later."

262   *Roberts' Best*

12
Roberts' Best

The year is 1955. It is the evening meal at the Roberts' family household. The family lives in a small single-family bungalow just to the west of Houston, Texas. This house is in the town of Alief. It is your typical small Texas town, lots of pickup trucks, cowboys, and boots.

"Daddy, Daddy, can we please turn on the air conditioner? Please, Daddy?"

"Now Sonny, you are correct. It is a bit humid. Tell you what, right after supper we'll drop all the windows, and turn it on. That will cool it down for sleeping."

"Daddy, Daddy, can I please visit grandfather Roberts this weekend? I love to sail his boat on the lake. He is teaching me to be a sailor. Besides he always has his air conditioner on! I love it. It's so cool."

"Now Harold Junior, just be calm. If your mother says it's ok, you can go over Saturday morning for the weekend. Let's go and ask your mother."

"I heard you two. Yes it will be ok. But Harold you will have to do your homework here or over there," Mom stated.

"How come he always gets to do everything he wants? What can I do?" Harold's sister Suzie complained.

"Now, Dear, you and I are going shopping," her mom added.

I guess you could say that the Roberts' family was a good old Texas country family. Harold Junior's dad was a tall and muscular thirty-year-old man. He was clean shaven and had a trim and short haircut. He worked for a local drilling supply. Oil drilling, that is. Sometimes he clerked and took orders, and sometimes he drove a big straight-bed, ten-wheeler delivering pipe and supplies to drilling rigs.

The little lady, Harold Junior's mom, was short and petite, very pretty, and had shoulder length brown hair. Mary was a couple of years younger than Harold Senior. Then there was Harold Junior's older sister, Suzie, who Harold loved to tease and aggravate. However, he made sure he did it discreetly. Suzie was ten years old, not too tall, kind of like her mom. Since she was two years older than Harold Junior, she made sure he didn't forget it. She was blessed with long brown hair, like her mom's, a style of the times.

Now we come to our star of the story, Harold Junior. A very sharp young fella. Harold was going to take after his daddy. Already at eight, he was as tall as his sister. Even though he was tall, he was thin and scrawny. Harold Junior kept his dark brown hair kind of short, but not a crew cut. He had a little bit to comb, and that away he sometimes had some sticking up in the back.

Saturday morning came soon enough. At the breakfast table:

"Well, Daddy, are we going to go over to Grandpa Roberts? I've got my homework done...well almost. But all I've got is some reading, and I can do it on the drive over. Are we going to go?"

Harold Senior looked at Mary over the steaming cup of coffee he was holding in both hands.

She nodded her head yes and said to Harold Senior, "I already called him and he will be looking for you two. Harold Junior, get your reading book and the day-bag of clothes and toiletries I packed for you. Your dad will be going soon, and brush your teeth!"

"See you later, Hon." Mary said.

The two Harolds went out of the house to Harold Senior's pride and joy, a 1950 Ford F-150 pickup truck. It was Midnight Black and had reversed Mercury rims on the rear, sporting large tires. He was running Oldsmobile star flippers on the front wheels. The one hundred horsepower engine had been hot rodded up to at least one hundred and twenty-five horsepower. It had high compression Edelbrock aluminum heads, dual carbs, and a three-quarter cam. It would certainly move. Oh, did I mention, dual exhausts.

They drove a couple of miles from the Alief area and got up on the Beltway. Now let's talk a bit about Houston, Texas, the fourth or fifth largest city in the US, booming because of oil refineries on the east side and a large shipping port there also. Probably also fourth or fifth in the USA for its port. This all made it big and growing.

They drove first north and then the Beltway turned due east. They passed and went over and under bridges everywhere. Houston, Texas also led the nation with its advanced freeways.

After they got to the far northeast corner of the city's outskirts, they left the Beltway and went a few miles north. They were now in beautiful oak and tall pine wooded country. Then they took a turn into a lake-side development that sold large wooded lots. The more fortunate ones were on Lake Houston.

Now Lake Houston was built in 1953, as the primary water supply for Houston. It was built by damming up the San Jacinto River. Its dimensions are approximately three miles wide by twenty one miles long, running north and south. One branch runs an additional twelve miles due west.

They turned left, drove up a dirt lane, and broke out into a clearing. It was Grandfather Roberts' lot. On it he had a two-bedroom woodland log cottage. There was a two-car garage right off to the side.

They pulled up and stopped. Harold Senior revved the engine once and then shut it down. As Harold Junior was getting out, he heard a yell coming from down by the water. There standing out on a pier waving was Grandfather Roberts. Harold Junior took off running with Harold Senior walking behind.

They could see that just a short distance off the pier Grandfather Roberts' sailboat was anchored. The dingy was tied to a post at the dock.

"Hi! Harold Junior, Hi, Son," Grandfather Roberts welcomed.

"Grandfather, are we going sailing?"

"Now hold your horses, Junior. First things first."

"Thanks for bringing Junior out, Son. I will bring him back in time for supper tomorrow."

"That will be great Dad. He's said he had some schoolwork to do. It's reading."

Grandfather Roberts was a little above medium height, and well built for a man of fifty-five. He had an average haircut to his brown hair, not too long or short. He had a shadow of a mustache which was a little darker than the hair on his head. He, too, was into the oil business. An oil engineer at the age of twenty two, the company he worked for had wildcatted by drilling wells and struck it big. Roberts' stock skyrocketed, and he had retired three years earlier to take care of his ill wife of thirty years, who went on to see the Lord a couple of years later. That is when he downsized by moving from interbeltway, Houston, buying this lot on the lake, and building the cottage. He and his wife had the sailboat docked at a marina at the end of the lake, so he just moved it over here.

"Well, what we plan to do," said Grandfather Roberts as he put his arm around Harold Junior, "we'll work some on the sail boat today, and after Sunday school and church tomorrow, we'll take the boat for a sailing and fishing trip on the lake."

"Oh, Grandfather, why can't we go today?" Harold Junior questioned.

"Because we've got some work to do on the boat. We've got to get it fixed so we can sail. If we have time we'll take the dingy and fish some around here."

"Yes, that will be fun, grandfather. But why do we have to go to church and Sunday school?"

"Now Junior, we need to thank the Good Lord for all of our blessings. You know we always do that. Now let's run along and go inside. Want to stay for some coffee, Son?"

"Just a short cup, Dad. As you know, it's a fair trip over here, and I've got to get some things from the hardware store, and then put them on our house. You also know, the repairs never stop."

"Tell me about It, Sonny," Grandfather exclaimed.

Harold Junior and Grandfather Roberts could hear the '50 Ford pickup heading out as Harold Senior was shifting the three-speed floor shifter through the gears.

"Well, Junior, let's head out to the pier and do our repairs."

They took the dinghy out to the sailboat and brought the boat over to the pier and tied it up. Then they did the work on her, or mostly Grandfather Roberts did the work as Harold Junior tinkered. The sailboat, *Roberts' Best*, was a very nice craft, a twenty-eight foot sloop, mast a few feet forward of center with two sails.

"Junior, let's grab lunch. Then we'll take the dingy out rowing and fishing."

"Yes Grandfather, let's do it!" Harold said clapping his hands.

"Junior, you will have to help me make these sandwiches. You know I'm not the best cook, I need some help. Then tonight we'll eat out."

"Tell you what, you make yours, and I'll make mine!"

Harold Junior proceeded to pile on the peanut butter and strawberry jam, then banana slices and more peanut butter.

"I've got some ice cream in the refrigerator for dessert, so save some room," Grandfather grinned.

"Okay," Harold Junior said, as his mouth stuck together.

They cleaned up, brushed their teeth, and headed out to the pier.

"Here, Junior, you carry your pole and this pail of bait, and I will carry my fishing pole and this tackle box."

They put their gear in the dinghy. This dinghy was a small boat about eight feet long. It could be pulled along behind or placed on the rear of a fair sized sailboat. It was propelled by two small oars and was used to run back and forth between the anchored sailboat and the pier.

"Now, Harold, the first thing we have to do is put our life preserver vests on," Grandfather instructed.

"Why, Grandfather?" Harold asked.

"Just in case we fall out and can't swim, like you."

"Oh," Harold said.

"Now we'll row out a'ways and then go up that way," Grandfather Roberts said as he pulled hard on the oars.

Harold Junior was sitting in the rear, taking turns first dragging the tip of his pole in the water and then skipping his hand over the ripples from the boat.

Then he got a new idea. "Grandfather! I could row for you. That way you wouldn't get tired."

"Well, Harold let's let you try."

They swapped seats, and Harold Junior tried to row. That was when they started going around in circles.

"Ok, Harold, listen up. Pull both oars at the same time towards your chest. Then push down, put your arms out in front, raise them, and the oars will go down, then pull together again."

Harold Junior tried and tried. He did make some progress. However, it wasn't long until he said, "There Grandfather, it's your turn."

"Thanks for your help, Harold. Let's start fishing right here. We will let the boat drift. Let's bait your hook with this worm."

"I can do it," Harold said very independently.

Together they got it accomplished.

"While you are fishing for a blue gill, I'm going to cast this spoon out and see if any large mouth bass are biting. Harold, you use that side of the boat, and I will use this side."

"Grandfather! Grandfather! My pole is bent. I got one!" Harold Junior yelled.

Grandfather put his rod down. "Let me help you. Pull the pole up. Look it's a big blue gill," Grandfather said excitedly.

Z... Z!...Z! Grandfather's reel sang.

"Now I've got something!" he hollered, as he grabbed for his shaking reel which was starting to move across the seat. He started to reel in his line. "That's the way, Harold, get it in the boat," Grandfather said as he slacked off his line and looked around.

Z...Z...Z! There it went again. A big largemouth bass broke the surface on Grandfather Roberts' side of the boat. It rolled up and over as it dived down with a splash.

Z...Z...Z! He fought the reel as he wound it in. The drag was letting some line out. It was a big one!

"It's in the boat, Grandfather. It's flopping all over the boat. What should I do?" Harold Junior screamed.

"Keep your cool, Junior! Just put your foot on him until I get this bass reeled in."

Ka-flop! Ka-flop! The blue gill flopped all over the boat bottom, with Harold Junior trying to stomp him. Grandfather Roberts was concentrating on the biggest bass he had ever seen in this lake! It came up to the side of the boat.

"I forgot the net!" Grandfather Roberts exclaimed. "Well here goes nothing." He gave a big yank, and the clunker bass flew up out of the water, over the side of the boat, and onto the floor. Now there were two floppers.

Grandfather Roberts grabbed his glove and stringer out of the tackle box and took care of that problem real fast.

"Harold Junior, what do you think. We both caught big ones."

"Yes, Grandfather, very big ones!"

"I don't know about you, but I've had enough fishing for this day. Let's row back, clean these fish, clean up ourselves, and go out to eat supper. What do you think?"

"Let's do it, Grandfather Roberts," Harold Junior said with much enthusiasm.

They rowed back and tied up at the pier. Grandfather Roberts had a fish -cleaning stand nailed to a tree near the pier. He started by showing Harold how to scale the two fish. Of course when Harold Junior scaled, it was scales flying everywhere. It looked like a snow storm.

"Now I'm going to gut and clean the fish. Be careful of the knife Junior. Stand back!"

"Grandfather, is Grandmother in Heaven?"

"Why, yes Harold. She loved God."

"I remember her a little bit from when I was three. Will I be able to see her in Heaven some day?"

"Why yes, Harold. But you have to be sure you are going to Heaven."
How do I be sure, Grandfather?"

"Well it's easy Harold. You have to just believe and do three things."

"What are they, Grandfather? I want to be sure."

"Well, number one, believe that Jesus is the Son of God who died on the cross to save us. Number two, realize that you are a sinner, make mistakes, and ask Jesus to forgive you of all your sins, and number three, ask Jesus to come into your heart and make you a new person."

"Grandfather, I believe and want all those three things. Now am I going to Heaven some day?"

"Yes, Harold Junior, I believe that you just made God very happy."

"That's good! Now can we go to supper?" Harold Junior said with a cheer.

The next day after Sunday school, church, and a home-made fish dinner. "That was good fish, Grandfather. Now are we going sailing?"

"You bet, Harold. Let's get down to the pier and get going. They rowed the dinghy with their snacks and cokes out to the *Roberts' Best*.

"Do you want me to pull up the anchors, Grandfather?"

"Yes, Harold. Remember to turn the cranks in the front and rear, and then put on the locks. I'll check you."

"All done, Grandfather. Take a look."

"Real fine. You're going to make a good sailor. Now let's get these up. We're fortunate since it is a sloop we only have two sails to worry about, the mainsail here in the rear and the headsail there in the front. I like to call it the jib."

"Why do they call it a sloop, Grandfather?"

"Well mostly because it just has one mast. See this big pole here going straight up. It's called the mast. The big pole here lying sideways and holding the sail, it's called the boom. Now, let's turn these cranks. They will put up the sails."

"I can do it Grandfather."

"Ok, show me, Junior. I'll help you if you need it."

Up the two sails went and the boat began to move. The *Roberts' Best* was steered from inside a small cabin just in the center of the boat. Down below it had a very small galley, two sleeping berths, a head*, and some storage up front. It was a serious small sailboat."

"Let's get our life preservers on, Harold, and come down here so you can steer this boat."

"Ok, Grandfather."

"Now you will have to stand up on this step to look out. Here grab the wheel. Once we get out a little farther, we'll turn due north, and I will show you how to use the compass to stay on a northerly course."

"What's a compass, Grandfather?"

"It's this little thing in front of you, right here. One side of this needle always points north."

They sailed for about an hour due north. It was easy for Harold Junior since the main part of Lake Houston runs north-south for about twenty miles. At least ten miles of that was the wider part. Of course Grandfather Roberts was right at his side helping.

Clouds were beginning to appear in the southern sky, and the wind was beginning to pick up as Grandfather Roberts turned the boat around. Harold Junior had been playing around the bunks below and inspecting everything.

He came back to the cockpit, "It's getting windy, Grandfather. What happened to the sun? What are those big black clouds?"

"Harold, it looks like a storm is racing in. That's funny, I didn't see anything on the weather report about it."

They could see some boats to either side of them heading for the shore.

"Harold, hold this wheel for a minute. I'm going to drop the jib sail."

"That's the front one, right, Grandfather?" he asked proudly.

"You're correct. There it's done. Hold the wheel for a minute more while I secure the sail."

"There, that job is finished. You did well, Harold. Now we're going to get in a little closer to the shore and then we'll have to tack to go against the wind."

"What does tack mean, Grandfather?"

"Watch the boat's direction, Harold. First I go right...and then left. Watch the boom as it changes sides. See the wind, it is now letting us move forward against it, although not as fast as if the wind was at our back."

"Oh," Harold exclaimed.

It had become dark and foreboding. The wind was gusting. Every time they tacked left or right, the side of the boat was exposed to the wind, and waves would wash over the sides and splash both of them.

"It's getting wet, Grandfather!" Harold yelled as the wind took his words right out of his mouth.

"I know Harold, Just hold on, I can see our pier now."

They stayed on a right tack and came racing into the protection of their cove. Grandfather dropped both anchors. They got into the dinghy, and rowed hurriedly over to the pier, tied up, and ran for the house, life vests still on and dripping as the rain pelted them.

Inside the cottage: "Now, Harold Junior, it's hot showers and clean dry clothes for the both of us."

"The rain has stopped Grandfather," Harold said as he looked out the living room's front window.

"Good. Let's grab your day bag and go over to your house for supper.

I'm going to be hungry."

"I like this truck, Grandfather. It smells nice inside it."

"That's called the 'newness' smell Harold, It's from a new truck's seats and upholstery."

"Now buckle your lap seatbelt. We want to be safe."

The '54 Ford 150 took off real smooth. "How come your truck drives much quieter and smoother than my father's truck, Grandfather?"

"Harold it's newer, it's got an overhead valve engine, and an automatic transmission, and I'm not a hot rodder like your Dad."

"What's an automatic transmission, Grandfather?"

"It means you don't have to shift it. That means go from first to second gear like your Dad does when he moves that long rod on the floor. See, I just put it in 'D' here."

"What does the "D" mean, Grandfather?"

"Well it means "Drive. But what it really means is Go!"

"Oh," Harold Junior said, "What're all those bridges, Grandfather?"

"We just passed the Interstate Number Ten Harold. Those bridges and roads are needed when two big roads come together. We've just got a few more miles and we'll be at your home," Grandfather Roberts said patiently.

It had gotten real quiet. Grandfather Roberts looked over at Harold Junior. He had fallen asleep.

"Thank goodness!" He said under his breath.

The next day after school, Harold Junior arranged some lawn chairs and other items in the back yard. They kind of resembled the shape of a sail boat when he was finished. He got a plastic pan from the garden shed. He then went to the outside water spicket and filled it up half way with water. Why half way? Because that was just about all he could carry. He set it near his boat.

Suzie came out, "What are you doing?" she asked.

"I'm playing sail boat. If you want to play, have a seat and I'll tell you about my sailing in the storm yesterday with Grandfather Roberts."

"Ok, I have a few minutes, but make it quick!"

"Sit here in the cockpit of the boat. It's where you steer. Here, hold this steering wheel. It's from my old pedal truck, but it's what you use to tack the sail boat. You know what tack means?"

"No, smarty. Tell me."

"It's when you go from side to side to move against the wind."

"I knew that! Now get on with the story," Suzie said very indignantly.

"Now close your eyes so you can use your imagination. The story is coming. Now tack by turning right. Keep your eyes closed! The waves can now splash over the side of the boat and splash you."

Just then Harold Junior threw the pail of water on Suzie.

Sputter...Sputter. "What happened? Why did you throw water on me!" Suzie screamed as water dripped down from her wet hair and face and then onto her clothes.

"I just wanted to show you what happened to Grandfather Roberts and me." Harold Junior explained, a slight smile across his lips.

"I'm going to get you, you Do-Do!" she hollered.

Harold Junior took off running with a dripping wet sister on his heels. His long legs quickly out distanced his wet, angry sister. When she saw she couldn't catch him, she went stomping and still dripping into the kitchen.

"What are you doing, young lady? You're all wet. What happened?" their mother asked frantically.

"Mom, Harold Junior threw a pail of water on me," she said crying.

"Harold Junior! In the house, right now!" Mom hollered out the back door.

"What do you want, Mom?" Harold said very innocently.

"Did you throw a pail of water on your sister?"

"But Mom, I was just trying to explain to her about the storm Grandfather Roberts and I were in yesterday."

"Harold Junior, up to your room! Your father will talk to you when he gets home. Now Suzie, let's get some dry clothes on."

There were lots of sailing trips and fish fries with the Robert's family. One Sunday evening, Grandfather Roberts had an announcement. "Yes, the doctor said my sore lungs were an allergy. The pollutants from Houston afloat in the air with this high humidity is the result. I have to get out of this humidity and pollution. You know I'm not getting any younger, and this has really been bothering me."

"I will keep the lake cottage property and hopefully be able to return in the wintertime when the humidity is low. You will have the use of the lake site whenever you wish, and I hope you will watch over it for me."

"We're going to miss you, Grandfather," they all said.

"I'm going to miss you-all too. But I've got to go where I feel better. Now I don't want to be where it's cold. I have done some research, and

I'm thinking about Key West, Florida."

"Key West, Florida! Isn't that hot?" Harold Senior asked.

"No, surprisingly, if I get a place on the Atlantic, the ocean breeze will be great! I'm thinking about having the *Roberts' Best* trucked over to Galveston. I'm going to sail her from there along the Gulf Coast to Key West."

"Isn't that dangerous, Dad?" Mary asked.

"No, Mary, I'm sure it's more dangerous to drive on Interstate 10 in Houston. Besides, I'm going to write a book about my journey."

"That sounds so romantic," Mary commented.

"Why thank you, Honey," Grandfather answered.

"When are you going to start out, Dad?" Harold Senior asked.

"Son, I've got the boat in dry dock being checked over now. That means it's half way to being moved to the Galveston Marina. The boat fixer-upper should take a couple of weeks. I will get my supplies and things, and then I'll go with it and launch."

"Well, we'll have a bon-voyage party next Sunday then," Mary said lovingly.

"That will be real fine," Grandfather Roberts acknowledged.

The *Roberts' Best* was loaded up and trucked to a marina on Galveston Island. Grandfather Roberts had decided to leave his truck in the garage at the cottage. He had stocked his sailboat with five weeks' basic supplies. His boat carried forty gallons of fresh water, and he planned to stop at marinas along the way. His stops at evening would be because he was a crew of one and had to rest. Besides he wasn't in a hurry and wanted to find out about the Gulf Coast.

The following is an abbreviated version of Tom Roberts' book,

Gulf Coast Summer
One man's sailing adventure from Galveston to Key West

The research I had done on Galveston Island rewarded me with this tidbit of information. Galveston was originally inhabited by native Indians. The famous Spanish explorer Cabeza de Vaca's ship was wrecked on the island in November, 1528. In 1758 another Spanish explorer came along and named the island Villa Galvez in honor of the Count of Galvez from Madrid, Spain.

I stayed in the Galveston Marina and the surrounding area a couple of days. There were a lot of fellow boaters in all types of craft, from big cruisers to large sailboats. In fact, mine was on the smaller side. One good thing I noticed was that everyone was friendly and helpful. The first thing I was told that I needed was a Gulf Coast Water Travel Guide. The book I bought from the marina store was over five hundred pages. It consisted of charts and descriptions of every turn and stopping place on the Coast and most importantly the Gulf-Coast Intercostal Waterway.

By visiting around with the many boaters, one item I really found historically adventurous was the fact that two pirates had a lot to do with early Galveston's history. One was in 1816. Louis-Michelaury, a pirate supporting Mexico's fight against Spanish rule, sailed in and out of Galveston. The other was the pirate Jean Lafitte. He was a hero of the War of 1812 against the British. He had made himself the island's governor over all the inhabitants with a bunch of pirates. This may sound hard to believe, but these men helped with the early settling of Galveston.

During my stay on the island, I obtained as much advice as my mind could hold. Then the day came. I was really excited as I untied the *Roberts' Best* from the dock and headed away from the Galveston Marina. It was midmorning. I could almost picture the skull and crossbones flag flying from my mast.

I couldn't daydream forever. I was awakened from my trance by the waves and goodbyes from the many boating friends I had made the last few days as I sailed by them.

I was especially grateful for the designers and builders of *Roberts' Best.*

Roberts' Best route along the Gulf Coast Intercostal Waterway.

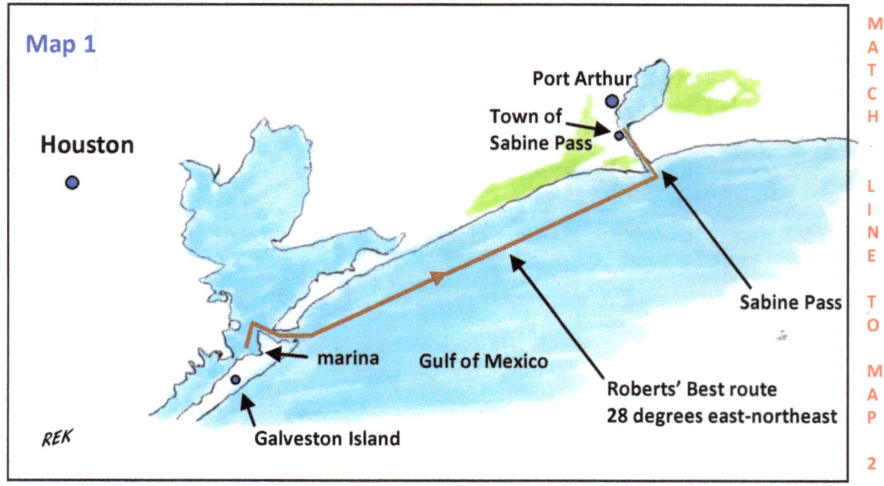

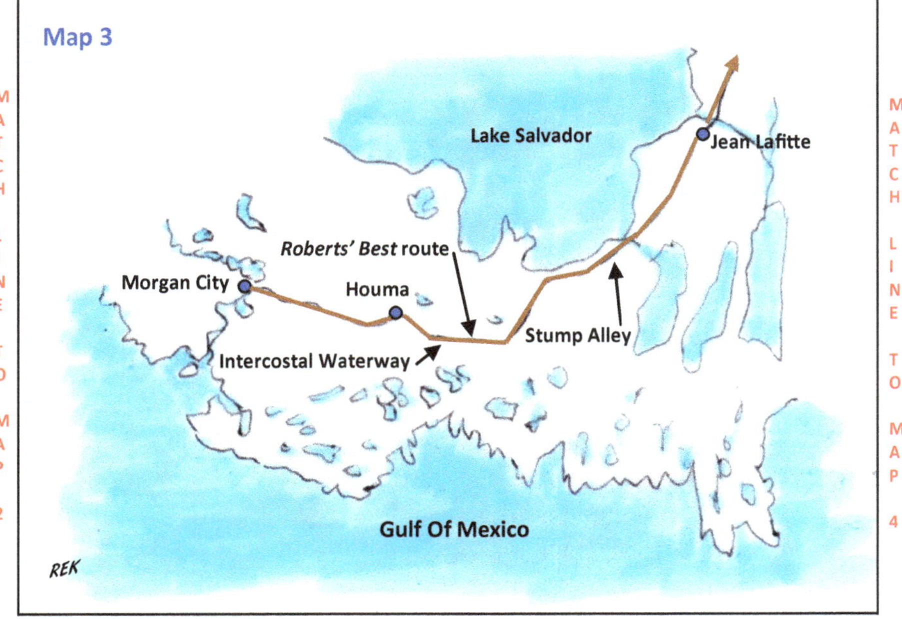

Map 2
MATCH LINE TO MAP 2
MATCH LINE TO MAP 3
Port Arthur
Marsh Island
Morgan City
Sabine Pass
Gulf of Mexico
Roberts' Best route
102 degrees east-southeast
(Ten hour trip)
Atchafalaya Bay
REK
Map 3
MATCH LINE TO MAP 2
MATCH LINE TO MAP 4
Lake Salvador
Jean Lafitte
Roberts' Best route
Morgan City
Houma
Intercostal Waterway
Stump Alley
Gulf Of Mexico
REK

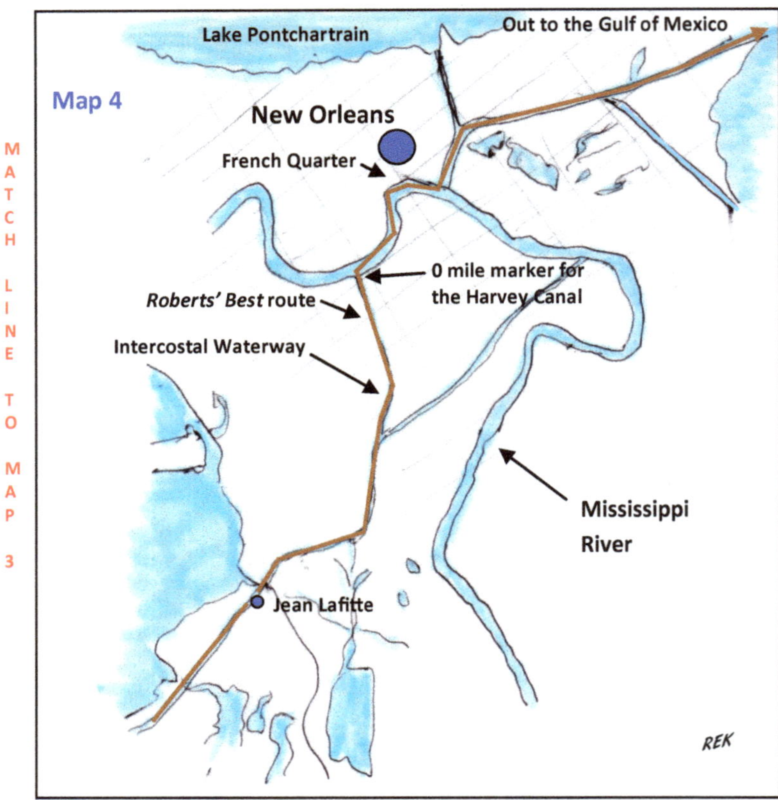

They had installed a twelve horsepower, two-cylinder inboard diesel in my great little sloop. It was going to save me in the many tight places I would find myself in on my adventure.

It was a sunny morning, and a nice breeze was springing up. As I pulled out of the marina I suddenly realized that I was not only in the Galveston Ship Channel, but also in the Inter-Costal Waterway. It was huge!

I headed north temporarily. It was just a short distance, only about a quarter of a mile and I was to take a right ninety-degree turn around the northeast end of Galveston Island to head out into the Gulf. As I made my turn right or starboard, I suddenly realized I was in the middle of the main ship channel entrance to the Houston port. Possibly that was why I was looking up at a large mountain of a ship coming right at me!

I immediately kept on turning, getting out of the huge oil tanker's way. I also remembered not to get too close to the shore or jetties because of the rocks. As he went past me and then his wake hit me, it felt like I was in the middle of an ocean!

That first emergency experience now past, I thought, what a way to start my trip! I flipped open my handy Gulf Coast Guide. I had made notes. I would have to use my math and lots of reverse thinking, because the Gulf Coast Guide was written from Key West to Houston, and I was going the opposite way.

The guide book said that if I went straight out from Galveston and then turned a magnetic east-northeast 28 degrees, in 49 miles I would be off Sabine Pass. This was the entrance to Port Arthur. I cut off the motor, put up the sails and was clipping along at eight to ten knots. What a glorious feeling. I was doing it!

The notes I had made warned me to keep a good look-out for drilling platforms and something called Christmas Trees. I found out that they are what is put on the drilling pipe after they hit oil. They stick out of the water, with all kinds of valves and pipes on them. I did keep a good look-out and saw many of them and kept my distance while maintaining my compass bearings.

As I went towards shore, I saw the flashing green and red markers. They marked the main Port Arthur ship channel. I turned in left or to port between the markers. I had decided to stay in the small town of Sabine Pass. It was on the Texas side of the channel. I dropped the sails and turned on the motor. It coughed a couple of times and then purred. On the Louisiana side was a large anchorage area. There were some big jack-up drilling platforms anchored in it.

Just past the little town were commercial docks. I pulled up just a little off of the dock. A guy was standing there. He looked like a boat captain, short, stocky, big arms, tee shirt, and jeans.

"Sir, would it be ok to anchor just off the pier here?"

"Yeah, it would be fine. No shrimp boats due in tonight. Most will be coming back in a'couple days. Just leave room for them to get past you. Where you out of?"

"Houston. I'm new at this Gulf stuff. Mostly sailed just in Lake Houston."

"A Newbie, huh? Tell you what, shut her down and anchor. Better use two cause of the wake from the channel. I'll show you a great restaurant. Don't look like much, but you can't beat the food!"

"I'll be right in," I exclaimed.

"Take your time. I've been working on my trawler. I need a break!"

I brought the dinghy in, tied her up, and shook hands with the captain. As we walked up the dock, he showed me his boat. It was a fair size, about sixty feet long. He had been shrimping all his life, and this was his home port. He was right. The restaurant didn't look like much, old weathered boards with pealing paint and one neon sign. It said, Sabine Pass Dockside Restaurant, Open. But the food, it was great! Talk about fresh fish, shrimp, and crabs, they had them.

It was a good thing it was early afternoon. It seems the captain wanted to take a long break! I told him I had to get an early start to make Morgan City by evening tomorrow. He said I could do it in around ten hours max. The tide would be in my favor. He also told me I should pass the green and red flashing channel markers and hold to a magnetic one hundred and twelve degrees east-southeast. I would just clip the south shore of Marsh Island. It's about eighty-five miles to the turn up into the Lower Atchafalaya Bay and River. After that it's about ten miles up the river to Morgan City and the Inter-Costal Waterway.

I bid the captain goodbye, and since it was early evening there was still plenty of light for me to find my way back. I had no trouble walking the short distance back past the piers, docks, and warehouse. I spotted *Roberts' Best* and rowed out. I checked my fuel and found I had used very little leaving Houston. I went to sleep fast because I needed to get up at the crack of dawn.

I woke up to the tune of my alarm. I had slept very well except for a couple of times when a boat went by too fast and it's wake put my boat to rocking. I had coffee and breakfast just as the sky started to lighten announcing the start of my day. I motored back to the flashing green channel marker and made my turn. Now I needed to hold this bearing. I wanted to clip the south shore of Marsh Island, not run into it or miss it entirely!

I immediately lost sight of land. At the max I was probably six to seven miles out in the Gulf. This was new for me. At the end of the third hour I could see land fast coming up on my port side. I thought, I couldn't be this close to Marsh Island so soon. I hastily consulted my charts and guide. No it was the forward part of Louisiana's heel. You can see it on any map. Louisiana kind of resembles a pirate's boot.

I kept my bearings but stayed out far enough to be clear of the shore waves. My maps told me on shore here was a wildlife area preserve, and it sure looked that way, no houses, piers, commercial buildings or any other signs. The interesting part was that the shore and sea birds were plentiful and beautiful.

During the fourth hour I was to keep my lookout for Marsh Island. It too appeared to be some kind of nature preserve. It was very green with huge flocks of birds. I was keeping off just enough and knew that I had about fourteen miles to the Lower Atchafalaya River channel markers.

There they were! It had been sixty-five miles, and I hit them right on the money! Thank You Lord! Then I realized I wouldn't be the only one turning up the river. Here came a commercial fishing boat. I found out that Morgan City is home to hundreds of fishing and work boats.

I dropped sails and started my trusty two-cylinder diesel. This trip of meandering the ten miles up the Atchafalaya River was really educational. The channel was well-marked and I want to thank the Good Lord and Louisiana State. If it wasn't for the markers a boater could lose their way. There were bayous, canals, rivers, lakes, and all kinds of water highways coming and going! There is a complete maze of ways to travel by boat all across the southern part of Louisiana. All of this was fifteen miles inland from the Gulf.

I also had to keep out of the way of the fishing and work boats as they came and went. This is where my VHF radio came in handy, really essential. I kept it on whatever channel it seemed every captain was using. The boat captains would call me by boat name and keep me posted on just what they were going to do.

Just a sort distance from downtown Morgan City the Intercostal Waterway came into the Atchafalaya River, on my port side. You can't miss the Morgan City waterfront because it has a huge concrete seawall to keep out the river's floodwaters. They have painted Morgan City right on the wall in large letters.

Right at the spot the Intercostal Waterway leaves the river was the Morgan City Public Docks. They were right under the two highway bridge spans.

I backed the *Roberts' Best* up right next to the dock. There were a series of pilings running along-side the dock. The dock looked like it would accommodate a boat of up to at least fifty feet. When one does this docking you need to put out fenders over the side so the fenders rub the dock and pilings instead of your boat.

I looked up. A man and a lady were lounging on deck chairs on a wide part of the pier. They looked about in their fifties. He was wearing a captain's hat.

"Oh, hi, I'm new at this. Left Galveston two days ago. I haven't been on the Intercostal before. Took the Gulf both days and came in from Sabine Pass this afternoon."

"Hey! That was a good day's sailing. We're heading the way you've come from. But we're just coasting along on the Waterway. Tell you what, we got in here last night, and we've been walking around the town today. We know a good Cajun eating place. Matter-of-fact, we're just getting ready to go to the Cajun Kitchen. How about coming along? It's only about a couple of blocks. By the way, I'm Jack Smith, and this is my wife and First Mate, Mary."

"What a nice invite. I'm Tom Roberts. Nice to meet you both, Jack, Mary. I'm sure ready to eat some good Cajun food!"

On the walk over to the Cajun Kitchen, I found out Jack had a home construction business in Pensacola, Florida. They had left the business in their son-in-law's hands and were on the second week of a month's water-cruise vacation.

We walked into the Cajun Kitchen and guess what, a Cajun band was getting ready to rock the rafters. There was a small dance floor in front of the stage the band was on. The band consisted of two fiddles, an electric guitar, and a washboard man.* There was a lady up front with a microphone preparing to sing.

As we sat down at a table, she said, "We're going to have a fais-dodo. So let's dance!" The music started, but no one jumped up to dance.

"Stop the music!" she said, kind of loud. "We need some dancers. It's easy. You, Sir," she pointed at me.

"Me? Ma'am," I said as I looked around for someone else she might be talking to.

She stepped off the stage, grabbed my hand and pulled me up. She was real pretty, so it didn't take much pulling on her part.

"Now watch my feet. Left, right, left, kick with the right. Right, left, right, kick with the left, and repeat."

The next thing I knew was, I was dancing, and the whole restaurant got up and did a fais-dodo.

After the dance, she said, "Thank you, Sir," as she went back up on stage and began to sing and rock to their Cajun music.

My two new friends and I sat down and had some great shrimp gumbo.

On the way back to their boats, Jack started laughing, "Tom, I didn't know what you were going to do at first when that Cajun beauty grabbed you."

"Jack, I sure have got more than I expected on this trip. You know, it's just started. I'm heading down to the Keys."

On their way back to the boats, Jack said, "Tom, if you need anything when you get to the Pensacola area, just call us. Here is my card."

"Why thank you, Jack, Mary. There is one thing I want to ask you. Where is the best place to get fuel?"

"That's easy. Just go up river under the railroad bridge. It's on the same side as we are now. You can't miss it, about a quarter of a mile. We're going to turn in. Have a good night, Tom," Jack said as he extended his hand.

"Thanks for everything," I replied.

The next morning I didn't wake up as early as I usually did. It had been a long day sailing the Gulf. It was morning, about eight, when I finally stirred. I cooked up some breakfast, cleaned up, untied, and slowly moved the *Roberts' Best* away from the dock and out into the river. Jack and Mary came up out of their cabin as I went by. I waved, and they acknowledged.

The fuel station was just where they had said. Under the railroad bridge up the river a quarter of a mile, and on starboard side, there it was, "Fuel and Supply." I was in luck. No one was at the pumps, so I eased right up to the dock.

A young man came out from the dock office and over to the pump,. "Need to fill'er up, Sir, I know it won't take much. Sailboats never do."

"Yes, thanks," I said.

"It only took eight gallons, Sir. That will be four dollars and twenty cents."

I counted it out, "Thank you, Sir," he said. "If you want to come up for supplies you can tie up to that dock right there. Sir, if I may ask, where you heading?"

"Well, Sonny, I'm new to this Intercostal Waterway, but I left Galveston two days ago. I'm heading to Key West. I came by way of the Gulf. Now I would like to turn up the Waterway and miss the lower part of Louisiana's Delta," I answered.

"Sir, ever considered a guide? I've been around these here parts all my life. Been on boats since I was twelve. I could guide you to New Orleans. I want to go there to visit my Grandma."

"Got any references? How much you charge? I never thought about it, but it is an interesting thought," I said.

"Yes, Sir, my boss said he would vouch for me and give me some time off. He will refer me. Tie up over there, and let's go see him. He's right there in the main office and store."

I moved the boat over to the other dock and tied up, then walked over and took a good look at the kid. He was clean-cut with decent clothes, blue jeans and t-shirt, average height and good build.

"Ready to go up and talk to my boss, Sir?"

"Son, what's your name? I'm Tom Roberts."

"Nicolas LeBlanc, Sir."

We went inside the office and store. It had some of everything… snacks, literature, and lots of boat accessories, even a VHF radio section.

"Boss, this is Tom Roberts. He might let me guide him up to New Orleans. Then I can visit Grandma. Can you give me a reference?"

"Nice to meet you, Tom. What you traveling in?" he said as he extended his hand.

"Got me a twenty-eight foot sail'n sloop. Wife and I used to sail on Lake Houston. This Gulf and Intercostal is new to me. I'm heading to Key West."

"So you want a reference for this young feller, hun? He'll probably get you lost off'n some bayou!"

"Now, Uncle Louis, don't say that. Tell him the truth."

Nicolas' Uncle Louis broke out in a big spasm of loud laughter. When he finished he said, "Tom, he'll do you real good. He's my nephew and he's been around boats since he was little, probably twelve I would guess. In fact he's guided about three different trips this last year. If he keeps this up I may start a guide service."

I said, "I thought there was something unusual about both last names being the same."

" Yes, I'm his uncle."

"Well Louis, what should I pay? What's the going rate?" I asked.

"What do you charge Nicolas?' Uncle Louis asked.

"Not much, fifty dollars a day and feed me. It shouldn't take us mor'n two, three days to get up to Orleans," Nicholas answered.

Louis broke out laughing again, "The fifty dollars a day won't hurt you, Tom. But he'll eat you out of house and boat!"

"Uncle Louis," Nicholas scolded.

"It's a deal," I said. "When can you start?"

"If it's all right with you Uncle Louis, right now. I've got a suitcase packed in the back of my car."

"Yes, kid. It's ok. Go on. Get out of here. But hurry back, and say hi to Grandma for me."

"Tom, I'll meet you at the boat. Got to get my suitcase," Nicholas said excitedly.

As we went downstream under both the railroad lift bridge and the two highway spans, Nicholas said, "Just as soon as we turn to port into the Waterway, keep a sharp lookout. There is a ferry crossing coming up. They will give us a visual signal or a horn if we can proceed."

Blat! Blat, Blat! Three high-pitched blasts emitted from the ferry at the dock on the port side.

"That's the all clear, Tom. Let's move!" Nicholas exclaimed.

"Nicholas, thanks a lot! You've already helped me. I would have never known what to expect next."

"Tom, next we've got the Bayou Boeuf Locks in a half-mile. They're twelve hundred feet long! We better hang our fenders over the side because the sides of the lock are rough! Let me contact the lockmaster on VHF, Tom."

"Lockmaster, this is *Roberts' Best*, twenty-eight foot sail'n sloop.
   Request permission to enter locks.
   Await instructions...over"

"Lockmaster, Bayou Boef, proceed.
   Ready for you, float the chamber...over."

"Lockmaster, thank you. *Roberts' Best* proceeding...over."

"Tom, we're to motor through."

"Nicholas, what is this lock for?" I questioned."We're not going up or down in water elevation."

"Tom, it's to keep flood waters out of the Waterway at certain times of the year."

"Well, that's two you got me through. What's next, Nicholas?"

"Tom, sit back and prepare to enjoy the most scenic section on the Louisiana Waterway. We're entering majestic nature at its best, cypress trees with Spanish moss, and for the next ten miles have your camera ready for our nation's bird, the eagle."

We did use up some film on a pair of eagles that we scared up from a tall cypress tree close to the canal.

"This looks like we've come into a lake," I noticed.

"It's true, now we're passing through a couple of lakes and soon the Waterway will also use a couple of Bayous," Nicholas stated.

At mid-afternoon we entered a straight-cut canal. "Tom, this area before Houma is all an oil and gas producing area, nothing around except canals, and oil and gas producing equipment sticking out of the water. Keep a sharp lookout."

"We're coming into Houma, Tom. There's a giant marina there with all the facilities. We can get water, fuel, our tanks pumped out, and ourselves filled up with good Cajun food. Then tomorrow if you want we should be able to make the forty-five miles to Lafitte."

"Sounds good to me, Nicholas," I agreed.

We eased into the Houma 'Downtown Marina'. "Now there's no fuel right here. But Tom, my uncle and I know the people running the oil and fuel depot just right over there. I'm going to call them and plan for an early refuel tomorrow morning."

"You've did it again. Thanks Nicholas. You've been a Godsend, by making this part of my trip a breeze. Now let's eat!"

True to his word and pre-planning, we fueled up early the next morning.

"Tom, this next ten miles is a 'No Wake Zone'.* We'll have to motor slow."

"Nicholas, what is that up ahead? It looks like the bridge is lying on the water!"

"It really is! It's the Bayou Blue Pontoon Bridge. Basically the road goes across on a barge. We need to signal him, one long and one short horn blast. Then we wait until he gives us a Clear-Go-Ahead. He pulls the barge with steel cables that are just under the water. We don't want to get snagged by those cables!"

The pontoon barge moved out of the way, then...Beep!

"That's the all clear. We can go now," Nicholas said.

Fifteen miles further we entered the area of a small Acadian town called Larose. There were small shipyards at either end with fishing trawlers and all types of pleasure boats lining the banks between. Again it was slow going with the "No Wake Zones'.

"That bayou there going south, is the Bayou LaFurche. It will take you to the Gulf in thirty-five miles," Nicholas informed me. "All along our port side is the big Lake Salador. After we pass the red-day beacons numbers four and two we've got to stay in the middle of the channel because that stretch is called 'Stump Alley'. There's all kinds of cypress knees along the sides of the banks and lots of hyacinths to foul our prop."

"I'll keep in the center, Nicholas. Thanks for the warning."

"Tom, we're approaching the town of Lafitte. Of course it's named after one of the most infamous pirates of the Gulf Coast. As can be expected, people always keep a lookout for his buried treasures."

"We could use some of that, Nicholas," I exclaimed with a laugh in my voice.

"Tom, we'll go a little bit out of our way to the right. It's down the Barataria Waterway. There are two good marinas there. Might as well take the first one. There's plenty of facilities there."

"You're the guide, Nicholas. Let's do it!"

The next morning: "Tom, we've got about five miles of homes with docks and boats next. Then we'll be in the Harvey Canal. It was dug by hand in the early 1720's. However it didn't go through the Mississippi levee. They had to unload their goods and carry them over the levee and reload on the other side. Thank goodness, today we'll use the Harvey Lock. It is also used for flood control and to prevent saltwater from getting into the marsh lands."

"Nicholas, it looks like we're getting into lots of commercial traffic. Look at those tugs and trawlers coming our way."

"Yep, Tom, keep a sharp lookout, and let's monitor the VHF radio."

"Hey Nicholas, I just heard a boat captain speaking French!"

That's right Tom. They still speak French around here. This is where the French Arcadians from Nova Scotia came in seventeen fifty five. They can speak both French and English and mix both languages up at the same time. There's the Harvey Lock up ahead. Let's call the Lockmaster on the VHF Channel 13."

"Lockmaster Harvey Lock.
This is *Roberts' Best*, twenty eight foot sail'n sloop.
Request permission to traverse lock...over."

"*Roberts' Best*, Lockmaster Harvey Lock.
Proceed.
Stay in center, give way to any commercial traffic...over."

"Oh my goodness, Nicholas, it's the Mississippi!" I exclaimed as we left the lock and entered the huge expanse of the Mississippi River. The center of the city of New Orleans was on the opposite bank.

The Mississippi River is one of the largest and longest waterways in the world. It is over two thousand miles long, draining from Canada to the Gulf. New Orleans was founded in 1718 by a French trading company and named for a French duke. Napoleon Bonaparte sold it to Thomas Jefferson's fledgling country in the Louisiana Purchase of 1803. It is one of the world's largest ports for both oil and tonnage and is renowned for its multicultural heritage, food, and music traditions.

"I guess I've gotten used to it, Tom. But you're right, it is a sight! What we're going to do is go right in about a mile, around the bend past the French Quarter and continue on the Waterway to the left. We'll be going through a lock which is similar to the Harvey Lock."

"Nicholas, do you have the time for a few additional hours of guiding? How about you and I do a brief tour of this here New Orleans?"

"Tell you what, Tom, since it's early, I'm going to see if I can convince one of the riverboat captains to let us tie up for a few hours. Right over there. I know those guys."

We cut across the wide Mississippi and up to a paddle-wheel boat that dwarfed the *Roberts' Best*. Nicholas was conspicuously standing up on the front deck of the *Roberts' Best*. He waved at the control house, and a guy stuck his head out.

"Hey, Nicholas, what-you-a do'n on that fancy sloop?"

"Hi François, can my friend and I tie up for a few hours?"

"We're just now leaving, it will be few minutes. Go'n up river to Biloxi. You can have it till we get back tomorrow."

"Stand clear and watch his wake, Tom," Nicolas cautioned as he waved to his friend. The gigantic paddle wheels began to turn and churn, throwing a volume of water high up into the air. I backed up aways, keeping a watch out for river traffic. As the paddle wheeler headed out into the Mississippi and upstream, I brought the *Roberts' Best* up to the paddle-wheel's dock. Nicholas jumped out and tied us up fast.

"How did you do that, Nicholas?" I exclaimed.

"When I stayed here with Grandma for a couple of years I worked part-time with those guys on the *Cajun Queen*."

"You sure have gotten around for a young guy!"

"Tom, let's lock up, and catch a riverfront streetcar to the French Quarter."

We walked across a park and up to a couple of railroad tracks. Just then we saw a 1945's era streetcar coming our way.

"This nostalgic streetcar is one of two different lines. The other one is the Saint Charles Avenue Line. We'll ride this one along the river, the

Historic 1945's era streetcar in the French Quarter

entire length of the French Quarter. Then we'll walk back through the center of the Quarter. We can get a good Cajun meal and listen to some fine jazz. Even though it's early afternoon, musicians will be playing. Why, there's someone playing music twenty four hours a day, seven days a week in New Orleans!" Nicholas exclaimed.

We got off at the end of the line near the French Market. Nicholas and I then wandered back through the narrow streets lined with three-story plaster-covered brick buildings. These buildings had wrought-iron balconies which looked down at us. We were on Bourbon Street when we had to stop and listen to the mellow sounds of a trumpet emitting from a restaurant door.

"This will be it," I said.

We went in and sat down to a Cajun meal and the music of a New Orleans Dixieland jazz band.

As we went outside, Nicholas said, "Tom, we'll walk the few blocks back to your boat. I'll tell you the easiest way to move on. It will be ok to stay here tonight. Now tomorrow, early if you can, you need to get moving so you will be gone before the *Cajun Queen* gets back. Just stay on the port side of the Mississippi. Watch out for the river traffic, and take the next waterway to the left. It's a lock and uses the same procedure we used for the Harvey Canal Lock. Notify the lockmaster and proceed at his direction. You will be in the Intercostal Waterway and it will turn to starboard shortly after you get into it. Then it is straight, and in ten miles you

New Orleans Dixieland at its best.

can continue on the Intercostal to Gulfport or slip out into the Gulf."

"Here we are, Tom."

"Nicholas, I want to thank you for the excellent guide service. Here is your pay and included tip. Also my contact information. I will recommend you highly to anyone. Good luck, and God bless you."

We shook hands and I watched Nicholas walk off into the bright colored lights of the New Orleans French Quarter, and then I turned to go to my *Roberts' Best*.

As I mentioned early on when I started my sailing adventure from Galveston to Key West, it would be an abbreviated version. I have rambled on too much already. If you are interested in the rest of my Gulf Intercostal Waterway sailing story, you will need to obtain my book:

Gulf Coast Summer
One Man's Sailing Adventure from Galveston to Key West.
By: Tom Roberts

Now I'm going to jump past Biloxi, Gulfport, Pascagoula, Mobile, Pensacola, Apalachicola, Tarpon springs, St. Petersburg, Sarasota, Naples, and Everglades City.

I'm now thirty-five days out from Galveston and in the Gulf heading towards the western Keys, just west of Marathon. In fact I am in the Big

Spanish Channel heading to Bahia Channel which will take me out into the Atlantic and the Caribbean.

I saw the markers for the Big Spanish Channel and slipped between. I was then on a slight angle east of south. There were a couple of small Keys I passed on the starboard side, and I could see big pine trees on the Key of the same name. It was a nice sunny and breezy day that I had been blessed with. Next I passed on the same side of a decent–sized Key called "No Name Key." It too had a pine tree forest on it behind the mangroves.

I was now in the Bahia Honda Channel. The old railroad bridge girder spans with the U S 1 Highway built on top was before me. I steered for the center of one span. I had ninety feet horizontal and thirty feet verti-clearance. It was no problem going between. As soon as I got through I could see the State Park boat basin. I entered it and went up to a slip. I was done for the day!

After eating, I walked over to the other side of the road and swam at the palm tree-rimmed sugar-sand beach which was on the western side.

The next morning, since I was a little anxious, (and that was because I was only thirty-five miles from Key West's western side, I got an early start. I untied from the dock slip and motored out of the boat basin. A few minutes and I was at full sail in the middle of the Bahia Honda Channel. At a marker designating the Hawk Channel and looking at the Atlantic, I made a course change of two hundred and fifty degrees west-southwest. I would be on that for at least thirty miles, til I was abreast of Key West.

This Hawk Channel was also the southern Keys Intercostal Waterway. With the ocean breeze heading inland, my sails were full, and I was clip-ping along at a comfortable eight knots. At the halfway point I was proba-bly about three to four miles out from the land. But the distance off the Keys was becoming gradually less and less.

Suddenly the air above me became alive with military aircraft landing and taking off. A quick glance at my charts told me that I was adjacent to Boca Chica Naval Air Station. I changed course a few degrees and now was heading due west two hundred and seventy degrees, which put me off the ocean side of southwestern Key West.

I could see the buildings of the island interspersed with waving coconut palms. I turned sharp to starboard when I got close to the red "Day" bea-con marker and headed for a flashing green lighted marker. I was now in the main ship channel, and it was well marked with buoys on either side. I had done my homework some time ago, as a matter of fact just as soon as

I had obtained my waterway guide. I was planning on docking in the Key West Bight* and renting a long-term slip at one of the smaller piers.

There it was, the flashing red 24 buoy. I cut on the diesel and dropped the sails. I let the boat float there as I rolled up and secured both of the sails. I could see my marina on the starboard side so I eased in, threw my fenders over the side, cut the motor off, and tied up.

"Where ya-all coming in from?"

I looked up. Across the dock was a Chris-Craft Cruiser. It was a vintage restored unit. There was a vintage guy in blue jeans, white shirt, and captain's cap sitting on a deck chair in the back of the Cruiser.

"Oh, hi, didn't see you there. About forty days out from Galveston," I answered.

"Ran the Intercostal, did you?" he asked.

"Yes, sure did! Moving to this island, if they'll have me. By the way, that's some boat you have there. Did you restore it yourself?"

"Yep. It's a nineteen thirty-five, twenty-eight foot Chris-Craft Model 557 Cabin Cruiser.* Got it off a guy near Homestead, Florida. He had it all tore apart. It took me and a couple of friends two years to restore it. I wasn't in a hurry. Just like you see me now."

"I like antiques. In fact that's how I make my money. *Honest Dave,* the antique man. I refurnish and sell antiques of all kinds. If it's old, and I like it, I buy it. If I don't want to keep it, I sell it, for a profit, naturally."

I stepped up onto the dock, Honest Dave did the same. We shook hands.

"Dave Crench, pleased to make your acquaintance."

Dave was of average height and somewhat muscular. His black hair was hanging out under the cap, but with his long sideburns, I could imagine he looked like Elvis.

"I'm Tom Roberts of the twenty-eight foot sail'n sloop *Roberts' Best.* I'm proud to meet you Honest Dave."

"How about a tour of your Chris-Craft? It's not every day I get this opportunity."

"Tom, I thought you would never ask. Step right in there."

"Wow! This mahogany wood is pristine. I like the Captain's quarters. Even a mahogany and brass six-spoke ship's wheel, and your chrome trim shines," I said admiringly.

"It wasn't easy. Lots of sanding and refinishing to the mahogany. Some of the chrome fittings had to be replated."

"How many will she sleep, Dave?"

"Take a look up front for yourself. Could squeeze in three if you had to. Not to mention the cross-the-transom cushion in the stern."

"Dave, what about power?"

"Well, Tom, that is what I like," he said as he pulled back the engine's cover. "This is a cruiser, not a speedster runabout. The in-line, six cylinder flathead is an original Chris-Craft ninety-five horse power "K" engine. It's all she needs. It's easy on fuel but will still move out because it's got a lot of torque."

"A great boat, Dave!" I complimented.

"What's your plans Tom? I don't know about you, but I'm hungry. I know it's early, but my stomach thinks it's late! I've been here about four days. I know a couple of good eating places only a couple of blocks from here. It's good, it's early, because we can eat and get back off the street before the town gets rowdy. What do you say? I'm buying. There is a small restaurant you might like."

"That was some good food. Thanks, Dave. I'm going to turn in. I had a long and busy morning. See you tomorrow."

Next morning, Key West docks in the Bight.

I poked my head out of my cabin.

"Hey Tom, so you're an early riser like me. Come on over. Had your coffee yet? I've got mine and yours ready to go. How about some eggs?"

"I'm coming right over, Dave. It's alright if I just call you Dave and leave off the Honest part?"

"Yep, Tom, that will be fine. Don't want the locals to get any ideas. Have a seat right there, and I'll rustle up your grub. Where you heading today, Tom?"

"Thanks, Dave. I've got to find me a place to live. I have this respiratory and allergy condition. It came from and was aggravated by the Houston pollution and the high humidity."

"What's wrong with living on your boat?"

"Well, Dave, a boat's fine, but I'm used to having a sturdy footing most of the time. A boat is great for recreation and getting away from it all for a few hours. But think, I've been the last thirty-eight days on the water. No, I need some land sleep."

"What you looking for, Tom? I've been looking around a lot. I could guide you around some, or at least show you the sights and all that I know."

"Well, to answer your first question. I need a good ocean breeze, no pollution. The answer to your second question is, yes. Show me what you know about this here island."

"You'll need to get your walking shoes on and come back and we'll start out!"

"Tom, if what you need is a lot of breeze, that means the Atlantic. Also since you like antiques, you need an old house. You've come to the right place, this island is full of them, real fine ones, and historic. You need a two-story with two to three porches on the second floor. Let's hail a touring carriage. Here's a horse and buggy, coming down the street right now. That way we can see everything at a slow pace. We need to get to the other side of the island. You need covered porches. They call them verandas here. It's when the porch roof is a continuation of the house roof."

"Hey, old timer," Dave said to the carriage driver. "We need a ride. My friend here is looking for an old house. It's got to be on the Atlantic. He needs porches on the second floor. What've you got?"

The carriage driver said, "Wooah Bessie," as he pulled tightly on the reins. "Well Sar, I know a dead-end street right on the Atlantic. It's called United. I think I saw one for sale on that street when I was passing by."

They stepped up into the carriage. "Let's go, Bessie, ge'up!" the driver said as he lightly snapped the reins.

"Driver, how could you be just pass'n by, when it's a dead-end street?" Dave asked with a smile in his voice.

"I must confess, Sir, there's this real pretty Miss living on that street, and you might have guessed it. I'm sure sweet on her!"

"Tell you what, oh by the way, what's your name, driver?" I asked.

"Franklin, Sir."

"I'll tell you what, Franklin, if this is the right house, you will get a tip big enough to take your sweetheart out to dine."

"Thank you kindly, Sir."

"Franklin, please take us through old town on the way over, so my friend Tom here can see just how historic and unique Key West is."

We went west out of the Key West Bight. Three blocks and Franklin said, "Sir, I'm going to take a short three-block around-about here and show your friend here Front Street and Old Mallory Square. It's the real old seaport front."

"There now, we're gon-a-go all the way down Whitehead Street. It's about eleven blocks to the ocean and our turn. We'll go right past the oldest house, Hemingway's house, the light house, and a lot of other interesting sights."

"You're doing great, Franklin, keep it up," Dave encouraged.

"Well, Sirs, here's our turn. It's on the left in the middle of the block."

"Feel that breeze, Tom," Dave said.

We pulled up in the front of a beautiful old Key West Bahamian style house.

"Look, Tom, it's got your porches, I mean verandas." Dave noted.

"It's too good to be true! Thank you, Dave and Franklin. Let's see if anyone's home. Franklin, rest awhile and stay with us till we find out anything. I'll pay you for your time."

"Yes, sir. I'll be right here."

Dave and I stepped down from the carriage.

Dave said, "Tom, I don't know if you know anything about this architecture, but these Key West old homes are all unique. In fact unique to Key West. This here beautiful little two-story baby is a three-bay Classic Revival. But they have added porches. See the separate roofs over the porches"

We walked up to and opened the picket fence gate, then went up the walk and the three stairs to the porch. The house was a light airy yellow trimmed in white, with some gingerbread.* There was a bell button next to the door. I pushed it.

Ding...Dong!

We could hear someone coming. The main door opened.

"Oh, hi! May I help you?"

"Yes Ma'm, we saw the *For Sale* sign, and I'm interested."

"Well, sirs, if you would have a seat on the porch there, I'll call the realtor. Be right back."

She came back out with a tray, glasses, a pitcher of lemonade, and some homemade cookies. "She'll be here shortly. They're only a few blocks away. I see your driver out there, would you like to take him some lemonade and cookies?"

Dave interjected, "Let me do it, Tom. That way you two can talk about the house."

He went out to Franklin carrying a glass of lemonade and a couple of cookies in a napkin.

The lady said, "Oh goodness me! I'm sorry I didn't introduce myself. I'm Kelly Albright. My husband is Naval Air and he's being reassigned."

"So nice to meet you, Ma'am. I'm Tom Roberts. Just got in from thirty-eight days sailing the Gulf Intercostal Waterway, from Galveston, Texas."

"My, so adventurous. Oh, here comes the realtor now."

A new '62 caddy pulled up, and a young lady got out. She and Dave were talking as they came up.

Dave said, "Tom, I'd like for you to meet Ms. Betty Thomas. She is probably the most knowledgeable and pretty realtor on this here island!"

He looked at Mrs. Albright. "Ma'am I loved your cookies and lemonade, but I didn't get your name. I'm Dave Crench. Purveyor of fine antiques, out of Homestead, Florida. This good man and I have our boats docked down at the Key West Bight."

"Oh, I'm sorry, Mister, Crench, I'm Kelly Albright."

The realtor, Betty Thomas, said, "Gentlemen, would you like to go in and look around?"

On the second floor, Betty Thomas said, "This house is unusual

Three-bay Classic Revival historic Key West house

REK

because of the porches all the way around. You will get both the view and the breeze off the Atlantic from this back porch. Not to mention, you don't have beach access, but nothing will be built between you and the Atlantic. When the Navy donates it to the National Park Service, it should be a public park along with Fort Jefferson."

"Ma'am, if it is reasonable enough, I'm interested," I said.

"That check is a draw on the Bank of Houston, Texas. It will be as good as gold!"

Betty Thomas replied, "Tom, give me two days to verify it, get all the paperwork ready, and we should be able to close in a week." She then looked at the owner, "Is that suitable, Kelly?"

"Why yes, Betty. I'm almost finished packing and will notify the movers just as soon as you let me know."

"Ms. Albright, any furnishings you wish to part with, just let me know, and I'll purchase them," I informed her.

The realtor, Betty Albright said, "We'll be in touch, gentlemen. It's been very nice."

Dave and I walked back out to Franklin, Bessie, and the carriage.

"Well, Franklin, you're taking your sweetie out to eat," I said, as I handed Franklin a very sizable tip.

"Thank you very kindly, Sir, Mister Tom."

"Really, I'm so thankful to you, Franklin. Well, Dave, what's next?"

"Do you have more time, Franklin?" Dave asked.

"Yes, Sir!"

"We need the full Old Town tour," Dave said with a flourish.

"Yes, Sirs! Hang on. Here we go."

"Franklin, we need some lunch," Dave said. "It made me real hungry watching Tom spend his money."

"There is a restaurant only a couple of blocks from here. Real good Italian food."

"Good. Let's take out, and then you can carry on with the tour. By the way, we're buying, Franklin."

"Thank you, Sirs."

We did the historic high spots, just stopping briefly at each one: Southernmost Point, lighthouse, Hemingway House, Oldest House, Aquarium, The Maine Memorial, and finishing up at the Turtle Crawls in the Key West Bight, right next to their boats.

"Franklin, it's been a busy, pleasurable, and successful day. We want to thank you."

"Sirs, I want to thank you! If you ever need me, you will see me and old Bessie here riding around the city. Also here's my card with my phone."

He and Bessie, clop, clopped off down the street.

"Tom, I know it's been busy, but if you're hungry, I'll buy. You need to see and eat at *Sloppy Joes.* I don't drink, and I'm guessing you don't either. However, they do serve a great steak and fries!"

"Dave, I'm for that. Now that I've got my house, thanks to you and

Franklin, I'm rested, not a care in the world. How do we get there?"

"It's only a couple of blocks from here, on Duval and Green. We can walk."

Sloppy Joe's was a one-story structure, right on the corner. In fact, it was kind of an open air establishment. It had many openings with folding double doors. There were five, six-foot wide openings right out onto the sidewalk and street. It was decorated inside with all kinds of paraphernalia, stuffed game fish, rods and reels, pirate stuff, boat hardware, and signed photos of all the famous people who had visited.

We went in and took a table between two doors off Green Street. "It's not very classy, but it's the place to visit when you're in Key West. Of course you know, Tom, that Joe and Hemmingway were just like this," as he crossed two fingers, "real deep sea fishing and carousing buddies in the 1930's."

"Is that right, Dave? I guess now that I'm an islander I will have to read up on the history. Sounds like you're on top of it!"

"Can I help you, Sirs?" the waitress asked.

"Yep, your steak and fries, please," Dave answered.

"I'll take the same," I added.

"Drinks, Sirs?"

Dave put in, "We're teetotalers, we'll take some sarsaparilla."

"I only have Ginger Ale," she answered.

"Yep," Dave and I both replied.

"Well, Dave tell me about your Homestead antique business."

"Tom, it's like this, I've been interested in and collecting antiques since as long as I can remember. Never could pass up a yard sale or an antique shop. I've got a couple of consignment locations, you know, antique malls. Also I'm set up in an old barn on the edge of the Everglades. That is my center of operations, furniture refinishing and tons of antiques I've bought over the years. I fixed me up a little suite in that barn, and I can hold up there and fix antiques to my heart's content. I also have a few other endeavors, such as flea markets where I sell authentic treasure maps to the tourists. Well, that was a mouthful. How about you, Tom?"

"Oil engineering. I started right out of college with a West Texas wildcat drilling company. They hit it big, crude oil, brought in a couple of wells right after I joined. I bought into the company, and we hit it big a couple more times. By age fifty-five I had a good share, so I sold out and then invested some in a few other companies. They also made it good. I guess I was blessed by the Good Lord. I'm not a millionaire, but I'm set up OK.

I've been tinkering around ever since."

"I've got a great son, daughter-in-law, and two grandchildren. Wife's with the Lord."

"Tom, I guess we have to take the good with the bad. Here comes our food. I'm famished!"

While Dave and I talked and dined, we didn't see the two men who came in one of the far door openings. They eased up to and sat at the bar.

"What're you guys drinking?" the bartender inquired.

"We'll take a couple of Sloppy Joe Specials."

They were dressed a little sporty, though not so wild they stood out, because in Key West, anything goes. Hawaiian shirts peeked out from under their light-colored sport jackets. Tropical dress pants and leather sport dress shoes finished their attire.

One was tall and thin, the other, kind of average height but stocky and with a scar across his forehead. Both had black hair and were tanned. The tall one had a faint moustache.

"There they are, Vince, the two guys I told you about. The one with the long side burns and pony tail has got that old Chris-Craft. He thinks it's a cruiser, it's just an old tub! Ha, he should see ours, then he'll know just what a cruiser really is!"

"What about the other guy?"

"He's got a small sailboat, one mast, about twenty-eight to thirty feet. Heard that he sailed down from the Houston area."

"They got any dough?"

"I haven't had any time to look into it. But it looks like the sailor may have bought a house down by the end of United Street."

"How do you know that, Frank?"

"He and Chris-Craft rode that tourist horse and carriage down there, went in, and a realtor showed up. Course it had a *For Sale* sign out front. When the realtor dame came out she had some papers in her hand and was smiling."

"Well, check 'em out. You know, even Chris-Craft may be loaded!"

"I'm on it, Boss."

Back at the Key West harbor on the pier: "So what's your plan, Tom?" Dave asked.

"The realtor will naturally verify the check. So, I'm going to touch base with the owner, see if she wants to part with any furniture. I'll live on this boat until I can move in, sooner better than later. Then I'll complete the furnishing of the place, and see if I can talk my son into coming for a visit. Hopefully, he will leave my grandson for a two-to-three week visit."

"Let's see, that will be in a month to five weeks. Tell you what, I'll call you and come back and then we'll tour, cruise, and sail around if you want?"

"It sounds good to me, Dave."

"Good. But what I need to do is go back to Homestead and make another bunch of money! I'm going to get go'n in a few hours. I return up the Intercostal and cut through at Pigeon Key under the Seven Mile bridge. You know it goes right up the Bay side."

"Yes, I do remember seeing that on my Intercostal Guide. Dave, it's been fine. Thanks for the help, and call and check back. Here's my card. I should have a phone by then. You'll have to call information."

They shook hands, and Dave went into his boat and started to get things organized. About an hour later, Tom heard the Chris-Craft engine start up. He looked out of his cabin as Dave pulled away from the dock. They both waved, and Dave headed across the harbor and turned south towards the Straights of Florida and the Hawk Channel.

In the realtor's office: "It didn't take us long, did it Tom?"

"No, a real short time indeed. You're half a week ahead of schedule."

"You sign right there, Tom, and also initial where I've marked the red x's."

"Now, Kelly, you sign here and initial right there. Tom, here are the keys to your new home. Congratulations to you both. Kelly's on her way to join her husband in San Antonio, and Tom is the proud owner of a beautiful Key West historic home on the Atlantic," Betty, the realtor said as she beamed.

"Not only that," Mrs. Albright the home owner said, "except for a few keepsakes, Tom is going to take the furniture off my hands. My dear husband says new furniture is going to be purchased when I get to San Antonio!"

"I guess everyone is happy, pleased, and content," Betty exclaimed.

"We sure are," we both agreed.

"Well Betty, Tom, I must run, the few things I kept shipped this afternoon, and my bus leaves early this evening," Kelly said.

"Bye, and thank you," we both said as she hurried out the door.

"Tom, what happened to your friend?" Betty inquired. "Was it Dave Crench?"

"Oh, he had to go back to Homestead. Something about he had to make some more money! But he said he was coming back in a month or so.”

“Oh, that will be nice. Could you give him my card?” She handed it to me and extended her hand. “Hope you enjoy your new home, and welcome to Key West.”

It was only six blocks from the courthouse area where the realtor’s office was and my new home on United Street. As I was about a block away walking to my new home, I saw someone wave from a cab. It was Mrs. Kelly Albright. I returned the wave as she passed by heading toward the bus station.

I walked up through the white picket fence gate and to the front door of my new home. I tried the key, and in I went. In the front was a living room and sitting room. A hall ran down the center, and in the rear a kitchen was on one side and a dining room was across the hall on the other.

I walked straight out the back door. The back yard was extraordinary, a profusion of bushes and plants greeted me, most of them bearing all sorts of gorgeous flowers, none of which I knew the names of, or recognized. There were two especially exquisite coconut palms towards the rear of the lot. I could see all the way to the majestic Atlantic and hear the breakers in the distance. The sea birds, gulls, terns, and pelicans were present throughout the scene, and that breeze, I thought, this is just what I needed.

Now, the upstairs. There was a nicely constructed flowing staircase leading up from the front door. In the front were two bedrooms with a shared bathroom in the hall. The same hall ran from the front to rear. The back bedroom or master had a small bath. Across the hall was an open area combined with the end of the hall. I’ll make this my office and write my book here, I thought.

All the windows were tall, some floor to ceiling, and all had Key West horizontal slatted shutters. Out on the spacious porches, second floor, the ocean breeze is delightful, I thought.

“This is it!” I said out loud.

“Hi Harold. It’s Dad. How you doing?”

“Fine, Dad. Last we heard, you got to Key West. You all set up, got a house?”

“Yes, son. I’m sitting pretty on the back upstairs porch. Got the phone cord stretched from my office in the back to this lounge chair. Hey, I’ve got a proposition for your family. I’m buying. How about you rent a

Station wagon and drive to Key West? Spend a few days, leave Harold Junior for two or three weeks, and Ill fly you all back. Can you swing a week or so? Certainly those oil companies can spare you for just a little old week or so, can't they?"

"Well, Dad, it sounds tempting. Tell you what, let me talk to Mary and then my boss and get back to you."

"Dad, it took us a day more than three. We stopped in New Orleans, rode the trolley train, and then saw the sights. We followed the coast as much as we could, swam, and picnicked a couple of times. Then we stopped in Sarasota, you know the Ringling Brothers Circus and the Ringling North Mansion and Art Museum? After that it was the Glades, Keys, and here we are."

"Yes Grandfather Roberts, I really liked the Trolley Train, and the circus. The swamp, it was real scary! Those big white birds with long necks and bills, wow! We even saw an alligator. But the bridges to get here, over the ocean, there must have been a million! Right, Dad?" Harold Junior said with much gusto.

"Not a million! You're crazy!" Suzie exclaimed.

"There were too! A million," Harold Junior shot back. "Right Dad?"

"No, there weren't!" Suzie said, stamping her foot.

"Now children, settle down," Mary injected.

"Grandfather Roberts, when are we going fishing? I want to catch a shark or a sailfish. I read about them in the encyclopedia."

"Now, Harold Junior, take it easy," I said. "First, we have to get you all settled. Let's take these suitcases upstairs. Harold and Mary, that front bedroom right there. Suzie, you have your very own room across the hall. The bathroom is second door in the hall right there. Harold Junior, back here with me. You get your very own couch here in my office. You see, I'm right there in that bedroom."

"What a nice home, Dad," Mary complimented. "I just love the plants, flowers, and the Atlantic view! Those porches are exquisite."

"Well, my great family, since you have driven so long, tonight you-all just rest. I'm cooking and serving. Then tomorrow, we're going to tour the island. I've got a surprise for you."

"Tell us, Grandfather!" Harold Junior and Suzie both begged.

"It is a surprise. You'll both see tomorrow."

"Grandfather! Grandfather Roberts! There's a horse and buggy parked in front of the house!" Harold exclaimed.

"I know, it's for us. That's Franklin and his good old horse, Bessie. Don't forget your cameras and snacks, let's get loaded. They're going to take us touring the town of Key West. We're going to see the sights."

"Franklin, nice to see you and Bessie. You are right on time, Thank you. This is my family. Let me introduce my son Harold, and wife Mary. This is my granddaughter, Suzie and grandson, Harold Junior."

"Pleased to make your acquaintances. Let me help you in."

"Won't your horse run when you drop the ropes?" Harold Junior asked.

"No she won't, young fella, I bet'cha. She is trained. In fact, she is the best behaved horse on this whole island!"

"Now you four sits in the back there, and this young man is going to help me drive old Bessie."

"Look at me Mommy, Daddy, I'm way up here!"

"You're not so smart. Don't fall off." Suzie said in reply.

"Hold on folks, off'n we go," Franklin said.

I put in, "You know your way around, Franklin. We're with you."

Franklin took the route he had originally toured Dave and me on.

"Ladies and Gentlemen, this here is the farthest south you can go in the good old U S of A. It's called the Southern Most Point. Now that house there, the pretty yellow one with the red roof and tower, it's the southern-most house. Now we're going up towards town to the…"

"Light house!" Harold Junior piped in. "I see it!"

"Why, young fella, you will make a good tour guide," Franklin inter-jected.

"Can we go to the top, Grandfather?" Harold Junior asked.

"If your father says it's ok and us old folks can make it, I think it will be ok."

Franklin pulled up and stopped, "Whoa, Bessie."

"Wait for us, Franklin. We'll be down in a bit."

It was a total of eighty-eight steps up to the top of the lighthouse and the walk-around, but the view of the entire island was worth every bit of the climb. We all came down, we older ones looking a bit tired.

"Now across the street is the Hemingway house," Franklin said.

Before he could go on, Suzie added, "He was a famous author. He wrote a lot of books. My teacher talked about him."

Harold Junior interjected, "He's not so great. Grandfather is writing a book too!"

"Now, Harold, I won't ever be as famous as Mister Ernest

Hemingway," I admitted.

"Now, here on the right is the main entrance to the U. S. Navy Base," Franklin went on.

"Grandfather Roberts, can we stop and see the ships?" Harold asked.

"Harold, we can't just go on in. See the two sailors with guns guarding there? You have to have Navy business for them to let you in," I explained.

"Ok, I would like to see the ships. What kind do they have?"

"There are lots of submarines and a big ship they call the Mother Ship. It is a tender and it takes care of, and repairs the smaller submarine ships. Tell you what, when we get by the water, we'll look for Navy ships, I promise."

"Coming up on the right is the oldest house in Key West. It was built in1823." Franklin pointed to it, and stopped in front.

"It sure is old. It needs some paint, huh, Dad?" Harold observed.

"Well, son, they don't paint it because then it would look new," Harold Senior explained.

"Mister Roberts, you may want to stop for lunch because next will be the aquarium," Franklin cautioned.

"Good idea, take us to a place to eat, Franklin."

"Yes, sir, how about right over there?"

"I hope they have hamburgers and fries, and I need a Coke!" Harold Junior exclaimed, "Look, they have tables outside on the sidewalk. Can we go there?"

They all said ok, except Suzie, naturally. "This doesn't look very good! Don't they have any of the fast food places like we have back home?"

"Now, Honey," Mary said. "This is Key West and every eating establishment is a mom and pop, or one-owner situation. That's the uniqueness of it. We're going to eat here, on the tables, on the sidewalk. I think it's quaint. You'll like it."

The waiter came out with many flourishes and ta-da's and took their order. I could see Franklin had taken the carriage and Bessie down the street so they would not interfere with the sidewalk café and people wouldn't bother him for a ride.

I pulled the waiter aside and said, "If there's anyone that can run a coke, hamburger, and fries down to Franklin and Bessie there, I've got a big tip for them."

"I'll take care of it, Sir. One of the bus boys can do it," he said with a grin.

"Thank you," I said.

"That was a great meal. Let's get on with our tour. We'll walk down to the carriage there," I pointed.

We loaded up, and Franklin said, "Next is the pirate house right there."

"Do pirates live in there now? Will they capture us?"

"Now, Harold Junior, settle down. That is where some pirates lived a long time ago," Harold Senior commented.

"Now we're going to go about four blocks to Front Street by the main square and docks. That is where the aquarium is. You are about to see lots of tropical fish," Franklin informed them.

They all came out of the aquarium, "See, Grandfather Roberts, I want to catch one of those sharks, only bigger. Why didn't they have a sailfish? There was just a dead stuffed one on the wall."

"Well, Junior, a sailfish is a game fish. It would be hard to keep one in an aquarium tank," I answered the best I could.

"Yah stupid!" Suzie broke in.

"I'm not stupid," Harold Junior replied.

"Yes you are. Yah...Yah...NaYah!"she teased.

"That's enough! Both of you!" Mary commanded.

They loaded up, and Franklin asked, "How about the Turtle Crawls and the Bight? They can see where you gots your sail'n ship."

"Another good idea. Thanks Franklin," I agreed.

"Look! I see *Roberts' Best*." Harold Junior stood up and pointed.

"Careful, Harold Junior. Sit down or you will fall off of the carriage," Harold Senior warned.

"First we are going to look at the Turtle Crawls," I said.

"Look at those big turtles swimming around. I would like to ride one!" Harold Junior exclaimed.

"You couldn't ride one of those big turtles. They would bite your foot off, and then sit on top of you," Suzie teased.

"Could too!"

"No, you couldn't'!"

"Now both of you settle down," Mary had to intervene, again.

"What is that boat with the big masts? Is it a pirate ship?" Harold asked as he pointed at the sailing ship tied up to the dock on the other side of the turtle pens.

"Harold Junior, that is the A. M. Adams. It's a turtle ship out of the Cayman islands. It catches these turtles and brings them to Key West to the Turtle Crawls," I said.

"I still think it looks like a pirate ship," Harold Junior insisted.

They walked over and out on the dock where the *Roberts' Best* was tied up.

"It looks like she did okay on the Gulf trip, Dad," Harold Senior commented.

"She is a good boat and a real fine sailor. Also that diesel engine really saved me!"

"Are we going to go out to catch a sailfish, Grandfather Roberts?" Harold Junior asked enthusiastically.

"Not today, Sonny," Harold Senior put in.

"Now we're going to get Franklin and Bessie to take us back to the house. We need a rest. Tomorrow we'll take a sailboat ride around the harbor and part of Key West," I said sympathetically. "We'll fish another day after your family leaves to go back home. You're going to stay with me a couple of weeks, Junior."

"O...k, Grandfather Roberts," Harold Junior sighed.

"Home, Franklin. You and Bessie have been superb! We all want to thank you." As everyone said with me, "Yes thank you, very nice, great!"

"Old Bessie and me just wants to help. You have been my greatest customers."

"And friends," I put in. "Now tomorrow we'll need a ride to the boat

The A M Adams tied up at the dock after unloading its catch of turtles.

The A. M. Adams flying both the Cayman Islands and U.S. flag.

in the morning. How about 9:30, Franklin?"

"Yes sir, we'll be there," Franklin answered, as Bessie shook her head and blew air from her nostrils. It was a coincidence, but they all laughed.

Franklin and Bessie were right on time the next morning

"There they are!" Harold Junior yelled.

"Not so loud, pipsqueak!" his sister commanded.

They loaded up, and thirty minutes later they were on the other side of the island at the Key West Bight.

"Thanks, Franklin. Check back in a couple of hours, around twelve. It's just going to be a harbor tour, a short trip."

"Yes sir, Mister Roberts. See you-all then."

Unknown to Tom:

As they loaded up they didn't notice two guys in Panama hats, light pants, and Hawaiian shirts sitting nonchalantly on a dock-side park bench.

"There they are, Vince. The whole family down from Texas. This old guy, Roberts, must have some dough. He's got a nice sailboat, buys a house cash, pays for the whole family to come down here, and doesn't work. Might be easy pick-in's."

"Frank, check into it. What else you got? Any new boats come in?"

"Ok, everyone, put on your life vests," I instructed.

"Yah, everyone. You too, Suzie!" Harold Junior put in.

"I know. Smart guy!" She answered.

"Now, we'll motor around at first. I want to go out of the Bight, and then we'll head south and look at the Navy Base to see what we can see!" I said. "Keep your eyes on the land there everyone. What do you see?"

"There it is!" Harold Junior screamed, "It's the

One of the crew was working on the side of the A. M. Adams turtle boat.

Mother Ship, a tender. Look at the one, two, three submarines."

"Ok, smart guy, we know you can count," Suzie said.

"Now, we're going to go around the southwest corner of the island. You can see the old Civil War red brick fort there. I pointed, "It's called Fort Zachary Taylor."

"Are there civil war soldiers in it now? Can we go see it?" Harold Junior asked.

"Now it's abandoned. But it's a National Park and Monument. We may go and see it next week, Harold Junior. You and me."

"Look, I see the Southern most house!"

"Now, Harold Junior, hold on to those rails. Don't jump around," Harold Senior warned.

"We're in the Hawk Channel now. Let's put up the sails. Harold Junior and Senior, up the sails, man the sail cranks."

"Like this, Daddy," Harold Junior proudly showed everyone, since he had learned how to raise the sails at Lake Houston.

"Now we'll just turn around and sail back to where we came from." I cautioned. "Watch the boom as it comes around."

We sailed back, dropped the sails, and motored into the harbor. Franklin and Bessie were there waiting. The two guys were gone.

The next day, mid-morning:

"Dad, We're going to drive up to Miami, drop off the rental station wagon at the airport, and fly back. It's non-stop on a Turbo-prop. We'll call when we get in," Harold Senior informed everyone.

"What's a Turbo-prop?" Harold Junior asked.

"I was going to ask the same question," I said. I guess it's a new type of aircraft engine," Harold Senior answered, "Supposed to be pretty fast."

"You-all have a safe trip," I said, as they all hugged, that is all except Suzie and Harold Junior.

"Now, Harold Junior, mind your Grandfather, and I love you," Mary said as she hugged him.

"Yes, Mom," he answered.

They all got in the vehicle, waved and drove away. We watched as they turn left onto Whitehead Street, go to Truman Ave, turn right, heading towards Roosevelt Boulevard and straight out to U. S. One.

"Junior, let's go in, clean up a bit, do some wash, eat, and we'll make some plans."

"Grandfather, couldn't we eat and make plans, instead of cleaning?"

"I wish we could, Junior, but we don't have a housekeeper. We are the cleaners."

Harold Junior was playing out on the porch, in the back. "Grandfather, you need a porch swing like you have back at the cottage."

"Sounds like a good idea, Harold Junior. Tell you what, we need two, one in the front and one in the back here. We'll order them today, and see if they can put them in tomorrow. We'll have them put on the ground floor. I don't want you launching off into space!"

"It's going to be fun, Grandfather."

"Give me a few minutes, Harold. I'm going to be on the phone."

Harold Junior didn't answer. He was playing around in the backyard, digging in the sand, and rolling a green husked coconut around.

"Dave Crench speaking, Antiques my specialty."

"Dave, that you? This is Tom, Tom Roberts."

"Oh hi, Tom. Excuse me, but I always have to put in my advertising specialty. How you doing?"

"My grandson is here. The family left this morning."

"You want to kick around some, Tom?" Dave asked. "I did some real neat work on my Chris-Craft. Wait till you see it! Tell you what, I got a few business deals to close. I'll leave tomorrow afternoon and get there the day after, afternoon late. Don't want to hurry my old antique. See you at the Bight. Oh, by–the–way, what's your phone number? I'll write it down."

"295-8763," I answered. "Give me a call and your time of arrival and we'll meet you with Franklin's carriage."

"Who was that, Grandfather Roberts?"

"A guy named Dave. He's coming down in his Chris-Craft Cruiser day after tomorrow, in the afternoon."

"What's a Chris-Craft Cruiser, Grandfather?"

"Instead of trying to describe it, I'll show it to you when he gets here. I'll want to tell you, it's a cool looking boat. Now, I'm going to call the hardware store to see about the porch swings."

I dialed the Island Hardware. There was a buzz, a click, and the line seemed to go dead. I was just about to hang up and try again when, I heard, "You called the Island Hardware?"

"Why, yes. Is this it?"

"What can we do for you?"

"I need a couple of porch swings. I would like them delivered and installed tomorrow morning, if possible."

"Let me check, Sir." It took a long time, but finally the person came back on. "Sorry sir, had to check stock. Tomorrow in the morning. Two porch swings installed. Your name and address sir?

"Tom Roberts, seven United Street, Atlantic side. Dead end street, yellow with white trim. 295-8763."

"Thank you, Sir. Your installer will be Frank. About ten am."

I noticed a strange click as he hung up.

"Harold Junior, they're bringing the porch swings tomorrow in the morning."

"Great, Grandfather Roberts! I bet I can swing so high, I'll touch the roof!"

"I don't know if you should go that high. You might turn over and fall out," I cautioned. "Tell you what, Junior, let's get our swimming trunks on, and get our towels. You know only three blocks away right next to the Southern-Most house, is the South Beach. We need to go for a swim."

They walked to the corner of Whitehead Street and turned right and walked a short block. Then, all they had to do was go around the Southern-Most house, and there was the South Beach. It was a small beach that had been the main beach for the old-town people for ages. Of course Harold Junior really liked the snack shop.

The next morning a pickup truck pulled up at ten sharp. A guy came up on the porch and rang the bell.

"May I help you?" I asked.

"Installer with two porch swings for Tom Roberts."

"You must be Frank from the hardware store?" I asked.

"Yah, I'm the guy. Where you want these things? I'll get my guys to bring them up."

"Tell you what, one goes right here," as I pointed, "facing out towards the street. Right between these bushes, so we can look out. The other in the back."

"'Just one second. I'll get the guys started. Hey, youse guys. Bring me one here," he hollered.

They both carried the swing onto the porch, "Right here, in between these bushes," Frank ordered as he pointed.

Now, where'ya want the other one?" Frank asked.

"Let's go to the back of the house, this way. "Will there be enough room to bring the other one through here, down the hall?"

"Yah, plenty of room," Frank answered.

He looked around the house as he walked down the hall. He seemed to be observing all he could. "Nice layout you've got here, Mister Roberts."

"Thank you. Now, the other one goes here. We can get a view of the Atlantic between those palm trees," I pointed to the location.

"Right, got'cha. I'll tell the guys," as he headed back through the house. "Hey youse guys! When you get done there, I'll show you where the next one goes."

I had followed Frank back to the front. "Frank, I would like to pay you. Let's go to the kitchen table, and I'll pay you cash, if I've got it." We sat down.

"I prefer cash," Frank said. "Let's see," he wrote on a pad. "Two porch swings at twenty-four fifty each plus fourteen dollars each to install. That's seventy-seven dollars. Don't worry about the tax, it's included."

I pulled a roll of bills out of my right pocket, "I've got it exactly."

"Here's your receipt." Frank had written the individual costs on the pad, and then scribble signed it.

"You don't have an Island Hardware receipt?" I asked.

"No, Mister Roberts, I'm a contract installer, work for myself."

Just then the two guys came back carrying the other swing, "Where ya want this, boss?"

"Let me show you. Right there, facing the Atlantic. Make sure it's got the view."

Suddenly Harold Junior appeared. He had been upstairs playing in Grandfather Robert's office. He was making believe he was writing a book. He had only gotten the operator on the phone one time and was really surprised when it happened. She had told him he shouldn't play with a phone. It was just afterwards he heard the noise of the two men installing the rear swing.

"Who are you? What's happening?" he asked.

"Hi, kid. I'm Frank, I'm putting up your porch swings. I've got the front one up. You want to see it?"

They went to the front, and Harold Junior sat in it and proceeded to give it the full test.

"Not too high, Harold Junior," I cautioned.

"We're done, Boss," the two guys came out the front door.

"Ok, we gotta' go. "Thanks, Mister Roberts. "Bye kid," Frank waved to Harold Junior.

The three got in the pickup and roared off down the street.

Unknown to Tom:

In a swanky hotel on the east end of Key West:

"I tell you, Vince, he's got some dough. You should have seen the roll he pulled out of his pocket. Paid me in cash. Also, I've got some more info from Texas. He lived in Houston, something about oil money, stocks. That's all they could tell me. He's also got a grandson visiting.

"I'll tell you, Frank, listen up. I've got an idea. By the way, Frank, how did you know he needed the swings?"

"Easy, I've got a guy running phone taps on a couple of targets."

That's good work, Frank," Vince commented, "Now here's the plan, "We've gotta' move fast. The kid may go home to his parents soon. We're gonna take the kid, and get some money for his return."

"You mean kidnap, Vince?" Frank exclaimed.

"Well kind of borrow the kid until we get some dough for his return. If they cooperate, nobody gets hurt. Now, you swing by the house with one of the guys. You see the kid out front, you get out, and while you're easing up to the kid, your man goes to the nearest phone booth and calls the gramps. You grab the kid and presto, you're gone!"

"Sounds like a plan, Vince. I'll start casing the place tomorrow."

"Hi Tom. It's Dave. I'm calling from the Bahia Honda State Park."

"That means you're only thirty five miles away."

"Yep, should be there in a couple of hours."

"Fine Dave, we'll meet you with Franklin and the carriage."

"Yes, Harold Junior, to answer the question you're thinking, we're going to see the Chris-Craft boat."

"Grandfather Roberts, are we going to go for a ride?"

"Harold Junior, I'm sure Dave will take us for a ride. Probably tomorrow."

Harold Junior and I were standing on the dock next to *Roberts' Best* when we saw the Chris-Craft heading towards us. Dave waved out the side window. He then skillfully eased up to the dock. The same slip he had last time was available. He revved the engine, and let her idle. I thought I could hear something different about the engine. I then grabbed the bow line and made it fast to the dock as Dave did the same for the stern.

Harold Junior was jumping up and down, "Yea, a speed boat! We're going to go very fast!"

Dave motioned for me to step in. We shook hands, "Good to see you,

Dave was heading across the bay towards the docks with his 1935, 28 foot Chris-Craft Model 557 Cabin Cruiser.

Tom. Now just who's this little man?"

"I'm Harold Junior," Harold put right in. "That's my Grandfather Roberts. Who are you?"

"Why, Harold Junior, I'm Dave, the speedboat man. I'm so glad to meet you. I've heard you're a great sailor!"

"Yes, that's right," Harold Junior said proudly.

"Tom, let me show you my engine compartment. It's had a makeover," he opened the hatch. "Take a look at that!" He pointed to the engine.

"Why, it's got three carburetors!" I exclaimed.

"Yep, got them at an auction. Triple down-draft carburetors, and there's two more things. But you can't see them, a hot three-quarter cam and a new three blade prop with a pitch designed for speed. This ninety-five horse power Hercules KBL flathead six is now rated for one hundred and thirty-one horse power!”

“I got a great price, a real steal! I couldn’t pass it up. A marine mechanic I know needed some oak furniture I had. It was an even swap! You know, Tom, a little more horsepower and that great three-blade prop, for a boat like mine, means more torque and that equals more speed!”

“We’ll have to try it out,” I suggested.

“What you say, tomorrow morning after breakfast?” Dave suggested. “But right now I’m famished. I could use some food!”

“I figured that. So Franklin dropped us off and will pick us up back here in a couple of hours,” I informed him. “We can walk a block or so to our favorite eating place, and then Franklin will take us home. You’re welcome to spend the evening with us or we’ll be back to see you tomorrow morning.”

“You know me, Tom, thank you for the hospitality, but I love my boat!”

“Hey, guys, when are we going to eat?” Harold Junior asked. He was sitting at the captain’s chair and turning the wheel.

They both laughed, “Come on, Harold,” Dave said, and we three headed for Sloppy Joes.

Next Morning:

“Hi, Franklin,” I said.

“Hi, Franklin, Hi Bessie,” Harold Junior said.

“He includes old Bessie. That’s a good boy you have there, Mister Tom,” Franklin stated.

“Thank you Franklin. We’re going to be out till mid-afternoon. How about looking for us about three.”

“Yes sir, Mister Tom. Me and old Bessie will be there.”

They rolled up to the Bight. Harold Junior was off running towards the two boats. Tom could see Dave up on the dock.

“She is all warmed up and ready to go. Get in, put on your life preservers, and hold on,” Dave welcomed them. “We’re going on a tour about the island. I figure we’ll go south past the Navy Yard, into the Hawk Channel, and along the entire south side of Key West. We’’ll stop at a marina for lunch at the cut between Stock Island and Key West. If you see a place to fish along the way, we’ll try our luck.”

“Can I drive? I know how. I steered our sailboat on Lake Houston!” Harold Junior put in.

Dave exclaimed, “I didn’t know that. How about as soon as we get into the Hawk Channel? First I want to go in close to the Navy breakwater. Maybe we’ll see some of those big boats.”

"This motor is purring like a kitten, Dave," I exclaimed.

"She really pulls along. Watch, I'll get her up on a plane," he said as he pushed the throttle forward. The six cylinder responded; the bow came up and then leveled off, and we were moving along at a good pace.

"Look there. That Coast Guard boat in front of the Navy base harbor entrance," I pointed. A Coast Guard boat was flashing a red light. Dave cut the motor.

"I guess they want me to stop. Oh, that's why. Look, a sub!"

"It must be going out on patrol," I said. "Come here, quick, Harold Junior. Look at the submarine."

It came out past the Coast Guard boat and turned south towards the Atlantic. Then it started a slow dive. We could see it disappear as the water washed over it. The Coast Guard flashed a green light, and the three of us in the Chris-Craft waved as we went past it. Some of the Coast Guardsmen waved back.

"Wow! A submarine, Grandfather. Mister Dave, thank you for bringing us out to see it."

"You're welcome, Harold Junior. Now let's get on with our tour."

We cruised along the entire southern end of Key West, which was about four miles. We could see the Civil War Fort Zachary Taylor, the southernmost house, and the East Martello Tower which was a small supporting Civil War fort on the east end of Key West.

"I'm going to drift a minute, and, Tom, let's bait up those rods. You two might latch on to something. Bait's right there."

"Ok, Dave, I've got it."

"Wow! I'm going to catch a shark!" Harold Junior exclaimed.

It wasn't a shark. But a couple of big red snappers really bent our poles. We caught them as Dave moved along trolling real slow.

"Dave, you will have to come by the house tonight for fried fish," I invited.

We motored up between Stock Island and Key West, and Dave said, "There's that marina with the good restaurant. How about lunch?"

"I need a hamburger, and fries, and a Coke," Harold Junior put right in. That afternoon, after the boat ride and fish cleaning.

"Grandfather Roberts, I'm going to swing on the front porch."

"OK, Harold Junior, I'll be right down."

Harold Junior went out to the front porch, where he proceeded to put the porch swing to the ultimate test. A pickup with two guys was cruising down Whitehead Street. It stopped at the corner of United Street. From there they could see the Roberts house and the porch swing.

"Frank, it's the kid," the driver said.

"Yah, I see. Go make the call, and make it snappy!"

"I'm on it boss," the driver answered as Frank jumped out, and the pickup hurried off.

Frank moved fast, then slowed down and nonchalantly walked up to the porch. He made sure he was off to one side so someone in the house looking down the hall towards the door couldn't see him.

He stepped up on the porch, "Hey, Harold, you're swinging pretty high!"

Harold scuffed his shoes a couple of times and slowed down, "Who are you? I'm not supposed to talk to strangers."

"Harold, I'm not a stranger. I'm Frank. Remember, I put this swing up for you."

"Ring! Ring!" The phone rang, exactly according to plan.

"Oh, now I remember."

"Harold, the reason I came by is I know where a pirate ship is."

"Really! Where is it?"

"Just a little ways over there. If we hurry we can see it, and get their flag and swords. But we got to hurry!"

"I could go and tell my grandfather."

"No, we don't have much time. See my truck just pulled up. If we hurry we can go over there, get the swords and pirate flag and be right back."

He then took Harold's hand, and they hurried out and got in the truck.

"Harold, this is Sam. He knows how to get to the pirate ship real fast."

"I sure do, Sonny." He eased out slowly and headed down Whitehead Street towards the Turtle Crawls.

The turtle schooner looked dark and kind of eerie anchored against the dock. Sam had given the captain and crew some money to rent it for the entire evening till the next day. A private party he had said, and don't bother to clean up.

Sam pulled the pickup up to the curb. Frank and Harold got out, "Look, Harold, none of the pirates are here. We'll be able to get in real fast, and get their swords."

"Sure looks spooky," Harold Junior exclaimed.

"Don't be afraid. I'm not worried," Frank said.

Frank took Harold's hand. They went out on the dock and crossed over the gang plank onto the turtle schooner. Just then, on the other side of Sam's pickup a carriage pulled by an old sway-back horse driven by

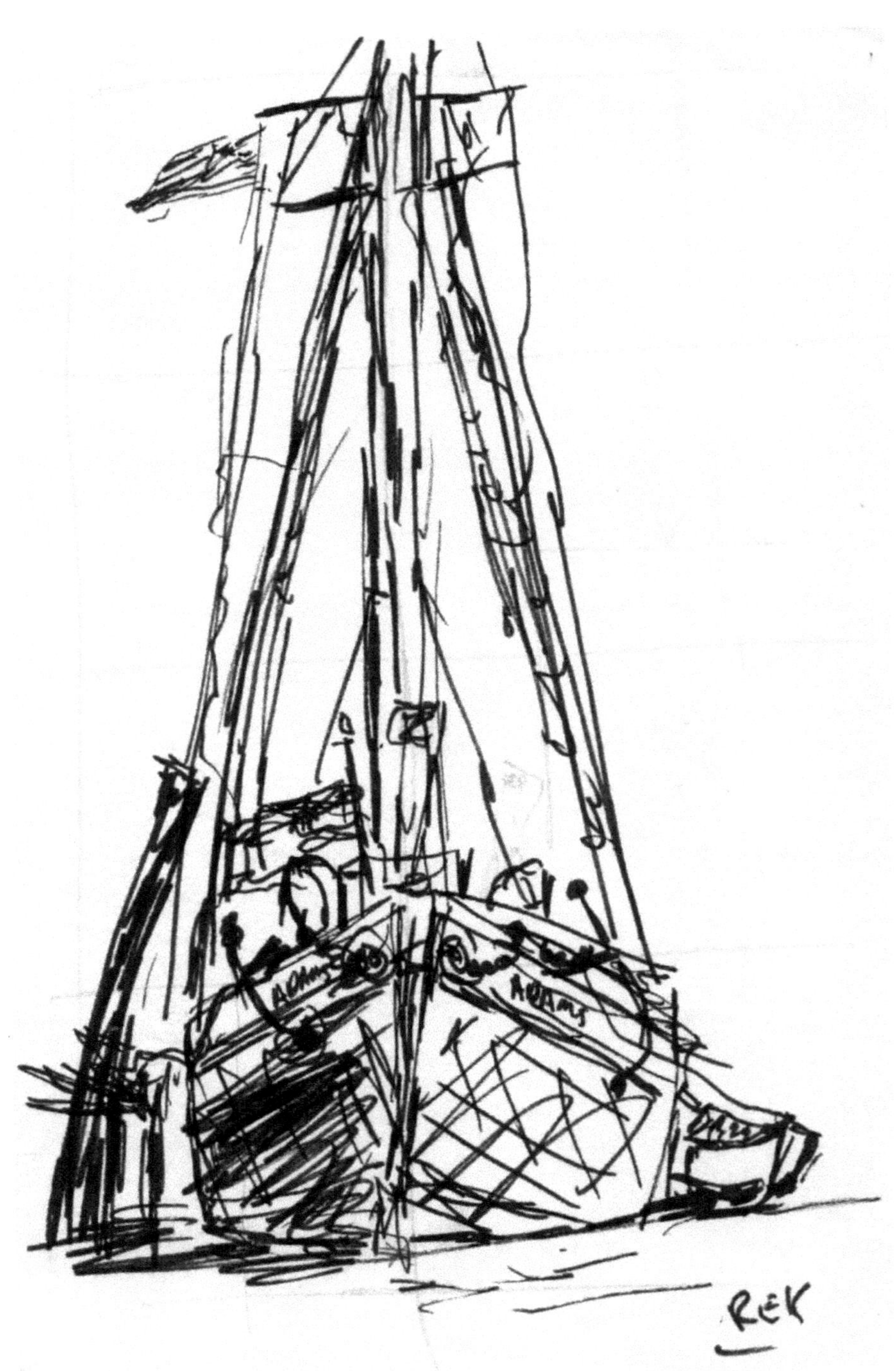

The A. M. Adams turtle schooner tied up at the dock at night.

316 Roberts' Best

Franklin went clopping by.

"Harold, the pirates' flag is down. I bet it's in the captain's cabin with their swords. They must be at the pirate's house."

"That's right. I remember seeing the house with my mom and dad."

"Here, I've got a flashlight. Let's go down to the captain's cabin. There it is. The door right there," Frank said as he shined his flashlight around.

Frank opened the door, and they went in. He saw an old light hanging in the center of the room. Frank pulled the cord.

"There, Harold, let's look around."

"I don't see any flag or swords," Harold said. "Hey, what are you doing?" Frank grabbed Harold. It was all he could do to tie Harold's hands and feet together. Harold got in two kicks to the shins and a punch in the stomach before he was subdued.

Frank said ouch two times and ugh once. He dragged Harold onto a bunk. Be quiet kid, or you will walk the plank, and the sharks will get you." He pulled the cord to put out the light. He hurriedly went out to the waiting pickup truck, slightly limping and holding his stomach.

"What's wrong with you?" Sam asked. "Kid slug you?"

"Shut up, and get out of here, to a phone booth."

They drove about four blocks. "There's one. It's kind of out of the way Boss."

"Keep the motor running."

Dial, Click...Click...Click, Dial, Click...Click...Click.

He put in a coin...Ding!

Ring! Ring!

I had been looking for Harold Junior all over the house and then around the yard. I was about to go next door.

Ring! Ring!

"Hello."

A muffled voice said, "Tom Roberts."

"Yes, who is this?"

"Don't worry. Just listen, we've borrowed your grandson. Nothing will happen to him. We just need a little dough, I mean cash. Now get ten thousand dollars in hundreds and put it in an old shoe. Leave it outside, on one side of the door to the lighthouse on Truman. Drop-off time is seven PM tonight. No later! You've got plenty of time to get the cash. We're not charging you very much. Now listen up, do not go to the authorities! We'll be watching."

I looked at my watch. It was four o'clock. I ran upstairs and rummaged through my sock drawer where I hid my cash. I counted it out. I had a couple of thousand dollars in hundreds. I stuffed it in my pants pocket and went over to the phone. I had to get over to Dave's boat. Dave would help me.

Then I heard it, Clop Da...Clop Da...Clop. It's Franklin, I realized, passing by to see his sweetie. I ran downstairs, out the front door, and into the street.

"Franklin! Franklin!"

"Yes, Mister Tom. Whooo Bessie!" He said as he pulled on the reins.

"Can you get me to Dave's boat. Right away? It's an emergency!"

"Yes, Sir! Jump in. Let's go, Bessie! Gitty Up!" Bessie hadn't heard that command for some time, and she perked right up and proceeded to move out.

"I'm going to cut over to Simonton. It's a straight shot," Franklin said. We pulled up. "Wait here, Franklin." I jumped down and ran out onto the dock.

When I got to Dave's boat, there was Dave and the realtor lady, Miss Betty Thomas sitting on the backseat of Dave's boat.

"Dave! Oh hi, Miss Thomas. Dave, I've got an emergency!"

Dave got up, "What's wrong, Tom?"

"They kidnapped Harold Junior. They want money. I've got some. What should I do?"

"Now, Tom, get yourself together. Go slow, and we'll make a plan. It will be all right! We got time."

This time I explained slowly, and both Dave and Betty Thomas listened intently.

As they were talking, Franklin came up. "Mister Tom, you didn't have time to tell me what was the trouble. You say someone took Mister Harold? Let me tell you what I saw earlier. This guy and a little boy, about Mister Harold's size, both backs were turned to me, couldn't see faces. They walked out on that turtle boat dock and then went onto the boat.

Dave said, "That's where they're keeping him. No authorities. They may be watching. We'll do the drop-off, and then make like we're going to your house, Tom to wait for a call. While they're picking up the money, Franklin will bring us back here. Then we'll take this Chris-Craft and board that turtle boat from the water side. They won't be expecting us!"

"Now let's see, how much money do you have, and then we'll get an old shoe. Wha'cha got, Tom?"

"I've got a little over two thousand in hundreds."

"Just a second." Dave went into the cabin and came back out with a wad of bills. "Use these," he said, as he ruffled the money.

"Dave, I can't take your money!"

"Here Tom, take a look at them."

I took the stack, "Why, it's Confederate money!"

"Fooled you, huh?" Dave smiled. "They'll fool them too. Here, put half of your hundreds on top and the rest on the bottom. Now, wrap them in this paper with a rubber band. Presto. In the shoe they go!"

"Now Franklin, let's us guys go down to the lighthouse. We need Betty to stay here. We're going to need her to drive this here Chris-Craft for the boarding party and get away!"

They drove down Simonton and turned right on Truman. Franklin stopped the carriage in front of the lighthouse.

Dave jumped out. "I'll take the money up. Be right back."

Dave went up to the lighthouse door and put the old shoe down in the grass touching the base of the structure. He then looked around and hurried back. Franklin started old Bessie up and headed the carriage back to United Street. Tom and Dave then ducked down, and Franklin went right back Simonton to the marina.

"Ok, guys, let's get the Chris-Craft started up. Franklin, you watch the turtle boat and if there's trouble you call the authorities."

"Yes, Mister Dave. Me and Bessie will get a little closer with this carriage, so we can keep a lookout."

At the lighthouse:

"I got the shoe, Vince," Frank said, as he jumped into the car.

"Let's go, Sammy," Vince said and then asked, "the money in it?"

Frank said, "It looks good as he unwrapped and thumbed through it."

"Let me have it," Vince grabbed the bundle of bills and cut the stack in half. "Confederate money! They scammed us!"

"What do you mean? Give it to me. There's some bills. They put a thousand on top and a thousand on the bottom."

"Sam, quick, to the boat. We've got to get the kid. We're not going to the dock. We'll board seaside and get him out of there. We'll get our dough one way or the other. No dumb amateurs are going to rip us off!"

Dave started the Chris-Craft as Tom and Betty untied it, stowed the

Dave took the old shoe with the money up to the lighthouse door.

cables, and pulled the bumpers. Dave backed away from the dock, did a 180 and headed across the Bight.

"Here, Betty, take the wheel. I've got to go into the cabin one sec."

He came back out brandishing a handgun, and stuffed it into his belt.

"What ya got there, Dave?" I asked.

"It's a Colt forty-five, Civil War six-shooter. No shells though. Here, check it out," he said as he handed it to me. "Might come in handy. Now here's the plan. We're going in right next to the turtle schooner and do a 180 heading out, Betty driving."

"Don't worry, Tom, I used to drive my dad's sixty-foot shrimp boat," Betty put in.

"Then we'll quickly ease up to the side of schooner. We'll be up on our deck. Betty will keep it running as we go over the side and board the schooner. We'll check it out, search it, and God willing, will bring Harold Junior out. Tom, we take no prisoners! Get in, and get out!"

The turtle schooner loomed up as a dark foreboding shape alongside of the dock. It was silhouetted by the city lights. There were a few tourists walking about on the main part of the city park. They pulled up, did the 180, and Betty professionally slid the Chris-Craft up to the side of the schooner.

"Boost me up, Tom," Dave said as he reached up and grabbed on to the side rails of the schooner.

Dave flipped over onto the deck, reached down, and pulled me up and over.

Now we were both on the deck. The turtle schooner was rocking sideways to and fro from the Chris-Craft's wake.

"This way. There's a hatch under this canvas," Dave said.

We went down below deck. Dave pulled out a flashlight and shined it around.

"There in the rear, the captain's cabin. Must be in there," Dave said as his flashlight shined on the door.

We advanced towards the door, Dave with a flashlight in one hand and Civil War six-shooter in the other.

"Check it out, Tom," Dave suggested.

I went forward. "Someone's blocked it from the outside."

There was a board across the opening with a rope tied to the handle. Tom twisted the board and opened the door. It was pitch black, except for a faint illumination coming in from the two small portals in the rear of the ship.

"Harold Junior! I hollered.

"Mm...Mm! A sound was heard from over by a bunk.

Dave's flashlight spun around exposing Harold Junior lying there. Tom ran up and pulled off the rope from Harold's feet and started working on his hands.

"Grandfather, I'm so glad to see you. That guy is really bad! He said he would help me find the pirate's swords and flag. He lied!"

Dave cautioned, "Tom, we got to get out of here!"

Dave led the way out the door and up through the hatch. I took Harold by the hand and then lifted him up to Dave. Out on the deck, we quickly crossed over to the sea side. Dave jumped down to the Chris-Craft's deck, took Harold Junior from me, and grabbed me as I let myself down. We scrambled back along the narrow sides of the Chris-Craft's cockpit and down onto its lower deck.

"Go! Go!" Dave said.

As he said it, Betty pushed the throttle forward and the Chris-Craft plunged into action, churning up waves and wake.

"Back to our dock, Betty," Dave hollered.

Half-way across the Bight, we suddenly saw a large cruiser skipping across the waves of the Bight and quickly coming up behind us.

"There they are now, Vince. It's that guy with his antique tub." Frank pointed at the Chris-Craft.

"They're coming from the schooner. They must have the kid. Faster, Sam!"

"It's a big cruiser behind us. It must be the kidnappers. Give it some gas, Betty!" Dave hollered as he watched the cruiser bearing down on them.

"I don't think we'll be able to beat them to the dock. Betty, let me take over. Everyone put those life preservers on! They're under the backseat's cushion. I've got an idea." Dave slipped in behind the wheel.

Betty had pulled the throttle back some as we were approaching the dock. Now Dave pushed it all the way forward. The Chris-Craft's bow went up, then the boat began to plane and skip across the waves.

"What happened, Sam? The tub's pulling away from us, "Frank asked.

Vince ordered, "Pour it on, Sam!"

"OK, Boss."

The two boats went around the western point of the Bight, the big cruiser slowly gaining on the Chris-Craft, both motors screaming and the boats skipping across the harbor's waves. They began a turn to the southwest, the big boat now right on top of the Chris-Craft.

"Hold on, and get down!" Dave commanded, as he suddenly spun the wheel hard to port. He cut the throttle by half. The Chris-Craft pulled a tight circle, skipping sideways, the motor revving a couple times as the prop came out of the water. Dave kept turning a full circle.

The big cruiser was turning on a larger radius, even as Sam fought to keep behind the Chris-Craft. It ended up with the cruiser making a 180 degree turn. But Dave had made a 360, putting him heading back the way he was going. He pushed the throttle full ahead. The boat again rose up and planed.

I looked back. The cruiser had finally got straightened up and was coming on after us, but way behind. Dave passed Malory Square on the port side and turned straight for the entrance to the Navy submarine basin.

I said, "Dave, we're heading straight for the Navy base!"

"Yes I know, I want to get arrested by the Navy."

"Oh," I acknowledged.

We entered straight in between the two break-waters. The cruiser was throttling down.

"What's those guys doing, Vince?" Frank asked as he holstered his gun.

"They're not so dumb. They're getting back up by the U. S. Navy. Let's get out of here, Sam!"

"They're slowing down, not following us in, Dave," I stated,

Suddenly we were lit up by a brilliant spotlight. It was blinding to all of us. Dave cut the throttle to an idle. The Chris-Craft dropped down from its planing and settled in the water, rocking with the waves.

"Ahoy there! You are trespassing on U. S. Navy property. Prepare to be boarded," a loud speaker bellowed out.

As the Navy patrol boat came up close to them, Dave said, "Keep your hands up in sight, guys. Don't want any trigger-happy sailor to start shooting."

The patrol boat came up touching. A lieutenant scrambled onto the rear of the Chris-Craft. It was now very crowded. There was a stern looking sailor with a big gun standing on the side of the patrol boat's deck looking down at us.

"Good evening, gentlemen, I'm Lieutenant Simmons. Why, hi, Miss

Thomas. What are you doing here?"

"It's like this, lieutenant. It started out this evening as a date, dinner, and a boat ride. But it soon turned into a kidnapping, a successful rescue, and a wild boat race!"

Before anyone else could say anything else, Harold Junior put in, "When that guy who lied to me tied me up, I prayed to God to help me, and Jesus sent Grandfather Roberts and these people to save me!"

Author:
This story is fictional. Any resemblance to any person or place is purely coincidental. The historic sources are in the Author's Notes of Definitions and References in the rear of the book.
(However, *Honest Dave* Crench, the Antique man's speech and mannerisms bears some resemblance to David Kranich. Dave is my brother who does live in Homestead, Florida. He is an antique seller and restorer extraordinaire.)

Author's Notes of Definitions and References

P 16   Fathometer: brand of sonic depth finder
(Webster's New Universal Dictionary Random House, 1996)

P 16   fathoms: A nautical depth measurement of 6 feet.
(Webster's New Universal Dictionary Random House, 1996)

P 16   dynamometer: A device for measuring mechanical force.
(Webster's New Universal Dictionary Random House, 1996)

P 17   knot: A unit of speed equal to one nautical mile or about 1.15 statue
miles per hour.
(Webster's New Universal Dictionary Random House, 1996)

P 17   speed of 8 1/2 knots   atlantic-cable.com

P 17   foresail: Front sail on the front mast.
(Webster's New Universal Dictionary Random House, 1996)

P 20   Mr. Herber Elroy Arch   schoonerwesternunion.blogspot.com

P 20   finish the boat.   schoonerwesternunion.blogspot.com

P 20   German U-boats   schoonerwesternunion.blogspot.com

P 20   captained the Western Union.   schoonerwesternunion.blogspot.com

P 20   National Register of Historic Places   wikepedia.org

P 20   movie *La Armistad*   wikepedia.org

P 21   Key West and be restored.   schoonerwesternunion.blogspot.com

P 21   Florida legislature in 2012   fla-keys.com

P 21   202 Williams Street   Internet search

P 21   charitable events.   schoonerwesternunion.blogspot.com

P 26   planing   (of a boat) to rise partly up out of the water at high speed.

P 26   Albatross: Is a large ocean bird with a wingspan as great as eleven feet.
Its long, narrow wings allow it to glide for hours and thousands of miles
without flapping its wings.

P 34   No Name Key   keyshistory.org/NoNameKey

P 42   Survival Manual   *FM21-76, US Army Survival Manual.*
                                 Reprint, Dorset Press, 1999

P 43   Military time: Is the same as civilian time up to 12 noon. Then just keep
        counting, such as: 1:00 in the afternoon would be 1300 etc. There is
        never any confusion as: did they mean 1 PM or 1 AM?

P 45   K-rations   usarmymodels.comARTICLES/Rations/krations
                                 Wikepedia.orgwiki/K-ration

P 52   Opa-Locka   aplaceinforidaonline.com/library_opa-locka

P 55   C-46 and C-54   Air America at the Bay of Pigs
                         Dr. Joe F. Leeker

P 55   Douglas A-26   wikipedia.org/wiki/Douglas_A-26_Invader
                                 napoleon130.tripod.com/id306

P 57   range   This firing range is in a field far away from any
                         human activity. It has targets and places for operators
                         to take a weapon's firing position.

P 58   red flags   Standard universal warning sign on a firing range.

P 59   paratroop shuffle   It is not a full step. It is a short scuffling forward. It
                         comes from one of the jumpmaster's sequence of
                         commands as the parachutists under his command
                         prepare to jump out of an airplane, "Shuffle to the
                         Door."   themilitaryview.com

P 61   strafing run   To attack by airplane with machine-gun fire.
                         Webster's Unabridged Dictionary, 2nd ed.,
                         1996 Random House

P 61   *Vaya con Dios*   Go with God.

P 68   M41 tank   urrib2000.narod.ru/Tanques3-e
                                 combatreform.org/airbornebayofpigs

P 69   Zapata swamp   wikipedia.org/wiki/Zapata_Swamp
                                 International Journal of Wilderness
                                 Volume 4, Number 2, Zapata Swamp.

P 73   **Bay of Pigs**

Szulc, Tad & Meyer, Karl.
The Cuban Invasion,
The Chronicle of a Disaster.
New York, N.Y.:
Ballantine Books Inc., 1962.

Persons, Albert C.
Bay of Pigs,
A Firsthand Account of the Mission
by a U.S. Pilot in Support of the
Cuban Invasion Force in 1961.
Jefferson, North Carolina:
McFarland & Company, Inc., 1990.

Johnson, Haynes.
The Bay of Pigs,
The Leaders Story of Brigade
2506.
New York, N.Y.:
Dell Publishing Co. Inc., 1964.

Lynch, Grayson L.
Decision for Disaster,
Betrayal at the Bay of Pigs.
Dulles, Virginia:
Ballantine Books Inc., 1962.

Wyden, Peter.
Bay of Pigs,
The Untold Story.
New York, N. Y.:
Simon & Schuster, Inc., 1980.

Trest, Warren and Dodd, Don.
Wings of Denial,
The Alabama Air National
Guard's Covert Role
at the Bay of Pigs.
Montgomery, Alabama:
NewSouth Books, 2001.

P 77   shell middens   refuse heap

P 78   blunderbuss   A muzzle loading early gun. A musket.

P 93   Midwater Trawling   Trawling off the bottom.
                                      wikepedia.org/wiki/Trawling

P 93/94 Shrimp: Pink, Brown,
        White and Royal Red   Stockislandflorida.net/FFLRoyal Red Shrimp

P 94   Seagoing Trawler   staugustinelighthouse.org/LAMP/-
        Greek style shrimp boat   Heritage_Boatbuiling/St_Augustine

P 94   Diesel Engine Sales Company (DESC)   "Same as above"

P 96   ways   A track leading from where a boat is being worked on down to,
                and into the water. Used to launch the boat.

P 97   skipjack   A small single-masted sloop-   Article from:
                    type sailing ship.   Henn, Lt. William.
                                                         Caught on a Lee Shore.
                    Oppel, Frank & Meisel, Tony.   *Pleasures and Perils of*
                    Tales of Old Florida.   *Cruse on the Florida Coast.*
                    Edison, New Jersey: The Century Magazine,
                    Castle Books, 1987.   June, 1893.

P 100   outriggers   The long metal posts that extend out the sides of the trawler. They help to spread the nets.
staugustinelighthouse.org/LAMHertiage_Boatbuilding

P 102   aft   Rear of the boat.

P 102   wake   The ripples and waves put out from the movement of the boat.

P 102   helm   The cockpit is where the steering takes place.

P 102   galley   The kitchen part of a boat.

P 104   USS Bushnell   floridamemory.com

P 104   Mid trawl   Mid-water (pelagic) trawling is a method of trawling where the net is not dragged on the bottom, therefore not damaging the sea floor. One species of fish is usually the main target.
wikepedia.org/wikiTrawling

P 104   otter boards   The otter boards are made of wood and are the size of doors. They provide horizontal spread of the net while in the water. One is on each outer edge of the net.
wikepeia.org/wikiTrawling

P 106   hold   The below-deck area where the catch is kept for storage. They have both ice and refrigeration.

P 106   by-catch   Any part of the catch that is not used, small, or illegal.
Wikipedia.org/wiki/Trawling

P 106   Calico scallops   Found at 30 to 1,300 feet along the Continental Shelf. Deep Sea Trawl Fisheries of the Southeast US and Gulf of Mexico

P 111   centerboard   A keel or flat board that can be raised or lowered on the bottom of a sailboat. It helps guide a boat and keep it from flipping over. It slides up into a water tight compartment when not in use.

P 111   tack   Go from side to side to catch the wind.

P 111   bilge   Inside bottom of a boat. Water will accumulate there in all wood boats, either leaking through the wood sides or from the deck down.

P 114   refraction   Bending of lightwaves in the water.

P 114   weighed anchor   Pulled it up off the bottom (marine term).

P 116   turtle stampede   Turtles rushing off of a beach to the safety of an inland lagoon to evade a storm.

Oppel, Frank & Meisel, Tony.
Tales of Old Florida.
Edison, New Jersey:
Castle Books, 1987.

Article from:
J. M. Murphy
Turtling in Florida
1890.

P 131   German U-boat Type VIIC
         wikipedia.org/wiki/German_Type_VII_submarine

P 132   kilometer   1000 meters or .62 mile

P 132   36th Street Airport   wikipedia.org/wiki/Miami_Army_Airfield

P 132   Enigma Electro-mechanical Rotor
         Cypher machine, German Navy   wikipeia.org/wiki/Enigma_machine

P 132   British unit   cryptomuseum.com/spy/b2

P 135   Cost of clothes in 1940   halglatzer.com/tdts/1940

P 140   Miami Beach Training Center
         wikipeia.org/wiki/Miami_Beach_Training_Center

P 146   CIC, Counterintelligence Corps
         wikipeia.org/Counterintelligence_Corps

P 157   mortise and tendon joint   A rectangular groove in a piece of wood, in which a mating piece of wood has a protruding piece just a bit smaller. These fit together to make a connecting joint.

P 158   Commodore David Porter   keyshistory.org

P 158   bowsprit   A wooden pole projecting out from the front of a sailing vessel. It is used to support the ropes and tackles to assist in holding the front mast and sails.

P 158	gaff rigged	Triangular sails above the main sails on both masts. wikipedia.org/wiki/Schooner
P 158	raked	an angle to the masts to the rear to support the force of the wind against large sails. cindyvallar.com/pirateships
P 158	quarter-boats	small boats that were stored on the deck of a ship.
P 158	Teredo worm	A shellfish that looks like a miniature clam. It attaches itself to the wood on the bottom of a ship and opens. The Teredo worm will then bore into the ship's hull. Keith Wilbur *Pirates and Patriots of the Revolution* Okd Saybrook, Connecticut Globe Pequot Press
P 158	sloop	A sailing ship with a single mast. It has sails fore and aft with a jib sail in the front. They were light and agile. cindyvallar.com/pirateships
P 159	"Heaved the log"	A knot was tied every 50 feet 8 inches on a long line. A weighted wooden quarter of a circle, 5 inches in radius was thrown out and the knots were counted. This gave the knots per hour or speed of the boat. Keith Wilbur (See above, *Pirates and Patriots of the Revolution*)
P 162	Red Holes	keyshistory.org/farming.html
P 162	bromeliad	Tropical American plants having long stiff leaves and showy flowers. Family named after Olaus Bromelius, Swedish botanist (1639-1705) (Webster's New Universal Dictionary Random House, 1996)
P 162	Smooth Cayenne	The most common variety of pineapple producing deep yellow fruit. keysnews.com/node/72193
P 165	frigates	Large naval military vessels
P 165	Bienvenido a bordo	Come aboard

P 167   con leche   with milk

P 173   grape   Small round balls of metal about 1/2" to 1" in diameter. anti-personnel ammunition.

P 175   square rigging   Rectangular sails that go across the width of a vessel

P 176   Man-of-War   Naval military vessel

P 177   narrow bladed hoe   https://hart.purdue.edu/new crop/Morton pineapple

P 777   breach   Rear loader

P 177   muzzle   Front loader

P 181   bringing the flag down   surrendering

P 181   heaving to   pulling over to be boarded.

P 183   breeches buoy   a sling with one seat which is hung over the side of a boat

P 190   lee side   Side protected from the wind.

P 190   hawser   Heavy rope for towing

P 190   capstan   A machine for winding in rope. t works in a horizontal direction.

P 193   oil cloths   raincoats

P 199   A. M. Adams was last seen.

Key West Marine Historical Society   Article:
Official Quarterly Publication   Reprint from the Atlantic Fisherman 1940
Vol. 8, No 1   Fall 1997   *The Story of Green Turtle Soup*
Florida Keys Sea Heritage Journal   Page 11, mid-bottom of page.

P 199   (History and topography of the Cayman Islands
                        Smith, Roger C.

                        The Maritime Heritage of the Cayman Islands
                        Gainesville, Florida
                        University Press of Florida

P 201   Christopher Columbus   keytocayman.com/history/dates-in-history
           Las Tortugas,   burtwolf.com/program-blog
           the turtles   Wikepedia.org/wiki/History_of_the_-
                               Cayman_Islands
                               Newworldencyclopedia.org/entry/-
                               Cayman_Islands

P 201   Sir Francis Drake   keytocayman.com/history/dates-in-history

P 202   Alligartas   Wikepedia.org/wiki/History_of_the_-
                                    Cayman_Islands
                                    Newworldencyclopedia.org/entry/-
                                    Cayman_Islands

P 202   careen   Beach the ship, take ballast and heavy items off, tie a
                                    block and tackle rope to it, pull it over on its side,
                                    scrape the barnacles off the bottom, and make repairs.

P 207   switchback   The trail goes from left to right , turning back on itself
                                    to gain altitude.

P 210   How to tan a gator hide   aligatorhuntingequipment.com/tan.html

P 226   tack   Sailing back and fourth against the wind. It allows the sails to
                   catch the wind and the boat to move against it.

P 231   station curves   The cross sections to show the ribs of a boat.

P 232   draw shave   Flat blade with handles on each side. Used to shave
                          wood.

P 232   keel   Main wood support that runs along the entire center
                          bottom of a boat.

P 232   animal glue   Made by boiling down animal and fish parts.

P 232   tree nails   Small round sharp hardwood pieces used as nails.

P 234   herbivores   Plant eaters.

P 237   block and tackle Pulleys and ropes to multiply the force
                          to pull or lift.

P 238   launching ramp cut into costal rock
                   explorecayman.com/george-town—its-sites-of-historical-
                   interest

P 238   oakum   Tarred fiber, made from old ropes or virgin hemp or jute.
                          wikipeia.org

P 244   shoals   Shallow places along a coast.
                           Webster's Unabridged Dictionary, 2nd ed.,
                           1996 Random House

P 246   helm   wheel and steering area.

P 251   filibuster   one who engages in an unauthorized military
                           expedition into a foreign country to support a
                           revolution

P 269   head   A name for a boat toilet

P 280   washboard man   A rippled stainless steel sheet worn on the musician's
                           chest with straps over his shoulders and played with
                           two spoons.

P 284   No Wake Zone   Go slow, don't make any waves.

P 290   Bight   A body of water bounded by a curve or bend in the
                           shore of a sea..
                           Webster's Unabridged Dictionary, 2nd ed.,
                           1996 Random House

P 290   Chris-Craft   Chris Smith was the founder of Chris-Craft Boats. He
                           built his first wood boat in 1874 at the age of 13. In
                           1881 he and his brother formed a partnership and
                           began to manufacture boats. In 1941 they produced
                           military boats: patrol, rescue, and utility launches for
                           the U S Army and Navy. By the end of the war Chris-
                           Craft had built more than 12,000 boats.

P 293   gingerbread   House wood ornamentation mostly on the rails and
                           porch columns.

Watercolor
And Sketch
Reproductions

Any and all watercolors and sketches in this book are copyrighted. They may be purchased. They will be printed from the original on high quality 60# watercolor paper. They will be centered on the paper.
All originals are 8 1/2" or smaller.
Prints on 5" x 7", 8 1/2" x 11", 11" x 17".
All prints will be signed.
Contact via E-mail for pricing.

For purchase contact: bobkranich@att.net
P. O. Box 50, White Post, Virginia   22663

Other Books by Bob and Joanne Mary Kranich

Jesus Loves Us All   Poems by Jane Kranich

The Adventures of Froggie and Grandma   Three children's books in a series.

The Jane Kranich Story   Bob's mom's life story.

A Walk Across Florida   Bob's 750 mile and 5 and 1/2 week hike from Georgia to Key West, Florida.

James The Young Brown Pelican   A young brown pelican learns that there is more to life than he realized. Trust and Faith in God is essential.

Isn't That Interesting   The building of a B & B, Maria's Garden and Inn as well as the life of Peg Perry. Includes Religious Stories by Peg Perry

Grandpa Builds His Grandchildren A Rocking Horse   A 32 page full color book which will show and tell your children how a rocking horse is built. They will see Bob using all of the tools he needs from saws to paint brushes.

About the author, Bob Kranich:

In 1972, Bob decided the United States needed a backpacking magazine. He laid out and published the first backpacking magazine, *American Hiker* in June of that year.

In 2001, he published two of his Mom's poetry books and a children's sequel. In 2015 after three years, he completed the writing of his adventure and first full-length book, *A Walk Across Florida*. The same year he published his mother's fully illustrated poetry book, *Jesus Loves Us All*.

Bob is at this time writing two books. One is a Revolutionary War era adventure featuring children in Boston during the British occupation. The other about his grandson restoring an old Chevy truck.

He graduated from Sam Houston State University in Texas with a BS in Mechanical Design and a MA in Management. Today he works in the mechanical engineering field. He also builds wood projects in his shop at his house. One of his great loves is watercolor painting.

Bob lives 10 miles north of the Shenandoah National Park. He is happily married to his wife and editor, Joanne.

bobkranich.com
bkranich.wixsite.com/bobkranich